# The Woman from Snowy River

Inspired by a true story

**ANN CONNOLLY**

**The Woman from Snowy River**
First published in Australia by Ann Connolly 2025



A catalogue record for this
book is available from the
National Library of Australia

ISBN: 978-1-7642989-0-2 (pbk)
ISBN: 978-1-7642989-1-9 (ebk)

Typesetting and design by Publicious Book Publishing
Published in collaboration with Publicious Book Publishing
www.publicious.com.au

For my mum, Helen, who was a beautiful,
gracious and courageous soul

# Prologue

*On the South Atlantic Ocean, East of Argentina, 17 September 1874*

She could never have prepared for this storm.

Fear was her master. It governed every breath in, every breath out. She feared for her life but would sacrifice her own without thought, in exchange for the lives of her six children.

The smell and taste of salt sickened her. Carrie Hedger looked in turn to her four- and seven-year-old daughters, one on each side of her. They clung on, their fingers digging into her, seeking safety she could not assure them of. Their mouths formed an O-shape, their screams swept up to mix with the deafening winds, smashing waves and groaning timbers.

With each roll of the ship, the thick ropes looped around their waists that bound them to a bunk, pulled, bruising and breaking their skin. Below the bed, ankle-deep water colder than the *Snowy River* after the snow on the mountains had melted, swirled around their cabin.

Nature was fighting to claim them—to send all onboard to the bottom of the black-as-coal ocean. But it had underestimated the human spirit that could fight on and on.

Carrie's husband, George, was one of the men manning the pumps. He had refused his sixteen-year-old son Edward's move to do the same, insisting he stay with his mother and siblings. Carrie had seen the flash of vexation in Edward's eyes and knew the time she had dreaded had come—her firstborn had stepped over the line from childhood into manhood.

She peered through the dim light to look upon Edward. He had finished tying his fourteen-year-old sister, and eleven- and nine-year-old brothers to the opposite bunk. Carrie watched what she knew in her heart would happen, unfold. Edward did not loop the rope around his own waist. He did not tie himself to the bunk. He stepped back from his siblings, and was flung immediately to the floor as the ship fell on its side into a trough between waves. He clawed his way back to hang onto the bunk, his wool trousers and waistcoat sodden, his white linen shirt glued to his sun-browned skin.

Carrie caught a glimpse of his face as he turned away from the bunk to dash for the cabin door. But it told her nothing. Edward had done as his father had instilled in him—masked any fear, any emotion, within.

She threw out her arm in a gesture that begged him not to go. But he did not see her. She could not stop him—her boy she had watched not long ago, throw caution to the wind to swim his horse across the wide, fast flowing *Snowy River*. He had made up his mind to defy his father and take his turn pumping water from the ship.

Carrie's lips moved quickly in a silent prayer for Edward. She pulled her daughters even closer to her sides. She turned her head to use her eyes to offer what comfort she could to her children on the opposite bunk. She would always do whatever she could for her children. But had she failed them by bringing them on this ocean voyage that was so different to her first?

# Chapter One

*Port of New York, 25 October 1855*

Sixteen-year-old Carrie shivered. She had donned her warmest clothes as her mother, Louisa, had told her to, but it was proving no protection against the chills that were created not by the late autumn weather, but by the imminent onset of her first ocean voyage.

Carrie stood on the wharf, looking up at the packet ship towering above her, its name, *B.R. Milam*, emblazoned on its bow. Ships were not a new sight to her. She had lived in an apartment in Brooklyn, and her mother had often brought her to the East River to see the ships, their sails furled or unfurled as they glided out of, or into, port.

But today she was to step onto this one before her. To journey to Australia—a country she knew nothing about except from the few remarks her stepfather, Amos, had passed, which had lit a wick of excitement within her.

A soft touch on Carrie's arm startled her. She turned to receive an embrace from her sister, Anna. There was a minute or two of warmth, and the familiar smell of lavender perfume to, perhaps, last a lifetime. Words were not possible when they parted. Tears trickled down their faces like cool drops of water from a tap.

Anna placed a brown paper package tied with a sapphire blue ribbon into Carrie's hands. Carrie pulled the package to her chest, clutching it, for it was a lifeline to what she had always known.

Next to embrace Carrie was her brother, William. She was not as close to her brother as she was to her sister, but she did not doubt his rare display of affection was heartfelt. He offered an envelope, through which she could feel coins inside—a significant gift when he was a careful manager of money.

As she watched Anna and William say their goodbyes to their mother and nod at their stepfather, restless feet betrayed her urge to run away. An impulse to abandon her carefully packed trunk of clothes and books that waited for her onboard, and go backwards to their home, rather than forward to where she had a persistent feeling her future lay. How she wished Anna and William were coming on the voyage, but as adults establishing their own lives, they were to remain in New York.

Her mother linked her arm with Carrie's, drawing them both towards her stepfather, whom they followed up the gangway at the slowest of paces they could manage, the small heels of their boots tapping on the boards.

Amos led them to the side of the ship closest to the wharf to wave a final goodbye to Anna and William. Carrie smiled at him to hide her shyness at this act of consideration. She turned away quickly to search for her siblings among the crowd below.

Carrie's mother was the first to spot Anna's grey bonnet, and pointed her out. Carrie followed her mother's example of a restrained wave. She clutched the wooden railing with her other hand to refrain from expressing her sorrow at leaving them more demonstrably.

Carrie gripped the railing more tightly as she saw Anna and William turn away after waving back.

Louisa took Carrie's hand in hers. 'Come, Carrie, we must go below. To linger will be more difficult.'

'Mother,' Carrie said, prepared to plead for longer, but as she looked into her mother's eyes, she saw tears and understood her mother was also pained. 'Yes,' she nodded, saying no more, and gently squeezing her mother's hand.

As they once again walked behind Amos, Carrie allowed the sounds on the wharf to soak through her befuddlement over what she was experiencing. Women's voices, happy and sad; men's voices calling instructions and farewells, and the clip-clopping of horses' hooves.

Those sounds, and the smell of New York—a smell she could not find the words for at that moment—stayed with her as she descended the stairs into the hull of the ship.

***

Carrie had known they would be travelling in steerage, but had not known what that meant until she arrived at the bottom of the stairs and faced a non-partitioned area that ran the length of the ship. In the centre was a long table of simple construction—planks of wood with bench seats formed from more planks. On either side of the table lay a row of two-high bunks.

A damp, musty smell greeted her. Her mother sighed beside her, like someone resigned to their fate. Carrie heard Amos whisper, 'No fuss now, Louisa,' in a stern voice. It had been a bone of contention between Louisa and Amos that they would be travelling in steerage. Carrie had heard them argue one day, her mother offering money to breach the gap to cabin class, but Amos had refused without explanation.

In an act Carrie had no doubt constituted a statement to Amos, her mother strode forward, Carrie's hand in hers, and selected their bunks from those that had not already been claimed. Louisa turned to place a wicker basket on the table and walked its length, introducing herself, Amos and Carrie to the other travellers, who were twelve in number. She invited them to partake in the cake she had made for the purpose of establishing friendly relationships with those they would share these quarters with for many weeks.

Carrie's admiration of her mother, always at a high point, reached a peak. Amos, who could occasionally be contrary, joined in the socialising, no doubt making his own statement to his dignified, determined wife.

*May no one realise the tension between them,* Carrie thought, for she was of an age—and timid nature—that fostered embarrassment.

When the cake was consumed, Amos said, 'Our trunks are stored below. We should seek them out and remove what we need for some days, until we are allowed to go to our trunks again.'

Carrie saw a brief look of displeasure cross Louisa's face, at the knowledge their trunks would be stored away from them. But Carrie heard her say, 'As you wish, Amos,' in a compliant tone. Amos nodded and led them to another set of stairs, narrower this time, which they navigated carefully to find themselves among crates and trunks.

When they located their own, Louisa turned to her daughter. 'Carrie, help me to change, thank you.'

This, at least, was not a surprise as it had been this morning to see her mother emerge in her best dress for an ocean voyage. Carrie's own best, but much plainer, dress was placed at the bottom of her trunk in expectation that it would not be needed until they arrived in Australia.

Louisa removed her shawl, revealing the full beauty of her ruby red, full-skirted, bell-sleeved dress. She bent to set aside her shawl and reach into her trunk for a blanket. Given there were several other travellers also retrieving clothes from their trunks, Louisa passed the blanket to Carrie to hold up so she could change discreetly.

For the briefest of moments, soft silk brushed Carrie's fingertips as her mother undressed, bringing a touch of joy to Carrie's heart in what was the strangest of times. Perhaps one day she would also own such a charming dress.

After changing into a simple woollen dress with a collar of lace, like Carrie's own, her mother retrieved another plain dress and chemise from her trunk. Carrie followed her example, retrieving the same for herself from her own trunk. Carrie also took out a book and her Bible she had placed near the top of her trunk. She knew that reading, along with the very feel of a book in her hands—as well as the guidance held within her Bible—would help sustain her through this voyage.

Of her mother's three children, it had been Carrie who had demonstrated an appreciation for the written word—an ability to draw words together. Her mother had gone to considerable lengths to further Carrie's education when she had realised her interest and ability. She had bestowed upon her bright daughter a treasure to comfort and benefit her to an extent that was somewhat foreign to herself.

When they retraced their steps to steerage, the atmosphere at the table had changed in their absence. Quiet prevailed over the noise the travellers had created when they had come onboard. Even the two child passengers sat still, grasping their parents' hands, eyes wide, lips pinched together, as all sat waiting for the ship to sail.

Carrie's fingers pressed down on her closed book, their tips pale and numb, as she too sat quietly. Finally, ropes that bound the ship to its mooring thudded onto the deck, and men's voices, muffled by the layers of wood in between, were heard in instruction and response.

Carrie fidgeted in her seat. 'Mother, may we go up on deck to farewell New York?'

Her mother opened her mouth to speak but Amos spoke first, 'No child,' he said.

Carrie did not respond to Amos. Her intention was not to be rude, but her need to see New York another time was all too consuming.

'Mother, please?'

Louisa stood, facing her daughter, 'Yes, Carrie. Come, we will go,' she said, 'For a brief time only.'

The men on deck rushed to and fro, too occupied to concern themselves with Carrie and her mother's presence. Louisa and Carrie moved to the starboard side of the ship. *How solid New York is,* thought Carrie. *Solid and large*, its orderly lines of brick buildings stretching for as far as she could see.

*Did she belong on this boat, or to the city before her?*

The ship rocked as it moved, the ground beneath her gone, like the certainty of the life she had always known.

***

Carrie sat beside her mother, administering what care she could. Sea sickness had struck Louisa the day after the Port of New York lay behind them, despite the sailing being smooth. For her part, Carrie had found the gentle swaying and complaints of the timber as the ship moved through the ocean, comforting rather than troublesome.

As an oddly organised child, she had soon established a daily routine, which included cooking the food provided onboard for the three of them. Although her mother's want of food had disappeared, with encouragement, Carrie had discovered Louisa would partake of sips of water and bite-sized pieces of bread, which she was able to keep down.

Carrie picked up her book to read to her mother in the hope that continuing the story of *Jane Eyre*, by Charlotte Bronte, would distract her from her sea sickness. And, as they did each day, the two children travelling in steerage, came to stand close by to hear more of the story. Carrie had discovered their names were Arthur and Mary, aged eight and six, and that they could not read. But their peering at the pages of her book told her they were curious. So today she had a plan. When her mother dozed, as she usually did after a short while of being lulled by Carrie's voice, she would teach the children some letters, to start them on a journey of learning to read and write.

She was doing so at the table when the children's parents came to see, making her fleetingly nervous that she was doing wrong. Until a nod from their father and a sweet smile from their mother, that warmed Carrie like sunshine, told her otherwise.

Carrie and the parents watched as the children turned the pencils she had given them, in their hands. Each ran a finger along its length, touching its tip, intrigued. Carrie held her own pencil between thumb and forefinger, and Arthur and Mary copied her. She lowered her pencil to the piece of paper in front of her and inscribed the letters M-a-r-y. She turned to the girl. 'This is how we write your name.' Two sets of eyes gazed back at her in wonderment. 'And now your name, Arthur,' she said as their eyes swung back to the paper to watch her work.

'Today, we will practise writing the letters of your names. So, Mary, you try this letter to begin …' Carrie pointed to the 'M'. '… and Arthur, you try this one,' she said, pointing to the 'A'.

She took it in turns to stand behind each child, reaching over to hold their hand to guide the pencil as a shaky letter wormed its way onto the paper. Mary wriggled with excitement while Arthur stayed motionless, spellbound by what he had managed to do.

Quite some time slipped by as the children's heads bent to their task of copying each letter of their names, showing Carrie they were quick learners.

Tiredness finally arrived, with little Mary wavering first. 'Would you like to learn more tomorrow?' Carrie asked. 'Yes, please,' they chorused.

'I will keep the pencils, but you can take your paper to show your parents what you have done.' Carrie barely got the words out before the children ran in the direction of their mother and father.

'That warms my heart,' she heard Louisa say from the bunk behind her. 'You have a way with children, Carrie—as well as reading and writing, it would seem.'

Carrie walked over to her mother, who peeled back her blanket and sat on the edge of the bed. 'I do believe I am feeling improved. Should we try for a walk on deck?'

'Yes, I think we should,' Carrie replied, gladdened by her mother's request and the touch of rose in her cheeks. It would be the first time her mother had been on deck since they had sailed.

Amos must have heard Louisa's request too, for he came over from where he had been sitting playing cards with other men, to help his weakened wife climb the stairs.

The air on deck was fresh and warm. Louisa surprised her daughter by releasing her bun and tossing her head, the light breeze capturing her lustrous sable hair, lifting it off her shoulders. She laughed, catching Carrie's eyes, in a wordless dare for her to do the same, which she did. Amos joined in the frivolity, reaching out to touch Louisa's hair, which she allowed him to do. It was a tender moment between the three of them, broken by a sailor's cry of, 'Whale aft! Whale aft!'

Casting her weakness aside, Louisa clutched Carrie's hand and walked swiftly to the stern of the ship. Louisa, Carrie and Amos arrived in time to see the whale haul its colossal form from the water. It created an arc darker than the ocean, before crashing back down, giving them but a glimpse of an upturned mouth and two fins that looked too small to propel the size of its body.

As Carrie watched in awe, a memory of her father, Nathaniel—who had passed away seven years ago—came to her. A time when he had shown her a drawing of a whale, his voice coming alive in her head as though he was standing beside her now. 'Beyond our imagination, Carrie, that is what the sailor who saw this creature told me. Beyond our imagination.' And the sailor had been right. *How could this animal be? Was it truly God who had made it?*

The whale appeared again, as suddenly as it had disappeared below the waves, its giant tail in the shape of a 'T' rising out of the water, slapping down with a great force that sent spray flying towards the boat. Carrie tasted salt on her lips. The whale was close this time, and Carrie sensed the danger. *What if it hit the ship? Would it put a hole in it and end their lives here, where they floated alone, where there was no one to help them?* They had not sighted another ship for days.

She understood now that the sailor's cry was a call to action—to watch, to protect the ship and all onboard. Yet the sense of wonderment at seeing the creature dominated the fear that simmered beneath her skin, like a cooking fire, which gave comfort but could flare without notice if care was not taken.

'A magnificent beast,' she heard Amos say.

But it was not a beast to her; it was a creature that set alight within her a love of nature.

# Chapter Two

*Jindabyne, Autumn 2018*

The hands that clasped the tattered book were frail, transformed by age to a bony, wrinkled version of their former selves; their prominent veins a passing-of-much-time record in themselves. But their appearance belied the internal strength of their owner, who had a firm grip on the old book and the treasured memories it conjured.

Diana raised her eyes from the hands of her elderly mother, Maggie, to the still-beautiful face above. To the caramel-coloured eyes that had dulled a little from the pain that came with life, but which still sparkled when the joy searched for each day was found.

She waited for her mother to speak. She would let her have the time she needed to find the words that sometimes took a little longer to find in her mind nowadays. The moments of silence sat comfortably between them, until her mother smiled and began.

'It is time for me to give this to you, darling,' her thin arms reaching out to place the book in Diana's hands. 'My mother gave it to me, her grandmother to her. Now it is yours.'

Its heaviness did not surprise Diana. In her mother's hands, the tome had looked as heavy as it now felt. Glancing down, Diana's nose, which tended to be over-sensitive, detected a faint mustiness as she ran a hand over the warped board cover, the faded green cloth of which was either thread bare or missing in places. A word or two was faintly visible, but she would need to retrieve her glasses from her handbag to have any chance of deciphering them.

'When I was a little girl, your grandmother would read to me from this book each night,' said Maggie. 'When I was very young, I would insist on scrambling up on to her big bed by myself. I can still feel her hands around my waist as though it were only yesterday that she bent down to give me a quick boost up so I wouldn't protest.'

Diana watched her mother's face light up with the love she carried within for her own mother, and the happiness those special times still gave her, over eighty years later. She knew her mother and grandmother had been exceptionally close. She had seen and felt the peace reminiscing brought before.

Diana loved these times when glimpses of her mother's childhood were revealed. Ten years ago, when she had still been caught up in her world of focusing on her marriage, her career, and her own daughter, Bella, she would not have thought to ask her mother about that time. She had barely had enough energy to do everything she needed to do. But since the changes to her life in recent years, her mind had weaved its way to an enquiring interest in the past. One or two family members' stories had revealed themselves through the magic of the internet, like a detective mystery unravelling before her eyes.

'Often we would both fall asleep,' continued her mother, 'then I would feel Dad's big, strong arms scoop me up, and pull me against his chest. I would hear the tap-tap tapping of his footsteps on the polished wooden floor as he carried me to my bed. He would tuck the blanket around me so tightly I would sleep like there was no tomorrow,' she chuckled, unselfconsciously hugging herself.

The specialness of the gift she had been given placed an instant burden on Diana. What if, somehow—and she didn't know how—she became responsible for its loss? She hadn't known this book existed until a few minutes ago when her mother had asked her to retrieve it from her cupboard when Diana had told her about her growing interest in family history. She didn't know what the book nestled in her lap was yet, but she knew she didn't want to take it away from her mother when it meant so much to her.

Diana rose from the lounge where they had been sitting side by side, their knees angled towards each other, close to touching. She lowered the book onto the antique writing desk nearby. Her mother's love of card and letter writing was on display through the open pad of coloured note paper, news and well wishes sweeping across the page in big-looped, curly letters.

She returned to kneel in front of her mother, linking their hands. 'Mum, I can't thank you enough. But why don't you keep it with you? You might like to read from it again.'

'Oh darling, I have done that many, many times. I want you to have it. From today, it is yours to treasure and pass on when the time is right. Please keep it now.' The appeal in her mother's eyes convinced Diana that it was, after all, the right thing to do.

'Okay, Mum. I promise you I will do my best to take care of it. Do you know any more about the book?'

'Only that it was a gift to Marmie—that's what my sister and I called our mother—from her grandmother when Marmie was four. Great-grandmother was born in New York. Did you know that?' Diana shook her head in an *I had no idea* fashion. 'My mother was named after her; they were both Caroline Amelia Hedger. 'Family rumour has it, Carrie the first—they both had that nickname too—took this book with her on an ocean voyage and she was shipwrecked.'

Excitement bubbled upwards within Diana. 'Shipwrecked? Mum, we might be able to find out about that using the internet.'

Her mother pulled her hands away, clapping them together, the knobbiness of her knuckles making the sound she produced a soft one, like a muffled clap heard through water-blocked ears. 'Wouldn't that be a treat?'

'Yes, Mum. It would indeed.'

# Chapter Three

*Sandridge (Port of Melbourne), 24 January 1856*

Carrie sat on her bunk bed. The time had come to open the parcel her sister, Anna, had given her on the wharf in New York. Her resolve to keep it until their arrival in Australia, to mark the occasion in a special way, had faltered more than once during the three months of ocean voyage. But she was pleased she had used restraint.

She untied the bow, imagining her sister creating it with nimble fingers. The sapphire silk slipped through Carrie's fingers, coming to rest on the floor before she retrieved it and popped it into her pocket. She had decided that on occasion she would wear the ribbon in her hair to have a reminder with her of Anna and the love they shared.

One corner of the brown paper wrapping of her gift had torn, a glimpse of leather poking through to tease her. She was the only person who sat quietly in steerage, a hive of activity swirling around her as though people were surprised that they would soon be stepping off the ship. Whereas Carrie had replaced most of her belongings into her trunk the day before, in preparation for departure.

Carrie folded back the brown paper, a gasp escaping when she saw a leather-bound journal, a sheaf of quality writing paper and a fountain pen. Aware of their value, she wondered how Anna had managed such a precious collection. She picked the pen up, its metal surface cool in her hands, its sharp end pricking her finger.

She placed it aside and opened her journal. '*My Dear Sister. May you one day look back with fondness, on the words you write here. May your words be a record of an adventure that creates treasured memories. I eagerly await your letters. Your affectionate sister Anna.'*

They were the right words to say. They added to the sense of excitement and relief Carrie felt at having arrived in Australia. And for the moment, they removed the tiredness that had found her towards the end of the journey, despite having found her sea legs early on.

'Carrie, it is time to go on deck,' she heard her mother say from close by.

'Yes, Mother. I have one more thing to do though, please?' she said. She removed several sheets of paper from her sheaf, and hurriedly moved along the row of bunk beds to where Arthur and Mary, the children she had been teaching for weeks now, waited with their parents. 'Arthur and Mary, will you keep practising your letters and numbers for me if I give you this paper and …' she paused, withdrawing two pencils from her pocket, '…these?'

Warm arms wrapped around her as the children responded in unison, 'Yes, Miss Carrie. Thank you, Miss Carrie.'

Joy took hold of her. She would miss the children, but knew they had their own adventure in front of them. Their mother had told Carrie their family was off to the goldfields at Ballarat to make their fortune.

'If there is a school, we will make sure they attend,' said their mother. 'Thank you, my dear, for what you have done for them.'

A call to disembark rang out, loud and clear, allowing only enough time to clasp hands before going their separate ways.

The dry heat that met them on deck was as stifling as an unwelcome visitor. Carrie felt her mother swoon beside her. Amos took a step forward to catch his wife in his arms. In the harsh light of their first Australian Summer, Carrie was struck by the paleness of her mother's creamy skin, several thin veins visible beneath. The voyage had been difficult for Louisa who had rallied occasionally, but the heat when they reached the equator and the long weeks of sea sickness, had seen Louisa dependent upon her bed and Carrie for her care.

Standing on either side of her, Amos and Carrie guided Louisa down the gangway. With her arm around her mother, Carrie felt her thinness and the looseness of her dress. She looked to her stepfather. *Had he noticed the same?* But Amos was casting furtive glances, searching around for what, she did not know.

It was a relief to feel the solid wharf beneath her feet, but everything around Carrie swayed. She realised it was her that was rocking back and forwards. Despite his attention being distracted, her stepfather had become aware of this. 'You will find your land legs soon, lass. Step carefully for now.'

She nodded in response, a wave of dizziness coming over her. A cry of 'Mind yourselves' snapped her out of it as two labourers staggered their way down the gangway, their faces flushed with the effort of carrying a trunk twice the size of Carrie's own. Carrie stepped forward, feeling a bump to her side. She turned to the sound of a strange language and the sight of a man bent over, hands clasped together as though in prayer. His hair hung down his back in a ponytail as black and shiny as her mother's jet necklace. When he lifted his face to hers, his almond-shaped eyes seemed to smile at her, bringing a smile to her own face before he bowed again and moved away into the crowd of people that swarmed the wharf.

She had not seen a Chinese man before. And she had not expected to see one here, although she had heard Arthur and Mary's parents talk about how Chinese people would be on the goldfields at Ballarat. *What else can I expect? Who else will I meet?* Carrie pondered as she began to walk the length of the wharf with her mother and stepfather. She knew they would meet Amos' son, also called Amos, and that they were to stay on his property a long way from Melbourne. But she did not know where the property was or for how long they would stay. 'A visit,' her mother had said, with no amount of time mentioned. *How long was a 'visit' when it took three months to voyage to Australia?*

Carrie was distracted from her thoughts by the toot of an engine, box carts of trunks and cargo trailing behind. The engine was like nothing she had seen before—small enough for the man standing on the rear platform driving it, to come close to matching its height. It ran along narrow tracks, which split the wharf down the middle. This, she declared to herself, was a day for unexpected sights!

At the end of the wharf stood a weatherboard train station. Her stepfather busied himself, ensuring their trunks were unloaded from a box cart on to the train that would take them into Melbourne. Carrie looked back at the port that reminded her of the busyness of the one she had left, both of them with many ships bobbing on the water, skeletal masts towering above.

The journey to the Melbourne Terminus was fleeting, giving her a glimpse of buttery sand dunes and clusters of buildings, her appetite whetted to discover more. But perhaps not the smell which greeted them when they stepped onto the platform that stretched out before the weatherboard station of the terminus.

'Fish,' whispered her mother, in her direction, bringing her handkerchief up to her nose.

'Aye,' said Amos, who had long demonstrated he missed nothing. 'A fish market warmed by the heat of a summer's day, is next door to this station.'

'Pa!' a voice rang out and they turned to see a younger version of Amos dashing towards them. That they were kin could not be doubted, with their thick heads of slate-grey hair and bushy beards framing their faces. They *looked* as similar as their names. But Amos the younger—as Carrie had decided to call him—had a lightness in his eyes and a curl to his smile that signalled a difference between father and son, though Carrie knew not what that was yet. She did know, however, that she was drawn to him from first impressions. *Was she to call him her stepbrother?*

'Welcome ladies,' he said, his hand still locked in a tug-of-war shake with his father's.

'Thank you,' Louisa and Carrie chimed together.

'I look forward to hearing about your voyage, but for now I have a buggy waiting to transport you to where we are to stay, and a horse and cart for the trunks. Pa and I will take the cart directly there. But I have asked the buggy driver to travel up and down Swan Street and others so that you may see something of Melbourne city on your first day here.'

This was exactly what Carrie was hungry to do! *Could he tell that a desire to explore was swirling within her?* A desire she was struggling to not let surface in her efforts to behave as a young lady should. *Was she failing in this? Or was this a sign of differences between father and son?* Consideration of others was a common, rather than occasional, occurrence in the younger man who had now claimed back his hand and was reaching into the pocket of his waistcoat. He withdrew a coin and presented it to Carrie.

'This is a half sovereign. If you wish to take tea, mention it to the driver and he will take you to where you can do so.' He swept his arm to the side to guide them to the buggy.

Carrie only had a moment to look at the coin that lay in her hand, its gold surface reflecting both the gleam of the sun and the generosity of this new person in her life. That he gave the coin to her, not her mother, intrigued her. Carrie concluded that it was meant as a welcome gift to her, and the significance of the kind gesture was not lost on her.

Without thinking, Carrie stepped forward and rose on to her toes to place a light kiss upon Amos' whiskered face. He did not blush, but smiled at her. Her mother did not draw back at the inappropriateness of Carrie's action, for she knew her daughter—organised she might be, but a touch of impulsiveness had also revealed itself on several occasions.

With her first Australian coin held onto tightly—an unexpected symbol of hope for happy surprises in this country—Carrie climbed into the buggy. She was immediately grateful for the canopy that shielded she and her mother from the sun bearing down upon the packed earth of the road, like flames licking at chopped wood in a fireplace.

Rather than tea, she would have liked a cup of coffee, made the same as her mother had prepared each day in their apartment in Brooklyn. But she had learned on the ship that, in line with British custom, the English settlers here preferred tea.

Her need for refreshment was subdued by the exhilaration she felt when the driver giddy-upped his horse and the buggy pulled away from the station into the throng of Melbourne. They passed men on horses, their wide-brimmed hats tipped low over their foreheads, and other carriages and drivers that their driver acknowledged with a tilt of his head. Women and men walked along the edges of the road, the men top-hatted and carrying canes, the women sheltered under parasols Carrie imagined came from Paris—a place she dared to think she might one day see. *What a dreamer you are sometimes,* she told herself.

Carrie tore herself away from the sights to better absorb the sounds of this new world, by closing her eyes. She heard their horse whinny as the hooves of another tapped a beat on the dirt road, the wheels of the buggy it pulled scraping a path to its destination as their own would do once their tour was over. She found all the usual noises people make when going about their business, comforting. They were no different here than they were on the side of the world she had come from, apart from new accents she knew would take her time to decipher. She sniffed the air, grateful that the fish market lay behind them. *Did Australia have its own smell like New York? What could it be? Or was she being fanciful again?*

'I am surprised,' said her mother, causing Carrie's eyes to snap open. 'So many people, sturdy buildings and oh my, that church.' She pointed to where she wanted her daughter to look.

The church was indeed another surprise. Not because Carrie did not expect this country to have churches, but because she had known so little of what to expect that everything was turning out to be a surprise. As it clearly was for her mother too.

'St James, Mam,' said the driver, the first words he had uttered to them. 'It be finished in 1847, Anglican. Presbyterian services be held there too—and school.'

'Thank you,' Louisa and Carrie chorused again, turning their heads as they passed by to see more of the single-storey, pitched roof brick building, fronted and dwarfed by a square bell tower. 'Perhaps we could attend,' said Louisa, hope high in her voice. As people of faith, they were grateful for the Sunday services on deck during their voyage, but they longed for the spiritual surrounds provided by a place of worship.

Carrie squeezed her mother's hand. 'We must talk to the men, perhaps they can arrange that for us.'

'Would you be parched?' asked the driver. 'Mr Crisp thought ye may like refreshment.'

Carrie was indeed parched, his question bringing her attention to the dryness of her mouth. But who was Mr Crisp? *Was he their host at their accommodation?* she pondered.

'Thank you, but not today,' she heard her mother say, having made the decision for both of them, which was not unusual when a daughter was still considered a child. But at sixteen, Carrie did wish she had more say so. She certainly felt capable of at least contributing to decisions even if she was not going to be allowed to make her own.

She would not oppose her mother's decision, of course; she would express her thoughts in a look. But she was stopped before she could compose that look, by concern for her mother, the paleness evident upon disembarking the ship, having worsened.

Carrie could feel the edges of her gifted sovereign bite into her skin, so strongly was it grasped in her hand, but she knew that exchanging it for tea would need to wait for another day.

Soon, the click-clacking of horse feet on cobbled stone sounded their crossing of Princes Bridge. 'That be Yarra River,' said their driver, Carrie's nose twitching as an unpleasant odour reached her. The river was murky as well as smelly. Several semi-clad men were half immersed in it, bathing or swimming—which it was she was uncertain, until she saw tents on the river bank and decided they must be the bathers' abode.

She found herself suddenly nervous about what their own accommodation would be like, knowing that her mother needed somewhere comfortable to recover from the voyage. Their second floor apartment in Brooklyn, New York, had been far from grand, but her mother had made their four rooms a home to be grateful for.

Her fears were allayed when, with a 'whoa' from the driver, the horse and buggy came to rest in front of a white-washed picket fence. A compact area of bottle green lawns and a stone path lined with neatly trimmed rose bushes adorned with crimson and coral coloured flowers, led up to a polished wooden door set between two bay windows. A most solid-looking house stood before them.

The driver offered his hand to each of them in turn, and as their feet touched the ground, her stepfather, Amos, came from the house to greet them, his son following closely behind.

Stepping into the hall that ran down the centre of the house, was like how Carrie imagined stepping into a cool stream on a hot day would be. This was something she had not yet had the chance to do in her young life. Relief flooded Carrie, delaying the tiredness she felt was again knocking at her door, helping her to hold on to the stamina she felt would soon seep from her.

Amos the younger led them into a large room off the hall that was brimming with heavy furniture and portraits of people and landscapes that were foreign to her. Among it all sat a rather stern-looking woman perched stiffly on a polished leather settee. Beside her stood her equally stern-looking husband, formally attired in long coat and thick trousers. A vague thought of how inappropriately he was dressed for the weather, crossed Carrie's mind.

'Why my dear, you are exhausted,' said the woman when her gaze fell upon Louisa. The note of care in her voice told Carrie she had been too quick to judge this lady they had not even been introduced to yet and who, with layers of swishing crinoline, was quickly by her mother's side.

'Can I suggest tea in your room while you rest after your strenuous voyage from so far away?'

'Yes, that would be most welcome, thank you,' answered her mother, leaning on the woman's arm as she was led out of the room and along the hall.

'How kind,' said Carrie, to the men she was left standing alone with. 'Thank you.'

She was unsure what to do next, but her newly acquired stepbrother—if that was how she was to think of him—stepped in for her.

'Carrie, may I introduce you to Mr Abernathy, a friend and business partner of mine and our host for our stay here?'

'I am pleased to meet you, Miss Crisp,' said Mr Abernathy, 'your family is welcome in our home, and indeed any time you may find yourselves in Melbourne.'

*Crisp? But my stepfather's name—the name they had adopted upon her mother's marriage to him—was Vince.*

The risk of an awkward conversation was averted by Amos the younger, who looked at her pleadingly and said, 'Carrie, may I suggest refreshments and a rest in your room also, until the evening meal?' She nodded in response, her desperate thirst and fatigue usurping any immediate need to solve the mystery that had revealed itself like an unexpected cloudy day.

'I thank you for the warm welcome, Mr Abernathy,' she said. 'My mother will no doubt offer her thanks to you personally when she is rested.'

The tinkle of a hand-held bell rung by their host, soon brought a maid to escort Carrie to her room. As she turned, the half sovereign she had forgotten about, tumbled from her hand, Amos the younger catching it in his own before it could fall to the floor. 'You did not get your tea treat; keep this for another time,' he said, a tender glance passing between them as he returned it to her.

But there was not to be a next time. The coming days saw her mother needing rest. She emerged from her room for meals only. Carrie spent her time in the small library she had been invited to use, and the garden, when the heat would permit, at the back of the house. Here she interrogated the gardener, a craggy-faced, friendly, older man, about the plants, fruit trees and vegetables he grew. In New York, they had not had the opportunity to use the tiny communal backyard that serviced the three-storey apartment building they lived in, for anything other than the convenience of the outhouse and for drying clothes. They obtained what they needed from the grocery store a few doors down, which was where her mother had met her second husband, Amos. He had no doubt used his charm to catch Louisa's attention, as she had no doubt caught his.

And he was not the only one. Carrie had noticed, from an early age, that her mother caught the eye of many a person, male and female. For her mother was a beautiful woman who stood out from others. Her creamy skin needed no assistance—a natural blush rouged her cheeks, above which sat doe-like dark eyes with long lashes and long, thick hair the colour of a cloudless night sky. When Carrie looked at herself, the only similarity to her mother that she saw was her hair, below which sat a more rounded face, a longer nose and less plump lips. When she had once remarked upon her more stocky build, her mother had replied, 'Nonsense, you are lovely, more like your father, a special thing to be.'

Carrie and her siblings had lost their father to pneumonia, an all too common killer, when she was barely nine years of age. It was a cruel end that she had witnessed, for a loving father who left them well before his time.

She was standing in the garden, thinking of him, wondering if he too would like the garden as much as she did, when voices that could not be missed rang out. The two Amos' were arguing intently, and she could not fail to hear their words.

'You have been recognised, Father. You must leave.'

'And you would have me explain that to my wife how?' quipped her stepfather.

'Perhaps say we have purchased the supplies we need, and passage is available on a boat leaving tomorrow.'

'Tomorrow! Louisa has barely had time to rest, and Carrie no more chance to see the Melbourne we promised her she would.'

There was a pause, and she imagined her stepbrother's response was a sigh, his next words less forceful. 'It is unfortunate, I agree, but it is how it must be.'

***

'There is good news,' said her stepfather at dinner that night. 'I have secured passage on a ship to Sydney that calls into Two Fold Bay on the South Coast of New South Wales. We will be leaving in the morning. Earlier than we expected, no doubt, but I am desirous of seeing my son's property again.'

Carrie was aware this was not the entire truth, though what that was she could not fathom. She turned to see if her mother showed any signs of more understanding than she herself had, but her mother appeared quite shocked by the news. Louisa stared pointedly at her husband, as though this was the first she had heard of it. *Has my stepfather not paid his wife the courtesy of informing her before he made an announcement?*

Her mother opened her mouth as if to say something but closed it again upon seeing her husband's face turn away from her. 'Carrie, we must pack after dinner, in preparation for our departure.'

'Yes, Mother and …' She turned to their hosts, who looked as surprised by the news as her mother, '… thank you for your kindness. My mother has been able to rest, and I have enjoyed my time reading and learning about gardening. My mind is full of the amazement of growing from seeds.'

Carrie had not planned to slip a note of merriment into an atmosphere that had become strained. She had been raised to be polite and to give thanks, but it was her nature to show her excitement about new discoveries. That she did lighten the mood, did not escape her though, and she was grateful for the ensuing chatter and the look of gratitude on her mother's face.

# Chapter Four

*Where to start* was the question that came to Diana later that night when she had driven the two-hour journey home to Canberra, tired now, but nudged along by a story she felt lay ahead of her to uncover. The book itself was the obvious answer to her question. It's poor condition generated a sense of urgency within Diana that needed to be quelled.

Ignoring the mess in the kitchen—she had always been one of those cooks that used way more plates and utensils than was needed—she plonked down at the dining table and pulled the book close to her.

The musty smell floated back to her, as did her mother's words about the book: 'From today it is yours to treasure and pass on when the time is right.' *To pass on.* Heartache threatened to drag Diana down to drown in a river of tears. Without thinking, she swung around to the photo of Bella that had remained in its place on her sideboard in denial of their two year estrangement. *How could two years have gone by without seeing each other? How could their relationship have fallen apart so quickly after so many years when they were inseparable?* No answer lingered in the sky-blue eyes of her daughter; no answer lurked within Diana's mind that revealed itself now either. She had reached out when they had fallen out, but she should have done more. But even as that thought struck, she knew she had not been capable at the time of doing more than she did. She had barely been able to stand, living her life by the put-one-foot-in-front-of-the-other survival approach. It had been a time of shock, a time of truly not knowing if she could carry on.

The *briiing* of her mobile phone roused Diana from her reflections. She reached the kitchen bench as it vibrated its way towards the edge, in time to see her cousin Sophie's number on the screen. 'Hey you,' she said more cheerily than she felt. 'Hey you back. How are you down there in the Great Southern Land?' Diana puffed out her cheeks, giving herself a moment to compose herself, 'Good, yeah, really good …' she lied, '… and you up there in the land of our British forebears?'

'Good also. Perhaps even better than good. I have shuffled up the ranks another notch in the publishing world. I am loving it, currently spending my days immersed in historical novel submissions.'

A mixture of relief and gratefulness to her cousin swept over Diana. Sophie had given her an in to a topic that drew them away from Diana having to admit she'd been allowing herself to wallow over the state of her relationship—or lack of—with her daughter, to the great passion she and her cousin shared for stories.

She listened to Sophie chat merrily about the details of her new position and what she was reading before she said, 'And I may have something you are interested in too—a book Mum gave me today. A book given to her mother by her own grandmother.'

'So, that would be our great-great-grandmother. Wow! Tell me more.' Sophie's mum had been Diana's mum's only sibling who had passed away in her fifties from breast cancer.

'Well, it's in poor condition and I was about to try to decipher the title. Hang on a second, I will get the magnifying glass.' Those words brought raucous laughter down the phone, making Diana pull it away from her ear.

'How old are you again?' joked Sophie.

'Ha, ha, only fifty-six and don't forget you are not that far behind. It's not my eyesight, I swear. It is the cloth cover of the book—the writing has faded.

'Sure, I believe you,' said Sophie, barely able to contain herself.

'Okay …' said Diana, leaning closely over the cover, '… there seems to be a "The" in smallish letters, then "Beautiful Story", two words below I can't make out, then "Religious Th…" and some more letters that are too worn.'

'I'm on the internet, so let's punch in what we have. "The Beautiful Story … Religious Th..", right?'

'Right,' said Diana, distracted now from her heartache over Bella, as she was drawn into another world.

'I've got it,' said Sophie. '"The Beautiful Story Golden Gems of Religious Thought." So, in fear of stating the obvious, clearly a religious book of some sort, published … oh drat, sorry Di, I have to go, that's my reminder alarm to get me out the door to a meeting. Punch the title in yourself and let me know what else you find out. This could be interesting. Love you.'

'Will do. Love you too. Bye.'

Diana didn't put her mobile phone down straight away; she wanted to hang on to the link with Sophie, to give it another minute for the wracking ache over her daughter to sink back to where it resided within her. *For goodness sake, get on with it,* she scolded herself, swinging her gaze back to the book.

*A religious book. That is nothing to be disappointed about. We're talking a long time ago that my great-great-grandmother gave it to my grandmother. Religion was a big part of life for just about everyone then, I guess. Exactly when was it published?*

As gently as she could, as though she was handling a cracked glass that could shatter at any moment, Diana turned the cover to find the page with the publishing details missing. *Drat!* She turned some more pages, too eager to stop to read, until she came to a coloured plate. It was protected by a thin piece of cloudy, parchment-like paper, which she peeled back with the tips of her thumb and forefinger.

Below lay a vividly coloured … *is it a war scene?* she asked herself. *No, more like a returning-from-war scene.* Five helmeted men, a copper-coloured breast plate here, a shield there, spears in the background. Two women and two children in flowing garb to one side, one child holding a basket of flowers, another blowing on two strange-looking flutes. *Greeting the soldiers by the looks of it.* At the bottom of the plate lay tiny writing, which she had not seen before. "And behold, his daughter (something, a small wedge of the page was missing) meet him with tumbrels and with dances." *So definitely a greeting of the soldiers by family.*

*What the heck is a tumbrel?* She would have to look that up. No, she was getting distracted. Part of doing family history she already knew was that one thing led to another and off you went on a completely different tack to what you had intended. She dragged her laptop towards her, punching in her password ready to get back to finding out about the book. But no, she had to know what a tumbrel was first for goodness sake. It's meaning appeared instantly—a cart, but she couldn't see a cart in the painting. *Oh well.*

*Diana, get back to finding out more about the book*, she told herself, speaking to herself less harshly this time, unable to deny the beauty of the coloured plate before her.

She punched in the book's title and up came a number of entries. She clicked on the first as she always did in her impatience to find answers. She ran her eyes quickly over the words, reading them out aloud. "Companion book to the Holy Bible ... narrative history of events ... golden gems of religious thought added ..." *Oh, looks like some are from 'great writers', whoever they are.*

Diana scrolled and clicked some more. "Published by W.L. Holloway, St Louis, Missouri, USA. 1887." And it was published by another company in the USA in 1888. *So, there was more than one edition. Whichever edition it is—the missing page makes it hard to say—it was published in the USA, so that ties in with great-great-grandmother coming from America.* Was she shipwrecked on the way out? Diana's over-active imagination immediately created an image of a woman bobbing about in the sea, gripping the book in one hand, her arm protruding above the waves, a bit like the Statue of Liberty arm thrust skywards. She shook her head. The book would surely not have survived that.

Diana picked up the book and held it against her chest. She was not religious, but this book offered her something else—a connection to women she had descended from. And one of those women she knew nothing about until today—only that she came from America and her granddaughter, Diana's grandmother, was named after her.

*What is her story? Why did she come to Australia? Why did she stay? How many children did she have? What did she look like? If there was a photo of her somewhere, would Diana recognise herself in her features?* So many questions swirled, then the book in her arms made itself known to her again for when she moved, it 'crinkled,' reminding her of its fragility.

She needed to get it restored. She knew it would bring happy tears to her mum's eyes to know this over-one-hundred-and-thirty-year-old book would forge on as a link to the past that had led to their own existence.

She punched in 'antique book restorers in Canberra' and up came one—just one. For some reason, she thought there would be more. She punched their number into her phone to call tomorrow.

*What next?* It would have to be bed soon she knew. The drive to Jindabyne and back was catching up with her. *Ancestry.com.au first though.* She would add her great-great-grandmother's name to the family tree she had recently started and see if she got any hits overnight.

***

Stepping through the door of the restorer's workshop was like taking a step back through time. Aged wooden tools dripped from boards lining the walls. Two waist-high, wide wooden benches occupied the centre of the room. It was a recollection of the scene she had conjured as a child while her mother read her the story of *Pinocchio*—about the wooden boy who had been crafted in his father's workshop—that came back to her without any effort to dig for it. *What was happening with her imagination? It was developing a life of its own.*

The delightful smell of leather and wood, and a sense of wonder about how many books linking their current owners to the past had come through here, greeted her. At the same time, the welcoming smile of a woman, who was perhaps in her early sixties, did the same.

'Hi, Diana. I am Carol. I can't wait to see it. Even after all these years of restoring books, each one is exciting to me.'

'Do you do this alone? Is this your business, I mean? Not that I mean anything by that,' she stumbled, embarrassed by how that could be taken the wrong way. A warm flush crept up her neck.

Carol chuckled. 'It's okay, it's a natural enough question. My husband and I have been doing this for over forty years. Our love of books and history somehow led us down this path. We will probably be doing it until we drop, I suspect. Now, let's see what you have.'

'Oh yes,' said Diana, her head bent down as she pulled out the book she had placed in a pillow case for its protection—she couldn't think of anything else late last night before she fell into bed—and passed it over.

Carol lay it on a bench and opened it even more carefully than Diana had the night before. 'Brilliant, an old bible of some sort.'

'A companion to a Bible apparently.' She gave Carol what little history she had except for the shipwreck bit.

Carol peered at one page for a moment. 'Some water damage, I see.'

Diana's heart skipped a beat. 'Apparently great-great-grandmother was shipwrecked but I don't know anything about that yet.'

'A good research project by the sounds of it. Lots of cracker stories buried in the records.'

For the first time in two years, Diana felt a sense of purpose. It may just be a small thing—or not—to many people, but it was a glimmer of something fun, an intellectual pursuit when her brain had been in 'pause' mode, it seemed.

'Leave it with me. It will take a week or two. Would you like to insert a page about the book's history at the front? Emailing it through would be good,' she said, handing Diana a business card. 'If you give me your email, I will send you a quote.'

# Chapter Five

The sun was nothing more than a promise the next morning when Louisa and Carrie faced Mr and Mrs Abernathy to say their goodbyes. Carrie's stepfather and stepbrother had gone ahead with their trunks and supplies. Over Mrs Abernathy's shoulder, Carrie noticed the gardener hovering in the front garden behind them, trying to catch her attention with a hesitant beckoning wave of his hand. It pleased her, for she had been lamenting not being able to thank the gardener for his teachings.

An opening in the conversation allowed her to excuse herself and slip away, the gardener holding a package out to her. 'I heard you was leaving. Seeds, Lass, for when you have your own garden.' Delight replaced the lingering confusion Carrie felt about their sudden departure. 'Oh, why thank you! What are they?'

'A letter on each bag marks the season to plant. Let them be a surprise to you. Good luck to you, Lass.'

'And to you too,' she said, stepping backwards to the sound of her name being called.

She looked back after the driver had given her his hand to climb into the buggy, but the gardener had slipped away. As the buggy rattled through the streets, making its way back to the train that would return them to Sandridge, Carrie did not feel disappointment at seeing less of Melbourne than she had hoped, but excitement for the destination that awaited them.

***

Standing on the wharf, it was not her stepfather who looked nervous this time, but his son, who seemed unable to stand still, his eyes ceaselessly searching around them. Amos the younger's eagerness to depart was made apparent when he led them to the gangway before the call to board had rung out.

Bobbing in the water close by, were steamships, but once again they were travelling on a sailing ship, this one more worn than the one they had journeyed on from New York.

The dissatisfaction on her mother's face was plain to see, but she uttered no complaint. When they descended the stairs to their quarters, it was clear that cargo was this ship's main business, for while there were many crates tied together on deck, there were only a small number of bunks below.

As they waited to depart, the silence swam back and forth between the four of them, until Carrie could stand it no longer and, without asking permission, climbed the stairs back to the deck. She was gazing towards several ships with no masts that she could see in the distance when Amos the younger joined her.

'Why would ships have no masts?' she asked, turning to face him.

'They are prison hulks,' he said, quietly enough for her to barely hear. 'They have no need for sails, they do not move from where they are anchored.'

'I do not understand,' she said.

He shuffled his feet beside her. 'Old ships past their sailing days. In disrepair but thought good enough to house prisoners under wretched conditions.'

Carrie turned away from Amos to search the ships for signs of life. She saw none. The ships appeared abandoned and empty. Her mind struggled to accept the knowledge that there were indeed men below decks.

'An abomination,' said Amos, his voice strained with tension. 'Convicts and others, like Captain Melville, the bushranger, kept in irons. The worst of them in Victoria, they say, if you can believe what they say. No excuse to treat men so meanly, I say. Beaten, punished with confinement, the prisoners rarely see the light of day.'

Horror washed over Carrie like too-hot water. 'I can only begin to imagine what it is like for them, Amos. To be chained. To be denied fresh air. To swelter in this heat below deck. Are there many men on the ships?'

'From all accounts, the ships are overcrowded.'

Without intention, Carrie placed her hands together as though she were praying. Amos recognised this as a mark of her compassion and placed his hand upon her arm.

'Are convicts those sent from other countries, Amos?' She had heard other travellers talking as such, on the voyage to Australia.

'Yes, often punished with transportation to this country for doing as little as stealing a loaf of bread to feed their families.'

'A loaf of bread,' she repeated in her astonishment.

'Yes …' Amos said, '… or for not much more.'

'And what is a bushranger, Amos?'

'A man who robs, who steals gold, horses, coins, anything. A bad man, perhaps; some of the time. A desperate, hungry man more often, more likely.'

***

Silence had advanced to distance between her mother and stepfather, Carrie finding comfort standing on deck searching for sea creatures during the day and stars at night. Amos the younger would stand beside her sometimes, equally captivated by the dolphins that swam alongside the ship, their grey skin appearing slippery, eyes looking their way as if the creatures were watching them too.

'They seem to be smiling at us,' she said, the first day they saw the dolphins.

'Indeed, it appears to be so,' he replied, a wide smile of his own greeting her when she turned.

As the few days' journey continued, Carrie's affections for him grew. She wondered if it was the same for him. She liked his gentle and gentlemanly ways but *what would he find to like about her*? she pondered.

The last night of their voyage found them beneath a pitch-black sky, barely a star to be seen. But on the mainland, they could see a small fire here and there, on the beach or in the bush behind.

'Why are there fires?' she asked him.

'The natives light them to cook their food, to keep warm.'

Carrie turned to look at his moon-shaded face. 'Will I meet natives on your property?'

'If you are lucky, you will, yes. And I hope you are.'

'What are they like?'

'They are dark-skinned people—some very dark, others less so. They speak a strange, magical language I have not heard the likes of before. They roam the country, using caves or building shelter from bark, branches. They wear few clothes, a truly strange way to us, but not to them. In the cold weather, they wear cloaks made of possum fur.'

'What is a possum, may I ask?' Carrie said, to which she heard him chuckle.

'Of course you may ask. You may ask anything you like.'

'I fear I may bother you with many questions, but I wish to learn about this country, about its people and animals.'

'A possum is an odd but interesting looking creature. Around this size,' he said, widening his arms to his body width, '… with a bushy tail and big eyes and it makes a *grr-ing* noise like this.' It made Carrie jump when he mimicked it.

'The natives eat the meat and dry the pelt, sewing pelts together to make cloaks.'

'I should like to see a possum, Amos. And any other creatures I can.'

'I am sure you will, my dear. And you will see my property, which stretches to the mountains too. Do you ride a horse?'

'No. But I should like to learn. Is it hard to learn how to?'

'It can be. Give it time. And I will give you the right man to teach you.'

'Not you, Amos?'

'I fear the property will require my full attention when we arrive, but we will have you riding and exploring in no time.'

# Chapter Six

The sparkling waters of Two Fold Bay, star-shaped light twinkling on low-lying waves, greeted them the next morning. It put a smile on Louisa's face that made Carrie's body relax with relief. Perhaps her mother would feel better once back on land, her dislike of sailing now clear to all.

Whether she did or did not, the sight of several near-naked natives stole the smile from Louisa's face again, her mother not having had the benefit of Carrie's conversation with Amos the younger. Louisa clung to her husband, averting her eyes while searching his for answers. What he offered was a firm instruction to walk on to their accommodation.

Carrie's heart went out to her mother. She had begun to realise that a life of their usual routine in New York perhaps suited her mother better than her own eagerness to absorb what lay before them. As they walked, Carrie found herself stumbling along, so consumed was she by the tall trees she could see behind the slope they were climbing, with their faded-green leaves and branches beginning to droop in the building heat. A large, black bird startled her with its drawn out *aarrrgh* sound that tapered off and began again. *How much there is to see, I can only imagine.*

They would stay the night in The Crown and Anchor Inn before beginning the final stage of their journey to Maneroo, within which lay her stepbrother's property *Jimenbuen*. The Inn was a welcome sight when they reached it, puffed by the exertion of climbing the hill upon which it sat. It afforded a breathtaking view of the bay, the several ships which rested upon their waters, and the small settlement alongside.

The Inn was made of stone and timber, and its roof was crafted from shingles. The coolness Carrie felt when she stepped inside reminded her of when she had stepped out of the heat in Melbourne, into the Abernathy's home. A young woman, dressed simply in a plain calico dress, her head kept down, led them to their rooms. Carrie was relieved as much for her mother as for herself when she saw the rooms were well appointed, knowing the rest they would bring, although their stay would be short.

Alone in her small room, she stood at the window, staring out over the bay. It had been agreed they would rest for several hours before a light luncheon to be served in a communal dining room. But as inviting as her single bed appeared after the hard bunk bed on the ship, Carrie did not feel like resting. She was not reluctant to be alone. Her time in Melbourne when her mother had needed to rest, when her stepfather and stepbrother had been out collecting supplies for the property, and her hosts engaged in activities away from the house, had shown Carrie that she enjoyed her own company.

It was more that her mind was whirring with thoughts about what lay ahead. *What would the countryside be like? When would she see a kangaroo? Who else would she meet?* She had enjoyed the company of the gardener, their hands working beside each other in the gritty dirt as he showed her how to nurture vegetables and flowers. *Could she learn to ride? Was it always this hot?*

To distract herself, she removed the treasured gift of paper, pen and a small bottle of ink Mrs Abernathy had given her, from the trunk that had been delivered to her room. It was her hope that she could leave behind her here a letter that would begin its own lengthy journey back to her sister in New York. She sat at a small table to write.

*My Dear Sister Anna. I pray this letter finds you and our brother in good health, as we all are. There is much to tell you and I will begin with our voyage from home, the colour of the ocean ever-changing as our ship sailed further away …*

***

The next morning, Carrie woke early in anticipation of what was to come that day. She was dressed and packed before Amos the younger knocked upon her door, which she opened swiftly.

'Good morning, Carrie,' he said, '... tea and damper are to be served on the verandah if you would like to join us shortly.' Carrie had no idea what damper was but a good night's sleep had encouraged a hunger befitting someone about to embark on another adventurous leg of a journey. 'Good morning, Amos. Thank you, I shall be along shortly.'

Damper, she discovered, was a delicious bread, still warm from baking, its form circular and domed, it's crust broken apart using your hands and smothered with melting butter. Washed down with English tea, she felt satisfied and fortified for what lay ahead.

'Did you rest easy last night, Lass?' asked Amos Senior, his voice gruff from what Carrie suspected was over-indulgence in the liquor available at the Inn.

'Yes, I sank into the bed and slept soundly, thank you.'

'Aye, no such spoiling tonight though. We sleep under the stars or the bullock dray, if be needed.'

Carrie wasn't sure what a bullock dray was either, but she replied with a nod and a pleasant smile, feeling confident she would cope and hoping her mother would also.

'I have written to my sister. May I leave the letter here to travel to Sydney, and on to New York?'

'You may,' spoke her stepbrother, 'I have several letters that are to travel on to Sydney myself and have arranged for them to go on the ship that will leave tomorrow.'

'Thank you. Mother, do you have a letter as well?'

'No, not yet. I am uncertain as to what to say.' It was a comment which struck Carrie as unusual and it was clearly not lost on her husband who stood up quickly, saying 'We are to gather in half an hour at the front of the Inn.' He then walked away.

When they did gather, Carrie was taken aback by the immense size of the eight creatures that were tied to the largest cart she had even seen, brimming with nailed crates, hessian bags, their trunks, and barrels of water.

Carrie was drawn to the creatures and walked to the front of them. She reached out to touch one, avoiding its wet nostrils. It snorted loudly and threw back its head. 'Not that one, Miss,' said the driver of the team. 'He be the leader and he is not partial to touch.'

'Oh, pardon me,' she said, taking quick steps backwards. 'I would not want to upset him. I was taken aback by his size and magnificence.'

For a moment, it appeared the driver did not know what to say, *or perhaps he would say nothing*, she wondered, thinking her a foolish child. But a smile took shape among the wrinkles of his face as he removed his sweat-stained hat and inclined his head towards the bullocks. 'The one at the back, Miss; scratch that one behind its ears and you will make a friend.'

Carrie raised a hand to her mouth to stifle a giggle at the thought that a bullock could become her friend. She nodded her thanks to the agreeable man, before stepping respectfully away from the lead bullock and towards the suggested one. She reached out her hand to feel the stiff hair near its ear and proceeded to gently scratch, the bullock responding by turning its head on the side, a low, deep sound coming from its throat.

When done, Carrie turned to see her mother watching her in a way she had not seen her do before. Wordless surprise at her daughter's actions hung in the air between them, broken by Amos the younger, who stepped forward to offer Louisa a hand up to where she and Carrie would sit beside the driver.

As the hooves of the lumbering bullocks came down upon the dusty road, and the dray jerked forward, Carrie twisted in her seat to take a last look at Two Fold Bay. She breathed in the fresh sea air that was like an elixir to her. She would miss the vast swells of water she had spent many weeks upon, and the glimpses of land and other sailing ships provided from their own ship-bound vantage point. She knew they were heading inland, and she was intrigued by the talk she had overhead between father and son of the need to time their crossing of the *Snowy River*. She looked forward, at the great-sized rumps of the animals, their hips rising and falling, then she looked backwards again at the dray full of supplies, perplexed as to how they would manage a crossing. *Perhaps the river is shallow and narrow, the animals able to drag their burden, including us, through?*

Her contemplation was interrupted by the swift passing of her stepfather and stepbrother, each atop a sturdy mount. A glimpse of the feisty eyes and waves of muscles of the horses offered to her, on the men's way to lead the bullock dray. She watched, entranced at the obvious skill of both father and son in controlling their horses, one gloved hand gripping reins, the other a rifle, it's on-hand readiness frightening her. *Could we meet bushrangers?* An image came to her of desperate, starving, dishevelled men appearing unwanted from the trees that hemmed in the track they travelled along, preventing any escape for a cumbersome team of bullocks.

But by lunch time they had encountered no one. And the increasing temperature saw a rise in her appreciation for the straw hats and plain, brown muslin dresses she and her mother wore, kindly provided by Mrs Abernathy the night before their departure from Melbourne.

It was good to stretch her legs when they stopped by a creek to rest and eat. Carrie offered to take a turn dipping a wooden bucket into the creek to water the bullocks.

'Not too much, Lass,' called the driver as she held a bucket under the nose of the one she had befriended. 'They can drink from the creek we camp beside tonight. Only enough to keep them going for now.'

'I understand,' she said as the bullock's thick tongue lapped up her offering. Carrie stepped away, towards the creek again to refill the bucket for another animal.

As she bent to do so, a piercing crack rang out beside her. She dropped the bucket, placing her hands over her deafened ears, the voices calling to her appearing far away as though across a park. An acrid, burning smell assaulted her nose as Amos the younger arrived at her side and placed a hand on each arm to turn her towards him. He gave her a moment to recover, simply standing there, his strong hands offering her strength and security.

'What happened?' she yelled, due to her deafness.

'Snake,' he yelled back so she could hear, pointing to the ground where a gleaming black creature lay, made headless by the bullet.

'One bite can kill you. Watch out for them wherever you go. Stand still if you see one; they may strike if you move.'

She felt him pull on her arms in an effort to move her away, but she was drawn to the small scales that made up the lifeless body. She stared at them as though they were what prevented her from moving, instead of the fear that was causing her to shake as though the day was cold, and not hot.

She felt Amos remove his hands from her arms, and her mother's hands take their place. For as long as she could remember, she had known the gentle softness of her mother's touch. Comfort replaced fear as she heard her mother say, 'You are safe, my dear daughter. You are safe. Come with me.' And Carrie did as she was bid.

***

The coolness of the night was welcome as she lay beneath the bullock dray, close to her mother's side on a bed of blankets, their shawls draped over them, no pillows beneath their heads. The men lay in the open, around the small fire they had made from sticks and small branches they had collected. Carrie watched the tongues of orange flame reach up like outstretched hands, but she knew there was no danger—the men had shown her where a fire should be built out in the open. She watched until the flames died down, letting the day come to its end, falling asleep to the sounds of a hooting owl and the snuffles of the nearby bullocks.

***

Two more days of searing heat, crossing creeks, and rest beneath the dray, passed. She glimpsed dark-furred wallabies hovering on the edge of thick stands of trees, and kangaroos bounding across treeless plains, their long tails bouncing behind. One night, a possum whose closeness and blinking red eyes had woken her, made her wonder if it was as curious about her as she was about it. Each night, there were the calls of owls telling each other where they were in the dark, and each day there were colourful birds to sight and their loud calls to hear.

She found joy in touching bark peeling from trees, which reminded her of a person shedding clothes. The heady smell of eucalypt leaves became familiar and comforting to her. She learned from the driver how to make damper—dipping her hands into flour to mix it with water, salt and golden syrup, taking heed as to when to cover the sticky mound in the ashes of a fire.

But during this time, that was replenishing to her, she watched her mother grow pale again, while offering not a word of complaint. One day, she heard her stepfather whisper, 'Not long now, my dear,' telling Carrie she was not the only one who was concerned.

On the fourth day, the road wound its way through field after field of boulders that looked like God had opened his hands and dropped clusters of grey buttons from the sky and allowed them to fall where they would. The bullocks grunted as they swung from right to left, following the turns of the rutted dirt track. Then they swung to the right one final time to face a sight that saw Carrie clasp her hand over her mouth.

'That be the *Snowy River*,' the driver said.

'Why, it is certainly beautiful,' she replied. Perhaps it was the heat of the day, but she longed to touch her bare toes to the water, to become part of what she was seeing. Her instincts told her the fast-flowing water represented danger, but she was mesmerised by the vista the river created, its wideness bordered by lines of the trees she now knew to call 'gums'.

With skills the driver had mastered, he brought the bullocks to a halt. Louisa moved restlessly beside Carrie, eager to alight. Her stepfather and stepbrother, who had ridden in before them, gave Louisa and Carrie their hands to help them down.

'Are we to cross the river?' Louisa said to her husband. 'Surely, we will drown.'

'It be safe, Louisa. You will see,' he said, as he took her arm.

'Perhaps you would both like to sit under the shade of a tree until you board the ferry,' Amos the younger said, a rim of red creasing his forehead from where his hat had sat these past few days.

Carrie looked towards the bullocks. 'The bullocks will remain here to rest before they journey back to Two Fold Bay,' said her stepbrother. 'Father and I will also remain until tomorrow when the carts for the supplies will come. A buggy will soon be here to take you and your mother to *Jimenbuen* today.'

'Thank you, Amos,' Carrie said, stepping forward to take her mother's other arm. As she and her stepfather helped Louisa to a fallen tree trunk to sit upon, her mother's trembling left Carrie in no doubt how uncomfortable she was in this new environment. But it was not so for Carrie, whose spirits continued to soar, the way they had each spring in New York when the birds sang their welcome to a new, more pleasant time.

As they waited, Carrie became absorbed in the sounds around her. Dried leaves crackled under the men's feet. Water swished downstream. The bullocks snuffled and the horses neighed, relieved, she imagined, that their journey had come to a halt. And there was the comforting voice of her stepbrother issuing instructions in his polite manner.

It was not long until trotting hooves announced the arrival of a buggy on the other side of the river. Carrie watched her stepbrother lift and wave his arm, a warm smile lighting up his face as he walked towards the river. Her stepfather returned to them, again offering his arm to his wife, supporting her to rise, walk and step gingerly onto the ferry—a punt—which would see them to the other side. He helped Louisa sit upon a plank of wood suspended in the middle of the boat, and Carrie joined her mother.

The punt was flat-bottomed and square-ended, and Carrie could feel the water pulling at it as they began their crossing, the river challenging them to a game of tug-of-war that only one side would win. In this instance, she was confident that the tug would be mastered by the two men, one at either end, with their long, wooden poles.

Carrie resisted the urge to lean towards the edge, but still, she caught a glimpse of a tiny fish weaving its way through water as clear as the delicate diamond stud earrings her father had gifted her mother years before. While Carrie had grown up close to the East River of New

York, wider still than the *Snowy*, its waters were muddied by both ships and those living alongside it. Today was her first experience of water she could see through—water which tumbled over rocks and pebbles below and wrapped itself around greenery growing beneath and alongside it. For Carrie, it was a refreshing sight, a sight which made its mark on her heart. She hoped she would see the river again soon.

***

Carrie noticed a quizzical look cross her mother's face when Amos the younger led them to the horse and buggy driven by a woman wearing a dress as equally plain and practical as their own. She had a similar straw hat to theirs perched upon her head.

'Louisa, Carrie. May I introduce my wife, Elizabeth?' he said.

Like her mother, Carrie was intrigued and taken aback by Elizabeth. Firstly, because she—and not a man—was driving the buggy, and also because she was not as Carrie had imagined Elizabeth to be. For some reason—that she now queried why she had thought this—she had formed an image of Elizabeth as a refined woman who would certainly not be driving a buggy herself. But here she was in front of them, doing exactly that, and dressed in practical clothes like themselves. Carrie felt immediately drawn to Elizabeth as she had with Amos the younger.

The three women exchanged greetings as Carrie and her mother's trunks, which had been brought across before them, were loaded, and the men were farewelled. But as the horse took its first self-assured steps, wordlessness settled in. Carrie realised her mother had no energy to spare for such a thing, while she wanted only to take in the waves of hills that showed themselves around each corner and the glances of mountains that teased her with their nearby presence.

When the homestead finally came into view, the sun was close to setting. They came to a small creek that Elizabeth had to encourage the horse to cross. The creek bed was stoney and the buggy leaned to one side, Louisa sliding as though she might tumble. Carrie pulled her close, aware her mother's trembling had turned to shivers as the cold of the evening bit them—a warning of the harshness of nature in this remote place.

Elizabeth pulled up in front of the single-storey timber homestead, an enticing verandah stretching its length. A gangly youth of no more than twelve years of age seemed to appear from nowhere. He reached for the reins of the horse and whispered quietening words. A woman emerged from the homestead, paraffin lamp held high, a thick woollen shawl wrapped around her shoulders. 'Mary …' said Elizabeth, '… please help Louisa and Carrie down,' which she did, immediately removing her own shawl to cover Louisa's shuddering shoulders.

'Louisa, Carrie. This is Mary. She keeps house, helps with the children and she is also our friend,' said Elizabeth, joining the other women.

'Aye,' said Mary. 'And we all welcome you here,' she said.

'The night is cold,' said Elizabeth. 'Let us show you straight to your room, Louisa, so you may rest while Mary and I unload the trunks. The station men are droving. So, until my husband and his father arrive, we are on our own, with the exception of our stable boy, Henry, who will take care of the horse and buggy. Thank you, Henry,' she nodded, turning her head towards him.

Elizabeth and Carrie threaded an arm through each of Louisa's and they mounted the few steps on to the verandah. They were guided by Mary, who had picked up the lamp she had rested on the ground. They passed through the front door, the lamp casting enough light for Carrie to see the shadowy shapes of heavy wooden furniture—a long table with chairs, a sideboard, armchairs. And an unlit fireplace. They turned from that large room, down a hall and into a bedroom where sat a wrought iron bed upon a polished wooden floor. A thick eiderdown and two plump pillows reminded Carrie of a story her father had told her of when weary travellers had come upon an oasis in a desert.

Elizabeth struck a match to light a candle that sat in its holder on a small wooden table to one side of the bed. Louisa lowered herself on to the bed with as much dignity as she could muster, a vague smile the only effort of appreciation her exhausted body was able to generate.

'We will fetch the trunks so your mother can dress for the night. I suggest a good night's rest before the exertion of a bath, in the morning, is called for,' said Elizabeth.

'Yes, thank you,' said Carrie as the women stepped from the room, releasing Louisa from the need to stay upright, her eyes and the world soon closed to her for the night.

Dragging sounds and the muffled voices of Elizabeth and Mary came to Carrie as she sat on the end of her mother's bed, waiting to retrieve a nightgown from her trunk and attempt to replace her mother's dusty dress with its soft cotton. The notion that she could help with the trunks struck her, so she joined the women outside where Henry held a wooden bucket of water to the horse so that it might drink while the women worked behind it.

'I have not done this before, but I am willing to assist if I can,' Carrie said.

'That is kind and welcome, Carrie,' said Elizabeth, 'The luggage is heavy, but we women have learned to find ways to manage when the men are away. Working together, when we can, is one of them.' So together, the three of them heaved and dragged until one trunk was in her mother's room and the other was in the small room next door that was to be Carrie's for her stay. It was a satisfying but not easy task, and having changed her mother and herself into nightgowns, she fell gratefully into bed and into a deep slumber.

# Chapter Seven

The mug of cappuccino, flavoured sweetly with caramel syrup, that was warming Diana's hands, was probably heading her towards diabetes. Or so she thought—primarily because she had been having one, two or three times a week for over a year now. But she didn't much care even though she knew that one day not too far away, she would have to make the decision *to* care and make a change. Right now though, she would not deny herself the comfort it brought her as she scanned the surrounding view over the iconic lake, designed by Walter Burley Griffin, that was central to Canberra. With the sun shining, the water in the distance sparkled blue, its surface appearing flat from the café at the National Arboretum that hovered, a bit drone-like, over the scene of the arboretum plantings, hilly terrain, thick bush, and water.

The *man*-made lake had been designed by the man it was named after. But it was only recently that Diana had read about the *woman behind the man*—to use the oft-used phrase. Three short words she suspected hid a trillion stories cast aside in the wake of men's tales.

In the case of the lake—or the city really—that woman had been Marion Mahoney Griffin. She was an architect like her husband, whose watercolours of his designs had been critical in him winning the international competition in 1912 to plan Australia's national city.

Each time she looked at the lake, Diana thought of Marion. And today there was another American lady who came to mind—her great-great-grandmother, Caroline Amelia Hedger. *Forgive me g-g-g, your full family description and name is a mouthful, so from here on in, I will call you by the affectionate name you were called, of Carrie.*

Perhaps it was because she was a woman too—*of course, it was*—that Diana was so interested in Carrie's story. But even when she had found out what she had this morning about her great-great-grandfather, while her mouth had dropped open, not long afterwards her mind had drifted back to Carrie and what *her* life had been like.

Brewing a camomile tea had been the only thing she had done after the obligatory bathroom stop that morning before she jumped on to *ancestry.com.au* to see if Carrie's name had brought up any hints. Nothing. Her heart sank. She reminded herself it was early days. But while there was nothing on her, there were several hints under her great-great-grandfather, George Henry Hedger. *Forgive me g-g-g*, she thought again, *let's just call you George.* It struck her that perhaps she was going bananas, having conversations with people, even if only in her head, who had died a very long time ago.

She noted George was on a number of ancestry member's family trees. She would go back to those, but she clicked on the hint that turned out to be his obituary. Her eyes skimmed to a sentence that made the world go silent for a moment. '*...was generally regarded as the original of Paterson's "Man from Snowy River"*' *What?!* Diana had to confess she was not that into poetry, but it was hard to imagine a person in her age group—and others—who was not perfectly aware of *that* poem. Afterall, who hadn't had to study it and recite it during their school years?

*So, was George the inspiration for Banjo to write that poem? Could that be possible?* The obituary in front of her seemed to be saying so. She read on.

> *One who knew him well said that as a stock-rider and bushman no one was comparable with him. He was born at Hobart in May 1883, and came to the Monaro district ...*

And that was as far as she got before the alarm on her phone trilled, telling her it was time she headed out the door. In a moment of late-night inspiration, she had decided to adopt her cousin Sophie's use of alarms to keep her focused on doing things rather than risk languishing. But she feared it would be like a New Year's resolution, and not be a roaring success.

Now, as she sat at the table at the arboretum, she tipped the last drops of the delicious coffee into her mouth. The warmth from the cup had seeped away as she had gradually drained it. She reminded herself that something else apart from family history awaited her. Today she was going to do something she wanted to—that she needed to—but had been unable to bring herself to do for the year she had been coming here. It was simply out of fear that the pain would be too great to bear.

She stood and pushed her chair in to nestle against its small, square, companion table, before walking slowly to the side door imbedded in the wall of floor-to-ceiling glass that framed the view she loved of the lake and surrounds. She hesitated for a mere moment before stepping up to the double glass door which opened when she approached. She strode with purpose to the Bonsai collection displayed like the precious art it was, behind a protective stone wall.

The gate was open, a smiley volunteer perched nearby upon a stool. Diana returned his smile. She took a breath in as she walked towards the Bonsai, but she couldn't bring herself to go directly to where she had last stood with James on their last outing. So, she ambled along, reading and failing to comprehend labels, but still absorbing the beauty of what lay before her. And then she was there. The world receded until it was her, a miniature Japanese Maple 'forest' and James's face before her—in her imagination. She saw the curl of salt and pepper hair that dangled over his forehead, forever uncontrollable. The olive-ness of his skin, a testament to his Mediterranean heritage. The sensual lips that she had been powerless not to kiss, that spread into the most glorious smile, two bracket-shaped creases having appeared as the years had rolled on. She saw the slightly too-large nose and the wide-set, dark-chocolate eyes that had lured her years ago into wondering what lay behind.

'This is my favourite,' he said.

'I thought that one was your favourite,' she said, pointing behind her.

'It was, until I saw this one,' he said, placing his hands on her hips to draw her closer to him. She could feel those hands now as though this moment was not a remembered one at all.

He had always been so affectionate, so hands-on. She had known how lucky she was. Or thought she was—until he was gone. A call at her work. He had collapsed. An ambulance had been called. She arrived at the hospital and waited. Tests. Time. A stroke. There was danger of another. And another had come. And he had left her.

Weeks followed of keeping it together, of being strong through the kind words and gestures, the funeral, of supporting others in their grief. Tears kept at bay. Screaming on the inside. Anger ate its way through the misery, like woodworms creating tunnels. Anger at James for leaving her. He was slim, he exercised, there were no heart conditions in his family. At fifty-eight, he was too young to go!

She looked upwards, his face as clear to her as the sky that shone above. Perhaps it was the unexpected warmth of the autumn sun that heated her soul, whatever it was, a sliver of joy touched her being too. A happy memory finally reached within to release a smile; not a tear, but the first truly-meant smile for two years.

She was glad she had come here. She would come back again. And again. To re-capture that memory and precious moment with her husband. All she could do was hope it would never leave her like he had.

# Chapter 8

Pale light touched Carrie's eyelids on its way to shine its rays upon the framed painting opposite the small window in her room at *Jimenbuen*. The painting was the first thing she laid her eyes upon when she woke. A stocky horse, its front legs in the air, a bearded older man astride, reins in one hand, a whip in the other. *Who is in control?* she questioned. *The rider or the horse? How can I hope to ride a creature of such strength.* She remembered her stepbrother's words, 'I will give you the right man to teach you.' Well, all she could pray for was that whoever he had in mind, the man would be patient with her—very patient indeed.

She sat up suddenly as another thought struck her. They were here! After months of planning and journeying, they were here—the destination they had set out for, and she was eager to start exploring her surroundings. Her hand had gripped the doorknob before she realised she was still in her nightgown. She kneeled to her trunk, sifting through the carefully folded layers, to find her simple cream cotton dress with lace trimming that she had last worn in Melbourne. She would need to wash the brown muslin dress she had worn on her journey here. It lay crumpled on the floor, the smell of dust from the dirt track wafting up to her nose, making it twitch in irritation.

Dust had ingrained itself in the creases of her boots too, so she tip-toed out of the room with them in her hand. She gave into the temptation to form her first daylight impression of her surroundings by stepping out onto the verandah that stretched the length of the house.

Like the *Snowy River*, what lay before her took her breath away. There was not another homestead or structure of any kind within view.

What there was, was a vista of rolling hills—a valley nestled at their feet, all clothed in golden, swaying tall grass. There were forests of gums at the top of the hills, and glimpses of blue-hazed mountains to one side. Her senses were having trouble separating all the smells sent her way, but the crispness in the air—*mountain air feels different somehow*—was a type of refreshment she had not previously encountered.

'Morning Lass,' boomed her stepfather's voice behind her, making her jump, which he did not apologise for. She had not heard the men arrive with the supplies and realised it must be quite late in the morning.

Carrie still avoided calling her stepfather anything. She had not decided upon what she was comfortable calling him yet. As far as she knew, his courtship of her mother had been brief, and their marriage—which was announced one day *after* it had taken place—had been unexpected. No invite issued to her or her siblings.

But Carrie could not deny the smiles she had witnessed this man bring to her mother's face after the heart-wrenching grief of losing her beloved first husband. So, she had said nothing and kept her own grief, her own memories of the father she would never forget, locked within her as though she had thrown away the key that would unlock the door and let them out.

'Good morning. This view makes my heart sing,' she said, taking them both by surprise for she had not shared such an intimate thought with him before. There was a pause before he replied, 'Aye, it is grand, but some say lonely, a lonely place to be.'

'I don't feel lonely. Do you?'

'No, Lass. I find comfort in the ranges. Luncheon awaits if you follow me,' he said, bringing the conversation to a close, which saved each from possible awkwardness. He opened the door to the house for her and she followed him through a back door and along a short dirt path towards a separate, smaller building. 'This is where the cooking be done, away from the house in case a fire were to catch,' he said.

A laughing child toddled up to Carrie as they entered, wrapping her arms around Carrie's leg, such was her young age. Carrie placed a hand on the girl's silky curls, their touch reminding her of the silk of her own mother's fine dress that one day she hoped to own one like. As the child turned her baby blue eyes to her, another giggle escaped. Her mother, Elizabeth who, in the light of day Carrie could now see was with child, walked over to them. She did not admonish the child for being forward, but rewarded her with a smile. 'Her affection has been forthcoming since shortly after her birth,' she said. 'Carrie, this is my daughter, Sarah, who will now try to pronounce your name in return. Go ahead please, Sarah.'

Her new little friend became serious, uttering two succinct syllables. 'Ka-ri.'

'We are practising her English,' said Elizabeth.

'And how well you are doing,' replied Carrie, bending down to address Sarah directly. Carrie was unable to resist scooping Sarah up into her arms, which the child allowed for a few moments before squirming to be put down again as two other children burst through the door, followed by two older children.

'And these ragamuffins …' said Elizabeth cheerily, nodding towards the tallest boy, '… are Amos, Elizabeth Ann, John, and Frances—in order of their birth. Amos, will you take your brother and sisters back out to play while we finish preparing their luncheon?' The children promptly turned on their heels, with Amos Senior—their grandfather—following them out.

*Another Amos*, Carrie thought. *About nine years old. So, Elizabeth had five children with another on the way!* Carrie managed to mask her surprise with a statement. 'Forgive me, I woke late. I have not seen to my mother.'

'There is no forgiveness needed,' said Elizabeth, stepping towards Mary, who had her hands in dough. 'Rest was needed after the journey you have all had. We are up well before the sun rises to get on with the day's work. We saw to your mother, who has eaten well and enjoyed her bath.'

'That is good news,' said Carrie, sinking into a chair away from the heat of the cooking fire.

Elizabeth smiled. 'And this morning we have been picking the first of the apples,' she said, her gaze directing Carrie's gaze to several wooden buckets sitting on the floor brimming with shiny red fruit. 'And we have milked the cow and collected the eggs. Would you like to try an apple while we make the damper for lunch?'

The sight of so many apples was a delight to Carrie, who had only had one or two before, in New York. A hunger descended upon her with insistence. She reached for one, and took as big a bite as she could, unaware that, picked straight from the trees, there would be none of the staleness of those that had travelled a distance to her plate beforehand.

Sweet juice trickled down her chin. She could only have dreamed of such crispness, such deliciousness, captured within a circlet of colour.

'We have more to pick tomorrow if you would like to join in,' said Mary.

'Oh, I would, indeed. I would like to help and learn about how they are grown. The gardener at Mr and Mrs Abernathy's in Melbourne introduced me to gardening and I am most intrigued.'

'Then we shall show you more,' said Elizabeth. 'How to bake them and preserve them too. But for today, I suggest you bath after luncheon and continue your recuperation.'

***

Carrie sat at a small, white wicker table on the verandah. After soaking in a tin tub filled with water warmed over the fireplace, and cool water that had been brought from the creek, she had been drawn back to the quietness and panorama the verandah offered. Bathing had cleansed her of more than the dust and perspiration of an overland journey; it had swept away any remaining tiredness and she did not feel like resting in her room.

She brought the steaming cup of coffee that Mary had surprised her with, to her nose. Its aroma was rich and nutty. She took a sip. Mary had added cream and sugar, reducing its bitterness. It was delicious and the cup was soon emptied. She picked up her pen, dipped it carefully in her little bottle of ink and began to write a letter to her sister.

*Dear Anna*

*I have so much to tell you! Firstly, that we have arrived and it is beautiful here. The property is named Jimenbuen, which …'*

The sound of pounding hooves broke into her concentration. She looked up to see a man riding his horse hard along the dirt track before the homestead. His hat was low over his forehead, a bushy beard the only other detail she had time to see, in his haste.

*Goodness,* she thought. *What would require him to ride so?*

The rider disappeared behind the homestead and Carrie returned to her letter, attempting to put into words the view she sat before.

'Who are you?' demanded a voice that boomed so loudly she came close to slipping from the chair she sat upon. It was a distinctive voice, capable of upsetting her calm in an instant it seemed, for she felt agitated at the rudeness directed at her.

'I, sir …' *Why am I even using that term of respect with such an impolite man?* she wondered momentarily. '… am Carrie. I am a guest in this …' But she got no further for as she stood to size up to him, she raised her eyes to the most alluring, handsome man she had ever lain eyes upon. And it was his eyes that, without her permission, were pulling her down into a depth that appeared to reside within him—one that she could not even begin to fathom.

The hat in his hand, and the bushy beard, told her this was the man she had seen upon his horse only minutes ago.

A bead of sweat chose that second to drop from his chin onto sun-browned skin made visible by a shirt opened to several buttons below. His chocolate-coloured hair was tousled, his cheeks sat high above a sculpted chin, and she caught a glimpse of redness in his beard. Carrie's heart thumped, causing her to be as furious with *it* as she was with him.

She gathered herself to stand her full height, which didn't help as she found herself face to face with his glistening chest. 'And who, may I ask, are you?' she tried but failed to boom back, refusing to be intimidated further.

'Head stockman,' he said, refusing to take his eyes from hers, to allow her some dignity in this exchange.

The image of the older stockman in the painting in her room, formed itself in her head. 'Young, aren't you to be a *head* stockman.' She did not mean it to be a question, and he did not answer it. Instead, he let it hang in the air between them, until a smile began to curve the corners of his mouth, spreading until perfect teeth were revealed underneath.

Her fury with him grew for as if rudeness had not been a big enough offence, now he appeared to find her entertaining!

'George, there you are,' came Amos the younger's voice as he rounded the corner of the homestead, followed by his father. 'It is good to see you man, how go the stock?'

As the men spoke, Carrie observed their closeness. They slapped each other on the back, and her stepfather grasped George's hand with both of his. Confused and quite shaky from her meeting with George, Carrie's only desire was to remove herself. Without their noticing, she slipped back into the house to the quiet of her room.

# Chapter 9

For several days, in the cool of early morning, Carrie enjoyed picking apples in the orchard with Elizabeth and Mary, the children playing chase around them. Mary had given Carrie her first lesson in milking a cow, her attempt causing them both to fall into fits of laughter, the cow herself kicking out, clearly not amused.

Carrie and Mary were preparing apples to preserve when Amos the younger arrived. 'Carrie, are you ready to learn to ride? You may begin this morning if you so wish.'

She was no longer certain if she did wish, and she was definitely not sure if the ability was within her, but his enthusiasm and customary generosity was not to be resisted. 'I am,' she declared, with far more confidence than she felt.

'Good.' And she was glad for he seemed pleased. 'Wear something suitable and we shall meet here in an hour.'

***

Changed into her brown muslin dress, Carrie and her stepbrother marched beyond the orchard to where the stables and a stockyard she had noted from the orchard, were.

*May whoever is to teach me be kind and patient*, she pleaded.

Six men stood along one side of the stockyard. Carrie could hear a horse whinnying and stamping its hooves beyond, but the men obscured her view of what was happening within. When she and Amos reached the stockyard, the men parted to make way for them—in time to see George swing his leg over a caramel-coloured horse that was displeased about him doing so.

The horse reared back, its front legs stabbing at the air. The muscles in George's arms, exposed by his rolled-up sleeves, rippled as he hung onto the reins to gain control that it was obvious, even to her unknowing eye, the horse did not want to relinquish.

At the same time, her body betrayed her again. The sight of George in all his masculine glory made her heart thump, her knees tremble and her mind cloud with inner turmoil. She did not understand what was happening to her. She cared about whether the horse was in distress, but she could not take her eyes from a man she didn't think she even liked!

Carrie clung to the rails in front of her for the long time it took George to master the horse. When he rode it around the stockyard, the other men cheered, including her stepbrother who, as the other men drifted away, said, 'Let's begin your lesson.'

'Amos, I cannot ride that horse …' she exclaimed, taking a step away from the rails, '… it is almost wild, and I have not set one foot in the stirrups yet. And who is to teach me?'

Her stepbrother roared with laughter. 'Carrie, my dear, George will teach you, of course. He is our best rider, and you will learn upon a different horse—one tamed long ago. That beauty George just rode, is a brumby recently driven from the mountains.'

'Do you have more than one George working for you?' she asked, fearing she knew the answer. She sensed that her hope of a kind, patient man to teach her had fled into oblivion. Amos laughed again and patted her affectionately on the shoulder.

Still facing her stepbrother, Carrie became aware of George's presence, an earthy smell setting her senses on alert. When he stepped into view, she glanced at him, moving her gaze over his shoulder at the still jumpy brumby being led away to the stables, its spirit reduced, but not broken, by the man before her. From her brief look, George appeared as dismayed as she felt at the prospect of teaching her. Then, to her annoyance, he smiled at her. It was a charming smile, like the one he had given her on the verandah. But she was not at all convinced by it.

'I will leave you to it, George. Carrie tells me she has not been on a horse before.' George nodded, saying nothing, keeping his opinion on that to himself.

Carrie and George stood for a few moments until they were alone. 'Come …' he said, '… to the stables to meet your horse.' He left her with no choice but to trot behind him as his lengthy strides required.

The morning was still young, the stables cool, and soft snuffling noises of horses feeding came to her as she entered. George stopped at the second horse along, its long-lashed, encircled hazel eyes rising to look directly into Carrie's. She reached to stroke its muzzle and the horse did not flinch, seemingly welcoming her touch as she welcomed the bond she already felt would grow with this horse.

'You should be able to ride this one,' George boomed, 'the two older children have learned on it.'

*Did he mean to offend her?* Probably, but she had no intention of allowing him to.

'She is beautiful. What is her name?'

'The children named her *Pony*. She was caught as a foal with her mother in the mountains. That is why she is tame enough even for you to ride.'

Now there was *no* doubt in her mind that he meant to offend! She decided the best approach was to ignore him.

'What do I do?' she asked, managing to keep the fury from her voice, she hoped.

'Before you can learn to ride, you must learn how to look after her,' he said, turning to grab a pitchfork and thrust it towards her. 'Clean her stall, put the old straw and droppings outside on the two piles, and give her new straw from over there.' He pointed to a mound of it. Then, he promptly turned and walked away, out of the stables.

She would *not* let him defeat her. She would give Pony the cleanest stall of all. She would show him! And she did. For when he returned two hours later, he nodded at her efforts, failing to hide that infuriating smile at her grime-y appearance. Straw was stuck to her clothes and in her hair, and the bun she had tied high on her head had sunk to her neck, wisps of hair dangling around her neck.

'Good, I will call for you another day, when I have time,' he said.

Carrie marched back to the homestead, weary, back straight, head high in case he was watching. She flopped onto the nearest chair when she made it into the cookhouse. She looked up to see amused expressions upon Elizabeth and Mary's faces. Movement caught Carrie's eye, and she turned to see her mother standing in the corner, an aghast look upon her face.

'Mother, how happy I am to see you,' she declared.

'And how surprised I am to see you in your current state, Carrie. What have you been doing?'

'I thought I was to learn to ride today, but *that* man—George—made me clean a stall in the stable. Apparently, I have to learn to look after Pony before I can learn to ride her,' she said, shaking her head from side to side.

Chuckles escaped from both Elizabeth and Mary before they could prevent them, which perplexed Carrie. But the sight of her mother on her feet again, having recovered from the journey, brought her joy enough to put their reaction to the side.

'Come to the verandah with me, Mother,' she pleaded, '… to look at the view—if you have not seen it yet this morning.'

'No, I have not,' her mother replied, allowing Carrie to take her hand in hers and lead her from the cookhouse and through the homestead.

'When I first stood here, the view took my breath away. There is so much to see,' she exclaimed.

'But Carrie, there is nothing. Where are the other homesteads? Where are the grocery shops? Where are the people?' The look of dismay on Louisa's face took Carrie aback.

'Look. You can see the mountains over there.' Carrie pointed, her need for her mother to see what she saw—to feel what she felt—consuming her. 'And the creek is down that way. And there is an orchard and vegetable garden behind the house. There is a great deal to enjoy here.'

'I am not used to this,' replied her mother, her voice barely a whisper. 'It is unusual. But I can see how it has struck you, so I will try to find the beauty in it.'

Carrie thought she could not love her mother more than she did in that moment as they stood contemplating their surrounds, her mother's eyes searching for beauty. She stretched out an arm to wrap around her mother's shoulders. She would try hard to help her mother find it.

***

It was the youngest of the Amos-named family members who delivered a note to her the following day, which read 'Stables, sunrise tomorrow.' Customary of his rudeness, she knew it had to be from George, and it was certainly a temptation not to follow his instructions. But her pull to Pony, and the determination to learn to ride—if for no other reason than to prove herself to George—had her dressed and stroking Pony before George made an appearance. He offered no greeting. 'Today,' he said, 'you will learn how to feed her, when to water her, when to let her out into the field.'

'And today you will teach me to ride,' she said defiantly, drawing herself up to him.

'When, is my choice to make,' he bit back.

'And it is *my* choice to tell Amos you are not being co-operative,' she tossed back at him, only to be met with that most infuriating of smiles again. *He likes it when I stand up to him. What an odd man he is. Damn him for being handsome! If only he had a large wart perched on the end of his nose.*

She watched him walk away, believing he was leaving her, but he grabbed a bridle from the wall and tossed it to her without warning. She caught it, refusing to fail and allow it to fall at her feet.

'Put this on to lead her around the stockyard.'

***

Carrie had been content with George's compromise. At least she and Pony would move outside the stable. Nevertheless, it turned out to be frustrating for he gave her no instructions, taking joy, she presumed, in her struggle to teach herself how to put the bridle on. When she had finished, or so she had thought, he sashayed over—for he had a distinctive, loping sort of walk. He made several adjustments, nodded and thrust the lead rope in her hand, pointing outside. She then successfully managed to walk Pony around the ring to exercise her and was very pleased with herself, although tired from the exertion of meeting George's challenge more than anything else.

***

Carrie had come to her room to change out of her dusty clothes and wash her face from the bowl of water Mary refreshed each day, when she could not fail to hear the raised voices of her mother and stepfather next door.

'I am trying, Amos! I am trying very hard, but I do not like it here. There is nowhere to go and nothing for me to do. There is no town to visit, no other people to see.'

'Louisa, you know I must be careful not to be sighted by many. Otherwise, I would take you to Sydney, despite the long journey needed, but I cannot.'

'Yes, I do know you must be careful, but I do not understand why. You should tell me why.' The pleading in her voice caused Carrie's heart to ache for her mother.

'You must try harder,' Amos said, ignoring his wife's plea. 'You must!' his voice was forceful and demanding. 'Your daughter is having no trouble settling in. She busies herself each day. You must find ways to occupy yourself.'

'But I am of no use. I am not good at picking and bottling fruit, and my reading is too poor to help the children learn. Carrie is a good teacher: I am not.'

A knock at their door saved her mother from what was surely further difficult admissions for her. Carrie heard her stepbrother and stepfather talk in hushed tones that drifted away as they walked along the hall to leave the homestead. She knew they were to ride into the mountains, but she had no idea how long they would be away for.

Her stepfather's comments about not being seen confused Carrie. Like her mother, she did not understand why that was so, or indeed why he used a different surname to his son. What she did know was that she must hurry—she must go to her mother, she must help her adjust, she must do that for her. Her kind, loving mother that had always been there for her. She must begin to return the favour.

# Chapter Ten

Diana had been chasing information on Carrie and George for the last week, aware that hers was a haphazard approach to family history research. She was certain there was a more systematic way than her '*where would I look for that, maybe there, worth a go, can't hurt*' stumbling-along approach. Still, she had managed to uncover quite a bit, probably—*definitely*—in more time than it would take someone who actually knew what they were doing. Someone who had done courses, read books, etc—but what the hey, she was enjoying herself, enjoying the chase, enjoying feeling like she imagined a detective would, following leads where they took her.

Instead of dreading the light announcing a new day, wanting to stay tucked up in bed, pushing the world and her heartache away, Diana was up, showered and breakfasted by nine. Either ensconced at the dining room table with her laptop and a growing pile of printed-off paper or off to the National Library of Australia to ask questions of computers, librarians, old newspapers, and microfiche. She tended to be a creature of habit, finding herself a tad annoyed if the desk she liked at the library, tucked quietly by the window—again with a calming lake view—was already occupied.

Today, she was visiting her mother again in Jindabyne, eager to tell her what she had found out and to ask a question that might help her research. Diana always felt at ease in her mother's house. Somehow each room echoed the love and warmth of the person her mother was, injecting Diana with strength each time she was there. On a clear day, she and her mother would sit, sipping coffee or tea, eyeing the smidgen of lake they could see from the lounge room. Beyond the lake was the rise of Hill Top, an area of a number of properties, reminding them of the range of mountains to be seen close by.

Diana and Maggie were sitting looking at the view now. Diana lifted a forkful of the 'soft-as' sponge cake her mother had made, to her mouth. Strawberry jam and cream oozed spirit-lifting deliciousness. 'No wonder the Country Women's Association—the CWA—keeps asking you to make these for their stalls. People must flock to get one, Mum.'

'Well, they have never been returned to me when a stall ends, so I see that as a good sign. Now what is it you are excited to tell me about? What has happened?'

If her mother was hoping for a sign that things were improving between Diana and Bella, she did not show her disappointment.

'Well, more information has come up on the ancestry website about the Hedgers, and I have found out Carrie and George's, and six of their children's, dates of birth. It appears there may have been a couple more children too, though I haven't found any details yet. Did you know they had that many children?'

'No, but even larger numbers of children were the norm back then, I think. And child mortality too.'

'How sad,' said Diana.

'I can't imagine what it would have been like to birth and care for so many in an isolated area, large distances between neighbours, I'm presuming.'

'Would there have been a doctor for when they gave birth, do you think, Mum?'

Diana watched as her mother closed her eyes for a moment. 'A memory of your grandmother talking about other women helping, midwives riding to help, is in here somewhere,' she laughed, tapping her forehead with one finger.

'Midwives! I will see if I can find anything,' said Diana. *Hopefully I won't forget. Note to self—buy a bag-size-friendly notebook to carry around with me.*

'Also, I have managed to find and order George and Carrie's marriage certificate and all the six children's birth certificates. From the

*Birth, Deaths and Marriages* website. They offer emailing them, so it shouldn't take long. Maybe they will tell us something.

'I suspect they will,' said her mother, proffering another piece of cake, which Carrie didn't think for one second of not accepting.

'Mum, would you know Carrie's maiden name?' I'm thinking that might help us find out exactly when and how she got here from the other side of the world.'

'Yes, darling. I think it was Marsden or Marston.'

'Did you ever go to where they lived on the Monaro?'

Her Mum chuckled. 'They had passed before I was born, but I remember going to where their eldest son—my grandfather, Edward—lived. My Aunty Hilda and her son, Noel, lived there some of the time. Dad would drive us. The property was called *Middleview.*'

'That would have been a very long trip from Crookwell in the Southern Tablelands, where you lived as a child.'

'It was. Very tiring, but worth it to see Mum and Grandfather ride out across the paddocks, side by side, Grandfather challenging her to keep up.'

'So, Grandma was a horsewoman? I didn't know that.'

'She was. I would listen to her tales of riding all over the *Snowies* as she grew up. Did you know Grandfather Edward used to give me a sixpence when we visited? He had a supply of them in his waistcoat pocket. And he was an elegant dresser. Not a hair out of place. I would rush outside to watch him mount and ride out to check on his stock. Twice a day, without fail.'

'A stockman, like his father,' said Diana, slightly distracted by the realisation that in researching Carrie and George's lives, she was learning more about other family members than she had expected to. *One thing leads to another*, she reminded herself.

'Mum, George's obituary says he was the original *Man from Snowy River*. Do you think that your great-grandfather, my *great-great-*grandfather, could have been the inspiration for Banjo Paterson's poem?'

'Well, apparently they rode together and went fishing together.'

'Mum, you never said!'

'Because I had forgotten until now. I heard that when I was a child. Give me a break, it's been a lot of years,' she scolded.

So that's why her mother had not flinched when Diana had told her about the possible link with Banjo Paterson. Somewhere in the back of her mind, she already knew.

Maggie looked away. Diana knew what this was—it was her mum pondering. She turned back. 'There were a lot of stockmen, drovers, in those days, weren't there? So, perhaps there were a lot of *Men from Snowy River* that Banjo met—which inspired his poem,' she said, shrugging her shoulders, flashing her glorious, cheeky smile at Diana.

# Chapter Eleven

By late February, Carrie was riding. She could barely believe it, though some embarrassing experiences had been had. When she had asked if she would be riding side-saddle, she was greeted with uproarious laughter from George. 'I would like to see that in the mountains, Miss,' he said.

When she had strapped the saddle on to Pony for the first time, it had slipped to hang under her belly and there was more laughter from George. And yet more when she had mounted Pony for the first time. The horse had moved off before she had thrown her leg over and she had landed on her bottom in the dust, the ache coming from there nowhere near as bad as the humiliation she had felt. Still, she had ignored the background laughter, dusted herself off, retrieved Pony, mounted her and ridden around the stockyard, her back straight, her chin tilted upwards in defiance.

Despite Carrie's best efforts, her attraction to George was growing, and no amount of telling herself it must not be, made any difference. *Why, despite his unpleasant personality, do I seem to actually like him? Why does my body react so?* she had pondered on more than one occasion. She had become accustomed to her heart thumping, her knees shaking when she saw him—but pleasant feelings in her breasts and below had surfaced when he stood close to her. And a wanting, that was shocking to her, to feel his body against hers had begun. It was strange. It was new. It was exhilarating and mysterious. But most of all, it was annoying.

Today, Carrie sat with her mother upon the verandah, having offered for them to write a letter to her brother and sister together. 'What would you like to say to them?' she asked.

'I am grateful that we write together as I am unsure what to say, Carrie. I do not want to worry them. Perhaps after your greeting, you could tell them about learning to ride a horse. Or do you think that would worry them?'

'No, I think they would find it most entertaining, although I hope they will take my efforts seriously.' Carrie's response gave them both the opportunity to share a light-hearted moment when there had not been many of those despite both of their attempts to find joy for her mother in their surroundings.

Carrie was now bringing her mother to the verandah each day so they could share the changing view it provided of sunrise and sunset. She had walked with Louisa in the fields and to the creek. She had involved her in reading to the children. She had taken her to stroke Pony's coat and talked to her of a picnic they could ask to be taken on, to the *Snowy River*. But still, she could tell that the smile on her mother's face was not a portrayal of how she honestly felt, but an exercise in pleasing others, including her husband, so as not to cause disagreements.

'I will say the words and you write,' said her mother cheerily, distracting Carrie from her thoughts, 'then we can read it together and hope it will make them happy.'

*Dear William and Anna,*

*Mother and I are well and wish the same for you. We sit together upon the homestead's verandah wanting to tell you about ...*

***

In the soft light of dawn, Carrie had thrown her leg over Pony, unaware that she was on her way to becoming a competent horsewoman. She followed George on his own horse, out of the stockyard and away from the homestead, envious of the trousers he wore. They were no doubt more suitable for riding than her muslin dress. *But, if I was wearing trousers, would the comforting warmth of Pony's flanks, where they rubbed against the bare skin of my legs, feel the same?*

George had told her they would move into a trot, so she was not frightened when his horse did so, and Pony followed suit. She concentrated on the subtle rise and return to her saddle she had practised in the stockyard, and the sense of freedom that washed over her as she rode for the first time unbounded by the stockyard. It was like when she had sought solace on deck from the claustrophobic confines of steerage on her journey from New York and felt relief in the wind that brushed her face and rustled her hair.

She realised she would be happy to do this ride alone, but was glad she was sharing it with George, even if she didn't understand why she felt that way.

They arrived at the creek, George not looking back at her, before he nudged his horse forward with his heels. Pony did not hesitate to follow his lead. The horses remained sure-footed through the shallow water, sand and pebbles below, and easily climbed the small rise on the other side. Again, George did not look back at Carrie, but continued on across an open plain, sweeping through tall, golden grass that stroked his horse's legs. The trotting turned into something faster she did not know what to name, but she enjoyed its pace all the same.

When George reached the base of a hill, he stopped, dismounted and waited for Carrie to pull her horse up. He placed his hands around her waist as she lowered herself to the ground, a surprise that sent a pleasurable sensation pulsing through her body. She turned to face him, his own face inches away, her eyes level with his lips that parted as though he may bend to kiss her own. But he did not. He stepped away from her. He returned to his horse to remove a strapped blanket and a bundle, which he laid out upon the ground.

Carrie still clung to the reins of her horse, unsure what to do as there was nowhere to tie Pony up, the trees being at the top of the hill. 'You can let go,' George said, 'she will not go anywhere; the horses will stay with us.' He sat down upon the blanket, untying the bundle, revealing damper and cheese. He then waved her over, and Carrie was quite certain she should be offended by his lack of verbal invitation when all he said was, 'Breakfast.'

That he should think to provide for her as well as himself, was perplexing to her. She had not seen consideration from him and believed that in teaching her to ride, he was doing as bid by Amos the younger. That there was no other motivation. She lowered herself to the ground and took the bread and cheese he held out to her, biting into it as hunger created by exercise, gripped her. The damper was fresh and took her back to the campsite on the journey from Two Fold Bay, where the dray driver had taught her how to make it. The cheese was velvety, with an acidic aftertaste. She held what remained to her nose, a milky smell bringing an image of the cow she had milked yesterday, to mind. A second bite. *Had he made this damper himself this morning?*

'It is Mary we have to thank. I asked her to prepare our breakfast,' he said.

*Had she spoken the question she had asked herself, out loud.?* 'Oh. How kind. I will be sure to thank her when we return.'

'And the cheese is made from the milk of sheep, not cows,' he said.

'Oh, how did you know I was thinking about cows?' she replied, trying to mask her intrigue about his perceptiveness of her.

'I did not. It makes sense, that is all. You like the cheese?'

'I do. I more than like it; it is delicious. I have not tasted one like it before.'

'If you want to see it made, ask Amos—not his father, that is. He is readying himself for a trip to Goulburn for supplies and he takes his cheese with him to sell when he goes.'

'Yes, thank you. I will. I would enjoy that.'

For the first time, the awkwardness between them slipped away. They sat in comfortable silence, enjoying more of the damper and cheese. George passed her a canvas water bag and she gulped eagerly. There was no breeze, and the heat of the day was building. Carrie leaned back, closing her eyes to listen for the bird calls she knew, among the ever-present chorus of high-pitched humming cicadas. A peaceful feeling washed over her.

'We best get back. I have a full day's work ahead. Perhaps a longer ride next,' said George, a crack in his deep voice as he rose.

'To the river? To the *Snowy River*?,' she said, pulling herself up quickly, the glee in her voice unmistakeable.

As George bent to collect the blanket and remains of their picnic, he said, 'We will see.' Carrie sensed him putting distance between them again. He then said, 'You would need another horse. The *Snowy* is too far for Pony.'

'Is there another horse I could ride?' she asked, trying not to let disappointment in his apparent reluctance, seep into her words.

'We will see,' he said again, this time more firmly, as he swung his leg over his mount and, rougher than she thought was needed, pulled on the reins.

He had not offered his hand to help her mount, but she felt no need as her determination was a match for his. The sudden springing of a brisk breeze though, brought with it a sting to her eye, causing her to slip from her stirrup. Pony took her weight as she listed towards her. Before she could right herself, George returned to her side, leaning from his horse to place an arm around her waist, lifting her onto Pony.

Carrie was grateful but insulted at the same time, that he had thought she was not capable of righting herself. And among the feelings that battled it out within her, was knowing that his arm around her felt strong and calming like when her father had held her as a child when she was upset by some small thing that had soon been forgotten.

Without warning, George removed his arm and brought a hand to her face, a ridged, work-hardened finger flicking whatever it was that had removed itself from her eye, back into the wind. 'A seed,' he said. She expected him to ride away, but he did not. Instead, he used his finger to trace a line from her cheekbone to her lips, her skin burning with sensation. It was an act of gentleness and seduction she had no experience to know how to respond to. Not that he gave her a chance, for this time he did ride away. He turned his horse towards home and left her sitting upon Pony, her mind and body numb.

She waited for him to put some distance between them. Then she bent to whisper soothingly into Pony's ear and gently nudged her into a trot. As she neared the homestead, she saw George peel away to ride back along the track on which she had first seen him appear on his horse.

George's finger may have taken the seed away from her face, but it had not removed the musky smell of him that lingered. It teased her senses. Back in the stall, she tried to mask it by burying her face in Pony's mane and breathing deeply, but when she pulled away, it was still there. It still linked her to him whether she wanted to be or not.

# Chapter Twelve

A scream Carrie had not heard the likes of before pierced the air as she walked towards the homestead. It frightened her. It told her a woman was in pain. It made her run towards it, to help, with no time to think of how she might do so.

She burst through the back door and into the living area where her mother was crouched on the floor, Mary at her side. Neither of them looked at her, their attention focused entirely upon Elizabeth lying on the floor, her knees raised and bare, a pool of blood on the floor between her legs. 'Carrie, thank God,' said her mother. 'Take the children to Henry, the stable boy. Ask him to care for them, then come back here as quickly as you can. Fill a bowl with warm water and collect clean rags on your return.'

Carrie looked over to where the three youngest children were cowering in a corner, arms wrapped around each other, eyes wide open, staring at their mother, who screamed again. Carrie covered the few steps to them quickly. She scooped Sarah into her arms, taking hold of Frances' hand and nodding to John to follow them away from the distressing scene. They ran to the stables, where Henry, recognising the urgency, took the children from her, asking for no explanation. He had no doubt heard the screams. Carrie knelt to face the children. 'Stay here with Henry until I come for you. It will be alright,' she reassured them, despite not knowing if it would be. She ran back to the cookhouse. *Thank goodness, the water is still warm in the kettle,* she thought.

It must have only been a brief time that she was away, but it seemed longer until she was with the women again. 'Wipe her forehead, Carrie. Hold her hand.'

'Yes, Mother,' Carrie replied, positioning herself to be able to do so. 'Mary, bring a sheet from the nearest bed,' her mother said. Mary dashed from the room, returning swiftly. Louisa placed the sheet under Elizabeth's hips. 'Now, boil water, Mary,' Louisa said. 'Pour some over scissors and bring them to me in a bowl. Bring a length of string also.' Mary scurried off to the cookhouse.

The smell of blood permeated the air. Carrie swooned for a moment before another scream curdled the air. 'It is too soon,' cried Elizabeth, 'the baby will die,' she howled.

'Listen to me, Elizabeth,' ordered Louisa. 'The baby is coming. I can see its head. There is no choice. You must be strong.'

Her mother's own strength instilled the same in Carrie. She gripped Elizabeth's hand, their eyes meeting. 'Have faith. My mother and God are here with us,' she said. A slight nod was the reply she received as Elizabeth panted before another wave of pain took hold, her cry reduced this time.

'Carrie, I need you here,' her mother said, a shake in her voice conveying a hint of the panic that must surely be embedded in the need to take control of such a distressing situation. 'There may be more bleeding after the baby,' she whispered, 'I will need to pay attention to Elizabeth. Can you catch the baby as it arrives? Wrap it in your shawl, but be careful not to move far, until I can tie the cord and cut it.' Like Elizabeth, all Carrie could do was nod. She could not pretend she was confident at all.

The sight between Elizabeth's legs was a shock, but it did not frighten Carrie for that part of her mother that enabled her to focus on the task at hand, was within her daughter too.

Carrie was aware of Mary's brief presence beside them, then her movement to kneel beside Elizabeth to take on her former role of comforter. Among the sounds of childbirth, no other words were spoken, until her mother cried, 'Push! One last time, Elizabeth. Push!' and a bloody child slid into the world and into Carrie's hands.

There was no time for wonder for they knew Elizabeth's life was at risk. Carrie did as her mother bid. She lowered the child—a girl—onto an edge of her discarded shawl and gently folded it over to provide warmth while her mother concentrated on what may come next. But more blood did not spill, only the tears of relief from four women who had worked together as needs must.

The child squirmed in Carrie's hands as Louisa turned to part the shawl, tie string around the thick chord that still bound her to her mother, then cut it so the child could begin her separated life.

'Place the child in Elizabeth's arms,' Louisa said, turning back as another mass slid from Elizabeth's body, caught by the bowl Louisa held. Carrie could see that it was not another child, but she did not know what it was. The sight of it made her feel light-headed and, through a dull haze, she heard her mother say, 'Mary, take the baby,' as the world went dark.

***

Carrie woke on her bed, a vague memory of being half-carried rising to the surface of her mind. A faint cry—the cry of a baby—came to her, then the warmth of what she knew was her mother's touch made its way from her skin to her soul.

They smiled at each other, understanding how much love can be shown in a smile.

'I am sorry, Mother.' Her voice was so distant to her own ears, it sounded like it did not belong to her.

'There is no need for that. What you saw is good. It is what sustains a child within its mother, and it comes away once it is no longer needed. It is all quite amazing, don't you think—the birth of a new person?'

Carrie did think so. She knew that she had unexpectedly learned one of life's great lessons when she had least expected to. 'How is the child?' she asked.

'Remarkably well for one who made its entrance early, but perhaps not as early as Eliabeth thought,' said Louisa. 'You must rest now, Carrie. Elizabeth needs to do so for some days while we assist Mary with the care of her and the children and the chores. So, you must be on your feet again soon.'

***

Carrie woke to watch the shadow, caused by the setting sun, make its way down the painting of a stockman upon his horse, on her wall. The clomp of a man's boots passing by her closed door, distracted her. Amos the younger was home to see his new child, to embrace his wife, as she had witnessed him doing once or twice when they thought they were alone. The memory brought a smile to her face and a tingle to her body as another memory took its place—George's gentle touch upon her cheek. *Is this romance I am experiencing?* she asked herself, sitting up. *Am I too young? Should I be wary? Should I stay away from him? How can I when I long to be near him? What would be the point of loving him, when we may return to New York one day?* She sat on the edge of the bed, put her head in her hands, overwhelmed by these questions that bubbled within her, like the water she had watched many times now, come to boil over the cookhouse fire.

# Chapter Thirteen

Her stepfather's words came clearly to Carrie through the wall that separated their rooms. 'Louisa, I will not stand for this. It is a ride to the river that George wishes to take your daughter on, no more. He is not planning to run away with her! You are being unreasonable. I have known him since he was a child. He is a man of honour. He will do your daughter no harm.'

'I will only agree if you accompany them, and that is my *final* word, Amos.'

'American women ...' he humphed, '... who speak their minds too freely,' he declared as he left their room, slamming the door behind him.

*Did this mean she was to see the Snowy River again? To ride out with George again?* Several weeks had lapsed since she had last seen him. Several weeks of untold jobs caring for the children and doing chores, while Elizabeth recovered from the difficult birth of her youngest daughter. There had been no time for Carrie to think of George. Exhaustion claimed her each night as she tumbled into bed, sometimes called to rise during the night, to a crying child.

She had done her share, and happily so. Perhaps, now that Elizabeth was recovered and back on her feet, this would be her reward. *Her reward? What happened to being wary?* she asked herself.

The tap of a lighter walk led its way to her door, a gentle knock eliciting a 'Come in,' from her. Louisa entered the room.

'I come to tell you that you are to ride with George and my husband to the *Snowy River*. I presume that is what you would like?'

Carrie went to her mother and placed her hand upon Louisa's arm. 'Yes, I long to see the river again, Mother; it stole my heart when we crossed it.'

'Are you certain it is the river that has stolen your heart Carrie?'

'I …' she stammered, '… *do* love the river, though I have only seen it once. And Mother, I will ride a different horse; it will help me learn to be a better rider.'

Louisa walked to the window, her face turned from her daughter. 'Why you should wish that when we will soon, I pray, return to New York, I do not know,' she sighed, 'but if it gives you pleasure, that is what I care about. You have worked hard. You have been most helpful these past weeks, and you deserve a light-hearted moment.'

Carrie rushed forward to embrace her mother, who held her daughter as tightly in return. 'I trust you will be on your best behaviour,' she said before turning towards the door, then turning back again. 'Carrie, you are young. You do not know yet that not all men are to be trusted. You must be wary.'

*Wary.* A word she had used herself in her mind. Yes, she must be wary.

***

They rode single file, her stepfather in the lead, George behind him. Not for the first time did Carrie wonder about the relationship between them—she had not forgotten their grasp of hands when she witnessed their reunion that day upon the verandah when she had first met George. There were now three men prominent in her life, each with different surnames, and still no explanation forthcoming as to why that difference between the two Amos' existed, or why George was clearly more than someone who worked for them.

Contrary to how it could feel, Carrie was glad of her stepfather's presence today, for while her mother's advice to be wary was alive in her mind, she was not convinced she could trust herself in George's presence. The pull towards him was stronger than anything she had known before—even the love for her family.

Her stepfather had scowled when she had thrown her leg over the horse and had turned to George and said, 'You must teach her to ride side-saddle for when she is in polite company.' George had nodded, proffering no opposition. A sign of respect, perhaps even affection, she assumed.

Carrie felt the horse's eagerness to be on its way beneath her, its jitteriness causing her to doubt her ability to control him. The horse was a taller mount than Pony—a gelding she had watched George lead into the stables the night before, from where she did not know. But once upon the track from the homestead, Carrie's joy of riding, the oneness of horse and rider she had grown to love, the sharing of power its rippling muscles conveyed to her, caused all doubt to dissolve. Her senses were alive to where she was and what she was feeling.

Autumn had arrived, bringing a refreshing coolness to the air. The movement of riders and horses created a light wind that brushed her face and neck. Carrie wanted to be closer to her horse. She lowered her face towards its mane to inhale the smell of its hair. She righted herself, the broad shoulders of George's back catching her eye. She noted the way he rode with ease, one hand on the reins, his total control of the horse evident once again. The sight of a rifle in his hand still made her twitch. *Was it necessary? Were there still bushrangers around?* Then she remembered the crack that had rung out as her stepbrother had saved her from the bite of a snake on their journey from Two Fold Bay. She may not like it, but a rifle seemed to be a necessary accompaniment in their lives.

They rode in silence, the men not looking back at her. But the very act of them not doing so added to her confidence—that they did not think she needed their help. Carrie liked the sense of freedom that created. It was a type of freedom she had not experienced before. She laughed to herself at how much she had experienced in so short a time, compared to her sheltered childhood in New York.

It was a distance to the river, but it did not seem so, so immersed was she in what she was experiencing—and her thoughts. She was almost surprised when they arrived, the sight of the wide, clear-water river bringing more joy to her heart.

She dismounted on her own, not waiting for the men to signal if or where she should tie her horse up. She led her horse to the river to drink, then tied him to a nearby tree. As she turned from her horse, the sound of stirring took her by surprise. Her eyes fell upon a small group of dark-skinned women sitting further along the river bank under a tree, one nursing a child at her bare breasts, others with toddlers in their laps or standing beside them. Her breath caught in her throat. Their beauty and the beauty of the scene before her—of them sitting quietly by the magnificence of the river—disarmed her of any words.

The women rose, the nursing child not disturbed by the movement. Carrie looked directly into the eyes of the child's mother, until the mother chose to look away and follow the others along the riverbank.

'I did not mean to disturb them,' she said as George came up to her.

'You have done no harm. They are peaceful people. They know me well.'

She followed him down to the river's edge, where her stepfather removed their lunch from his saddle bag. Carrie had watched Mary pack a fine luncheon of sliced roast meat and cheese, and slices of apple pie, its pastry crisp and dotted with sugar. It made her wonder about what the Aboriginals ate, how they survived. Not for the first time, George appeared to know what she was thinking, for he said, 'They live off the land, like we do, but have different ways.' He did not say more, and she did not expect him to. She was becoming accustomed to his man-of-few-words way. She would like to know more though.

***

Amos, George and Carrie sat on the riverbank in companionable silence, enjoying Mary's fare. A row of large rocks dotted their way across the river a little upstream. The water flowing over them made a soothing gurgling sound as it curled into a foam of bubbles below the rocks. One, then two magpies carolled in a nearby gum, the tree's bark peeling in strips as though eager to leave and take their place upon the ground below. A white cockatoo, its fine wings stretched wide, feathers outlined by the sun, screeched above her, causing her to startle then laugh a little at her response to a sound she thought she had become accustomed to. She took a deep breath inhaling the earthy smell of the soil and grass she sat upon. She tried to think of descriptive words she could enter into her journal.

A sudden urge—like the one she had felt when they had crossed the river in the punt on their journey from Two Fold Bay—to touch the water, to feel its coolness, its very being—arrived. She jumped up to kneel beside the river and reached her hand towards the water, lowering it slowly into a coldness that took her aback. It was bracing to say the least, but she unlaced her boots and immersed her feet just the same. Within a minute, numbness began, so she removed her feet, tucking them under her skirt, relishing the feel of bare feet upon the ground as she sat upon the riverbank.

George came to sit at her side. 'The water comes from the mountains, too cold to swim in, unless it is summer.'

'I did bring my bathing costume from home—New York that is. Perhaps we will be here next summer and I can swim then,' she said.

'I would like that. Perhaps all from *Jimenbuen* could come and we could have a mighty picnic beside a mighty river.' Carrie rose to twirl around, her skirt swishing, in another unaccustomed display of emotion.

She heard George laugh, then felt his hands pull her towards him, tight up against his body. She looked up to see him smiling at her. But it was a different smile—a smile not expected of him, of the person she thought she knew more about now, but who, planned or not, confused her more as time passed by. He leaned towards her, his lips close to hers.

'George!' boomed her stepfather. 'It is time to return, I believe.'

Despite the warning in her stepfather's voice, George delayed stepping away from Carrie long enough for a look to pass between them that sent the words of caution, '*Be wary*' scurrying from her mind.

***

Their first stolen kiss was several weeks later, and wariness was still nowhere to be seen. Carrie was tending to Pony when strong hands gripped her waist and spun her towards him. She reacted by pulling away from him, out of arms reach. She did not know if it was how she had been raised to protect her virtue or a previously unknown temptation to tease that made her do that, but either way, George took little notice. He pulled her back to him, pressing his body against hers. He said nothing until after their lips had touched and lingered upon each other. It was a gentle kiss, the antithesis of an urgent need communicated through his hands that had moved to surround her. She leaned back in his arms, to look into his face, the gentleness of his kiss transposed there.

'I have missed you,' he said, breathing heavily.

'I have also missed you,' she replied. 'I did not know you were to be away.'

'Neither did I until Amos sent me.'

'Which one?'

'The younger, though I suspect he was instructed by his father.'

'I heard words between them and my mother, about you and me. When they thought I was not nearby. My mother was angry at what she was told.'

'And what was she told?' he asked, as he walked her to a bench seat cut from nobbly wood.

'Their words were not clear, but my mother's tone was not a pleased one.'

'We should give them time,' he said, 'to accept that we have found each other. We should meet in private.' Carrie's eyes communicated her consent.

***

From then on, it became a game of waiting, anticipation and excitement for the next time she would feel his arms pull her out of the view of others, to kiss her longingly and ever more passionately. She returned his passion. It was beyond her to hold back. But he did not ask, nor did she offer, to take things further than kisses and embraces. Once though, his hand had brushed against her breast, and she thought she would faint from her need to feel his skin against hers.

# Chapter Fourteen

Diana's eyes closed against her will, the book on Banjo Paterson falling from her hands to whack her in the face, startling her awake. 'Ouch,' she yipped, sitting up. *Serves me right for reading in bed so late at night when I am bound to fall asleep.*

It was a thick book, and she was halfway through. From what she had read so far, Banjo had been riding since he was a young boy, and all over New South Wales, so there would have been countless encounters with stockmen, she imagined. He was much younger than George, her great-great-grandfather, so *if there had been a 'ride' like in the poem, would Banjo have witnessed it or more likely heard about it?* she contemplated. She made a mental note to search for books and articles on theories of who *The Man from Snowy River* was—in the notebook she would *definitely* buy tomorrow.

Meanwhile, the book was adding fuel to her imagination about what life was like in the 1800s. *But what about the women? Can I find writings by every day women from that time that tell things from their perspective? Add that to the search list, Diana.*

***

Diana was filling her cousin, Sophie, in over another long-distance phone call from London. Sophie called once a week now, her own interest in their great-great-grandparents' life stories growing incrementally with each fact Diana discovered, a bit like a climbing rose bush that steadily creeps upwards.

'So …' Carrie said, knowing Sophie was eagerly awaiting her next words, '… today I received George and Carrie's marriage certificate.

It's a bit hard to read but I can make out their names alright, and Mum was right. Carrie's surname was Marston. It lists the church they were married in as *Christ Church* in Cooma, so I am planning on having a look at that. Not sure when it's open though.'

'Why not try the Cooma Visitors Centre? They might know.'

'Good thinking. I will do that. From the internet, the church looks small. I'm thinking it is perhaps not used as a church anymore. Maybe there is a caretaker who would let me inside?'

'I hope you can go inside. Imagine standing where they married. I am envious,' Sophie droned.

'I will definitely take photos and send to you, Soph.'

'Fabulous. What else have you got?'

'Well, to finish with the marriage certificate, I was surprised to see Carrie's mother isn't listed as being present. Where it says, "In the presence of…", I can make out an Edmund something and an Ann something and there is a cross beside George's name so maybe he couldn't read or write. What do you think?'

'Well, a lot of people couldn't read or write in those days. Here's hoping you will dig up more about George's background as we go along.'

Diana liked her cousin's use of the word 'we'; it made her feel less lonely than she had felt since James's passing.

'But …' Sophie chimed in, '… why no mother present at their wedding? Gosh, maybe they eloped. That could mean her mother didn't agree!'

Diana smiled. She had come to that possibility herself, but it was good to hear Sophie express the same thoughts. 'Yes indeed. And the date on the certificate is as clear as day. It is 30$^{th}$ July 1856. Which leads me to something else exciting—I found a New York State Census record dated 25 June 1855, which lists Caroline Marston (16); her mother, Louisa Marston (46); and siblings, William (22), Anna (20) as well as an Emma (23), George (2) and Sarah (1) — perhaps William's wife and children? And the address is Kings, Brooklyn City.'

'Wow! More evidence that the family name is Marston, but critically for us, a date. Carrie was in New York in 1855 but married in Australia in July 1856. That's a big leap!'

'Exactly. So, what do I do now, Soph?'

'Ship records. Ship routes. From New York to where—Sydney or Melbourne?'

Diana sighed. 'No idea. Or where to look.'

'That's easy—the National Library, State Libraries, jump online. Check arrivals, passengers, origin New York.'

Diana sighed again, this time in relief. 'You're a treasure, Soph. Thank you.'

'No altruism happening, I'm afraid. I want to know too.'

'No problem with that from this end. It's great to share this with you.' Like all the times they had exchanged reviews of books they had read, each of their 'To Be Read' piles added to afterwards. Both of them still preferred the feel of a book in their hands to eBooks, even though they could see the sense in electronic books too.

As they said their goodbyes, a memory came to mind of their childhood dream of owning a bookshop. They would chat about how full of stories from around the world it would be. Bookshelves lined with old and new books mixed in together to show they were of equal value in lots of ways. The bookshop would be full of colour—coloured walls, book and movie posters, old comfy chairs, an eclectic mix of coffee cups for the free coffee and tea, and home-made biscuits on offer. A veritable kaleidoscope of colour; real and imagined experiences, all to encourage people to add to their lives by enjoying books the way she and Soph did.

*Ah, what a dream. Chances of it becoming more than a dream? Zero. Oh well.*

***

Hitting herself in the head with a book was becoming a habit. So was them being thick books. This one was Edward Rutherfurd's *New York*. A factional novel (Diana called it) because it combined facts and imaginings to create a story. It began in 1644 and ended in recent times. It had lain before her a period of time and place that had been a mystery to her, mainly due to a lack of interest if she were honest. Anything she had seen on television or in movies highlighted the density of buildings and people in New York, which made her claustrophobic tendencies claw their way towards her senses.

Before diving back into the book, she had spent several hours searching online for the likely route the ship Carrie had sailed on would have taken. She concluded—rightly or wrongly, for she was not *at all* confident—that New York to Melbourne was the route to use as the foundation for her research. That the ship may well have travelled down the coast of South America, swung around the Cape of Good Hope of South Africa, then down the coast of Western Australia and under the belly of mainland Australia, to finally arrive in Melbourne.

Images swirled in her head—like an eddy in a river—round and round. Drawings and images she had found of ships and the Ports of New York and Melbourne from the mid-eighteen hundreds threw themselves into the mix. The images created a fast-flowing collage of what Carrie may have experienced just trying to get to Australia, let alone what happened afterwards. *I'm thinking my great-great-grandmother was one adventurous, strong woman. And more.*

The smack of the book, and her thoughts, made sleep a while away, so a hot chocolate was her destiny tonight, she concluded, along with more trawling, this time of the State Library of Victoria's website. With the milk gently warming in her smallest saucepan, she hunted in her pantry for the blob-of-chocolate-on-a-stick-thingy she had fallen prey to at a local market stall. She peeled the cover off, swished it through the milk, the chocolatey colour making her mouth water in anticipation. One sip—*Oh My, why on earth didn't I buy six of those?*—coated her mouth in pure pleasure. *Who cares about the sugar? Not me. Not tonight anyway.*

Diana took her cup to her table and opened up her laptop. She was quickly on the State Library of Victoria's website. It struck her that when she and Sophie had narrowed the arrival time to between 1855 and July 1856, it hadn't seemed like a long time—but it certainly did now. Already, she could see that ships were coming and going all the time. And she didn't even know the ship's name.

As she flailed around the site, she came across an *Assisted and Unassisted Passenger Lists 1839-1923* link and felt a thrill-of-the-chase feeling bubble up. She clicked and punched in Carrie's full name. Nothing. She had multiple stabs at arrival dates. Nothing. She punched in Carrie's mother, Louisa's, name. Nothing. Multiple stabs at arrival dates again. Again, nothing.

A groan escaped her. The effect of the hot chocolate was wearing off and bed was looking appealing. She stood up, knocking a bunch of papers to the floor. *Definitely time for bed,* she thought. As she bent to scoop the papers up, her eyes were drawn to the piece of paper on top. Carrie and George's marriage certificate. A word jumped out at her. *Jimenbuen*, or something like that. Above it were the words, 'Usual place of residence'. *Jimenbuen* was written twice. *Where they both lived? A property maybe?*

She punched the name into her web browser. A pastoral property, not far from Dalgety. And a place called *Snowy Vale. Was this a lead? Just maybe, just maybe.*

# Chapter Fifteen

Carrie stood in the orchard at *Jimenbuen*. The weather had turned cold. A carpet of leaves that had fallen from the apple trees lay upon the ground, and a carpet of snow lay draped across the mountain tops. Her shawl was no longer enough to keep her warm, so layers of clothes lay underneath, making her movements more cumbersome.

George was away again. Again, without warning. She yearned for his company. She yearned for his touch. Cascades of rain had kept her inside for days and now that she had seen to Pony, she would make the most of the rains end and take herself for a walk across the fields.

She skirted the homestead and crossed the dirt track in front of it. In her eagerness to leave, she had not told anyone what she was doing. Carrie held her open palms out at her sides to feel the weight of tall, wet grass, drooping from their burden; the thick skirt of her dress prevented its touch upon her legs. She reached the creek, bending so water glided over her fingertips, which tingled from its sharpness.

A *wooshing* sound caught her attention but not in time to stop the wall of water descending upon her from catching at her feet, sweeping her along as she flailed about. Her limbs became numb as she fought to keep her head in the air. She failed and went under, icy water flooding her mouth. She surfaced, spat the water out, and went under again. The weight of her sodden clothes dragged her down. This time she kept her mouth closed, and pushed upwards until her head broke through the water. She gulped for air. She could feel herself losing consciousness, her body failing her will to live. She slipped under again. Then something strange—she flailed again, fighting whatever was grabbing at her, until she had nothing left within and the light faded.

Carrie woke, wrapped in warmth, to the sound of horse hooves thudding nearby. *Was she dreaming? Had she lost her battle to live?* Strong arms scooped her up. She gave into their comfort. She opened her eyes to see a blurry form of George's face above her before different arms—brown arms—were around her, lifting her, until George held her again. She felt movement and heard a single whinny, as the world slipped away again.

***

Beneath her hands was a softness she woke stroking. There was a weight to it that was unfamiliar. She heard her mother's voice and struggled to open her eyes.

'Carrie, oh Carrie. I am here. You are safe. You are in your room.'

'What happened to me?' she heard herself ask, a shivering overtaking her body as memories of coldness engulfed her. 'George. Where is George? I want to see him.'

'Quiet now. You must rest. Drowning was nearly your fate. You must not go out on your own again without saying.'

'I want George,' she demanded in a voice that even to herself, did not sound like her own.

A shadow stepped forward and showed itself to be her stepfather. 'I will fetch him, but you must do as your mother says. Louisa, broth would do her well while I bring the boy,' he instructed.

*The boy? Who is the boy?* she wondered in a drowsy haze. *Does he mean George? Could it be that her stepfather had known him since he was a boy?* She would ask. And she would ask more. There was a vastness of knowledge she did not have about the man she had fallen in love with. A drive to find out settled within her as she sipped rich, beefy broth from a spoon her mother placed before her.

'I am sorry, Mother. I did not mean to frighten you.'

'Well, you did. To lose you would break my heart.'

'I frightened myself too. I thought I would die,' she said reaching for her mother's hand.

'We must be grateful to God that you did not, Carrie.'

'And to who saved me. Who saved me, Mother? I remember arms around me, but that is all.'

'I do not know,' she said, hearing the creak of the door as her stepfather entered, followed by George, hat in hand.

'George! Who saved me, George?' she asked as he pulled a stool up to the side of her bed. His hand crept towards hers, but a cough from Amos stopped it from touching hers.

'The women. The dark women you saw by the *Snowy River.* They were there when you were swept away. They wrapped you in this to warm you.' His hand stroked the fur that her own hand had begun to do so again.

'It must be valuable to them. We must return it.'

'It is. Many possum skins that they sew together, with strands of kangaroo skin. They have moved on now until after the cold weather. I offered it back to them, but they would not take it. It is their gift to you.'

To have been given such a gift, one they must surely need during winter, brought tears to her eyes. 'I will treasure it always.'

'And I will collect possum skins for when they return.'

The return of her mother to her bedside signalled the conversation between George and Carrie had come to an end. But Carrie had one more question to ask, which she did hastily. 'I remember now. It was you, George, who came on your horse, to bring me home. How did you know to come?'

'Your absence was being talked about when I arrived at *Jimenbuen.* I offered to search for you,' he said, his hand, seemingly having a mind of its own, reaching out to grasp hers.

She grasped it back with what strength she had. 'Thank you,' she said, there being no need to say more, the look between them conveying what Carrie felt.

They had pushed it as far as they could. 'She must rest now,' said her mother firmly, giving Carrie permission to relinquish herself once again to the tiredness. She closed her eyes, and as sleep came, she heard George's footsteps as he left the room.'

***

Carrie's recovery took weeks—many days spent resting and reading, George's absence keenly felt while he drove cattle to market in Victoria. On a day that belied the closeness of the coldest time of the year, she sat on the verandah writing to her sister.

*Dear Anna,*

*Your letter arrived causing great excitement. Mother and I huddled together to learn news from home, relief washing over us to know you, William and his family are well.*

*Winter is not far from us now and I have an inkling that the coldness will be like what we have known in New York. From the verandah, I can see the snow creeping down the side of the mountains, snailing its way towards us. The chill in the air greets us each morning, lasting throughout the day, giving the two older children of our hosts, Amos and Elizabeth, little time to play outside.*

*Life in this place of rugged beauty is in some ways the opposite to what we experience in New York. There are no greengrocer or butcher shops close by; goods that are needed must be produced here or carted from Cooma or further away places, such as Goulburn or Sydney. The town of Cooma is a day's horse ride away, but we have not visited there to date, so I cannot report upon its appearance.*

*I have become adept at horse-riding I have been told, and it brings great joy to my heart to ride across the valley, creeks and as far as the mighty Snowy River. The fondness I have found for my mount 'Pony' has been a welcome surprise, but there is another surprise that I wish you were here to advise me on. I will share it with you – and only you – and it is that I have become undeniably attached to the man who has taught me to ride. His name is George.*

*He is a man that confuses me, for at first, I did not like him at all, his manner can be brisk and to the point of rudeness. But a gentleness to his nature showed itself as unexpectedly as you might imagine. And since that time, the affection between us has grown.*

*Mother is aware of the growing affection between us and has told me to be wary, that not all men are to be trusted. Wariness escapes me when I am close to him though, it simply vanishes, as my heart beats noticeably and my legs shake at his nearness. I am overcome when he is near. Dear Sister, please tell me, do you know if that is what happens when you meet the man you are to be with …*

***

'I do not like it Amos,' Carrie heard her mother declare through the wall between their bedrooms.

'Keep your voice down, Louisa. Do you want everyone to hear our business?'

Carrie was certain her mother would not appreciate him telling her what to do, but her mother's voice dropped, causing her to push her ear against the wall to hear more of their conversation.

'Amos, I fear there is a danger that Carrie has fallen in love with that man. We are to travel home to New York, and she is to come with us, do you hear?'

'I could hardly not hear, Louisa. You are standing in front of me preventing my escape from this small room we share! Move aside, I am needed elsewhere.' The door creaked and closed behind him as he departed.

*New York.* Her mother had given no indication that she wanted to leave so soon. Were they, after only four months, to make that arduous voyage across the ocean again? The thought made Carrie sway. She lay her hand flat upon the wall for support. Perhaps she was not fully recovered from her ordeal, or perhaps it was the thought of being dragged away from George—for dragging is what they would need to do to remove her from him.

Discontent must have lain within her mother these past weeks while Carrie had misconstrued her silence as settling into life at *Jimenbuen.*

If her mother gave it more time, surely she would see that there was a future for them all here in Australia? That is what she must do, she realised, she must choose the right time to talk to her mother about giving this new country more time. She would reason with her. Her mother would surely listen to her; they had always been close.

***

'No, Carrie,' Louisa said stiffly. 'There is to be no more talk of us staying longer. I have told Amos I will not remain. New York is my home. I cannot bear the isolation here for longer than it takes to organise our passage.'

'But mother …' she pleaded.

'I will not hear any "buts" about it; you are a child, and you will return with us.'

'You discredit me, Mother. I am not a child; I am soon to be seventeen and I have my own mind.'

'Believe you me, young lady; marriage is the sole reason by which you will strike out away from me, and *that* man is not in a position to marry you. He cannot provide for you. His background is a mystery to us and so is his religion.'

# Chapter Sixteen

Carrie flung herself into George's arms when they met in the stables. Several days had passed since the conversation with her mother. A tension had hung in the air between mother and daughter, like the wall that separated their bedrooms. The distress within Carrie had built as the days passed without a resolution to their conflict.

George wrapped his arms around her protectively. He kissed the top of her head. He allowed her time to shed tears before he spoke. 'What is it, Carrie?'

'It is Mother. We are to leave, to return to New York. She hates it here. Oh, George, how can I leave when I love you?'

The words she spoke were not planned—were not even set in her mind. Her hand flew to her mouth to cover where the words had come from. George stood, still and stiff. She dared not look into his eyes, out of fear that she may witness rejection there.

She closed her eyes, then felt his fingers on her chin as they lifted it upwards. 'Carrie. These past weeks away from you have driven me mad. I rode hard to get you out of my mind, but could not.'

His words were like an elixir, her body concocting a magical feeling that dissolved her uneasiness. *He loves me also!* But instead of saying so, he said, 'Ride with me tomorrow morning. I have something to show you. We will be away most of the day.' Then he slipped away when they heard footsteps approaching the stables.

***

George had left her perplexed as to what he wanted to show her. The *Snowy River* again? He knew how she cared for it. Or could it be the mountains? Had he guessed they were beckoning her to be among them?

He said nothing else again this morning when she found him saddling Pony, his own horse ready to ride. He leaned to kiss her, using one hand to release her hair from its tight bun—a gesture which brought the delight of the touch of his fingers upon her neck. To break the moment, for they needed to leave, she raised her hand so he could see the muslin-wrapped food she had prepared for their lunch. He took it from her and placed it in his saddle bag.

He knew she needed no help to mount Pony, and did not offer it. They saw no one else as they left, her trust in him complete as they began their journey to where only he knew.

She rode a little behind him, rejoicing in the rawness of the air that whisked around her, that flowed through and lifted her hair. Pony's breath misted, as did her own. The horse felt strong beneath her, between her legs, as eager as she was to fly across the fields. The sounds of their horses' hooves and early morning bird calls heightened her senses.

George stopped and waited for her. But she streaked by him, laughing, hearing him laugh in return at her brazenness. They played that game across the fields until she halted and he pulled up beside her, allowing their horses and each other to catch their breath as their horses moved into a walk.

'I had never heard an American speak until you,' he said, taking her by surprise with what he chose to talk about.

'I did not know that. Did … *do* … I sound strange to you?'

'Yes, you did. But I am accustomed to it now,' he said, leaving her unsure if he liked the way she spoke or not.

'I was used to how the English sound—my stepfather for one, and other English people in New York also. But in Melbourne I heard a way of talking I thought strange too. Like yours,' she teased, 'which I learned to attribute to those born in Australia. You were born in this country, George?'

'I was. In Van Diemens Land. Many miles away. Over the ocean from Melbourne.'

It did not escape her that he shifted in his saddle, appearing ill at ease, but she could not help but ask more. 'Is that where your parents are? How did you come to be here?'

'My father is dead, and my mother married again. I was brought here. That is all, Carrie,' he said, abruptly ending their conversation. He dug his heels into the flanks of his horse, again riding it more forcefully than she thought necessary, as he pulled away from her.

Even in her youth, Carrie was not fooled by his statement of there being no more to tell. She hoped one day he would reveal his story to her, but for now it was enough to be with him in this new world of love and the beauty of their surroundings.

A forested rise came into view. Not a mountain, but it had a height to it still. Her eyes were focused upon it, until she noticed a dwelling as they drew closer, that sat below it. A hut made of different-sized pieces of stone. A roof of rough-hewn timber. A chimney at one end. A tiny slab hut to the side, and a larger one behind. They dismounted and tied their horses to a wooden railing built for that purpose.

'Ironmungy,' George said. 'This place,' waving one arm around him, 'is called Ironmungy. I had an offering to look after cattle here during the winters, stock not sold at market. I built this,' he said, walking towards the hut before turning back to her. 'We can live here, if you will have me.'

She had taken one step towards him when his words caused her legs to fail her. She could not have been more shocked. 'Are you asking me to marry you, George?'

'I am. You might like to see the hut before you give your answer.'

She nodded, her young age, this time, leaving her lost as to what else to do. She followed him through the sturdy wooden door, a small glass window to one side of it.

The rich, familiar smell of gum reached out to her, delicious and welcoming as she stood upon the floor crafted from trees. A large, single room surrounded her, and a pot hung over a pyramid of kindling in the fireplace, ready to be struck alight. She imagined them here, warm, safe from the snow, nourished by what she cooked and the warmth of their bodies.

'Outside,' he said. One word and again she followed, to the smaller hut, filled with wood, then to the larger hut, a stable, hay stacked to roof height at one end.

'I will make a bed, a table. You should make a list of what else is needed. We should make haste.'

She understood what he was saying. If she agreed to marry him, they must do so before passage was organised to New York to take her away from him. She would not be taken away from him! 'Yes. Yes! I will marry you, George,' she said, throwing herself into his arms. He pulled her to him as though he would never let her go.

'How? How are we to do this? Will you ask my mother and stepfather?'

George gently pushed her away from him, until he could look into her eyes. 'They will say no,' he said, his voice quiet. And she knew he was right. He lowered his lips to hers, a delicate touch that was in opposition to the physical strength of the man behind those lips. 'I know how, Carrie. Will you trust me?'

'Yes, George. I will trust you. With all that I am.'

***

*How can love be so wondrous, yet so tortuous?* When Carrie was with George, nothing else mattered. Her heart threatened to burst with happiness and longing. When she was with her mother—who was more content because of *her* plans to go home to New York—Carrie's heart threatened to shatter into pieces.

If she denied George, she would betray him—and herself. If she denied her mother, she would betray the woman who had loved and cared for her, all her life. Carrie's mind and heart were split in two, involved in their own battle—a futile endeavour when she knew that her future lay with George in the hut they would make their home.

To distract herself, and because being organised was reassuring to her, she worked on her list of what they would need to start their married life together. She watched Mary in the cookhouse more closely, noting what ingredients she used for different meals. She estimated how much flour, sugar, tea they would need to get them through this winter. Her list to give George grew.

A tributary of the *Snowy River* ran within walking distance of the hut. Water would be there for them. Milk? Perhaps occasionally from *Jimenbuen*? The same for cheese? Perhaps one day they would have their own cow. With all the goings-on, she had missed the opportunity to learn how to make cheese. She created a second list of things she must learn to do.

Preserves. Would Mary and Elizabeth allow her to take some? Vegetables. What could she grow? She would have to start her own garden. She rushed to her trunk, to the packs of seeds the old gardener had given her in Melbourne. Four packs for four seasons. *Would anything grow at Ironmungy in winter?*

Meat. She would have to rely upon George to supply that. There was a great deal to think through and prepare for. She would do what she could while she waited for George to arrange their marriage.

***

She didn't have long to wait. He came to her one day as she tended Pony. 'The bed is made, the table next.' He encased her in his arms. Her heart soared. She felt his need for her press against her. Of the physical side of marriage, she knew little—another learning to be had, led by him she presumed.

'I have a friend, Edmund,' George said, 'he will be our witness, and a woman we know, Ann, has agreed to be another. No permission is needed. You are of legal age. We will marry in the Christ Church on the edge of Cooma. We will take the buggy from here to the *Snowy River*, and the stable boy will come with us and return it. We will cross on the punt. Edmund will meet us with a cart. We will stay that night in Cooma, marry and return the next day to declare ourselves husband and wife to all here,' he said, sweeping his arm in the direction of the homestead. The following day we will ride to Ironmungy.

Carrie's head swam, trying to take it all in. His words heralded a change to her world that would change her life forever. 'When?' she asked. 'Soon,' he replied. 'I will send word.' She gripped his hand for the strength she needed from him. He returned her grip. She let go, to search her pocket. 'Here, a list of what we will need.' She held it out to him. He glanced at it briefly but did not appear to read it. 'And here, the coins my brother gave me. American. Will that help?' He took the coins, still in the brown envelope that her brother had given them to her in on the wharf in New York. 'Yes. Good,' was all George said, asking nothing about them.

He bent to kiss her, and left.

***

Carrie unknotted the handkerchief, the never-used gold coin lying shiny within, like a miniature sun meant to shine for her alone.

She'd made a decision not to give the coin to George. She had no reason to tell him about its existence, which had not arisen in any conversation. Her instinct was to keep it; a small amount, should she have need of it in the future. She did not know why that was her instinct. Perhaps because she did not know what her mother would do when they announced their marriage. Would her mother stay in Australia once she knew her daughter would not be leaving? Or would she return to New York as planned, putting oceans between them? Or was it that the coin, given so generously to her by her stepbrother who she had liked immediately, represented hope for what lay ahead, and she wanted to keep that symbol of hope to herself?

Whatever it was, the coin was her own treasure. She wrapped it up, tied another knot in the handkerchief it sat within, and placed it carefully back in her trunk.

***

The note to meet him was in her hands two weeks later. Two weeks of heartache over what she was to put her mother through, mixed with the anticipation of being with George forever.

'Tomorrow,' was all that was written on the note, in childish writing, as though Henry, the stable boy, had penned it.

They had met there long enough for her to know she was to meet him in the stables. She would take little. She would collect her things when they returned to announce their marriage. She sunk her hands deep down, to the bottom of her trunk, where she felt the soft cotton of her best dress that had lain there since she had packed it, in New York. It was not silk, like her mother's beautiful dress that she hoped to have one like, one day. But it held a loveliness of its own in its creamy colour and petite embroidered cornflower blue flowers at the hemline and high lace collar that sat snug against her neck. She placed it in a pillowcase along with a spare chemise, nightgown, her brush, and her Bible, and slipped it under her bed until morning.

# Chapter Seventeen

A blackness as dark as mourning clothes, engulfed Carrie as she tiptoed from her room with no lamp to light her way. She left the door open to avoid its tell-tale creak alerting her mother and stepfather next door to her uncharacteristically early movements. For days, she had agonised over the pain she would cause her mother. But the pull towards George and the adventurous life he offered was greater than anything she could have imagined. It was as though choice, and control of her own life, had been swept away, like the way she had been swept away when the creek had flooded. A modicum of logic not to do this had skulked in her mind, but a force she did not understand had caused it to retreat and it was nowhere in sight when she opened the back door of the homestead. She tilted her face upwards searching for bright stars to light her way.

But there were none, and she tripped, powerful arms scooping her up before she met with the ground. George must have been watching out for her.

If any doubt had been striving to rise to the surface again, its mission was doomed to failure, the warmth of George's body against hers, her desperate longing for him, having already replaced the past with the future. Their breath misted and mingled in the frosty morning air. He put a finger to his mouth to warn her not to talk. He took her hand in his. He walked her away from the homestead to where Henry, the stable boy, stood calming the horse harnessed to the buggy, with slow strokes of his hand. Still without words, the three of them climbed onboard, George taking the reins. A lift of his hands instructed the horse to move off through the touch of reins upon its back.

It was a long, eerie and cold journey to the *Snowy River*. The darkness, the ice in the air, seeped through to her bones. Carrie said a silent prayer to God when the sky began to lighten in the east. When the birds began to call and George pointed to the fog that hovered above the river like a blanket being thrown over a bed, Carrie looked to the heavens and smiled her thanks through chattering teeth.

The stable boy offered her his hand to help her down. George nodded to the boy, tilting his head in the direction they had come from. Henry climbed back up onto the buggy, expertly turning the horse around. Carrie raised her hand in farewell and watched him until she could see him no more, wishing she had some way to repay him for his help, concerned that one so young would make the return journey to *Jimenbuen* alone.

'Do you have regrets?' George said.

'No, I do not,' she replied, falling into his arms, his lips cold as they fell upon hers.

A whistle travelled across the water to greet them. A welcome sound, signalling the arrival of the next person who would help them—Edmund. George returned the whistle with one of his own, the sweep of the punt through the water the next sound to reach their ears. The clunk of wood against damp soil as the punt met with the riverbank, followed.

George led her the few steps they needed to take, holding onto her hand so tightly he unwittingly offered her reassurance that crossing the river on her way to be married was indeed her destiny.

She peered into the water as Edmund guided the punt through the current. There was not enough light to see the fish that swam within, or the pebbles and rocks she knew lay among the sand at its bottom. Still, that did not put a dint in the place in her heart that belonged to this river. *Will I come to understand why it has such meaning to me?* she pondered, but only for a minute, until punt met soil again.

Another horse and buggy were tied to a tree close by. This time it was Edmund who gave her a hand up before taking a small bundle from his coat pocket and pressing it into her hands. 'You be wanting some breakfast, Lass,' he said. 'It is not much—some damper. Enough for George as well. I have broken my fast.'

A smidgeon of warmth, perhaps imagined, came through the cloth. 'Thank you,' she smiled, making short work of her share and the share George declined. The food made her drowsy. The rhythmic clip-clop of the horses' hooves, the sway of the buggy in time with the horses' movement, and her thighs pressed against the two men she sat between, soothed her. She leaned her head against George's shoulder, and the journey passed in pleasant silence.

***

They arrived in Cooma late in the day, having stopped only for convenience along the way. The day had remained cold but blue skies and sun lightened their moods as their journey neared its end.

'Arrangements have changed,' George said. 'You will stay with our friend, Ann, tonight, above her father's store. I'll not have people blighting your name by you staying in the hotel with us before you are wed.'

Carrie reached to squeeze his hand, grateful that he had thought of that—for she had not—although now he had voiced it, she recognised his concerns were justified. Her only excuse for not thinking of the slur upon her reputation, was the power of her love for George that had swept away logic and wariness. But she would not dwell on that. If she did, she would be drawn to thoughts of her mother and the heartache that would have begun for her, with Carrie's absence from *Jimenbuen* no doubt noted by now.

***

Edmund turned the buggy in to the widest street Carrie had seen in her short life. She turned her head from side to side to take in the brick buildings that were similar, but of a smaller nature, to the ones she had seen in Melbourne. Weatherboard shopfronts lay among the brick buildings, a few souls gathered upon walkways outside.

Carrie had imagined what Cooma might be like, but it was more than the images that had formed in her mind. Images which were no doubt influenced by the isolation she had experienced during her months at the homestead and her lack of knowledge about Australian towns. Excitement simmered within for the adventures that lay ahead of her—that opened themselves to her from today—that would blossom from tomorrow, when she would become a married woman—her childhood put behind her forever.

Edmund pulled back on the reins to halt the horse in a more-gentle manner, Carrie noticed, than she had seen George do. The window displays of the store they sat before caught her eye, filled as they were with a variety of items, from a woman's shawl draped over a mannequin, to homewares and tools.

Two warmly attired women chatted under the eave of the roof which extended over the wooden walkway in front of the store. The women became silent as George gave Carrie his hand to step down from the buggy. They cast disparaging gazes up and down her. Carrie felt intimidated but nodded as she walked by. She received no polite acknowledgement in return. George and Edmund, on the other hand, chose to ignore them entirely. Their reaction confused Carrie. *Were the men used to such rudeness? Why would that be?*

The door of the shop opened, a friendly greeting proffered by the lady who emerged, beckoning them inside. 'Welcome,' she said, 'I am Ann. Come into the fire. You must need to warm yourselves—and quickly so.'

Orange flames blazed between the bricks of the fireplace set in a wall on one side of the store. Further conversation was delayed until they stood before it, hands extended to catch its warmth. As the numbness in Carrie's fingers turned to tingles, Ann excused her father, resting his aching limbs upstairs. 'Rheumatism,' she said. 'Aye, Ann, you do well to run the store on your own now,' said Edmund, George mumbling his agreement.

The corners of Ann's lips shaped upwards in a humble smile, her hand patting down her still-dark hair already held firmly in place by a tight bun at the nape of her neck. 'Stay here while I make tea. Or would you prefer coffee, Carrie, as I hear Americans like it? I do too.'

'Oh yes please,' Carrie cried, her enthusiasm escaping her before she could muster it into a more polite form, the thought of the taste and warmth of coffee heartening after the day's long, cold journey.

***

They lingered over the coffee and the meal they shared of rich, beef stew, after chairs had been dragged to the fireplace, and Ann's father, Alfred, had come downstairs to join them. George had kissed Carrie tenderly on the cheek before he and Edmund left for the hotel. 'Tomorrow we will be man and wife,' he whispered close to her ear. 'Tomorrow night we will be together,' he teased, his breath hot on her skin, her body pushing into his in response. A light cough from Edmund reminded George and Carrie they were in company, and his steps towards the door enticed George to finally follow.

'A nip of something for you, Lass,' Alfred said, as the door clicked closed, 'to celebrate your nuptials.'

'But father, she is a child,' declared Ann, her disapproval clearly relayed.

'In the eyes of the law, she is old enough to marry, to make her own choices,' Alfred said, his tone gently cutting off any retort from his daughter. 'Would you like a nip of port, Carrie?'

There was a part of Carrie that wished to agree with Ann, out of loyalty for the kindness she had shown, and a part of Carrie that wished to agree with Alfred, out of politeness for the offer the gentleman had made. It was her curiosity though about the taste of port, buoyed by Alfred's assertion that she was old enough to make her own choices, that saw her acquiesce.

An hour later, she made another decision. The small tumbler of port that had burned on its way down and gone straight to her head to make her woozy, had to be the cause of where she now found herself. She was submerged under the water in the tin bath she and Ann had filled in the back room of the store where the cooking was done, imagining herself to be face down in the *Snowy River*, gazing at its inner world.

As she sat up, her hair dripping wet, she was not at all sure she would try port again.

A soft knock on the door heralded Ann's arrival with a length of cloth for Carrie to dry herself with. Ann averted her eyes until this was done, and Carrie was dressed in her nightgown. Ann gestured to a chair in front of the fireplace for her young friend to sit upon, holding a brush in the air to signal her intent.

The touch of soft bristles on Carrie's scalp was as placating as the warm water of the bath she had just alighted from. The only sounds were the crackling of the fire and the hoot of an owl she imagined perched on a branch of a tree beyond the back door. It would have been the perfect end to a big day in her life, if only it had been her mother brushing her hair. A tear with no voice accompanying it, tracked its way down her cheek to silently disappear in the garment she wore.

# Chapter Eighteen

*Cooma, 30 July 1856*

Carrie woke to the sound of a soft knock upon the bedroom door. She sat upright, in quick fashion, still cloudy with sleep. She had not expected to sleep so soundly, given the excitement about her marriage that she had been unable to subdue when she had climbed into bed last night.

She was grateful Ann had insisted Carrie share her bed last night. Perhaps their quiet chatter had lulled Carrie to sleep. A sleep deep enough not to be aware of Ann leaving the room earlier, until she returned now accompanied by the sweet, milky smell of aromatic coffee and freshly baked bread.

'Good morning, Carrie,' Ann said, a twinkle in her eye and a delighted look upon her face. 'Nourishment to begin with, I suggest, on your special day.'

A flush of excitement swept through Carrie, any trace of sleepiness now vanquished.

'Yes, please,' she said, reaching for the tray Ann proffered. 'Why, you must have been up early to bake this bread.'

'No earlier than usual,' Ann said, 'and slather as much as you like of the orange marmalade upon your bread. I have several more jars in our pantry.'

'Oh Ann, you have been so kind, so generous. You have asked no questions of me. Like why my mother is not here.'

Carefully, so as not to disturb the tray, Ann sat upon the bed and lay one hand upon Carrie's. 'I know enough. I know that George and Edmund are good men, and I trust that they would not have asked for my help unless it was needed. Now,' she said, rising from the bed, 'I will give you time to enjoy your breakfast and contemplate the day ahead.'

While Ann's words gave Carrie further reason to be grateful for her new friend, Carrie's own mention of her mother brought an ache to her heart that threatened the arrival of tears. She knew she was going to marry George. Nothing was going to stop her. She had made her choice. But to do so without her cherished mother present had been an unimaginable thought, until recently when her mother had made her disapproval abundantly clear.

Carrie tossed back her head. She would not dwell on what could not be changed. Fate had thrown she and George together. She must hang on to the hope that her mother would accept their union once it was done. For what else did she have but hope?

She picked up her mug of coffee and gulped it for good measure. She slathered marmalade onto a thick piece of still warm bread and bit into its sticky sweetness.

Ann would soon return to help her dress, and Carrie was determined her friend would not find a weeping bride.

***

George rode ahead of the buggy, on a mount he had hired. He sat tall in the saddle, turning once to cast his eyes in Carrie's direction, as he led them several miles along a curving track to Christ Church, where they would marry.

Ann squeezed Carrie's hand as Edmund pulled on the reins to bring the horse to a halt. A wrought-iron gate with a cobbled path beyond, that weaved its way to the arched doors of the little church, invited worshippers into God's house.

So much smaller than the churches Carrie had known in New York, its majesty was none the less. The church was made of blocks of hand-hewn stone, cut to a size a man could lift. Its roof was steeply pitched and made of wood slats, and a tower soared above the doors, reaching for the heavens, a metal cross sitting at its top. The church was a fine sight, sitting as it did among forested rolling hills and a nearby babbling creek.

George came to the buggy and lifted Carrie down, his hands around her waist, the skirt of her dress billowing with the petticoats underneath that Ann had loaned her. For a moment, they stood, facing the church, all tension removed from their expressions. George led her to the gate and along the path. He pushed both doors open, and they stepped into the entrance of the church, its floor made of pieces of slate. Edmund and Ann followed.

Carrie closed her eyes and prayed for forgiveness—for marrying into a faith that was not her own; for marrying without her mother knowing.

As planned, George and Edmund proceeded into the church while Ann prepared Carrie. Ann removed the thick woollen shawl Carrie had journeyed in this morning, ran her hands over the skirt of Carrie's dress to straighten out any creases, and brushed her hair. George had requested that Carrie wear her hair out.

Ann placed a Bible in her hands. The Bible that had been a gift from Carrie's father, Nathaniel, and that Carrie had chosen to have with her on her special day—to have something of her father with her. Around her wrist she wore the sapphire blue ribbon she had kept from the parcel her sister had presented to her on the wharf of New York.

Edmund returned to her side, his elbow held away from his body, to allow Carrie to link arms with him. 'Ready Lass?' he asked. 'Yes,' she smiled. They stepped into the nave of the church, turning to walk the short aisle that lay between six rows of wooden benches.

Inside, the church was as beautiful as it was outside. Rendered walls of white, broken by tall, narrow, recessed arched windows, through which Carrie caught a glimpse of an eagle circling upon the wind. In stark contrast to the white walls was the dark wood of the exposed roof, no ceiling in between, and the thick wooden beams the roof rested upon.

George stood before the reverend at the tiny altar, his back turned to Carrie until she neared. When he turned and looked at her, the love in his eyes made her heart sing. The reverend allowed them a few moments before he began, the sound of wind howling around the little church on this cold winter's day.

The reverend introduced himself and welcomed Carrie. He was not one to linger, it seemed, for the service was brief and their marriage was sealed with a thin band of gold George placed upon Carrie's finger. A record of those present was then taken.

Her first surprise, as a married woman, was to find that George could not write. When the reverend asked him to make his mark upon their marriage document, Carrie watched him struggle to form a cross. *No matter, I will teach him,* she thought, knowing that she was capable of doing so. She smiled to reassure him all was well.

It was a tender moment between them, a look of relief passing across George's face. A moment soon broken by the sound of men on horseback arriving in haste. George left her then, to rush outside, raised, angry voices soon coming to her—voices that belonged to her stepfather and stepbrother.

'Tell us we are not too late, George,' demanded Amos the younger.

'You are not,' George replied, fury fierce in his voice, 'you are in time to celebrate our marriage. It is done.'

Carrie made it to the door as fist met face—the fist of her stepfather connecting to her husband's face. George fell to the ground. 'Stop,' she screamed. 'I beg of you, stop!' They did, though their faces were turned to the reverend, who peered down upon them from the doorway of his church.

His steely voice matched his steely gaze. 'Take this away from God's house,' he insisted, his authority recognised and respected by the younger Amos, who pulled his father from his position of leaning over George, still prone on the ground.

'Our apologies, Reverend,' he said. 'Father, come. This is to be dealt with at home.'

# Chapter Nineteen

*Bingo!* There it was, on three pieces of paper laid out before her—proof that Carrie had arrived in Melbourne from New York on 24 January 1856 on a ship called the *B. R. Milam*. An entry under *Shipping Intelligence* in *The Argus* newspaper listed the arrival of the ship on that date, and a handwritten passenger list showed she had travelled in steerage. The third document was a typed translation of the list of passengers. Diana had obtained the passenger list and translation from the Assisted and Unassisted Passenger Lists held by the *Public Record Office of Victoria.*

Both lists showed she had travelled with her mother and a man named *Amos Vince*—and that they had all used the name *Vince*. That is why Diana had not been able to find anything under Carrie and her mother's surname of Marston!

Diana was positively bursting at the seams with excitement and eagerness to fill her Mum and cousin in. She picked the papers up as though they were treasure and put them in her bag before closing her front door on her way to drive to Jindabyne to visit her mother.

As she drove, she thought about the last two days at the National Library of Australia. She had sniffed her way from one lead to another, like a hound dog on the chase—not that she liked that image much—uncovering the story of Amos she was quite sure she could not have dreamed up herself. When she had seen Carrie and Amos' names side by side in a paragraph of a family history book written about one of his daughter's, she knew she had hit pay dirt.

Diana glanced quickly at their own piece of family history treasure—the one-hundred-and-thirty-year-old book—beautifully restored—that she had picked up late yesterday. *Perhaps Mum will be more excited by that,* she wondered. With everything whirring in her mind like a whirligig, the trip soon passed and she tapped on her mother's front door before she walked in.

Her mother's home was quiet. Unusually and worryingly so. Usually, there were sounds coming from the kitchen as her mother prepared a pot of tea or coffee for them and laid the sweet treats she had made on one of her colourful Italian pottery platters. But not today. Diana peered into the kitchen. No Mum. She walked to the lounge room and at first thought *No Mum* there either. Then she noticed a tuft of silver hair near the top of her mother's favourite armchair.

She tiptoed over and whispered, 'Mum.'

Her mother jumped a little. 'Oh, sorry darling, just a nana nap as they say.'

Diana's concern grew. It was only ten o'clock in the morning; her Mum's nana naps were usually confined to the afternoons.

'That's okay, Mum. I am early today; I have so much to tell you—and show you. But first, I will make us a cuppa.'

Her mother made to rise. 'Oh, I can do that. No fuss. I am just a little bit tired today.

'How about we do it together then?' Diana said, hoping she was managing to leave the worry she felt out of her voice.

'Now, don't treat me like an old lady, Diana. You know I don't like that. But …' she hesitated, '… for today, I will take you up on your offer.'

Diana came close to making the mistake of moving to give her mother a hand up, but stopped herself in the nick of time, distracting them both by digging into her bag and extracting a packet of biscuits. 'And I have your favourite *biscotti* from your favourite Italian bakery in Canberra,' she said. A flush of rose colour touched her mother's cheeks, relieving Diana's concern. *It's okay,* she told herself. *Mum is okay, a little tired that's all.*

***

Sweet peppermint tea and even sweeter biscuits consumed, it was Diana's turn to pass over the restored family treasure to her mother, the way her mother had passed the book to her several weeks ago. Maggie's hands trembled as she held the restored book then steadied as she placed it on her lap. For a few seconds, she stared at it, running her eyes over the front cover. How the restorer had replaced the original barely-hanging-together front and back cover and spine, then attached what could be salvaged of those to the new board, Diana could not fathom. But the restorer had done an excellent job.

A tear slid down her mother's cheek, landing on the book. 'Oh,' she said, reaching for her lace handkerchief to wipe it away. She turned the book over, noticing that the splotches of water damage were still there. 'There is history in those marks, Diana.'

'Yes, Mum. I believe there is too. But Carrie didn't have this with her on her voyage out to Australia. My research has found that she arrived in Melbourne on 24 January 1856 and this book wasn't published until 1887 in America, so how did she get hold of it? I wonder if it was sent to her?'

Her mother turned the pages of the book and stopped at the same colour plate Diana had. Maggie's brow creased into a frown as it often did when she was concentrating. 'I remember now. One time when your grandmother and I were looking at this, she told me that Carrie had sailed back to New York. perhaps it was then?'

A chill of thrill raced through Diana. *Another voyage!* Did grandmother say when, Mum?'

'No, I don't think so.' The frown was still there, so Diana knew to wait. 'But Carrie's son, Edward, went too, because when I was a little girl, I remember him saying so. And you said the book was published in 1887 so is that a starting point to look for records of another voyage?'

Diana whipped out the notebook she had *actually* remembered to buy and jotted that down, though she doubted she would forget such an exciting new lead. Still, writing things down was helping her to decide what her next research step was. 'Yes, great idea, Mum.'

'The first voyage darling, can you tell me about that please?'

Thirty minutes went by as Diana described her own 'voyage' of discovery, only pausing when she got to the man Carrie had arrived with. She took a deep breath. 'Mum, Carrie and her mother, Lousia, did not sail out from New York on their own. They were with a man called Amos Vince. The three of them came out under the name of Vince.

'So, Louisa had remarried then?'

'Yes, she had. I found a *United States Dutch Reformed Church* record showing Louisa and Amos married on 22 October 1855. But …' she paused before she delivered the punch line, '… his real name was not Vince. It was Crisp. Amos Crisp. And he was an escaped convict.'

Her mother placed the book on the table in front of her and looked at Diana with a glint of excitement in her eyes. They were both enjoying this bonding session over family history. 'Gosh, do we know anymore?'

'We do. Hold on to your hat,' Diana teased. 'Amos was transported to Australia from England for stealing a watch. His first wife and two children followed on another ship—apparently that happened sometimes. There were more children, then she died, poor thing. He remarried, but his second wife died not long after.'

Her mother shuffled in her seat. 'Another poor thing.'

'I suspect there were many women who did it tough, Mum.' Her mother nodded, saying, 'They were a hardy lot I would say, Diana. They would have had no choice, but to be.'

'Part of Amos' long story is that he ended up getting a Ticket of Leave but down the track he fell foul of the law and ended up in Hyde Park Barracks in Sydney. He apparently escaped in 1836, possibly with the help of his adult daughter. I got that and more information from a book written on the history of the Cartwright family. Amos Senior's daughter, Elizabeth, married a Cartwright. Guess how?'

'No idea, but I'm thinking it had to be creative,' her mother chuckled.

'Indeed. The theory is his daughter took clothes into the barracks, and he left dressed as a woman!'

It was a hearty laugh that escaped her mother now. 'What a man, so to speak. A real character.'

'Exactly. And after he escaped, he made his way to Launceston and sailed off, under his mother's maiden name of Vince, to England. He ended up in New York working as a grocer, where he met Louisa. And it looks like he was quite a bit older than Louisa. How's that for a story?'

'Amazing. But why come back to Australia?'

'You are so on-the-ball Mum. I'm not completely sure, but he got himself into trouble in New York. I found a New York record of him being pardoned—and fined one hundred dollars—on condition he left the county. That was dated 12 September 1855. He married Louisa on 22 October of that year, and they sailed from New York three days later on 25 October 1855.'

Her mother raised her eyes to the ceiling. 'Surely that had to be the reason they left New York then. But why Australia? Why take the risk of coming back here and of being re-captured?'

Diana shuffled to the edge of her chair. She leaned towards her mother as though there was someone else in the room she didn't want to hear what she was saying. 'Turns out he had a son—also named Amos Crisp—who, it seems was a respectable settler on a large, remote property near the *Snowy River* and *Snowy Mountains*, called *Jimenbuen*. Amos Senior, Louisa and Carrie went there from Melbourne. And Carrie and George's marriage certificate gives their residence as *Jimenbuen*.

'So, his son's property offered him an isolated place to be, away from troopers or whatever they called the police then, and others who might identify him. And, if I remember correctly, *Jimenbuen* is along the road from my grandfather's property, *Middleview*.'

'Yes, on both counts. *Jimenbuen* would have been a safe haven for Amos Senior. I have been thinking they probably hot-footed it out of Melbourne once they arrived in case he was recognised when he returned to Australia.'

'I can imagine it would have been a long journey from Melbourne to the *Snowies*, by horse-drawn dray.'

'That's one way they could have got there. There was also a ship that sailed between Melbourne and Sydney, and vice-a-versa, that stopped at

Two Fold Bay and sometimes Tathra. We now refer to Two Fold Bay as Eden more often than not, I think. Ship would have been quicker than by dray, I think. The old hotel people stayed in at Two Fold Bay is still there.'

'Then what? Only two-three nights overland to the *Snowy River*?'

Not for the first time, Diana thought how she and her mother's ways of reasoning things out was the same. 'That was what I was thinking too. Or perhaps it took a bit longer.'

'Must have been a jolly big shock. I can imagine New York was already a bustling city at that time, then bang, there you are in the middle of the Australian bush with barely a soul around and the danger of a bushranger or two popping out or a snake biting you on the backside as you saw to your ablutions, as they used to say.'

'Indeed! Not to everyone's liking I could understand.'

A pause, followed by her mother rubbing her hands together, told Diana her mother had something else to say, so she waited. 'Darling, I am quite sure …' her mother said firmly, '… that Bella would like to hear all this too.'

The mention of her daughter's name brought back the familiar ache in Diana's heart. For the life of her she did not know how to close this gaping wound that was her separation from her daughter.

Nor—in this moment—did she know what to say to her mother. So, she took the easy way out and nodded, then distracted them both again. 'I printed out photos of New York and Melbourne for you to see what they were like in those days—the 1850s. I couldn't find a drawing of the ship they came out on but I found another one of a packet ship, which might be something like the one they voyaged out on. But how about another cuppa first, Mum?'

Always a gracious lady, her mother had the grace to say nothing more about Bella. 'Yes, please, this time an Earl Grey, I think.'

***

When Diana returned, her mother was napping again. Diana's heart threw in an extra beat. *What if* thoughts turned up uninvited. And how would she cope with the loss of her beloved mother, without the support of her also beloved husband and daughter? She literally shuddered.

*Calm down, Diana. Napping is a good thing at Mum's age. She may be in her early eighties, but she's still managing here on her own. She's still okay.*

She picked up the photos she had ready for her mother and immersed herself in her own imaginings of the experiences of her great-great-grandmother.

Diana's imagination was still doing its thing when her mother woke and whispered to her, 'Darling, it's time for you to leave if you want to stick to your travel rule of being home before dark. Can you leave the photos for me to look at please?'

'Of course, Mum. I will make you a fresh cuppa before I go and how about I pick up more biscotti for my visit next week?'

'Yes please, that would be delightful.'

# Chapter Twenty

Carrie stood before her mother—alone.

When they arrived back at *Jimenbuen,* George had insisted on accompanying his wife into the house, but Carrie's stepfather and stepbrother demanded he remain in the stables. George only relented when it became clear more blows could be thrown from men he had years of connection to, and a deep respect for.

Louisa's eyes were downcast, as though there was a creature crawling on the floor that had caught her attention. 'Mother, please look at me,' Carrie pleaded. But her mother's head did not turn towards her. Louisa remained where she sat. 'Mother, please, I love him. I had no choice but to marry in secret.'

Her mother's body stiffened, revealing barely suppressed tension. 'No choice? No choice? How dare you, Carrie! You are my daughter. You could have come to me!'

'No, Mother. I could not. I heard you through the wall. You were determined to return to New York. You were troubled by my relationship with George.'

'As you have proven I had every right to be!'

'Mother, please listen. I love him. He and this country are my destiny. I have known for some time.'

Louisa stood, her face turned towards the wall, her back towards her daughter. 'The marriage will be annulled, Carrie, and we will return to New York as soon as passage is secured. Go to your room and do not leave it except for necessity.'

Carrie opened her mouth to refuse, to insist she be treated as a married woman, and not a child. But the look in her mother's eyes as she finally turned and brought them to her own, stopped her. For within them, she saw a level of grief she had seen only once before—when Louisa had lost her first husband, and Carrie had lost her father.

Carrie said no more and left.

***

Carrie paced her room—a room which had offered her quietness and comfort since her arrival at the homestead, but now felt like how she imagined a gaol cell would feel. She desperately wanted out. She wanted to run to George, to ride with him to Ironmungy. She was angry with her mother, but heartbroken for her at the same time. She searched for a resolution but could not find one. She searched until her feet began to blister from the rubbing of the leather of her boots. She searched until she fell, exhausted, upon the bed.

A soft knock upon her door woke her as night fell. Mary tip-toed in, carrying a lit candle and a bowl of soup she placed on the small bedside table. She said nothing until she left and returned with a hunk of bread. 'Come Lass, you must eat,' she encouraged, taking Carrie's hands in hers to encourage her to sit up.

'Oh, Mary. What will I do?'

'You must give them time. I have watched the love grow strong between you and George and have no doubt that your mother watched it too. It frightened her, with her not biding this place, with her longing for her home.'

Mary placed the bowl of soup in her hands; the seeping heat warmed Carrie's soul. 'Yes, I understand.'

'Nourish yourself there, Carrie,' Mary said, handing her a spoon. 'Potatoes, turnips, carrots, chicken broth. I made it for you and George.'

'Oh Mary, where is he?'

'In the stables. He refuses to go. I will take him a bowl soon. Is there a message I should give?'

'Oh yes! Tell him what you said to me, that we must give them time. Thank you, Mary. I would kiss you but this soup smells so good; I would really like to eat it now.'

'Then *I* shall kiss *you* and go to George,' she said, leaning in to gently do so on Carrie's forehead.

***

*Surely a week is enough time*, thought Carrie, as she paced her room once again. Enough time for her mother to muse on Carrie's words—to accept her decision to marry and stay in Australia.

She knew from Mary that her mother had taken to her bed, seldom emerging from the room. She knew this to be true for when she had finally left her own room to sit upon the verandah, seeking solace in the scenes of nature before her, or spent time in the cookhouse with Mary, she had seen no sign of her mother. Neither had she heard conversation through the wall that adjoined their bedrooms that would give her any knowledge of what was occurring. *Had the reverend been consulted about an annulment? Had it occurred without her say so?* Carrie's frustration grew each day, like an illness about to express itself in fever.

A tiny stone tapped against the window of her bedroom, catching her attention. She strode over, George's face appearing from the dark. A single wave of his hand towards the stables and he was gone.

They had not risked a meeting. Carrie had watched him ride from the stables each morning, turning to wave where he thought she would be standing at her bedroom window. She had watched him return each night, his day of work done, not resting until she knew he would be too—until the glow of a lamp told her he was settled in for the night.

But she was done with waiting. She would take the risk of discovery, brave the creaking door and floor boards and go to him. Within a few minutes, she was in his arms.

'Enough,' he said. 'We have respected them, we have waited. It is time for us to be together as husband and wife.'

'Yes. When? How?'

'Tomorrow. At night, when they are sleeping. Bring only what you can carry.'

He bent to kiss her, the coldness of the night replaced with the heat of their shared desire. She could manage another day without him, but no more.

***

Carrie found her mother ladling out porridge for the children the next morning. She rushed to her side, her exasperation flung to the side, replaced by the joy of seeing her beloved mother up and about.

She reached out to hold her and Louisa allowed her to, but she did not put down the pot and return the affection. The stiffness of body that greeted Carrie shocked her. She took a step away.

'Mother, may we talk?' Her voice was a mere murmur.

'I am occupied, Carrie. There is much to do. Would you like porridge?'

*Porridge? What I want is to talk about my marriage with my mother!* were the words on the tip of her tongue—words that threatened to shoot out like a bullet out of a gun. But she glanced at the children, each smiling up at her, and fought for composure. 'No, thank you,' she said, knowing in her heart that those words were about more than sharing breakfast, that they marked an acceptance that the relationship between mother and daughter had changed forever.

***

Carrie ran her hand over the recessed letters on the front of her Bible. She closed her eyes, giving her mind time to allow a picture of the smooth, gold lettering to settle in place. She had carried this Bible from the other side of the world, carried it at her marriage, but tonight she would leave it behind, unsure about her choice to do so, unsure about what agreeing to marry into the Church of England would mean to her faith. *Would she find the gap in beliefs between this religion and the Baptist way she had known all her life, too great to accept? Would her mother—one day—come to accept her daughter's choice to step away from the religion that had sustained them both, including during the loss of her first husband—Carrie's father, Nathaniel?*

With her eyes still closed, Carrie brought the book to her face to breathe in its familiar smell of leather and fine paper. Then, sighting it again, she laid it gently in her trunk, nestling it in the folds of her cotton dress as an act of protection, until she could reclaim it.

She picked up her copy of *Jane Eyre* by Charlotte Bronte. Pleasant memories came to her, of teaching the children to read as they voyaged to Australia onboard the *B. R. Milam*. It was a journey that seemed so long ago now, but in truth was only a matter of months. She tucked the book close to her chest, struggling to do up the buttons that led from waist to neck. Underneath her dress, she wore a chemise and her night gown, and over the top of it she layered her apron and thick woollen shawl. She did not know when George could arrange for her trunk to be taken to Ironmungy, so as over-bundled as she felt, it gave her comfort to have some of her things with her.

She turned to leave the room, taking only a step or two, before dashing back to retrieve the handkerchief wrapped around her gold coin. Careful not to alert the household, she laid each foot gingerly upon the floor as she made her way from her room, along the hall, to the front door of the homestead.

As she stepped out onto the verandah, a hand that tasted slightly salty, clamped over her mouth. She gasped in fright until George's face, alight from a full moon shining upon it, came into focus, his expression as solid of strength as the mountains nearby.

She blinked twice to reassure him that she would make no sound and he removed his hand. He took one of hers to lead the way down the steps and away from the homestead. She expected a call to ring out from behind them, but no voice came. She expected to trip but George led her confidently away. Away at last, to her new home.

They sighted the shape of his horse, framed by moonlight, its breath smoke-like in the frigid air as they neared. George cupped his hands for her foot to rest in and she threw her leg over the horse. He bent to untie the reins, handing them to her. He needed no other assistance to mount, jumping straight from the ground to sit behind her. He removed a woollen scarf from around his neck to cover her nose and mouth to help keep her warm. He took the reins from her hands and gee-d the horse to move, hooves lifting and falling on crunchy snow.

The journey was longer than she remembered because of the slow pace they travelled at. At times, George walked beside the horse to ease its burden. Carrie began to wonder if they would ever see their hut, and when they did it was framed by the palest of glimpses of the coming day.

Soft flakes of snow began to fall as George lifted her from the horse in a gesture that was more practical than romantic given how long she had sat atop his mount in bone-chilling weather. He carried her to their hut, over its threshold and put her down before the fireplace.

His first words in their home were, 'I must stable my horse,' then he left her to look down into ash, where she wished a warming fire roared. A glint of orange, like a piece of amber, revealed itself. It caused her to drop to the floor, encumbered as she was by the layers of clothing she wore, that prevented a more graceful descent.

She blew a puff of air towards the coin-sized ember which glowed a little brighter, as did the hope for it to flare that sat within her. She coughed when she blew again, too hard this time, and ash rose to lodge in her throat. A wooden pail beside the hearth held twigs, which she broke into pieces, touching their ends to the ember. They smoked, catching alight. Her excitement grew as she continued her work, George returning in time to find her placing a log upon the growing flames.

They smiled at each other, reaching their hands towards the topaz-like flames. 'You did well,' he said, satisfying her need to show him she was capable of caring for them. He brought one of their two chairs to the fireplace. He placed his hands around her waist to persuade her to sit. 'A hot drink for warmth as well, I think,' he said, turning to hang a heavy, spouted kettle on a hook above the fire and retrieve tea, sugar and a surprisingly dainty looking teapot, from a rough-hewn stretch of wood, the only shelf in their hut.

Tendrils of heat stretched from the flames to twine their way around their home, making it cosy, while sips of tea warmed their souls. They sat together quietly until the teapot was empty, and the sun outside shone brightly through their window. Carrie felt content and peaceful.

George stood, and Carrie followed his lead, pressing her body against his. The time had come. They had waited long enough for this moment, longer than they should have had to, as a married couple.

His broad hands shook as he fumbled with the buttons of her dress. Perhaps he was as nervous as she was. She had assumed he had been with a woman before, but it was yet another thing she did not know about him. She helped him remove her dress. Other layers followed. He chuckled when he realised how much she had managed to conceal on her person, including the book which she placed upon a chair. Only the gold coin remained hidden from him in its handkerchief, nestled among her clothes.

She thought she may faint from the tension of the moment, from her desperate need to feel his skin against hers. She swooned and he clasped her to him. He swept her up and carried her to their wrought-iron bed. He slipped the last garment, her silky chemise, over her head, and peeled back the blankets for her to climb under. He was not ready for her to do so though, so he held her at arm's length. He pulled his eyes away from hers, allowing them to roam over her body. She felt no shame in her nakedness, only excitement and desire.

It had not been a choice to love him—she had been powerless on that score, but she was choosing to give herself to him here and now.

She lay on the bed, the security of the blankets forgotten, as he tore off his clothes, revealing his own nakedness and excitement. She did as he had done and let her eyes wander over his body. What she saw frightened her a little, but what was to happen did not.

They lay side by side. She sensed his urgent need. She did not try to slow him down when he could wait no longer and hovered above her, entering her slowly but not slowly enough to prevent her gasping in pain. She had not known it would hurt. She had simply deduced what she could from snippets in books she had read about the act.

She was not disappointed when it ended quickly with his groans. She was able to accept the experience for what it was and she was surprised when he was ready again, a short time later.

This time he covered her with feathery kisses. His lips lingered upon her breasts to take each of her nipples in his mouth. It was her turn to groan as he trailed his hand lower to parts she had not even confessed to herself that she had long wanted him to touch.

She gasped when he entered her, untold pleasure replacing the previous pain. She arched her back, welcoming him to stay. She did not want either the physical joy or the strength of his body within her to end. And when it did, they lay, sated, in each other's arms, falling asleep to the sound of birdsong outside.

# Chapter Twenty-One

Carrie woke to a different sound—a dragging sound. She sat up to see George positioning a tin tub near the fireplace. 'A marriage gift from Ann,' he beamed, picking up two wooden pails. 'I will fetch water so you can bathe.'

'I will come with you,' she said, bouncing from the bed to dress and take hold of one of the pails.

The world outside was veiled in snow when she stepped through the door. It was crisp and white and looked perfect to her. She followed George, stepping into the footprints he made in the snow. She swung around to look at their home, dwarfed by the hill above it, by the plains before it—a safe harbour in a sea of nature.

For an hour they trudged back and forward, earning a healthy tiredness, which was relieved for Carrie when she slipped into the water they had warmed over the fire. George sat nearby, watching her, love and lust in his eyes, while the light outside faded, heralding another night.

When she was done and dressed, he stood, subdued, reaching into his pocket to remove a small, paper-wrapped packet bound by string tied in a clumsy bow. He held it out to her. 'My wedding gift to you. It is not grand,' he said, apologetically.

Whatever it was, it already meant more than Carrie could express to him. It was the first gift he had given her, and it would remain the most important to her for that reason. She stood on tippy-toes, and stretched, in her bare feet, to kiss his lips. When he released her, she untied the string of her gift and unfolded the paper to reveal a beautiful pearl-shell hair comb. Its colours changed in the firelight from aqua to sea green as she tipped it from side to side. She gave it to him to put in her hair, but his efforts made them both laugh when it became obvious he did not know what to do. She took it from him, sliding it in place, moments before he scooped her up and took her to their bed.

***

A week passed. An intimate week that was theirs alone. A week of love making, of venturing out for water, kindling and seeing to George's horse. A week of sharing simple foods—damper and potatoes cooked in ash, morning porridge and slices of cold beef. Once or twice, Carrie allowed her mind to wonder why no one had come for them as she had expected them to, but she forced the thought away, refusing to let it intrude on their happiness.

They were naked again when they heard the sound of horses' hooves on crackling snow followed shortly after by the unmistakeable English accent of her stepfather. They moved like lightening to dress, George stalling to give her more time to do so by going out to meet the man Carrie knew George had a special bond with.

When a tap came upon their door, she was seated, her long hair swept back and held in place by her comb. She was unsure how she should behave. *Should she be meek and accepting of the harsh words that would surely come, for her behaviour of running away for a second time? Or should she prepare to argue, make a claim upon her independence in no uncertain terms to end their opposition to her marriage once and for all?*

It was not her stepfather, or stepbrother—whose voice she had also since heard—who came through the door though. It was her mother, looking weary and hunched, her beauty perhaps dulled by her daughter's rebellious behaviour. Or had Carrie missed the commencement of Louisa's ageing?

Compassion overcame her and she rushed to throw her arms around her mother, tears falling like raindrops from her eyes when the arms that had held her since she was a child wrapped around her too. She laid her head upon Louisa's shoulder, and for a moment she relished the restoration of their relationship. Until her mother stepped back and asked to sit down, a coolness in the tone of her voice.

'Mother …' Carrie said, her mother holding up both hands to stop her.

'Do not defend what you have done. I could not stand it. You have caused me great suffering. This …' she said, sweeping an arm, '… is not what I had intended for you. But you have made your decision. I assume he has taken you.'

Carrie bristled at her mother's words. 'No, he has not taken me. I gave myself to him. He is my husband!' she declared as she began to pace. 'And you gave us no choice. We waited for acceptance of our marriage, but it did not come.'

'You barely waited a week, Carrie. Perhaps if you had waited longer.'

'How much longer? Months? Would you have had me on a ship back to New York by then? We could not allow that.'

Her mother seemed to shrink in her chair. The life-long bond between them tugged at Carrie's heart strings again. She kneeled at her mother's feet, clasping her hands.

'I love him. This land is my new country, my home. Be happy for me, Mother.'

'I do not know if I can give you that. Your father—God rest him—worked hard to give us a better life than he had. Our apartment, room for all of us, enough coin for provisions for all of us. Now you choose this,' she said, sweeping her arm again, casting a critical eye over their humble home. 'But it is too late, you leave me with no choice but to accept your marriage and to pray for you.'

Carrie sat back on her haunches, at once offended by her mother's unkind words about their home and relieved by her acceptance of her marriage. Her hopes that their relationship was restored, were dashed. She could no longer deny to herself that change hung between them like an unwanted barrier.

Carrie wanted to bite back, to defend what her husband had provided for them, but her mother's sad and shrunken form stopped her. Instead, she made a silent pledge to always love her mother and be more considerate of the woman who she could see would always love and worry about her.

The door opened and George strode in, a frown creasing his smooth, sun-browned skin. 'You are needed outside, Carrie,' he said, raising his left eyebrow in that strange way he did. 'Gifts have been brought for you.' He left her questioning why that upset him. He was a proud man, she well knew. *Perhaps he had overheard. Perhaps he was also offended by her mother's inference that he could not provide for them?* Those thoughts were swept aside when Carrie stepped outside. They were exchanged for joy when she caught sight of Pony, a man's saddle upon her back. Amos the younger handed Carrie the reins and bent to kiss her upon her head. She threw herself into his arms, before a whinny and a gentle wet nuzzle from Pony distracted her. She turned to stroke Pony's ears and lay her face against the horse, relishing her familiar smell.

'You will ride to see us,' she heard her stepfather say, 'for your mother's sake at least.'

'I will,' she said, moving to embrace him too. He seemed embarrassed by her display of affection, remaining in her arms for no more than a moment before moving out of reach. 'We must unload the supplies then head back, Lass, before weather sets in.'

She nodded, marvelling at the bags of flour, sugar, winter vegetables, jars of preserves, and cast iron pot she had no doubt held one of Mary's stews. And last, but not least, her trunk, on top of which sat her possum cloak.

Her heart swelled. She had much to do, much to organise, which allowed her to put George's unease from her mind.

# Chapter Twenty-Two

When Diana had driven away from Jindabyne last week, she had done her best to apply logic to her concerns about her mother's health, but her concerns had kept niggling away at her as she drove home to Canberra, the way a surprisingly painful paper cut does. And now, six days later, her concerns about her mother were still foremost in her mind.

Walking through her own front door, after having taken herself for her first walk in months, Diana headed straight for the fridge, determined to distract herself by cooking a chicken curry. As she reached for the fridge door, the photo of her and James's old dog, Ridge, caught her eye. 'Not a very original name, was it Ridge?' she said out loud. Ridge had been a Rhodesian Ridgeback cross, and the name had come to both she and James at the same time when they had chosen him at the local RSPCA shelter. They had laughed at the time, and it made her chuckle now. They had shared so many happy times with their dog over the twelve years of his doggy life.

Diana held her cupped hands out in front of her as though Ridge's snout lay upon them—as it had when the vet gently administered the injection that would give their beloved companion a peaceful passing from this world. Ridge's eyes had been locked onto hers, conveying love, trust and a level of understanding that had come as a surprise, before a single tail wag marked his last moment with them.

How they had cried when the vet had left their home. The kindness of enabling Ridge to pass away in his bed, still pulled at her heart strings—an act of compassion that would never be forgotten.

Diana lowered her hands, and for the first time in years was struck by a desire to know the love of another dog. She had loved their dog so much—he remained present in her heart and mind to this day—that she had thought there couldn't be another. But here she was, longing to reach down and stroke soft fur, a long ear, a long nose—to feel the comforting warm body of a dog leaning against her leg.

*Perhaps I should. It will need to be in the one-day category though—for when I have tackled my finances and can afford to care for him or her.*

The possibility gave her the gift of calmness while she cooked her curry, allowing her to replace her worry about her mother with imaginings of long walks with her dog and night time cuddles nestled upon the lounge as she read or watched a movie.

***

Diana had enjoyed making the curry, made creamy by the coconut milk she had added, and enjoyed eating it even more so. She patted her satisfied stomach as she pulled her laptop towards her and opened her email. She scrolled passed the unsolicited messages encouraging her to buy more things, searching for something of interest. Her eyes opened wide when they fell upon an email from Births, Deaths and Marriages. *The first Birth Certificate of Carrie and George's children had arrived. Yay!*

She bounced up to switch her printer, that sat upon the sideboard, on, opened the certificate and printed it off, before saving it to her family history research file under 'Documents'. The OCD trait she suspected she may have a touch of, saw her save any documents in order of receipt.

Her eyes flitted up and down, back and forth, over the certificate, honing in on details. Mother Caroline Amelia, formerly Marston. Age 18. Birthplace New York America. *Yes!* Father George Henry Hedger. Age 21. *Yes, that fits in too.* Date of Birth of their child George Edward, 17 January 1858. Place of Birth Ironmungy, District of Cooma. She scribbled that name in her notebook to look it up on Google Maps. There was an 'X' against George's name as the 'Informant'. *So, he definitely couldn't read or write.* A nurse was present, a Biddy Rootsey, but 'No Accoucheur'. *What/who is that?* She punched it into the internet. *Okay, someone who assists in childbirth, possibly a doctor then, if a nurse is already listed. So, no doctor, as Mum and I suspected.*

Diana rose, moving slowly to the kitchen to boil the kettle to give herself time to process this thought. *Oh, Carrie. You must have been so frightened. Only eighteen years of age when you had your first baby. And no doctor to help you.*

Diana made and sipped her camomile tea, it's honey-sweet warmth readying her for bed. Tomorrow she would punch in the location of where their first child was born so she could see where they lived at that time.

# Chapter Twenty-Three

*Ironmungy, 17 January 1858*

Intense pain and a muddled brain wore down Carrie's resolve not to scream as the night inched its way towards dawn. She had bitten down on her wooden stirring spoon until her jaw ached from the strain. She had imagined herself riding Pony across the plains with George on his mount, as they had done many times, to check on the cattle under his charge. She had imagined too, the gift she was working for, lying in her arms. She had thought being present when her stepbrother's wife, Elizabeth, had given birth, had prepared her for birth, but now she knew she had been wrong.

Carrie's work-roughened hand gripped another work-roughened hand—that of her friend, Maria. They had met through their husbands, both stockmen. Maria was a woman of few words, but many kind ways who, far from cowering from the reality of childbirth, was unruffled by all it involved.

The last remnants of Carrie's resolve dissolved, and a blood-curdling cry hurtled from her mouth. A midwife known as Biddy, who was positioned between Carrie's knees, told her to push. Words that were not necessary as her body was not giving Carrie any option but to do otherwise. Maria wiped her brow with a cloth cooled in water from the creek.

The contraction eased. 'I am sorry I cried out,' she said to the air in between Maria and Biddy.

'Hush,' said the midwife in the matter-of-fact voice of one confident in what she was doing. 'You are close, your babe will be with you soon.'

Maria gripped Carrie's hand tighter. 'Did you hear, Carrie? It is almost done. Stay strong.'

Carrie saw the strength in her friend's face that no longer existed within herself, and borrowed from Maria, when the final contraction arrived, and her son slid out. The pain fled and euphoria took its place, her arms reaching for her first born to hold him against her breasts. His first cries were the most glorious sounds she had ever heard.

Tears flowed down Carrie's face as her son squirmed against her, the legs and arms she had felt moving inside her for months, now wet and warm against her skin. Maria leaned to wipe her forehead again, the summer heat building as the day awoke, her own tears mingling with her friend's.

***

George paced the verandah he and Carrie had built together, his newborn son nestled in the crook of his arm. 'George. We will call him George,' he declared, 'after my father and myself. As my first-born son, he will carry the name onwards.

'He is my first born too, George,' Carrie said, a touch of teasing in her voice. She had long ago accepted the practice of passing down first names. She was glad her husband had referred to his own father, for whenever she had asked about his parents again, he had chosen not to tell her anything more than what he had previously said—that Launceston was where George had been born and that his father had passed in Hobart Town.

George met her eyes, deliberately raising his left eyebrow as he was so often want to do. For a moment, Carrie let him be unsure of her mood, until she turned the corners of her mouth upward and saw him relax in return.

Carrie wished her mother could see this man that she loved, again. The heat of a summer day dampening his hair, his eyes softened by the love he felt for the child he held in his arms. If only her mother could see him now—rather than how Louisa and George had parted, angry with each other. Perhaps her mother's opinion of him would change.

Perhaps his opinion of her mother would also change and their joint love for Carrie and her newborn would bind them together.

Wishful thinking was all it could be though, as her mother had sailed home to New York months ago, just as Carrie suspected she may be with child. She had kept that to herself, choosing not to force her mother to stay when it was clear she needed to go. To go back to what she was familiar with, to the city that she was comfortable in, and the comforts it provided her with. And when the day of leaving came, Carrie had ridden alone to the *Snowy River* to embrace her sad-eyed mother, before the river swept the punt on which she stood—and part of her daughter's heart—away.

George's voice, framed by a thrumming chorus of cicadas, interrupted her thoughts. 'He will learn to ride as he learns to walk.' Carrie laid her hand on her heart as flutters of protectiveness unnerved it.

'He will ride beside me to round up brumbies. I will teach him how to break them in. And …' but Carrie cut him off before any images of their son tumbling from his horse formed in her mind. 'And …' she said, '… I will teach him to read and write, to enjoy the written word, to add numbers …' A wail from George Junior—who they had agreed to call by his second name of Edward—stopped her from saying more.

A scowling George handed her their baby to feed. She realised that without meaning to, she had reminded him of his illiteracy, her offer to teach him rejected on the occasions she had suggested.

Reclaiming the moment, he said, 'And he will learn to use a rifle. As you also need to do, Carrie. You have a child to protect now. You can no longer avoid it.'

# Chapter Twenty-Four

Carrie stood, the rifle a heavy burden in her hands. She did not want to kill, wound or threaten any animal or person. It was not within her to do so. But George was soon to leave her for a length of time while he drove stock to be sold in Victoria, and she knew he was right about her needing to learn to shoot.

In what was simply a last attempt to not have to learn *this* day, she asked him, 'What is it exactly that you think I must protect my son from with this rifle?' George sighed. He brought his hands to his hips, so his elbows stuck out, something he did when he was frustrated. 'Snakes.' A memory of the crack of a rifle fired by her stepbrother to save her from the bite of a black snake on their journey from Two Fold Bay returned to her again. 'And bushrangers,' George continued. And a memory of rifles held aloft on that same journey surfaced. 'Wounded stock, kangaroos for food ...'

Carrie relented. She aimed and pulled the trigger to stop hearing more unpleasant possibilities and was thrown backwards onto her bottom, pain blooming in her shoulder. George bent to lift her up, shaking his head, amusement in his eyes. 'Ready yourself before you shoot, Carrie.' They were words that resonated with her need to always be prepared. She stood, ignored her throbbing shoulder, listened to his instructions, and fired, this time hitting the bottle he had placed on a log. The bottle shattered and scattered across the ground. George swept her up in his arms, turning her in circles before placing her feet on the ground and bending to kiss her. His passion was hard to resist.

***

When they arrived back at their hut, Carrie rushed to take her baby from the midwife's arms, so keen was she to hold him after only an hour away. She brushed her lips against his soft downy hair, inhaling his sweet baby smell. She smiled at the midwife who had stayed for the week since the birth, teaching her how to care for her baby, taking over the household chores to allow Carrie to recover. How grateful she would always be to this woman who had also slept, uncomplaining, on a bed made of straw on the floor, away from her own bed.

The sound of horse hooves and the wheels of a cart upon the hard ground of the track to their hut made Carrie look up, for they were expecting a visit from her stepbrother. Amos was travelling back from Cooma today, and was to bring them supplies and mail, if there was any.

And there was! Knowing what it would mean to her, Amos held aloft a brown paper-wrapped parcel, before he climbed down from the cart. Her heart soared. It had to be rare news from her family in America! She rushed forward, retrieved the parcel, and held it close, thanking him for his troubles.

'No trouble at all, Carrie,' he said, the affection between them reflected in the look they exchanged.

Her son howled, wanting to be fed, so she turned away, leaving the men to unload and discuss cattle business.

As the baby suckled, she marvelled at the pull with which he drew milk from her breast. While the birth had been much harder than she had expected, the wonder of producing a new life had taken over as soon as her son had been placed in her arms.

She longed to open the parcel which sat beside her chair on the floor, its shape that of a book which she ached to see the title and author of. She hoped there would be a letter tucked inside its cover, but would it be from her sister or her mother? If it was from her mother, it would be the first she had sent to her daughter since her return to New York. Before she could find out though, she must ready her son to sleep in his crib and farewell the midwife who would ride off with damper and cheese Carrie had wrapped in cloth for her, to sustain her on her journey to the *Snowy River* and beyond.

***

The afternoon had fled before Carrie's eyes, her babe's needs and other chores making time vanish as though stolen by a thief. Supper served, dishes washed in a bucket of water fetched from the creek, her son asleep in the cradle her husband had made, she finally reached for the parcel that still sat on the floor and retreated to the verandah to see what was inside before daylight faded.

Carrie peeled back the wrapping paper, to reveal a copy of *The Count of Monte Cristo* by Alexandre Dumas. She ran her finger over the smooth, gold lettering etched into its leather cover. She had read about this story, which her mother had deemed not suitable, but this told her that her mother was not likely to be the sender. She searched among its pages for a letter, finding a thin, folded sheet, in her sister, Anna's, handwriting.

> *Dear Sister*
>
> *Finding myself with a few spare coins in my purse, I took the opportunity to acquire and send to you this book I recall hearing you tell our mother about not long before you sailed from your home.*
>
> *I hope this letter finds you well. Our mother and brother wish so too.*
>
> *As I write this, I imagine you heavy with child, the date and words of your last letter allowing me to establish the month you may be due. But perhaps you have already had your dear babe? How I wish our letters did not take months to travel between us.*
>
> *Please write as soon as you can so we know childbirth has not taken you from us.*
>
> *Your affectionate sister, Anna*

Carrie's heart sank. *Such a brief letter. Which said so little. And still nothing from Mother.* She slipped the letter back into the book. *I must focus on being grateful for the story I have to read,* she told herself as George came to her side.

'What have you there?' he asked.

'A brief letter and a book from my sister. How kind to send a story she remembered I had wanted to read.'

'What story is it you have wanted to read, Carrie?' he asked, the tone of his voice suggesting he was asking, not out of intrigue, but out of politeness.

Nevertheless, she saw a chance to engage him, with her offers to teach him his letters and numbers rejected to date. 'I know little except it is a tale of a wronged man, imprisoned for a crime he did not commit, who seeks retribution.'

George said nothing, his silence causing her to turn and gaze into his eyes. What she saw there puzzled her. *Sadness?* She became aware of him clenching and unclenching his fists. *Anger?*

'Will you read it to me?' he asked, his voice quiet, his request taking her aback. But a thrill ran through her. An interest at last! 'Yes. Will I begin now, while our son sleeps?'

George nodded and sat down upon the steps to the verandah. He looked away from her, across the vast plains, but she would not be discouraged, and felt her mood heighten.

She turned to page one.

***

From then on, each night, they sat together in their hut, their son asleep in his cradle beside them. George was silent as Carrie read, the gripping tale unfolding. When their son woke and needed her attention, George rose, making no comment, their sharing of the tale coming to an end for the night.

Carrie did not know what her husband thought of the story, but when the last page was behind them, she asked again if she could teach him his letters and numbers, and he nodded. The evenings from then on saw a slate board and chalk pass between them as George proved to be a good, if somewhat impatient, student.

The going was slow though, as he was often away. She was not quite nineteen years of age, left alone with her baby, a rifle she could barely use propped up beside the door, their nearest neighbour an hour's horse ride away.

Still, she was not frightened. Despite growing up in a city surrounded by people and activity, she felt at home among the plains of swaying grass and gum trees, the mountains in the distance framing her day-to-day life.

Not until—that was—dusk one night brought a stranger to her door. She saw him riding along the track, his rifle drawn, a ragged hat upon his head. With George away, she recognised the danger he was. Her heart pounded and her legs weakened as she took herself and her son from their verandah, bolting the door of their hut behind her.

The baby cried as she lowered him to the floor, sensing a change in her. She fumbled for a bullet, the first falling from her hands to roll along the floor. The second bullet she loaded, kneeling to the side of the door, her head below the window, out of his sight. But she knew he had seen her, and the baby's cries confirmed they were barricaded inside. So, she stood, moving further into the room, refusing to cower in her own home.

She heard the fall of his footsteps upon the boards outside and pointed the rifle at the door in case he should break through. She would shoot him! She would do anything to protect her child.

A low, gravelly voice, addressed her, 'Miss. I mean you no harm.'

She may be young, but she was not naive. She said nothing. Her son's cries stopped.

'Could ye help a man down on his luck? A meal is my need.'

Her head swung to the damper she had made on the table nearby, the cheese that sat beside it, ready for her supper. *Will you go away if I feed you?* she wondered. She had enough to share.

'You are alone, I see,' he said. His scraggly bearded face, one eye lowered by a ridged scar underneath, stared at her through the window.

She caught her breath. She braced herself, as George had shown her, ready to shoot. Her finger shook on the trigger. She pointed the gun at him. A bead of sweat ran into her eye, and she shook it away.

'I am a Mrs, not a Miss,' she yelled, 'my husband will return soon,' she claimed.

A chuckle met her. Strange behaviour from a strange man who had her measure. Again, she said nothing. And again, no cries came from her son.

'Who might that be? Your husband then, Miss?' he asked in a mocking tone.

'George Hedger,' she replied, proud to say his name, that alone giving her reassurance. How she ached for him to ride up the track at this very moment!

The stranger stepped back from the window, casting glances around. 'George Hedger? The stockman from *Jimenbuen*?'

'Yes, that is him. And he will soon be home,' she repeated for good measure.

The stranger stepped down from the verandah. 'I will take my leave, Missus,' he said, his eyes no longer engaging hers. Instead, they swept the land that surrounded him.

It struck her then that he was nervous. 'Wait,' she shouted, 'walk to your horse, wait there.' She rested the rifle against the door, within easy reach, dashed to the table, ignoring the knife there, to rip off a chunk of bread and break off a hunk of cheese. She wrapped it in the cloth the cheese had sat in, tying it roughly. She unbolted the door, tossed the package on the verandah, slammed the door shut, and bolted it again.

The stranger stepped forward, scooped up the food, and returned to mount his horse. Through the window she saw him tip his hat to her, turn and ride away.

She scooped her son into her arms, her head against his to hear his breath safely escaping him. She sunk to the floor, holding him too tightly, feeling him squirm against her chest.

***

Carrie stayed in the house the next day, leaving only to fetch water from the creek, her baby strapped to her chest with strips of linen, the rifle in one hand, a pail in the other. The few vegetables she had managed to grow would have to wait for water until tomorrow, when she hoped her fear of the stranger returning had abated.

The first winter they had spent in their hut, she had scraped back the snow and dug in the hard ground with a stick to plant the seeds labelled for the season, checking constantly for their appearance. But they did not poke their heads through, and with a sigh one day she accepted they were not going to. *Not all seeds grow here then,* she decided, understanding dawning that she had a lot to learn.

The sound and sight of another rider firstly heightened her fear that the stranger had returned before hope that it could be George, surfaced. It was not, but it was her friend, Maria, who had held her hand while Carrie had birthed her son. Like Carrie, Maria did not ride side-saddle, and she looked strong and confident, her hat held in one hand, reins in the other, her auburn hair released from the restrictions of a bun.

Relief washed over Carrie as tensed muscles relaxed. Maria dismounted, a tight embrace her greeting. The baby nestled between the two women made gentle coo-ing noises.

'Carrie. What is wrong? What has happened?'

'Oh, Maria. A man of rough appearance came yesterday.'

'A convict? Or once a convict?'

Carrie pulled away. 'Perhaps. I don't know. Can you stay and I will tell you?'

'It was indeed my hope to stay with you tonight. I am on my way from having attended another birth. I wanted to tell you about it and see how you are, with our men being away longer than expected.'

Maria placed her hat upon her head and reached for Carrie's hand. 'Pony will be grateful of another horse for company too,' she said. As they walked together towards the stable, words spilled from Carrie in their eagerness to be released, as though saying them could take the memory of the stranger away with them.

# Chapter Twenty-Five

Carrie sat atop Pony, her son strapped to her chest. It was his first time upon a horse, but he stirred little. *Chances are, he will grow to love horses, and riding, the way his father and I do.* An image of her son streaking across the plains came to her.

Maria had stayed for two days. The closeness of her friend when necessity saw them sharing a bed, when they had walked together to fetch water, when they tended their horses and prepared meals, had settled Carrie down. Their time together had also helped Carrie to be decisive about her friend's suggestion that she ride to *Jimenbuen* to stay with Elizabeth, her stepbrother's wife, for a short stay.

'Fruit will have been picked, and your help will be valued,' Maria had said, sealing Carrie's decision.

She travelled slowly, stopping to feed her son from time to time, making the journey a long but peaceful one, encountering no one along the way. She arrived at *Jimenbuen* late in the day, Elizabeth and Mary coming quickly from the homestead to welcome her and take the baby from her arms. They passed him backwards and forwards while Carrie led Pony to the stables to tend to her care.

When Carrie entered the homestead, she was surprised to see a woman she did not know holding Elizabeth's youngest daughter, Eliza, in her arms. A warm smile lit the woman's face as she moved towards Carrie.

'Carrie, this is our friend, Mrs Mary Anne Harnett, who is visiting from *Rosebrook Station* near Cooma. And Mary Anne, this is our friend, Carrie, who is married to George, our head stockman.

'It's a pleasure to meet you, Mrs Perkins. As we are both friends of Amos and Elizabeth, please call me Mary Anne.'

'Mrs Hedger,' corrected Elizabeth, jumping in, a pleading look passing between her and Mary Anne. The look did not escape Carrie, who had not heard the name Perkins before and was perplexed by its use in relation to her. The pleading look Elizabeth then turned towards Carrie further confused her but told her this was not the moment she should ask the question on her lips.

'Thank you, Mary Anne. It is a pleasure to meet you too,' she said demurely, aware that Elizabeth visibly relaxed at her side. 'Please, call me Carrie.'

The next three days were spent in agreeable company as the four women worked together to cut, wash, cook, and bottle boxes of fruit while they each helped with the children. On the last day, they churned milk to make cream and butter and sat down together to eat large slices of apple pie. Its pastry was crispy to bite into, the cream on top thick and oozing. Elizabeth's children's faces became dotted with the cream, which made them all laugh, before cloths were reached for.

The friendship between Elizabeth and Mary Anne had extended to Carrie and the embrace that passed between them when her new friend waved them goodbye to return to *Rosebrook Station* was warm and affectionate.

It was the next day, when Elizabeth was driving the buggy to return Carrie and the baby to their home, Pony trotting behind, his reins attached to the buggy, that Carrie finally summoned the courage to ask why Mary Anne had addressed her as Mrs Perkins.

'Dear Carrie,' Elizabeth said, her eyes focused on the track ahead, 'that is a question you must ask your husband, it is not my place to say.'

Lost for words, Carrie broke an awkward silence that hung between them by turning in her seat to look at the high-country mountains that were closer to *Jimenbuen* than Ironmungy. 'I have been here more than two years now' she said, 'but I have not ridden up into the mountains. I do long to be among them.'

'Then you must, my girl.' Relief and lightness was unmistakable in Elizabeth's tone. 'The baby will soon be old enough for you to leave him with us for a few days, then you can ride with your husband into the *Snowies.'*

Carrie pulled her son to her breast, feeling even more protective than she did each day at the thought of being away from him. But she knew he would be well cared for, so she let excitement flood in. She turned once again to look behind at the peaks that stretched towards the sky.

# Chapter Twenty-Six

Diana had been enjoying finding her way around the Monaro Pioneers website. So much history and people sharing stories of the families they were descended upon. All fascinating.

But right now, she was sitting at her dining table, frozen to her chair, like a finger stuck to an icy windshield. For on the laptop screen in front of her was a photo of Carrie—an actual photo of her great-great-grandmother! Diana could not take her eyes away from it.

The photo was grainy, but there was still a lot of detail to latch onto. Diana estimated Carrie's age to be in her early forties at the time the photo had been taken. Her hair was dark. It looked black but could be brown; it was difficult to tell in a black and white photo. Either way, it was dark, parted in the middle and pulled back from her face. Her hair appeared to be captured in a net (but that was a guess) at the base of her neck—a severe but practical way of wearing her hair. Her thin lips were not smiling, as Diana believed was the custom in early-photograph days. Her nose was shapely, the quality of the photograph not good enough for Diana to be able to 'look into' her great-great-grandmother's eyes.

Carrie was not a *classic* beauty, but she had attractive, pleasant features with an aura of strength about her. Although Carrie was seated, Diana could tell that her dress was voluminous—full-skirted—so that it was not possible to tell if she was slim or plumpish. The long sleeves of her dress were criss-crossed with braiding and there appeared to be a circlet of lace at her throat. *So much material, she looks trussed up! Was this photo taken in winter?*

Carrie held a handkerchief in one of her hands, which drew Diana's eyes to her slender fingers. *If the quality of the photo was better, would*

*I see calluses on your hands, Carrie, from all the hard work you must have done by that time, raising your children so remotely?*

Diana's mind wandered on, through a forest of questions and thoughts. She shared Carrie's dark hair, thin lips and slender fingers, and for some reason that was a comfort to her. *Did she have any of Carrie's other traits*? she wondered as she pressed the print button and dashed to her hall cupboard to locate the spare photo frame she remembered she had. Bringing it back to the table, she only had to trim it a little to make it fit the frame.

'There you are, Carrie,' she said, placing the frame on the table, 'and there you will stay as I keep looking into your story.'

Although it was late, Diana felt too excited to sleep yet, so opened up her email. Once again, amid the unsolicited mail, was another treasure—the birth certificate of Carrie and George's second child. She quickly printed the certificate off and saved it electronically.

The certificate stated that the date of birth was 18 July 1860, and the place of birth was Marinumbla. 'Where is that?' Diana said out loud, followed by, 'Oh, no Accoucher again. And no nurse this time! But there are two women's names.' So, no doctor, no nurse but perhaps neighbours? Women from nearby properties? Was this a case of women who relied upon each other during births that could kill them? What else could it be? She wracked her brain for a few minutes but could come up with nothing.

The certificate listed Carrie's age as 21 and George's as 24. And George's occupation was listed as a stockman. His place of birth was listed as Hobart, Tasmania. Interestingly, after George's surname of Hedger was '(alias Perkins).' *Huh? Why an alias? Or more to the point, a different name?*

Carrie's place of birth was listed as Jamaica, New York, United States of America. And the baby's name was registered as Sarah Louisa. *So, if George Edward was born in 1858, and Sarah was born in 1860, Carrie had two children under three when she was 21, and a husband who, as a stockman, was probably away a lot?*

A random thought flashed through Diana's mind. *Were you as happy as I was to have a girl, Carrie?* For a moment, Diana felt that overwhelming, life-changing joy she had felt when the pain of labour had suddenly come to an end and her own beautiful baby girl had been placed upon her chest. Then it disappeared like a waft of mist as the heartache of being estranged from her now adult daughter replaced it.

She dragged her mind back into *this* moment and rifled through a folder of print-outs to find an A3 map. She had Googled where little George Edward had been born—Ironmungy—and marked it on the map. Now she Googled where little Sarah Louisa had been born. *No* Marinumbla came up on Google Maps, but a Murranumbla did. She knew spellings of names and places and other things could often differ in historical records, so she decided to go with the likelihood that Murranumbla was where the family lived at the time of Sarah Louisa's birth.

She used Google Maps to tell her the distances between Ironmungy, Murranumbla and *Jimenbuen*—where Carrie and George had lived before their marriage—and realised that they were relatively close to each other. Short car rides in between nowadays—less than thirty minutes perhaps—but in terms of the horse or horse and buggy days, still not that far perhaps? Or perhaps it was?

Her eyelids sagged with the need to sleep that could no longer be put off, so she toddled off to bed, contemplating whether that meant George was still working for Amos Crisp, the owner of *Jimenbuen* then.

# Chapter Twenty-Seven

*The Snowy Mountains, October 1859*

George took Carrie's hand to steady her as they stepped from boulder to boulder. Such times, when her husband showed his gentle, caring side to her, meant the world. They galvanised her for the times when he was away, when she bore the responsibility alone, for their son, home and any stock that remained.

They came to a small pool of water among the boulders. A thin stream trickled over an edge, tumbling below. Carrie leaned over, feeling George's hands around her waist. 'Not too far,' he warned, 'the drop is more than it appears.'

She pulled back and they each chose a rock to sit upon, to let curiosity search the emerald and earth-brown colours of the forest that surrounded them, to let birdsong wash over them. To make the most of a rare occasion alone.

'It is beautiful here, George. Our first stop in the mountains is one that will stay with me. How … *when* did you find this place? A waterfall no less.'

'On my own first ride in the mountains. It was young Amos who brought me here. It was he who taught me to ride when I was a lad.'

Nerves tingled within Carrie. Here, unexpectedly, was the opening she had not found to ask George more about his early life. She had not forgotten about the family name 'Perkins' that Mary Anne had called her when Elizabeth had introduced them less than two years ago.

Carrie inhaled the refreshing air of spring, releasing it in a sigh. 'How did it come to be that Amos taught you?' she asked, her voice deliberately low in an effort to mask her eagerness to hear his response.

Silence met her. Enough time passed for her to think she may have upset him. Then he moved upon the rock, as though it had become painful to sit upon. She made to move herself, but his words stopped her. 'As I told you, I came from Van Diemen's Land. I was ten years of age when I was brought to *Jimenbuen* by a daughter of Amos Senior. A woman you have not met.'

'Was it a kind thing she did then?'

'Yes. I did not think so at the time, however. I was taken from my mother. Her name was Francis.'

Carrie caught her breath. A picture, as clear as if her son Edward was there with her, formed in her mind. A picture of him being taken from her, of her arms outstretched to him in a desperate plea for him to be given back to her. She shuddered and reminded herself that her nearly-two-year-old son, Edward, was safe in Elizabeth's care at *Jimenbuen.*

Her heart ached for George's mother as well as for George. *What had they endured to be taken away from each other when he was so young?*

'Why?' she asked. 'Why were you taken away from your mother?'

'My father died; my mother was with another man, John Hedger.'

The truth dawned on her. 'Was your father's name Perkins?'

He turned to her, a steely and not-all-together happy look in his eyes. She saw his own question mirrored within.

In explanation, she said, 'Elizabeth's friend, Mary Anne, called me Mrs Perkins when I visited *Jimenbuen* while you were away some time ago. That is where I heard the name.'

Carrie saw him clench his fists. 'Did she say anything else to you?'

'No. I asked Elizabeth, but she told me it was for you to say.'

His fists unclenched. 'She was right.' He waited. She knew he was deciding whether to tell her more. He made his decision. 'My father was named George Perkins. He was brought to this country from England, accused of a crime he said he did not commit. He died in an asylum, beforehand a prisoner in a gaol of violence and mayhem. After his death, my mother married a man named John Hedger and I was given his family name.' George stood, muscles taught. He punched the air with his fist.

The violent move took Carrie aback. *A convict. His father was a convict.* She remembered the day before their marriage, the women on the boardwalk of Ann and her father's shop, who had looked down their noses at her. *They knew, like Mary Anne did. How many people knew?* She had not been in Australia for long, but she had quickly gleaned that to be a convict, or the child of one, was not looked upon well.

George sat down upon the rock again, his body slumped. She reached to place a hand on his thigh. 'Why *Jimenbuen,* George?' He stood again. 'That is enough for today, Carrie,' and he began to walk away.

She followed him to their horses. He cupped her face, tilting it so that their eyes met, burning into each other's souls. 'Does being the son of a convict make you think less of me?'

'No. It does not,' she said, doing her best to convey her strong conviction. She stood on her toes to touch her lips to his.

***

Carrie woke, pleasant memories of their lovemaking the night before her first thoughts for the day. Among them, the hope that another child would come. Son or daughter, she would not mind, though now she had presented George with a son, the thought of a baby girl created a twinge of excitement within her. She stretched her limbs, careful not to disturb George. She lay on her side to watch her husband, to look at the sensuous mouth that had travelled over her body, setting her senses on fire, to enjoy the rise and fall of his chest, his breathing reassuring her that all was well.

Only a tinge of light penetrated the window of the tiny hut they had arrived at upon dusk the night before. There had not been enough daylight left to determine more than that it was set on a crest overlooking a valley. They had released their horses into the corral they would share for two nights, and collected kindle to strike a fire. The time that took had taken the last of the daylight from them. This morning, Carrie was eager to see what lay outside.

She slipped one foot out of bed, then the other, sliding her body out after. She saw that the fire had gone out, so rather than wait to dress in more than her chemise, she tip-toed to the door, thinking she would search for kindling and have a fire greet her husband when he awoke.

The first step she took saw her fall over a great big lump, winding herself as she landed. Her unintentional cry roused George, who appeared at the door to find her hauling herself up.

He reached for her, saying nothing, as was so often his custom.

'I fell over something,' she said, her eye going to where she had tripped, but seeing nothing. 'Oh,' she exclaimed.

'I would say, Carrie, that you met with the wombat that passes by this way on occasion,' George said, trying but failing to hide a smirk that crinkled the creases at the corners of his mouth. 'Look,' he said, 'there he is,' he pointed. Carrie twisted to see a large, furry, brown bottom waddling away from them.

'How do you know it is a *he*?' she asked, which caused her husband to make bare his amusement and release a laugh that echoed back at them across the valley.

'That, my dear, is a good question, but I have a question of my own—what are you doing outside in your chemise at this hour?'

Carrie dusted herself off, somewhat embarrassed, but now fiercely hungry—the fresh air she presumed. 'I came in search of kindling so you would be warm when you woke, but I confess I want to see more of what is out here.'

George scooped her up in his arms and carried her to where they could see down into the valley. His feet were bare, but he pushed leaves and sticks away before he set her down.

*Is it cloud or mist?* she pondered, searching for the answer by stretching out an arm as though she could touch what lay in front of her. Fine moisture attached itself to the raised hairs on her arm, early sunrise casting light upon the hairs. For a moment, that distracted her.

The answer she sought came from the man standing at her side. 'The mist will clear soon, in time for our ride. Shall we breakfast?'

She did not want to breakfast, to return to the hut and make their porridge and tea. She wanted to stand here, perhaps sit, perhaps on her own, to welcome the raw beauty of the world she was dwarfed by—a wonderland of sight and sound that brought peace and calm to her soul.

But she did not protest when George scooped her up again to return to the hut. Her duties as a wife called, and the day ahead of them would be her reward.

***

They struck out from the hut with a sense of purpose, although they had none other than to introduce her to the mountains she had longed to be among since she first set eyes upon them from *Jimenbuen*. George led the way as they walked their horses the short distance to the ridge above the hut where she looked in awe upon a bare-topped mountain that stood above the others.

George turned in her saddle. 'The tallest. First climbed to the top by a Polish man named Strzelecki in 1840. They say the wind is fierce there, with no trees to stop it.'

'Why are there no trees?' Carrie said, her burgeoning interest in plants and trees igniting her intrigue.

'I have heard it is too cold.' He walked his horse away from hers, to prevent—she sensed—her asking more questions that would delay their planned descent into the valley.

George knew this area well, Carrie could tell, choosing the right place to head his mount downwards. She respected his knowledge and followed behind, respecting too the slow pace he took for her benefit, as the forest with its thick layer of leaves, its fallen branches and rocks, unfolded ahead of them. The danger it represented caused a shiver entwined with a thrill to grip Carrie's body, heightening her sense of aliveness, of desire to conquer the challenge she was immersed in. She concentrated hard, noting each footfall of her horse, the sounds of hooves upon what lay beneath, and the soft snorts and tosses of head that told her the horse was wary of the danger as well. She felt the tension in the horse's body fade when they emerged onto the valley floor to dismount and rest beside a narrow river, frothy water flowing over rocks. The scene reminded her of the joy she felt whenever they visited the mighty *Snowy River.*

She rushed to George's side to embrace him, his cheeks ruddy, his smile wide, his aliveness matching her own. He was at home here. They parted to retrieve damper from his saddle bag, washing it down with handfuls of crystal clear, cold water scooped from the river.

Their plan was to ride further along the valley before climbing back up to the hut for their second, and last, night's stay in the mountains.

As they mounted and rode again, George came abruptly to a halt in front of her. He held his right hand aloft to instruct her to halt too. They sat still in their saddles, waiting, until a horse came into view a hundred yards away. It sensed them and threw back its head, stopping to stare in their direction.

Carrie could see the shine on its treacle-coloured coat. The horse stood alone but not for long, as other, smaller horses, seemingly unaware of the strangers ahead, gathered behind it. Tension hung in the air. George and his mount were as still as a statue.

Within the space between two breaths, it all changed. A strangled, defiant cry travelled down the valley towards them, as the lead horse, a stallion, reared, arching its body to twist away from them, its call to run beginning when its front hooves landed upon the ground. The herd followed, streaming behind, each animal releasing its own cry of alarm.

At the same time as the lead horse acted, so did George. He dug his heels into the side of his mount and rode off, not looking behind him to his wife. He matched the lead horse's speed, standing upright in his saddle, leaving Carrie in no doubt about the remarkable horsemanship he possessed. She watched as his hat flew from his head, as he and the herd thundered towards the end of the valley.

Carrie hung on to the reins of her horse, which was unsettled by the events but wanting to follow. It was a new mount George had led from the stables of *Jimenbuen* for her, that she did not know well. It was taller than Pony, who was being cared for by the stable boy in their absence and she did not have the confidence to let the gelding have his head.

She sat, not knowing what to do as the distance stretched between her and her husband. She stroked her mount's mane, leaning forward to whisper calming words, her own heart pounding in her chest. She trotted forward to dismount and retrieve George's hat that sat atop a tussock of grass.

She waited for an hour, fearful that an accident had befallen George. Then he came into view, riding sedately, belying the wild look in his own and his horse's eyes. She rode to him, wanting to throw herself into his arms. His eyes were still looking ahead when he spoke. 'Such a fine horse would make a fine racehorse, Carrie. A fine racehorse would make us pound o'er pound.'

# Chapter Twenty-Eight

Refreshed from a longer-than-usual sleep, Diana's first thought was *had she missed '(alias Perkins)' beside George's name on the birth certificate for his and Carrie's first child?* She scrabbled through her folder of growing information and found the birth certificate for George Edward. No '(alias Perkins)' reference was written anywhere.

*But what could that reference to a different surname mean?*

To Diana, it sounded like it meant there was another story to be discovered! Was her great-great-grandfather's surname actually Perkins, and not Hedger? Or did he have a shady past where he used an alias?

The obvious place to start looking into that, she thought, was a record of his birth. Which surname would she find?

She looked at both the children's birth certificates again. Both clearly stated their father's birthplace as 'Hobart Town Tasmania'. So, presumably she needed to search the Tasmanian *Births, Deaths and Marriages* website for a record of his birth.

The website was easy to find, but a few minutes of searching soon told her that those records from the era she was looking at—someone else's family tree on *ancestry.com.au* that had George's date of birth as 4 May 1836—had not been digitised. For a second, her spirit slumped like a profiterole that unexpectedly deflated when it was brought from the oven. Then she read that such records were listed on a *Tasmanian Pioneer Index for 1803-1899* and it was available at a number of libraries around the country.

She wrote those details in her notebook, left the website and headed to the National Library of Australia's website. She went to the amazing search engine of TROVE, punched in the name of the index, and up it came. Yay! She could view it in the family history section of the main reading room.

Diana grabbed her keys and bag and headed over to the library straight away. It was mid-morning, mid-week, and the quiet, peaceful atmosphere of the main reading room, with people with their heads down concentrating on what they were intrigued by, generated a sense of calm and contentment within her.

She enquired about the index, and a librarian led her to a desktop computer and showed her how to access it. She typed in the name 'Perkins' and up came a number of results. Her eyes skipped along until she found what she was looking for. Record 6770.

Great! But this was an Index of Records, not the actual records. How would she get that? She wandered back over to the librarian and joked about would she have to fly to Hobart to get it? Then the librarian thought of something—perhaps the baptismal record was on microfiche the library had? She followed him to a cabinet where he searched through a number of small boxes. He pulled one out, saying, 'Maybe this one.' He wound the reel of film on to a reader machine that sent images to the desktop beside it and within five minutes he and Diana were staring at her great-great-grandfather's baptismal record. Diana was quite sure the librarian took about a twentieth of the time it would have taken her to achieve that, and she expressed her gratitude perhaps a bit too loudly for a library. But he seemed to appreciate her thanks.

***

Diana was home again, her great-great-grandfather—known as George Henry Hedger's— baptismal record in her hand. It clearly stated his date of birth as Launceston—not Hobart—on 4 May 1836, his date of baptism in Hobart as 22 May 1836, and his parents as George and Fanny Perkins.

So, her great-great-grandfather was not a Hedger at all, he was a Perkins. Now, the '(alias Perkins)' on his daughter's birth certificate made sense.

*Did it matter?* she asked herself. Not to her, she could honestly say. But what had it meant for George? And, because Diana was even more interested in her great-great-grandmother's life, what had it meant for Carrie? And how did Fanny and George's child acquire the name Hedger? So here, in the comfort of her own home, she let her imagination take her to wherever it was going to go, like a horse that knew the tourist riding upon its back had no control over the route the horse knew it was supposed to take.

After a while, she concluded that the obvious reason why the surname of her great-great-grandfather had changed could be because his mother had remarried. Which, in those days, meant his father must have died. Clearly, she needed to know at least something of George and Fanny Perkins' own stories to find out what had happened.

Diana wandered over to the kitchen to make herself a hot chocolate—she had been back to the markets and bought a stash of the swirl-in-hot-milk-chocolate-on-a-stick thingies. She decided she would start by interrogating *ancestry.com.au*, as her skills at doing that had improved quite a bit lately. After all, it wasn't that hard once you spent some time investigating the website.

She carried her cup back to the table and pulled the laptop towards her, taking a sip of the rich, velvety chocolate treat, as the laptop did its thing and presented the internet to her. She remembered her days at university when there was no internet and she had spent hour upon hour searching for, ordering and reading books in the library. With that memory in mind, she doubted her appreciation of the internet would ever fall away.

She added George and Francis Perkins' names to the family tree she had created in the hope that some hints would turn up. She expected that would take a while, so she went to the search icon and punched in the little she knew about George Perkins first.

When a number of lines of results came up, she felt the familiar surge of excitement of another discovery ahead. She leaned back in her chair and picked up the cup of hot chocolate to take another sip, to give herself time to say to herself, *What are the odds it would be the George Perkins I am looking for?*

Quite high as it turned out—much to her amazement. She clicked on the *Australia Marriage Index* link and there was the record of George marrying Frances Doyle on 12 January 1836. She clicked on the *Australia Births and Baptisms* link and there was a summary of the birth of their child, George Henry Perkins, the date of which she knew her great-great-grandfather had been born on from the baptismal record she had come home with today from the National Library.

Diana's eyes widened when she clicked on the *Australian Convict Transportation Registers* link and saw that on 8 March 1833, in Rutland, England, George Perkins had been convicted. His sentence was listed as 'Life', and he was transported to Van Diemen's Land (Tasmania) on the ship *Isabella*, which sailed on 11 July 1833.

So, her great-great-great-grandfather was a convict! Nowadays, that was not something people reared back at upon learning. Many people in Australia were descendants of convicts. But she knew that had not always been the case. In the past, people were both ashamed *of* it and shamed *because* of it. *So, that had to have affected his son, and his son's wife, Carrie,* Diana concluded. *And what on earth was he convicted of?*

# Chapter Twenty-Nine

Diana rose from her dining room table and pulled back the curtains of her living room window. The dim light of dawn greeted her. She stood watching the light touch the shrubs, roses and the leaves of the big gum tree in her garden, the shapes of each becoming clearer as the light grew brighter.

She shook her head. She could not believe she had spent the entire night researching. Neither could she believe what she had found out. She'd gone back to *ancestry.com.au* a number of times but also to other sites, such as the *United Kingdom Archives*, *Libraries of Tasmania*, the *National Library of Australia's TROVE*, *newspapers.com*, and *Find My Past.*

She turned to look at the pile of paperwork she had printed out during the night. *Was she addicted to family history research? Or was it that the lives and stories of the people who had come before her—that if it wasn't for them she wouldn't have existed—both mattered and said so much?* For her, it was both, she decided.

She walked to the kitchen to make a strong, black coffee. She chose her biggest cup as with no sleep she needed a big slug of caffeine. She grabbed a jacket from a hook on the wall in the hall and headed out the back door to sit at the picnic table in her garden.

Before she had a warm shower and climbed into bed for a few hours' sleep, she needed to get the story straight in her head, in her own words. To help her concentrate and make the story real, she spoke out loud.

'Okay. So, in England, in January 1833, George Perkins went poaching with his two older brothers, John and Robert, and two other men. They made a poor decision to drink beer beforehand and take guns with them. Two gamekeepers ended up being shot—one seriously. The poachers were caught and tried. One of the two other men turned evidence on the Perkins brothers in return for his own freedom.

The eldest brother, John, who was twenty-six, was charged with firing a gun with intent to murder one of the gamekeepers. Robert, who was twenty-three, and George, who was twenty, were charged with aiding, abetting and assisting John.

The three brothers were found guilty and sentenced to be hanged. John was. But Robert and George had their sentences reduced to Life, and transportation to Van Diemen's Land. Robert and George were put on a prison hulk on the Thames River, where they both came down with fever. Robert died from the fever. George survived.

George was transported to Tasmania, arriving in Launceston in November 1833. Somehow, down the track, George ended up meeting Francis Doyle, who sailed from England in 1834 as one of 286 free women onboard the ship *Strathfieldsaye*. Francis, known as Fanny, worked as a nursery maid. Having been given permission to, George and Fanny married in January 1836. Their son, George Henry Perkins, was born on 4 May 1836. So, Fanny was pregnant when she married George.

George was apparently given work as a convict Constable in the colony, so that could have been how he'd had the freedom to come across Fanny? And you would think his role and marriage, as well as fatherhood, might represent an improvement in his life, but the number of criminal records for misdemeanours he went on to commit didn't make that look likely.

In 1844, George ended up being found guilty of theft and was imprisoned in the infamous Port Arthur for two years. The next record is of a pardon from his life sentence, dated February 1853.

So, he was finally free. But—and Diana heaved a great, full-of-emotion sigh—the remaining records are a report from the New Norfolk Lunatic Asylum after his admission in December 1853 and of his death in May 1854. The report had been difficult to read. Perhaps nowadays, George would have been diagnosed with a neurological disease? Or could he have suffered a brain injury, perhaps even been beaten? He was only forty-one when he died.

Diana got up from the picnic setting and, still talking to herself, strode around her garden. She hoped the neighbours weren't listening; she probably sounded like she had lost the plot.

'So, where had all that left Fanny and her son? Well, Fanny remarried two years after George died. But it was clear she had taken up with another man years before. The record of the birth of a daughter registered to Fanny and this man in 1842, was evidence of that.

And the man's name was listed as John Hedger!

So, Fanny's first child—George Henry Perkins—had been given his step-father's surname.

Not only that—John Hedger was a convict too. And which ship was he transported from England on? —*The Ocean*—the same ship, the same voyage, that Amos Crisp had been on.

And the last record Diana had found had been a passenger list for a ship that had sailed from Tasmania to the mainland in July 1846 and on it were a Crisp, and a George Hedger. That had to be her own great-great-grandfather, George Henry Perkins, who had been given the surname of Hedger.

The Perkins-Hedger-Crisp dots had joined!

# Chapter Thirty

Crumpled now from being in her pocket, Carrie placed the envelope on the table, smoothing it out. The letter allowed her a minute to step away from this day in Australia and bring New York back into her life, if only for the briefest of interludes.

With shaking hands, she slid the thin piece of folded paper from its protection and read:

*Williamsburg November 7th 1861*

*Dear Sister*

*I now take the opportunity of writing to you a few lines hoping you are well as we are at present. When you answer this letter, I would like you to tell me the reason why Amos Vince altered his name. Mother says you know the reason.*

*Our brother William and his wife Emma send their love to you and George and your children.*

*Mother wants you to write where you live and how you are getting along dear sister.*

*Dear sister that hair you sent me in your last letter I am going to have a ring made and have that hair put in.*

*When you write you must tell me if you intend to come home, we would all be very glad to see you and your children. You must kiss Edward and Sarah for me.*

*Dear Sister, I do as I please and have everything I want, and I wish you could do the same.*

*In this letter you will find my likeness and if you will answer my letters as fast as you get them, I will send you all of our likenesses. William and Emma are going to have their likeness done for you.*

*Mother has given us five hundred dollars and mother says that if you were here with us she would be happy to do the same for you.*

*Dear Sister, I could write you a great deal more but I am in a great hurry and that you can tell by my scribbling. Good dear sister.*

*I remain your affectionate sister.*

*Anna*

Carrie rose. She returned the letter to its envelope as she covered the short distance to her trunk. She kneeled to add the letter to the others from her family, bound together by the length of sapphire blue ribbon that had once been wrapped around the gift Anna had given her on the wharf in New York.

Her feelings about the letter were mixed. It was gratefully received, bringing relief that her family in America was well. But she did not believe it was her place to tell her sister why their stepfather had changed his name—it was their mother's, whose husband he was. Perhaps her mother had referred Anna to her out of politeness, not wanting to tell a tale about a person Carrie and George were connected to, not through her stepfather's relationship with her mother alone, but through Carrie and George's close association and friendship with his son, Amos the younger; and his wife, Elizabeth. Carrie suspected that may well be the case and she had a loyalty to uphold to the man her husband often worked for, who assisted George to shelter and put food on the table for his family.

For those reasons, she would not answer Anna's question about their stepfather, Amos Senior—or Amos Vince, as he called himself. She did know the answer. George had given her the answer some time ago. And—casting her eye around their hut, its size hardly enough to contain her growing family, hanging hessian bags all that portioned off their sleeping area—she would keep her address as care of the post office in Cooma, and say little about their circumstances. A memory of the sadness that crossed her mother's face when she had cast her own eyes upon their first hut at Ironmungy, returned to her.

But she would share the brightness that her son's riding prowess and Sarah's sweet nature brought her, and she would thread honest words through her writing about being uncertain as to when they would have the opportunity to voyage back to New York.

She would write about George's striving to purchase and breed cattle of his own. Perhaps that would give her family in America some comfort that they were doing well. It was, after all, what George hoped to do, even though they did not yet have the means to begin doing so yet.

But she would not write about her choice to be baptised into the Church of England. Her own baptism had taken place in between her son Edward's and her daughter Sarah's. In the church where she had married George. Her decision had pleased her husband, but she knew her decision to step away from the Baptist faith she had been raised in, would not please her mother, and she did not wish to add to her mother's disappointment in her.

Carrie decided she would not give up hope that one day she could face her mother again and sooth the pain she had caused her by choosing to marry a man against her mother's wishes and remain in a country her mother could not stay in.

# Chapter Thirty-One

Diana hit the 'Send' button on an email to her cousin, Sophie, in England. She was sure it wouldn't take Sophie long to get back to her once she read the story Diana had attached, the one she had said out loud to herself in the garden yesterday and spent time typing up after she had woken from her long catch-up sleep.

As she had typed, she had made no attempt to push the thoughts and feelings that surfaced for each person in the story, and the toughness of the lives they had led, from her mind. She had let her feelings become part of what she told Sophie. Doing so somehow felt like a fitting tribute, especially to George and Fanny Perkins and their son George Henry, Diana and Sophie's great-great-grandfather.

The tragedy of George Perkin's life, a convict held on a prison hulk before being transported to Tasmania for a crime there was suspicion he did not commit, followed by him being in and out of trouble for years, before a sad death in a lunatic asylum, was difficult enough to grapple with on so many levels. But what had it been like for Fanny? Unable to rely upon her husband with a small child to care for in the hostile environment of a convict colony? Diana could imagine that Fanny hadn't had any other choice but to turn to another man, even though her husband was still alive at the time.

When Diana lingered upon that thought, a surge of annoyance bloomed into anger at how often in history women's choices had been dictated to them by the situation they found themselves in. And it wasn't as though it wasn't still happening in various countries around the world.

Diana sucked in a big breath and puffed it out. She went to close her email when a new message flashed on the screen. Another one from *Births, Deaths and Marriages*. Attached were two files that she quickly opened. Two more birth certificates! She printed them off and lay them on the table. Not for the first time, she wondered if it was time to get herself a desk, so her table could once again be used for its intended purpose of dining.

Carrie and George's third child had been a boy. His name was William and he had been born on 16 January 1863, at somewhere called Bobundra. Again, no doctor but a lady called Mrs Foster. Again, George Hedger was listed as 'alias Perkins'.

Diana picked up the next birth certificate. Another boy! Their daughter, Sarah, must have felt outnumbered by this stage. This boy's name was Charles and he had been born on 25 January 1965, at somewhere called *Jenny Brother*. Again, no doctor but the same Mrs Foster was present. No 'alias Perkins' this time though.

At the time of Charles' birth, the certificate listed Carrie's age as 25. *The nature of George's work being what it was, how often had Carrie been left alone, with four children to care for? How many women were in the same position*? Not for the first time, Diana thought how life in those days was not for the faint-hearted.

Diana's phoned pinged, indicating a text message. It was from Sophie.

> *Just read your email, not sure whether to be amazed at what you have found out or to cry.*

'Maybe both,' she typed back. 'Talk soon,' to which she added a heart emoji.

***

While Diana had been able to find Bobundra—where baby William had been born—on Google Maps, it had taken the help of members of the Monaro Pioneers—through their Facebook page—to be able to locate and map where baby Charles had been born at *Jenny Brother*.

Looking at her own map now—at the remoteness of the locations where the four of Carrie and George's children that she had birth certificates for so far, had been born—it was hard to escape the conclusion that the family had for some years moved from hut to hut. That was thought-provoking in itself, but in the process of pushing the internet for new information, another thing had come to light which was currently, as the old saying goes, blowing her mind.

For she had discovered there was a heritage-listed homestead, called *Snowy Vale*—built for George Hedger in 1874 that was not far from *Jimenbuen*—that the younger Amos Crisp had owned.

And it was yet another location for her map. All these dates and locations were helping her build a picture of Carrie and George's movements and lives. None of the locations were far from each other, but she reminded herself that it was horse-powered travel in those days, so the distance, of course, would have been thought to be much further then.

She sat back in her chair, pondering what else she would find out. And how now, perhaps she could visit, and find herself standing in a home her great-great-grandparents had once lived in! She was positively itching to see it!

# Chapter Thirty-Two

*Cooma, November 1864*

From time to time, Carrie would remember George's dream to own a racehorse, which was expressed to her upon his return from chasing the stallion in the *Snowy Mountains* several years ago. If hard work was the key to success, then her husband should have in his possession not just a fine racehorse by now, but a stable full of them. But he did not. The years that had passed had been years of him being a cattleman, a drover driving stock long distances to graze and to market, and a rider who rounded up and broke in wild brumbies. While always working for other people, including her stepbrother, Amos.

George had cast his eye in the direction of gold prospecting as well, but Carrie had refused his proposal to move his family to the goldfields of Kiama. It was the only time she had denied him, and he had not liked it. He had ridden off and not returned for two weeks, leaving her to suspect he had gone to the goldfields. When he returned, he had said nothing and neither had she. Whether he had come to agree with her that it was not a suitable place for them to be, she would never know.

And now he seemed determined to begin breeding cattle of his own, the purchase of his first steer having cost the price of the savings they had battled to gather.

Elizabeth's voice came to her, 'Carrie, come see this weave. It would do well for your dress.'

She and Amos' wife, Elizabeth, had come to Cooma to see Ann and buy supplies at the store she continued to run, following the passing of her dear father. Though they seldom had the opportunity to see each other, Carrie felt great affection towards Ann, who had been so kind to her on the eve of her marriage, providing companionship and shelter.

Carrie placed a protective hand on her stomach, the material of her dress stretched tightly across its ever-increasing girth. She wondered how she would manage with her fourth child on the way, given the circumstances they lived under.

Her purse contained a small number of coins, little left to spend on material after the meagre supplies she had placed on the store's counter. Still, she strode over to where Elizabeth and Ann stood, a length of the cloth pulled from its roll and drawn out between them, as though Carrie's limited coins were not of concern. As she looked upon the practical but soft muslin, Ann told her the price before she could ask, no doubt reducing its cost considerably for her friend. 'Thank you. It will do nicely,' Carrie said, lifting her eyes to convey her appreciation for the kind gesture that lay behind Ann's offer.

The bell over the store door rang as it opened. They turned to see a woman, who exuded confidence, march in, her tread loud on the wooden boards her feet fell upon. Atop her head sat a fine bonnet that framed her fine-boned face. Grey-green eyes made more striking by long lashes, settled upon Ann's. The woman paid no heed to either Carrie or Elizabeth as though they were not standing there at all.

Ann bristled, handing the muslin in her hand to Carrie. Ann stood to her full height, which was not grand, pointed her chin in the air, and looked positively defiant. But she did not move. She stood where she was, requiring the woman to come to her.

With no eyes upon her, Carrie cast her own over the woman's attire, noting the quality and expense of the rose-coloured cotton of her full-skirted dress cinched in at her narrow waist, and the circlet of lace at her throat.

'Yes,' she heard Ann say, in a terse tone she had not heard from her before. There was no attempt at introductions, equally strange from such a polite person as Ann was.

'I seek more cloth.' The woman's eyes locked upon Ann's, who held her glare. 'Do you have any silk?'

'I do not,' was the reply, which confused Carrie, who had spied a colourful length she suspected would suit this woman, under the counter when Ann had taken them past to make tea in her back room earlier.

The woman said nothing, taking her time to step away and walk around the store, Ann watching her every move until the woman opened the door and left with neither comment nor a backward glance.

A sigh escaped Ann, whose body sagged. Elizabeth and Carrie spoke at the same time. 'Who is she?' asked Elizabeth. 'A costly dress,' said Carrie.

'Yes, no doubt from ill-gotten gains. That, ladies, is Annie Clarke, sister of no less than the Clarke brothers, bushrangers at large, herself known to peruse before they strike.'

Carrie and Elizabeth gasped. 'Oh Ann,' said Carrie. 'Could they strike here?'

'If they do, I will have no choice but to let them take what they will. But I do not think they will do so. She comes, from time to time, to buy. I do my best to not sell.'

***

As Elizabeth drove them from Cooma, their supplies tied down in the back of the buggy, Carrie barely heard the sounds around her. The clip-clop of the steady gait of the horse, the creak of wheels, the melodious call of a magpie perched upon a tree branch they passed under, and the flutter of wings from small birds that flew past them, barely registered. Neither was there any chatter between them as there usually was when they were together. Carrie suspected that, like herself, Elizabeth was mulling over the unexpected encounter with Annie Clarke and whether the woman's appearance foreshadowed a threat from her bushranger brothers.

Carrie had heard and read about the Clarke Brothers and their gang. It was only recently that George had told her that there was a warrant out for their arrest. She knew their reputation was one of notoriety and ruthlessness. She had witnessed the rage reddening George's face when he talked about their thieving of fine horse flesh. Carrie knew they travelled from their station near Braidwood to rob coaches of their mail and passengers of their valuables. But what troubled her now was the knowledge that their sister, Annie, who had been known to peruse places her brothers robbed before they did so, had appeared in her friend's store when her friend lived alone above the shop. Carrie tried to comfort herself by remembering that her friend had seemed more defiant than troubled. She hoped Ann had not been putting on a brave face.

They came to a fork in the road, one way led to *Rosebrook Station*, where Elizabeth would stay overnight, the journey back to *Jimenbuen* too far at this time of day. They exchanged subdued smiles, Carrie relieved when she saw George driving their own small cart towards them, his horse kicking up dust as he drove it hard. She was eager to tell him what had happened. She was eager to describe Annie Clarke to him. She could not deny she was impressed by Annie's elegant appearance, and somewhat appalled by her harsh persona.

George slowed and pulled up beside Elizabeth's buggy. He tipped his hat to Elizabeth and treated his wife to one of his occasional smiles that still, after eight years of marriage and several children, made her forget much of everything else.

Carrie reached to clasp Elizabeth's hand before taking her husband's as he lifted her down. Although heavily pregnant, he had no difficulty lifting her up to sit on the seat of their cart, Carrie's hands feeling the bulge and movement of his muscles as he did so.

She waited a short while before she told him about Annie Clarke, surprised by his reaction of pulling on the reins to halt their progress and turn to her. 'She is a woman of wiles, not to be taken lightly, I hear.'

'That is my concern, George. I am worried for our friend that her store may be robbed, and she may be in danger.'

'It is of concern Carrie,' he said before flicking the reins and sending them on their way.

'What can we do?'

'I will talk to Edmund when I can. It was he who suggested she be a witness when we married. He will keep an eye out for her I dare say. He will keep her safe. He is fond of the woman.'

As they approached their hut at *Jenny Brother* late in the afternoon, they were greeted by their eldest son, Edward, who sat straight-backed upon his pony. A boy older within himself than the seven years of age he was approaching, Edward had taken to riding early and easily, already displaying some skill akin to his father. If George had noted it, he had not spoken of it, and Carrie suspected that an underlying expectation that his son would follow in his footsteps, was at the heart of George's lack of words.

But there were differences between father and son that were already evident. Her husband could be hard on his horse, whereas his son was gentle, talking softly to his pony, out of sight of his father. He understood his father well enough to know he might see it as a sign of weakness, which Carrie well knew there was little of in her first-born son.

On occasion, Carrie had observed her husband frown at his son's neat appearance, Edward taking care to comb his hair, always quick to dust down and smooth the clothes he wore after riding. His father, on the other hand, worried not about such things, his wind-ruffled hair and crumpled clothes after a day's work taking nothing away from his striking good looks and presence which filled any room he entered.

Carrie knew her son would dismount to help unload the supplies when they pulled up. His father would expect him to, but she knew Edward would do so regardless, for the future gentleman he would be had been made known to her before now.

She and Edward did not embrace, for her husband had scolded her when Edward was not quite four, for the softness she showed, telling her they must make him strong to prepare him for the hardships of life. Carrie offered no opposition. At the forefront of her mind was the harshness of George and his own father's past, along with the compassion she felt for both of them, despite there being no chance of her meeting his father who rested in his grave in Hobart.

Her friend, Maria, who had achieved her wish to become a midwife and who travelled far and wide to help isolated women birth their children, walked from their hut. Carrie's second son, her nearly-two-year-old, William, jiggled about in her arms, while his four-year-old sister, Sarah, skipped by Maria's side. William's cheery chuckle greeted Carrie as she walked towards them. Sarah ran, rushing into Carrie's arms. She turned her beautiful face upwards to her mother, her dark hair, the same colour as her fathers, was loose and curly.

While her son, Edward, was of a quite serious character, his sister was more so, an endearing frown of concentration appearing when bent over her letters or helping with chores. She had grasped her letters as quickly as her older brother, and it was a source of great joy to Carrie that when little William would fall asleep, her two older children would ask her to read to them or tell them the grand story of her voyage on the big ship from New York to Australia. Those were special times for the family, her husband sitting quietly beside them, listening without interruption.

While he could read, write and add numbers now, George had not shown a desire to read stories himself but was content to listen to Carrie's own life stories or those she read from books. Afterwards, he would scoop Sarah up in his arms, carefully lay her in her cot, tuck her blanket under her chin, and brush hair away from her eyes, preparing her for a comfortable sleep. Carrie wished he showed the same gentleness to their sons, but she understood why he did not, his belief that boys must be tough, strong within him.

As for Edward, he seemed to have accepted this. He showed no signs of resenting his sister, and though a gentler person than his father, he was not a soft boy. When scolded by his father, he would not retreat or cry but stand firm before him, legs apart in a stance which set a challenge to his father, who often left the disagreement where it sat, no doubt because of George's young age.

Carrie felt Sarah's head move on her swollen belly. 'Come,' she said quietly, 'Maria must be on her way, we shall say our farewells, feed William, and water our garden before we prepare our evening meal.'

'Yes. And I will help,' said Sarah, her head still resting against her mother's belly, her newest sibling nestled inside.

***

The rope handle of the pail pressed into the thickened, cracked skin of Carrie's hands as she stayed one step behind her daughter, who was diligently ladling water on to each plant in their small garden. The vegetables were struggling to find their way in this new garden that Carrie had not had time to enrich the soil of with vegetable peelings and horse manure.

This home was their fourth, in line with the number of children they would soon have. How it had pained her to ride away from their first hut at Ironmungy, the home that had given her a false sense of security. In time, it had become clear that her husband had to move to where the work was. This time they were closer to Cooma than they were to *Jimenbuen.*

At each hut, she had done her best to turn it into a cosy home for them, learning a little more with each garden she planted. The joy she felt when seeds became seedlings—including those from the envelopes labelled spring, summer and autumn that the old gardener had given her in Melbourne—lifted her spirit each time they appeared, as though a burst of energy had come with the first rays of a days' sunshine.

Sarah spun back around to her mother, her hand pointing downwards. 'Look, Marmie, shall I dig up the turnip?'

Carrie lowered the pail to the ground, making sure she did not spill a drop of the water, for it was a walk she felt was too far today to the creek to refill the pail. She kneeled beside her daughter, her belly making her movements awkward, to make a show of looking at the turnip and agreeing with Sarah's conclusion that the vegetable was indeed ready for the pot. Her daughter smiled, reached down to flick soil away from the base of the turnip, and pulled it from the soil. She stood, holding it, her look of delight telling Carrie that her daughter's interest in growing vegetables was blossoming, just as her own had.

*Perhaps, with more time and care, the garden here will do better than I thought*, she told herself as they finished their watering. Sarah proudly carried her treasure back to the hut to show the others.

***

Carrie's fourth child, Charles, was born weeks early after a quick, intense birth that saw her on her back for days to recover. The unexpected arrival had George away in the high country and their oldest son riding at night to seek help from the woman of the nearest homestead. By the time he returned with Mrs Foster, Carrie was holding Charles in her arms, content with his ruddy appearance, despite his untimely arrival.

Mrs Foster stayed to care for the children until Maria, Carrie's friend and midwife, rode up. The sight of Maria brought tears of joy to Carrie's eyes. 'He took me by surprise,' she said. 'I can see that,' said Maria, bending over to peel back a corner of the sheet Charles was wrapped in, to see his bright eyes turn in her direction.

'I will farewell Mrs Foster, then we will see how you fared and what needs to be done,' Maria said, her arm sweeping around the hut. Maria winked at Carrie, 'Already I can see he has his father's hair and good looks. And certain it is that George will be surprised to hear his newborn son's cries when he rides back in.'

# Chapter Thirty-Three

There was a lot to contemplate on the drive to see the at-one-time home of her great-great-grandparents and their children at *Snowy Vale*. On the passenger seat beside Diana, was the photo of Carrie she had put in a frame, that at the last minute she decided to bring with her as it seemed appropriate to bring a little something of Carrie to her former home.

From what Diana had been able to view on Google Maps, the heritage home looked considerably more substantial than a hut, so if it was built in 1874, perhaps their years of hut living had come to an end by then.

Anticipation at the further insight into their lives was pumping adrenaline around her body, as though she had been on a tearing bicycle ride. At the same time, dates were butting up against each other in her mind as she turned her thoughts to when a second voyage may have happened. The discovery of the Perkins stories had caused her mind and research efforts to veer away from her mother's revelation that Carrie had returned to New York, but it was now back on track.

She spoke her thoughts out loud, which was becoming a bit of a habit, she realised. 'So, Carrie arrived from America in January 1856, was married in July of that year, the book she passed on to her granddaughter was published in 1887, and logically somewhere in between or not long after, was the voyage back to America. Carrie's children were born in 1858, 1860, 1863, 1865, 1867, and 1870. And the *Snowy Vale* house was built for them in 1874.'

She was still waiting for the birth certificates of the fifth and sixth children from *Births, Deaths and Marriages*, to confirm the last two dates—she was simply going on information in other people's family trees on *ancestry.com.au*—but for now she would go with those dates.

Could Diana assume Carrie would not have travelled during those years of childbirth and having young children? She thought that was a fair enough assumption to make. Could she start looking for another voyage in the records from 1887 then work forwards, perhaps even backwards? After all, the book could have been sent to her from family in America. But that would not account for the water damage. *Umm, it's a mystery to solve that's for sure. And perhaps not all mysteries can be solved.*

She had done the drive along the Monaro Highway to Cooma so many times that she laughed at the thought that the car could probably drive itself nowadays. She would often stop for lunch in Cooma, but today she was keen to forge on, although by the time she arrived at the village of Berridale, the need to pick up a takeaway coffee could no longer be denied.

The coffee was piping hot, so she rested it in the cup holder of her car as she headed towards the small town of Dalgety less than twenty kilometres away. She had never been this way before and it wasn't long before the road became a dirt one that wound its way through rolling hills and paddocks, dotted with jumbles of granite rocks. Endless jumbles of rocks.

She pulled over to sip her coffee—no sugar this time—its rich bitterness warming her soul on this cool, nearing-winter day. She got out of the car, and walked in a circle to take in this land her ancestors would have travelled through—that they would have known well. An image of George riding his horse hell for leather, standing up in his saddle, skilfully navigating the rocks, came to mind, his waistcoat flapping, one hand on the reins, the other clutching his whip. Just like *The Man from Snowy River*, dare she think.

'You may well have come this way when you first travelled to *Jimenbuen*, Carrie,' she spoke out loud. 'You would have seen all these rocks too, and the mountains not so far away. What did you feel when you did, I wonder?'

There was no wind, no one else around, and no other car went by. The peace was restorative. The sky seemed so close, as though she could reach out and touch it. The connection she felt to long-passed family was growing, with visiting their home still to come. Speaking of which, she had better get a move on.

Ten minutes later, she drove into and around Dalgety, a small number of homes, an old pub, a small showground and a charismatic holiday park lining the river—*the river, the Snowy River. It must have been pivotal in the lives of her great-great-grandparents and their children,* she concluded.

She pulled into the holiday park and walked to the edge of the river. It was still quite wide, despite the impact of the Snowy Hydro Scheme. The clear water flowed steadily, and a little fish valiantly trying to swim upstream, caught her eye. She kneeled and cupped her hand in the water, bringing it to her mouth. Cold and refreshing, and nothing like tap water.

She stood to gaze at the bridge that sat high over the river. *No bridge when you arrived, Carrie. Did you cross on a barge-thingy?*

She returned to her car, crossed the bridge and turned onto Jimenbuen Road. She experienced more of the same openness-to-the-vast-sky and immersion-in-the-outside-world feelings. Seventeen kilometres later, she turned onto Matong Road and shortly afterwards passed through a gate that led to the heritage home, knowing that the property *Jimenbuen,* where she believed her great-great-grandparents had met, was about fifteen kilometres further along Jimenbuen Road.

She drove several hundred metres and pulled up at the homestead, recognising it from the aerial view Google Maps had given her. *Here I am,* she thought, feeling a mixture of excitement and nervousness.

*And how heritage it looks! Definitely something from the past.* She had never thought a lot about heritage buildings, but their value in understanding and appreciating the past, had now well and truly dawned upon her.

A woman, perhaps a bit older than middle age, dressed practically in jeans and a bush hiking type of zipper-at-the front jacket, came around the corner of the house, waving one arm in the air in greeting. As Diana got out of the car, the woman said, 'Hi. Diana, I presume. Welcome. My name is Ruby, and I am the long-term … um, *very* long-term actually … tenant here,' she chuckled.

Ruby's pleasant voice and face, framed by salt and pepper hair cut to a short length, put Diana at ease. 'Hi Ruby, it's nice to meet you. I can't tell you how much I appreciate being able to see the homestead.'

'Where your great-great-grandparents lived, is that right?'

'Yes, I believe so. Carrie and George Hedger and their children.'

Ruby smiled. 'Oh, I have heard quite a bit about them over the years, and their connection to the Crisp family.'

'Really! That's so good to hear. Perhaps we can exchange what we know as we walk around.'

'Good idea. Walk this way,' Ruby said, leading Diana to the front verandah of the homestead and in through a narrow door to what would be thought of as a small living room nowadays, an old, long, wooden dining table taking up most of the space. 'Are these walls original?' Diana asked, pointing to the close-together, well-cut, darkly varnished slats of wood.

'Mostly,' said Ruby, 'one or two have been replaced here and there over the years. Shall we go through to the kitchen out the back? You may know the cooking was done in a separate building in these homesteads, because of the risk of fire.'

'Yes, I read about that, and yes please, I am keen to see the kitchen,' she said, following Ruby to a door on the other side of the living room, from which they stepped onto a tiny porch and a short walkway that led to the kitchen, which was actually bigger than the living room. A table took up centre position in this room too, and an old fireplace that certainly looked very old to her sat to one side of the room, but in complete contrast the kitchen now also held a dishwasher, fridge and stove.

They lingered for a few minutes, Ruby remaining quiet, which allowed Diana to become aware of the stillness and lack of sound surrounding them.

Ruby gestured to another door and they left the kitchen to step outside where before them were several fruit trees, a small vegetable patch and six chickens happily clucking around, pecking at the grass. 'Apple trees,' queried Diana. 'That's right,' said Ruby, 'and rumour has it, this has been where the chickens—even turkeys, I heard—have been kept, and vegetables have been grown forever, so to speak.'

'Makes sense,' said Diana, 'and would you know about those rocks?' she asked, pointing to a long line of them that created an ending to the garden area.

'Apparently, there was a rock wall that surrounded this whole area,' Ruby said, sweeping her arms around. 'The garden, the kitchen and where the lambs were kept. The wall joined up with the back of the main homestead building and had a gate in it. Over here,' she said, walking back to the side of the kitchen where the old fireplace was on the inside, 'was a shelter for the lambs, and there was a brick oven too, so the lambs were warmed by the wall behind the fireplace and the wall of the outside oven.'

'Gosh, they certainly knew what they were doing,' said Diana, wondering now if Carrie had looked after lambs, chickens and turkeys too in her day. *Um, not so sure about the turkeys.*

'There is a creek not far beyond the wall—Numbla Creek,' Ruby said, pointing to the drainage line the creek represented. It's a dangerous creek, not much in it in the dry, but if there are downpours it can suddenly flood. I was in the back paddock one day after a lot of rain and this wall of water came swooshing down—a flash flood I think you call it. In the old days, they would have had to stay away from that creek after rain. And the one that runs through *Jimenbuen* too—that's called Matong Creek.'

'Yet another thing the pioneers had to deal with then,' said Diana, shaking her head. 'They would have had to be on the alert for so many things.'

'Indeed. Will we go back to the main building now?'

As they walked, they chatted and Diana found Ruby's understanding was similar to her own, which made her have a little more confidence in her research ability.

'This,' said Ruby, walking through a small door off the living room, is what was called the Parson's Room, for the use of the reverend who travelled to do religious services. It's pretty much been retained in its original wood floor and panelling state, like the four bedrooms I will show you. But next door there is a bathroom, relatively modern of course, for convenience.'

Diana revelled in the sense of history and connection to her ancestors she was feeling as they moved on through the rooms, that mostly opened off the front verandah, and a small second verandah to the side of the back porch. She didn't know if Ruby felt the same about her, but Diana was coming to really like this lady, who was taking time to show her everything and chat happily about times and people from the past. Ruby was also happy for Diana to take photos that she would be able to show to her Mum, Maggie.

Diana glanced down at her watch, surprised to see that she and Ruby had been wandering in and around the house for nearly two hours. Ruby had shown no signs of hurrying Diana along at any point, but a sense of guilt for taking up more of this kind lady's time than they had planned, overcame Diana. 'Thank you so very much,' she said. 'It's not easy to find the right words to express what it means to me to be here.' And Diana meant that, the sense of history, that without its existence would mean she would not exist, was quite overwhelming. A good overwhelming though.

They were standing near Diana's car now, the perfect place to say farewells, but Ruby surprised her. 'I have to admit to not being entirely open with you. I have been using this time to make a judgement about whether to show you something else. To give it to you actually, if you would like it, which I strongly suspect you will.'

A little taken aback, Diana managed to get out, 'Oh, why yes I would like to see whatever it is.'

'Right, this way then,' said Ruby, striding towards an old shed, tossing over her shoulder, 'it's a trunk that belonged to Carrie.'

Diana stumbled, managing to catch herself before she fell flat on her face. She managed to stay upright and keep hold of her dignity.

*Could I be so lucky? Could there be things inside it that would shed more light on Carrie's life? Things the trunk had kept safe for nearly one hundred and thirty and more years? Surely, I couldn't be that lucky.*

Ruby broke into her thoughts, 'This old shed was cleaned out years ago, and I found the trunk in the corner, under a pile of old hay, battered but not falling apart, with a barely visible name on it. Because of its obvious age and the name, I thought I should hang onto it, in case anyone it might be important to, turned up one day—and here you are,' she beamed, as they arrived at the shed.

Ruby took hold of the heavy horizontal plank that sat across the two doors of the shed and Diana rushed forward to help. They pushed the plank to the right until the left door was clear to open, which left them puffing from the effort.

As they walked in, Diana thought, *Ruby was right, it is an old shed—a very old shed. Could George have built this. Could it be that old?*

Dust motes swam around them, silhouetted like tiny flakes of snow by the light coming in from two windows and between gaps between the wooden slats of the shed that had been worn down by time. The smell of hay and the impacted dirt floor hung in the air, making Diana and Ruby sneeze at the same time, then share a laugh about doing so.

Diana looked around but the shed really had been cleaned out. It looked empty to her. 'Over there,' said Ruby, pointing to a far corner. 'I put a tarpaulin over it, in case any water worked its way into the shed.'

The tarpaulin was damp, and dread at possible damage to the trunk hit Diana, her heart thumping now. She removed the tarpaulin and kneeled to place her hands on the cold leather of the trunk. 'It's dry,' she said, a sigh escaping both of them. The tarpaulin had done its job.

A chunky brass lock, still committed to the task it was allotted years ago of keeping people out, was still doing its job. Diana pulled on it, hoping something might give, but no such luck. 'There's no key,' said Ruby, 'I have searched high and low.'

'Have you been tempted to crack it open? I would have been.'

'I won't lie, the answer to that is yes, but ethics got the better of me, when I looked at her name.' She pointed.

It was faded but it was there., 'Caroline Amelia Hedger.' A wave of dizziness came over Diana and she swayed. An arm, made strong from Ruby's years on the land, wrapped around Diana, steadying her. Diana looked into Ruby's weather-lined face and found herself hoping they would truly become friends.

'It's excitement, adrenaline and nervousness at what we might find,' she said.

'Well,' said Ruby, 'I have bolt cutters. Shall we find out?'

Diana nodded, 'Let's do it.'

Ruby left and was back within a few minutes, during which time Diana had said an out-loud apology to Carrie for breaking into her belongings. But Diana felt the timing was right as a need to piece together, and perhaps even write down, her great-great-grandmother's story, was growing within her.

'Ready?' asked Ruby, kneeling beside her again.

'Ready,' said Diana, not entirely sure she was. Would she be disappointed, or would there be *treasure* within?

A loud snap reverberated around the shed as the lock gave way and the job it had done so well for so many years ended.

Diana put her hands on the cracked leather and lifted up the lid. It creaked with age. They peered in. Fur. Animal fur. They both reached out to touch it. 'Possum,' said Ruby. 'Silky smooth, despite the years.' *Why,* was the first thought that came to Diana's mind.

Diana lifted it from the trunk. She stretched it out on the ground. 'A rug? Of possum skin and fur.'

'Oh … my … goodness,' cried Ruby, 'it's not a rug, it's an Aboriginal cloak. Possum pelts sewn together. Very important to Aboriginal people.'

Diana knew something of the cloaks from documentaries she had watched. But why did Carrie have one?

'There has to be a story behind that,' said Ruby. 'When your great-great-grandparents were here, Aboriginal people, whose country this was, would have passed through, to feast on Bogong moths, for example, in the mountains. Carrie must have had some contact to have such a valuable item.'

'Look, there is more,' said Diana, who reached into the trunk and pulled out a barely-together lace hanky tied with a knot, and a piece of folded, frayed paper.

'The light is better in the house. Shall we take them inside?' asked Ruby. 'We can have a cuppa while you look.'

Replacing the cloak in the trunk, they headed back to the warmth of the open fire, the day having marched on, the coolness coming off the mountains having made its way down to greet them.

'Hot chocolate?' asked Ruby.

'Perfect. I have recently rediscovered my love of the stuff,' Diana quipped.

Diana waited until Ruby returned and they had taken their first slurp of the rich, syrupy beverage. She reached for the hanky, which fell apart as she tried to tease it from its knot. Their eyes fell upon a coin, about the size of a ten cent piece. Diana picked it up, angling her hand to one side, then the other, catching glimpses of yellow beneath the tarnish it was covered by.

'It's gold,' said Ruby. 'It could be valuable.'

'It's heavy too,' said Diana, passing it over to Ruby. 'Why one gold coin?'

'There's another story,' replied Ruby, shrugging her shoulders. 'If you have this cleaned, you can start Googling once you can see the detail.'

Diana nodded. She picked up the folded piece of paper, frightened it might fall to pieces like the hanky. Its crispiness told her its fragility was not in doubt. Neither she nor Ruby said a word as she unfolded the paper.

It was a letter, the ink faded but readable. Diana's eyes shot to the 'My Dear Caroline' and from there, to who it was from. 'So, love from your affectionate mother. Louisa Marston.' She looked up. 'Ruby, it's a letter to Carrie, from her mother, my great-great-great-grandmother.'

'Oh, my goodness.' This was clearly a favourite saying of Ruby's. 'The trunk has given you three treasures now. Can you read the letter?'

'I think so.' And she began to read.

*Williamsburg*
*February 12th 1871*

*My Dear Caroline,*

*I write to let you know that I received your letter dated I think the 17th of December. I have not much to tell you at this time. I am feeling a little better of rheumatism. Your brother William's folks are all well and also Anna's. We are having a terrible snow storm today. I don't suppose I ever will know where you live for you don't tell or want to tell. I wish you would write to me every month for I get terrible uneasy if I don't hear from you. Mr Barnes I think he will get a letter from you in about two weeks after you get this letter, containing some seed from you. You must tell him what they are and he can call them what he has a mind to being they go in a strange country.*

*When the new line of steamers commence running as they now talk of, I suppose you will be coming home. It will be an easier journey anyhow. I think the snow tonight is about two feet on the level. Terrible travelling here. Are the rail car travelling in any of your country? I do wish you would write me particulars about things of your country and do tell me where you live. Have your likeness taken and send it to me, get one that looks just like you. Have one of your children taken if you can and please your poor old mother.*

*Love from your affectionate mother*

*Louisa Marston*

One read and Diana knew there was so much in that letter for her to think about. And another date to add to the ones she already had. She felt gobsmacked. Not only had she visited a home that Carrie and George and their children had lived in, and met someone she felt would be a friend, but she found three treasures that told her more. This also formed more questions in her mind. It was almost too much for her to process and as she glanced out the window and saw dusk approaching, she knew it was time to head off. She was continuing on to Jindabyne to see her mother and stay the night.

'Ruby, I must go. I am going to stay with Mum tonight in Jindabyne, and I have taken up so much of your time.'

'It has been a pleasure, Diana. Please keep in touch. My interest has skyrocketed with your visit and our discoveries.'

'I would like that too,' said Diana.

'I'll give you a hand with putting the trunk in your car. If we lay the back seats down, it might fit.'

'You are okay with me taking it all then? Taking it away from here?'

'Oh yes, no hesitation there. I believe it belongs with you.'

'Thank you so much,' said Diana, unable to resist giving Ruby a quick hug.

***

A sense of wonderment at the trunk and its contents that were travelling with her in the car, occupied her mind for the drive back to Dalgety and on to Jindabyne. There had to be some luck involved here; she couldn't claim her family history research skills were that good yet.

To find the current owner of the *Snowy Vale* property, she had simply tried the old-fashioned way of tapping into the white pages (available now on the internet) and punched in the name 'Hedger', discovering there were people of that name still on the Monaro, and she started randomly calling. People were friendly, and a few phone calls later she was talking to the owner, who gave her the mobile number for the long-term resident of the property—Ruby.

She would take the coin to an antique dealer when she got back to Canberra—for advice on how to clean it and how to determine its value. She was a realist; she had as much expectation of it having monetary value as she did of winning the lottery, but maybe there was something she could find out about it that would shed a touch of light on why Carrie had it. More than likely that was too big an ask of a single coin though.

And there was probably even less chance of her finding out why Carrie had an Aboriginal possum cloak in her possession, the question that cropped up in her mind being, *What is the right thing to do with the cloak now?*

The letter was a different matter. When Louisa had written it, Carrie's youngest child had only been six months old. That had to be too young to consider a long voyage—even if it was by steamer, as Louisa had referred to in her letter. The more Diana thought about that, and what a big deal ocean voyages were in those days, the more she was convinced Carrie would not embark upon such a journey at that time.

But—and it was a big *but*—the letter was evidence that Carrie's mother was not well and was pushing for her daughter to come back to New York to see her. It had, after all, been about fifteen years since they had last seen each other.

Intriguing too, was why had Louisa also appealed to her daughter to tell her where she lived? And to 'write me particulars about things of your country'. Was Carrie not writing to her mother very often? Was she not wanting her mother to know they were moving from hut to hut—remembering the *Snowy Vale* home was not built until 1874? And had Louisa barely absorbed any details of Australia when she had visited? Or had she pushed them from her mind?

As she pulled into her own mother's driveway, Diana thought, *How could George and Carrie have even paid for a voyage back to New York?*

# Chapter Thirty-Four

Diana juggled an esky and two bags of groceries that she had brought with her, as she opened her mother's front door. She intended to piece together spaghetti bolognese and salad for their dinner. But the delicious smell of roast chicken and roast vegetables greeted her, making her mouth water. The long day had created a fierce appetite, and the thought of her mother's finely-tuned-over-the-years, herb-enriched gravy was like a pied piper drawing her to the kitchen.

It was not her mother in the kitchen though. It was her daughter, Bella. For two years, they had not seen or spoken to each other, and Diana was clearly not the only one in shock at this unexpected meeting. Like herself, Bella was frozen, statue-like, where she stood at the counter, a pair of tongs in her hand.

Footsteps approached. 'Oh good, Diana, you are just in time to taste-test my gravy that I have been teaching Bella how to make.'

Diana cringed inwardly, obviously this was a set up. Her mother had dopped them both in it. She wanted to be angry with her mother, but the anger did not come. Presumably, it was the same for Bella, who moved to remove a spoon from the cutlery drawer, scoop it into the gravy, and hand it—wordlessly—to Diana.

Diana, equally graciously, took the spoon, raised it to her mouth and had to admit, it was very good.

'Lovely,' she said.

'Excellent,' said her mother, 'and after dinner we are going to watch *The Man from Snowy River* movie on DVD. You might like to fill Bella in on your family history news, darling. I haven't mentioned that yet.'

Diana followed her mother into the dining room, leaving Bella to put the dinner out on plates. 'Mum,' Diana whispered, close to Maggie's ear.

'Well, someone had to do something, darling,' her mother replied, mischief well and truly alive in her eyes and cheeky smile. All that was left for her mother to wrap up the point she was making was for her to wink at Diana, which thankfully she didn't do.

***

Dinner was as good as it smelt. Bella had shown no interest in cooking when she had lived at home, so this was a pleasant but confusing surprise to Diana. Maggie did most of the talking as they ate, chatting away to both of them, asking each of them questions, which they each politely replied to. By the end of the meal, Diana knew that Bella was contemplating moving back to Canberra from Melbourne, and that she had an interview next week at the Australian National University to be an anthropology tutor. *A good foot in the door,* Diana thought. Bella had studied anthropology at the same university, graduating with First Class Honours, then up and moved to Melbourne not long after James had passed away, taking temporary jobs in hospitality. Before that, she had talked about doing a PhD. Diana hoped this new job would be a step in that direction.

Memories of Bella's excitement about what she was learning when she came home from lectures, flooded back as though it was only yesterday. It had been such a happy time for she and James, as well as Bella.

By the end of dinner, Bella also had a potted summary of Diana's family history research. A hint of genuine interest poked through the stilted conversation between mother and daughter, like a ray of sunshine breaking through a cloud-crowded sky. Bella's reaction lifted Diana's spirits and she contemplated telling them about her visit to the *Snowy Vale* homestead, and the trunk. But her hesitation while she made her decision, saw Diana's mother change the topic to prevent an awkward silence. Her mother was on a mission.

'Right,' said her mother, rising gingerly from her chair, '*The Man from Snowy River* it is. Come on. I have a box of chocolates waiting for us in the lounge room.'

This time both Diana and Bella came close to making the same mistake of rushing to help Maggie up, and both stopped themselves in time. *She is like me,* thought Diana, *in some ways. But she has a classic beauty about her.* Diana noted that Bella's petite figure had filled out a smidgeon, and she looked healthier for it. Her blonde hair was longer, shoulder length, and her eyes seemed even more striking in their blueness than before. With an inward smile, Diana saw that her daughter's lips and nose were the same shape as her own—and as Carrie's had been.

The opening scene of the movie captured all their attention and they watched quietly, the box of Cadbury Roses chocolates passed back and forth between them.

Diana's head was not quiet though. Inside was like a fly-by of the Royal Australian Air Forces Roulettes with, *Is that how they were, is that how it was for them?* thoughts, zooming along, parallel to each other, in relation to George and Carrie.

*Was George clean-shaven like Tom Burlinson?* For some reason, she imagined him as having a bushy beard. Probably from photos of men she had seen from around that time. *Did George and Carrie meet the same way as Tom Burlinson and Sigrid Thornton did in the movie, when Tom was breaking in a brumby? Was the property in the movie modelled on Jimenbuen? Hang on, perhaps that was not a coincidence. Oh my gosh, Sigrid is American in the movie. Carrie was American. Could that be more than coincidence too? Could there be something of local folklore about Carrie and George that had found its way into the script?*

*Would they have spent time high up in the mountains in a hut, like Tom and Sigrid? Likely. Yes, likely. And would they have ridden together like Tom and Sigrid? Again, likely. If Carrie hadn't been able to ride, you'd think she would have needed to learn with living remotely and with him presumably away a lot.*

It was a long movie. Diana was tired from the day and mental gymnastics, but not as tired as Maggie, who had fallen asleep and was quietly snoring. Diana reached for the remote controls and turned the DVD player and TV off. 'Bella, I will wake her and help her to bed. You cooked dinner so I will clean the kitchen.'

'Okay,' was all her daughter said.

***

The sound of the dishwasher swishing along, getting on with its job, was a good sound in the silence that surrounded Diana. *One more task to go—the trunk.* There was no way she was going to leave it in her boot overnight when the car was parked in the driveway, even with the coin and letter safely ensconced in her bag. As tired as she was, she would not be able to sleep until the trunk and possum cloak were tucked away in her mother's garage.

She grabbed the remote for the garage and her car keys and went outside. She would have to drag the heavy trunk the short distance from her boot. Hopefully she wouldn't pull a muscle or ten, or damage the trunk.

It was a still night and no lights were on in neighbours' homes, so when the garage roller door squealed and squeaked its way open, Diana found herself cringing, closing her eyes tight in frustration over the risk of waking people up. She had the trunk half out of the boot, when the garage light came on and Bella said sarcastically, 'Is there a body in there? Do you have a confession to make, Mother?'

Perhaps it was the word 'Mother', rather than 'Mum' that triggered her—on top of her tiredness that had advanced to exhaustion—that made Diana snap. 'What a ridiculous thing to say, Bella! Of course, there's not a body in it.'

'Would you like a hand then?' asked Bella, meekly.

Guilt swamped Diana, the protectiveness she felt as a mother kicking in. 'I'm sorry. Yes, I would. Thank you.'

Together, they managed to carry the trunk and place it on a table in the garage. 'What's in it?'

Diana lifted the lid. 'It belonged to Carrie. I was given it today. It had sat for many years in an old shed at the homestead, not that far from here really, in a straight line that is, where Carrie and George and their children lived.'

She watched Bella's face light up. 'Possum. Is it a possum cloak? An Aboriginal one?'

'It is apparently. Well, I think so. I have never seen one before, except on TV.'

They lifted the cloak out and stretched it over the trunk. Bella reached to stroke it slowly and gently. 'Only one or two small patches of fur are missing. It is in very good condition. I saw one while I was doing my undergraduate degree at the university, but it was not in as good as condition as this one.'

'Especially when it was kept in a very old shed. This solid-as trunk has protected it well.'

'How do you know it belonged to Carrie?'

'Her name is on the trunk, so it appears to be a fair assumption. Carrie is your great-great-great-grandmother, you know?' to which Bella said, 'Well, I didn't know, until tonight. What will you do with it? Return it?'

'To whom?' Diana asked.

'To the right Aboriginal people. You could work that out.'

All Diana could do was move her head slightly from side to side in a *maybe* fashion. She had only just received the cloak. She did not feel ready to hand over this link to Carrie.

***

Diana was awake all night. Her conversation with Bella had generated mixed, confusing thoughts and feelings. It was almost as big a shock to—after two years of nothing between them—have had a relatively *normal* talk with Bella, as it had been to see her standing in Maggie's kitchen when she had first arrived. And it seemed so weird to have had that conversation, with no mention from either of them of the breakdown in their relationship. Yet, the fact that they had talked had instantly raised hope of a proper reconciliation and the ache in Diana's heart for her daughter as well as her need to reach out and pull Bella into her arms was all-consuming.

But they had both pulled away, ending their conversation with a simple 'goodnight,' both withdrawing into the two spare bedrooms.

And as Diana rose at dawn to make herself a coffee, she found Bella in the kitchen doing the same. But the distant look that passed between them told Diana that neither of them was ready to move on from the pain of the last two years.

As Bella silently poured her coffee, Diana noticed she was wearing the ring James had given her; and a different type of heartache, a longing for times gone by, assailed her. She remembered the day Bella had thrown herself into James' arms when he had given her that ring, a circle of seed pearls with tiny opals of pink, blue and cream in its centre, and how the three of them had been so delighted by the happiness of the moment.

Without thinking, Diana said, 'I have to get back to Canberra unexpectedly; forgot I had an appointment that I got a reminder text for …' which was a complete fabrication, '… once Nana has woken.'

'Okay,' said Bella, heading back to her room, coffee in hand.

***

By the time her mother surfaced, Diana had packed her overnight bag, dragged the trunk from the garage into her boot—on her own this time—and had fruit salad and yoghurt ready for all their breakfasts.

She left Bella's bowl on the bench and carried the others to the kitchen table, her hands threatening in their shakiness to tumble the bowls to the floor. She seemed powerless to stop a stream of chatter coming out—about the weather, what Bella and her mother might do in their time together, and finally her excuse for a quick getaway. She did not look at her mother, whose eyebrows she knew would be raised in scepticism.

Bella did not reappear as they ate the food Diana could not taste. Diana hopped up quickly to scoop up their bowls, put them in the dishwasher and hug her mother. 'Enjoy your week with Bella, Mum. Will give you a call in a day or so.'

'See you next week then?'

'Definitely. The spaghetti bolognese ingredients are in the fridge for tea tonight. Love you,' she said, knowing her eagerness to depart was clearly evident.

***

Arriving back in Canberra, Diana drove straight to the National Arboretum, foregoing a coffee in her rush to stand before what she thought of as James' bonsai. Her stomach lurched, and she thought she might lose her breakfast. She breathed deeply then blurted out aloud, 'I don't know what to do! I don't know what to do!'

She swung around, embarrassed by her public display of distress, but there was no one there. In a whisper, she repeated, 'I don't know what to do, James. Why aren't you here to help me?' a flash of anger surging through her. The anger was rare, guilt-producing and hard for her to deal with.

'I love her so much. She is my daughter. And you loved her too. I *still* don't know what I did wrong. I *still* don't know what to do. What was it? What do I do now she has come back?'

From behind Diana, came the sound of footsteps and two voices—men greeting each other. She turned, knowing her eyes were brimming with tears, forged a smile and walked quickly by and back to her car.

# Chapter Thirty-Five

*Rosebrook Station, 22 March 1866*

Carrie had a welcome surprise when George presented her with a fine bonnet to wear at the Cooma races. They had journeyed to *Rosebrook Station* in their cart the day before, one year old Charles snuffling in slumber against her chest, George nursing his rifle as he drove the cart, hesitant to say why he did so. Their three older children remained at home in the care of Maria who had brought her own child to visit. Once again, Carrie was grateful to her friend who travelled far and wide on her horse helping the women of the district during birth, often with her child strapped to her chest.

It was the day of the races and Carrie twirled in front of a full-length mirror, the royal blue skirt Mary Anne had loaned her fanning out around her, the petticoats underneath making a swishing sound. Her image in the mirror reminded her of a drawing she had seen long ago of a flamenco dancer, and something within her wanted to throw her hands in the air and dance just like she imagined a flamenco dancer would. Instead, she became still, running both her hands over the silk of the skirt. A picture of her mother in the beautiful silk dress Carrie had once coveted, popped into her mind. It was doing so more often as the time since they had been together stretched, but she was afraid that one day the image would not come easily to her.

As a mother herself now, Carrie's heartache over the pain she had caused her mother by placing great physical and emotional distance between them, created an understanding she had not had when she married George—as well as a growing need to be reunited. But how?

She reached to touch the lace at her throat of the white blouse she wore tucked into the skirt, a wide belt of black leather cinching her waist. She looked in the mirror again. Her mother would be pleased to see her in such finery.

A knock on the door pre-empted George's entry. He came to a stop a step or two into the room, when he gazed upon his wife. He came to her taking her hands in his, 'You grace me with a picture I will hold in my mind for all time, my dear.' His uncharacteristic poetic compliment touched and delighted her.

He kissed Carrie gently and led her by the hand to where Amos and his wife, Elizabeth, were waiting in their new buggy to transport them all to the races. Elizabeth handed her a pretty parasol when she climbed onboard. 'To finish your outfit, Carrie, how lovely you are!'

The two compliments so close together took Carrie aback. She was unused to such praises. *No wonder*, she thought, *I am usually dressed in plain, practical clothes suitable for a woman caring for her family, a dwelling, a garden, and animals*, all of which she loved to do despite the challenges that accompanied remoteness and making do.

The canopy over the dual-seated buggy protected them from the morning sun which was still quite hot in March. But she wanted to feel it on her face, to soak up its spirit-lifting warmth on this happy day. She leaned to the side so she could do so, availing herself of all the usual sights and sounds that the countryside gifted her. She turned back to see a smile upon her husband's face.

Hustle and bustle met them at the Cooma races. Acting in a more genteel way than usual, George, attired in dark trousers, waistcoat and white linen shirt, gave Carrie, and then Elizabeth, a hand down. He led them through a crowd to a table laden with fat scones, plump cream atop, jam peeking out from around their edges. He nodded to both ladies then left them to join other men who clustered to place bets on their favoured horse and rider. They saw Amos join George, having arrived after tying the horse and buggy up beneath the shade of a gum tree.

'Shall we?' invited Elizabeth, her eyes not upon Carrie but the two plates of scones being held out to them by a lady behind the table.

Carrie let a smile be her reply as she reached for one of the plates, uninhibitedly sinking her teeth into the deliciousness, cream touching her nose and, she noted, Elizabeth's too. They laughed, their delight interrupted by an older lady, her grey hair caught up in a tight bun on the top of her head that made her look harsher than she possibly was. Although, when the woman ran her gaze up and down Carrie, she began to have doubts about that.

'Mrs Crisp, how lovely you look,' she declared, ignoring Carrie's own finery. Carrie was not bothered, she knew the reason for the snub was George's convict heritage. She had experienced it on a number of occasions over the years.

'Thank you, Mrs Cook. Mrs Hedger and I had a most enjoyable time dressing for today.' Mrs Cook's only acknowledgement of the reference to Carrie was a slight lowering of her chin before she launched into a description of the hope she and her husband had for their horse running in the races today.

Carrie's mind drifted away from the inane conversation, to sweep around the crowd, immersing herself in the finery of others, men and women alike. Although she had no intention of doing so, she took several steps away to enhance her view and felt a bump to her side, the now-empty plate flying from her hand.

Uncertain as to who had bumped into whom, she turned to face the person to apologise, out of politeness, and looked straight into the grey-green eyes of Annie Clarke. No words passed between the two women, but a moment of recognition did. Annie made no attempt to retrieve the plate lying upon the ground, now in danger of being broken by surrounding footsteps.

Carrie bent to pick it up, righting herself to see the back of Annie's head disappear into the crowd. She became aware of her heart beating faster in her chest, and the voices around her diminished in loudness. *Are her brothers, the bushrangers, here? What should I do?*

She bridged the gap back to Elizabeth's side and tugged her sleeve gently, to alert her friend of her need to talk to her. A second, almost imperceptible tug, led to an inquiring glance from Elizabeth and widely opened eyes from Carrie. Elizabeth did her best to curtail her conversation with Mrs Cook but it took several minutes for her to do so.

'Carrie, what is it?' she queried when they could finally exchange words out of ear shot of the prying Mrs Cook.

'Annie Clarke. She is here. I saw her, she bumped into me. It was not until I saw her eyes that I recognised her. She is dressed plainly, not brightly as when we saw her in Ann's shop. Could her brothers be here? Could they be up to mischief?' The words tumbled from Carrie in a stream.

Elizabeth placed her hand on Carrie's arm. 'Are you certain it was her?'

'I am.'

Elizabeth took her by the hand. 'Search with me,' which they did, nodding to others as they were greeted, but not catching sight of Annie Clarke.

'Should we find Amos and George and tell them?'

'Yes, Carrie. They will be among the men over there,' she pointed, heading straight into the gathering of men.

Any thoughts Carrie had that the men would doubt her were put to rest by the swift action that was taken. Amos and George swiftly recruited others to search the crowd for signs of the Clarke brothers, their gang and their sister. But no sightings were made.

A sigh of relief escaped her when George returned and told her that although they had been sighted the day before watching over the racecourse from Bushy Hill, the Clarke Brothers were not believed to be present this day. Word, however, was spreading to keep an eye out for them.

Carrie allowed herself to relax again, slowly returning to her enjoyment of the day.

***

On the journey back to *Rosebrook Station*, Carrie gave herself time to wonder why Annie Clarke had attended the races. She didn't appear to be with anyone, her demure attire appeared to be out of character, and she had disappeared when Carrie had recognised her. In her own mind, it pointed to suspicious behaviour. Had the Clarke brothers been planning a robbery and been foiled by Carrie's recognition of their sister and the swift search the men had undertaken? Had Annie Clarke been casing the race meeting on behalf of her brothers, whose presence would not have been tolerated? Or was Carrie reading too much into it all? Could Annie have simply been there to enjoy the event, as Carrie, George and their friends had been? Had Annie dressed demurely to avoid being noticed when people were used to her elegant attire? Worry niggled at Carrie like an annoying insect bite. *Time to put such thoughts aside*, she told herself, *all is well.*

***

Late that night, muted conversations and laughter came to Carrie through the wall which separated the living area of the homestead at *Rosebrook Station*, and the bedroom given to her, George and Charles for their short stay to attend the races. Carrie was barely aware of those sounds for all her senses were focused on the baby at her breast. She gazed upon her son, inhaling the sweet smell of him, his suckling sounds offering knowledge that he was feeding well. She brought one hand to his head to touch his downy hair, leaning forward to kiss it when his eyes closed in sleepy contentment.

She knew that soon a fiddler would play his tunes, which would not bother her baby, growing up as one of four children. Charles was already accustomed to loud noises despite his young age.

A smile played upon her face, growing wider, smaller, wider again, at the memory of her husband's bolstered spirit when he had won some pounds on a winning horse. His mood remained joyous as they joined others gathered around a long table set up outside the homestead, under the stars, for a meal devoured by appetites fed by the excitement of the day.

Carrie had gradually succeeded in her quest to put any thought of Annie Clarke, her bushranger brothers and their gang, from her mind and was lifting her head from her son's when loud, violent voices tore through the night like unexpected claps of thunder.

Instinctively, she pulled her son closer to her chest, causing him to stir from the tightness of her hold. She sat rigid in the rocking chair, her ears searching for an answer to the disturbance. Despite their loudness, the words that followed were still muffled through the wall, but she gleaned enough for a sense of danger to come over her.

She stood, backing into a corner, considering the window as an escape route, but instantly recognised the risk its closeness to the front door of the homestead posed to her being seen. Her eyes dashed around the room catching sight of the space between the bed and floor, knowing she could slip in there, but not knowing if she could keep her baby silent to prevent their whereabouts from being discovered.

A loud voice boomed, loud enough for her to hear its demand for valuables. She closed her eyes and prayed that her husband, who did not suffer insults well, did not take it upon himself to quell that voice.

Opening her eyes, they fell upon the door. *If I can get down the hall to another room,* she thought, *I could climb through a window there and hide outside.*

She took a step towards the door, halting in her tracks when the doorknob turned, and the door creaked open. Her stomach lurched as nausea took hold. She backed into a corner of the room again, a need to run pumping through her body like a friend yelling at her to do so.

A slim figure, dressed in moleskins, a long-sleeved shirt, vest, a weathered, brimmed hat pulled low over forehead, a man's kerchief covering mouth and nose, entered the room. Attire to disguise the person beneath but there was no mistaking the grey-green eyes that met Carrie's. They belonged to Annie Clarke.

Annie lowered the pistol in her hand, but Carrie sensed the danger was still real. The pistol could be raised again, or Annie could call out for her brothers—for it must be them making demands for valuables in the room next door. The bushrangers she had feared were here.

Annie removed her hat and pulled down her face covering. 'No use pretending we do not recognise each other,' she said, taking several steps towards Carrie, their eyes fixed upon each other, until Annie lowered her gaze to the baby. 'Yours no doubt. A boy,' she queried.

'Yes. His name is Charles,' Carrie said, her voice croaky and shaky.

Annie stepped closer still. She bent her head to peer at the baby. Carrie pulled him closer to her breast to protect him, a whimper alerting her to his discomfort at her too-tight hold.

'I will not harm you, Mrs Hedger. Nor your child. I am here to search sleeping rooms for valuables while the gang relieve the guests of theirs.'

Carrie's eyes betrayed her, lowering to the wedding ring hidden by the baby's wrap. Annie noticed. 'Show it to me.'

'It is all I have.'

'And it is mine if I want it,' Annie smirked, raising the handgun from her side again, pointing it directly at Carrie.

Fury pounded down Carrie's fear, akin to a horse stomping a hoof upon the ground in opposition to being broken in. 'No! It is mine and you have no right to take it!'

'This,' said Annie, turning the gun from side to side in her hand, 'says otherwise!'

'You do not scare me. Fire that and you announce your presence for all to hear.'

'Including your husband, no doubt. But he cannot rescue you from out there.' She tilted her head towards the wall that separated them from the others.

'And you do not know my husband! He knows I am here with his son.'

Annie threw back her head and laughed, unconcerned about whether the sound would carry through the wall.

'You may keep your ring. I assume it is of little value.'

Carrie felt her face flush red. 'Well, you assume wrong. It is of great value to me,' she declared, putting one foot ahead of her to bring her closer to Annie, the barrel of the handgun inches from her chest.

Her opponent rose to the challenge. She did not flinch. She did not break eye contact. But she lowered the handgun to her side again. 'Value is not necessarily measured in pounds is what you are telling me?'

'Yes,' replied Carrie, her voice steady and harsh even to her own ears.

'You may be right, Mrs Hedger, and if you were a woman of wealth, I would deem you to be a patronising hypocrite. But you are not. You are the wife of a man tainted by convict heritage,' she lingered. 'I will therefore grace you with more attention than I otherwise would, with more respect than I otherwise would.'

Carrie knew better than to question how Annie would know about her husband's heritage, for she had experienced the far and fast spread of words, despite the stretches of distance in more isolated areas of the country. Just as she knew that Annie's parents were convicts transported from England.

'That is of no consequence to me, I do not heed the poor judgement of *some* other people. And I am my own person and should be considered as such. I demand it!'

Annie turned away, not allowing Carrie to see the look upon her face—to perceive her thoughts on Carrie's declaration.

The sound of a fiddler striking up a tune turned Annie around again, a smile playing upon her lips. 'A strange thing, wouldn't you say Mrs Hedger? A joyous tune during a robbery by bushrangers?'

'I would.'

'But I would not, for I know my brother's love of music. No doubt they will be quenching the hunger that comes from the events of tonight as well.'

'Why?'

'Why what, Mrs Hedger?'

'Why do you do it? This. Tonight. Why do you thieve from others?'

Annie's mood became sombre. Her silence left Carrie wondering if she was going to give an answer or not.

Annie moved to sit upon the bed. She placed the handgun beside her. 'To ask such a question makes me ponder if I was wrong about you. Do you come from money after all? American money?'

'We had enough and some extra, no more.'

'And now?'

Carrie raised her eyes to the ceiling, not wanting to betray her husband by admitting that the life of a stockman, his wife and children was not plentiful.

'A simple life, but we have what we need.'

'Perhaps if you had less, you would grasp what it is to have nothing in your belly—for days.' She paused to give time for this to be imagined, but Carrie did not need time; there had been days when supplies were few and it was not a big leap to perceive the horror of no sustenance, of not being able to feed her children.

Carrie said nothing. She returned her gaze to Annie, seeing anger in her expression, understanding that hurt and suffering lay behind it. An urge to comfort her arose but the presence of the handgun was a stark reminder of the threat Annie posed to her child and herself.

'Perhaps if you had not the support of the Crisps you would grasp what it is to be looked down upon and left to fend for yourself, as our family has been.'

Carrie remained silent, her chin tilted slightly upwards, her eyes locked upon Annie's, but conveying little to this woman whom she had unwittingly given an opportunity to voice what Carrie suspected she had held within for years.

The baby grew heavy in Carrie's arms and she shuffled from foot to foot to ease the growing ache in her back. She would not be drawn on her relationship with the Crisps, which had begun when her mother had married Amos Senior, her stepfather, and swelled into friendship with his son and wife. There was also the relationship her husband had with the family that had begun when he was a child, when they had given him the opportunity to earn a living as a stockman, uncovering a natural ability to master horses. They had been rewarded by his hard work for them and enduring loyalty. No, she would not reveal anything intimate to this woman who deemed robbery justified.

'Barefoot we were. A childhood with no shoes, ragged clothes, winters waking to frozen toes and fingertips, my mother trying to make damper and lard last for days.'

Sorrow for what no child should suffer pulled at Carrie's emotions—until they swung the other way when she heard Annie say, 'Perhaps if you …'

'Do *not* presume to know me! Do *not* presume to judge me! You have *no* right to do so!'

Annie flinched but kept on. 'I vowed then not to depend on others. To do whatever was needed. That is what *I* and my brothers do!'

Carrie sighed. Charles stirred, whimpering at not being settled for sleep. Annie rose and came to them, the fierce look that had covered her face a moment before, replaced by a smooth-skinned gentleness as she looked down upon the baby. 'Can I hold him?' she asked.

Carrie pulled her son closer to her breast again, saved from having to say no by a rowdy commotion outside.

'They are leaving,' Annie said as George's voice rang out, calling to Carrie.

Annie's eyes swung to the window. 'Go,' said Carrie, before he gets here. He will not understand.

'And you do?' Annie asked.

'Go. Go now!' Carrie urged, pointing to the door. 'That way, down the hall to the end room, out the window, otherwise you will be seen.

For a moment, they held each other's gaze. Annie's eyes portrayed her confusion at Carrie's gesture of kindness, before she nodded and left, leaving the door she passed through ajar. Carrie understood Annie's confusion, for she was confused herself—by her own actions.

# Chapter Thirty-Six

Diana paced up and down her lounge room, trying to calm down. It had been two days since she returned from Jindabyne, where she had come face to face with her daughter, Bella, unexpectedly. Two days of being unsettled, of taking herself for long walks along the paths that circled Lake Burley Griffin, of watching two series of *Downton Abbey* to give her mind a break from trying to work out what to do—how to reach out to her daughter. But still she had no answer, not even any options.

She had thought about talking to Sophie, but when her cousin had phoned, they had spent over an hour going over the Perkins' stories, empathy oozing from both of them. After that, the timing just hadn't seemed right.

Right now, what Diana did know was that she had to get it together. It wasn't helping her—she had barely eaten or slept—and it certainly wouldn't help her relationship with her daughter if Diana was a nervous wreck when she went to Jindabyne again on the weekend. She had promised Maggie she would be there, and she would not break that promise.

The laptop caught her eye, sitting on the table as though it was waiting for her to see it. She had been so out of sorts; she hadn't even checked her email. She sat, turned her computer on and signed in to email. *Birth, Deaths and Marriages* again. Her interest in family history flickered into life. The two remaining birth certificates for Carrie and George's fifth and sixth children soon sat printed out before her.

Two baby girls. Alice—who had been born at the same location as her brother Charles, Jenny Brother on 13 February 1867; and Fanny

Eliza—who had been born on *The Snowy Plains* on 24 August 1870. As usual, no doctor for either, but a Mrs Lawless was present at Alice's birth and a Mrs Kelly was present at Fanny's birth.

*Fanny*. Diana smiled. Carrie and George had chosen to name a daughter after his mother. George had been taken away from his mother at a young age, but this showed he had never forgotten her. And here was their tribute to his mother—the naming of a child after her.

Diana now had all six of the children's birth certificates that were available to order. She had remembered that she had seen on someone else's family tree on the ancestry website, two other children listed, but she had double checked and no birth certificates were available for any more children. Another mystery to keep in mind in case she could somehow find out more about that.

Receiving the certificates motivated her to search for the Monaro Pioneers on Facebook and leave a message expressing her appreciation for any information anyone may have on her great-great-grandparents. *Perhaps no-one would reply, but maybe someone will,* she thought. *Everything is worth a go.*

She went to the kitchen to make herself a cup of camomile tea, its flowery taste and aroma soothing her. She was starting to feel a little better and soon found herself perusing the local RSPCA website for rescue dogs. All those appealing eyes. If only she could take them all. As weariness overcame her, she realised her heart had made the decision before her brain had got there—one day she would adopt a rescue dog, who just might rescue her too.

# Chapter Thirty-Seven

Diana pushed the books of ship voyages aside in a movement of frustration. She was at the National Library of Australia again, searching, she felt, for a needle in a haystack! Whoever had come up with that saying had hit the nail on the head, she thought. *Another Aussie saying. Do I use those sayings often?* she wondered.

Anyway, it certainly was feeling like a close-to-impossible task to find any record of when Carrie had gone on a voyage to New York. But then, she was flying by the seat of her pants—*oh dear, another saying.* All she had to work with was the dates of Carrie's children's births (1858, 1860, 1863, 1865, 1867, 1870); the date the letter Carrie's mother, Louisa, had written conveying her hope Carrie would return to New York (1871); the date the 130-year-old book was published (1887); and Diana's assumption that the date of the voyage lay somewhere in between 1871 and 1887.

She couldn't think of where to look next. To distract herself, she moved to a computer terminal and punched 'George Hedger cattleman' in, when that popped into her head. A couple of entries came up that she had seen before—including his obituary, which claimed he was *The Man from Snowy River*—but a new one caught her attention. A court criminal record.

*What?* She leaned forward, about to click on the record, when her phone belted out her *Il Divo* ringtone. She glanced down. It was Bella's number. The first call from her daughter in two years. Another shock. She answered it, and said 'Hello' in as quiet a voice as she could.

'Mum, Mum, it's Nana, it's Nana!' Bella literally screamed down the phone.

Any thought of where she was disintegrated. 'Bella, what is it? What has happened? Try to calm down and tell me. Take a deep breath.'

She heard Bella breathe in and out loudly several times. 'I went to get some groceries. I came home and Nana was on the floor. She couldn't move, she tried to talk, and she couldn't, just a slurring sound came out.'

*No. This can't be happening.*

'Mum?'

Diana gripped the corner of the desk as hard as she could. 'Bella, have you called the ambulance?'

'Yes. Straight away. They came. They have taken her.'

'Taken her where Bella?'

'To hospital. In Canberra. They told me to follow, to bring some clothes and toiletries for Nana. I have packed a bag. Where are Nana's car keys, Mum? I walked to the shop this morning.'

Diana's head swam. She felt faint. 'In her bedroom, there's a little glass bowl on her dressing table. Bella, don't rush. Tell me you will sit for ten minutes before you drive the car. Remember, Nana is with people looking after her.'

'Okay, Mum. I can do that.'

'Good. I will meet you at the hospital. Canberra Hospital?'

'Yes. I think so. Maybe check.'

'Okay. Drive safely. I will be at the hospital when Nana arrives. You don't need to rush, remember? I will see you there.'

'Okay. I'll go now,' and then she was gone.

Diana ran back to the desk where the books on ship voyages were, grabbed her handbag, ran through the library, down the front steps, and across to the car park to her car.

***

Diana was in the waiting room of the Emergency Department when the ambulance pulled in. She pleaded to be let in to be with her mother and within ten minutes was sitting by her side. As soon as she saw her mother, she knew it was what she feared. One of Maggie's arms lay slack by her side, and one side of her mouth was turned down. A stroke. Her beautiful mother had had a stroke. Her heart didn't just sink, it plummeted like a rock thrown into a river.

A stroke. Like James. Again. She wasn't strong enough for this. But she had to be. She had to be.

She moved to the other side of the bed and took her mother's other hand, squeezing it gently. She looked into her mother's frightened eyes.

'I'm here, Mum,' she said softly. 'Bella will be here too, soon. The doctors and nurses will help you now.'

Her mother tried to speak but nothing came out. Diana's heart lurched in her chest. 'Best to rest, Mum. It will be okay.' This was something Diana felt a fraud for saying when she knew only too well it may not be. But she smiled anyway and felt her mother's hand relax in hers.

***

By the time Bella sent a text to say she was in the Emergency Department waiting room, the doctor had taken Diana aside and confirmed it was a stroke. Diana had returned with the doctor while he so-sensitively told Maggie and explained the treatment she would receive. Maggie blinked her understanding and Diana thought she saw less fear in her mother's eyes than before.

The little relief that provided, gave Diana the strength to explain to Bella what had, and what was, to happen, without breaking down.

'A stroke,' Bella said, 'like James.' The colour drained from her face, her lovely rose-coloured skin now as creamy white as thickened cream.

The reference to James was almost Diana's undoing. She turned away to prevent Bella seeing her face collapse.

'We might lose her too,' Bella cried out.

Diana turned back. She reached for Bella's hand, 'But we might not. It might be different. We must be strong for Nana. We must think of Nana and be here for her.'

Bella let the tears fall unashamedly. Diana waited, until her daughter said, 'Yes. We can do that. We can do that. What now, Mum?'

'They have given her a drug that, when given in time, can be very good for stroke victims. Minimise the damage. And she has had it in good time, thanks to you and the paramedics. You have already helped Nana and now we can help more by being by her side. They will soon take her to a ward, and we can be with her.'

'Yes, we will be with her. That will help her,' said Bella, gently nodding.

*My beautiful girl,* Diana thought. *Somehow, I will make us right again. Somehow it will all be right again.*

***

The crick in Diana's neck hurt like crazy. She had dozed on and off during the night in a chair beside her mother's bed. Bella had done the same in another chair on the other side of the bed. They both stood to stretch at the same time. 'Coffee?' Diana asked.

'Yes, I know where the café is, I can go,' Bella said.

Diana didn't protest. She thought it might be good for Bella to have a few minutes to herself. 'Okay, thank you.' She smiled her appreciation and received the touch of a smile back from her daughter.

As her daughter left, Maggie tossed in the bed, and Diana moved to her side. But the restless movements stopped, and her mother did not open her eyes. Alone, Diana pleaded silently, *Please, Mum. Don't go. Stay with us. Please!* She was still standing there, gazing down, thinking about how beautiful older women were, both inside and out, when her daughter returned, the smell of coffee entering the room a moment before her footsteps.

'Hospital coffee or not, that smells divine,' Diana said, reaching out an arm to gratefully take the takeaway cup from Bella.

'In Melbourne, I cart a KeepCup with me, but I am not going to feel guilty about a takeaway today. Not after an all-nighter,' said Bella.

'And an all-dayer yesterday. We have done well, Bella.'

They raised their cups to each other and smiled. 'And Nana. She has done pretty well too, Mum.'

'She has done the best of all of us,' Diana said, turning to raise her cup to her mother, whose eyes remained closed.

Bella dug into her bag and retrieved two sandwiches in triangular containers. 'Not going to feel guilty about the plastic these are in either,' she said, passing one over.

They ate and drank quietly, finishing just as the doctor and a nurse entered the room and asked them to step out. They paced nervously in the hall. The doctor emerged and nodded. 'You can go back in soon; give the nurse a few more minutes.'

'How is she?' Bella blurted out.

'Doing as well as can be expected,' he said.

*Why do doctors say that?* thought Diana. She wanted the facts!

'Her chances of recovery are good. Time, physio. She will be here for some days. Does she live on her own?'

'Yes, she does,' said Diana.

'I suggest that is something to think about,' he said, looking Diana directly in the eyes. 'I will drop by again tomorrow.'

'Thank you, Doctor. And the nurses too. Everyone is so kind,' said Diana.

***

Late in the afternoon, with more coffee and sandwiches consumed, and more hours of quiet bedside sitting having passed, Maggie's eyes opened, and she said her first discernible words, 'What time is it?'

Diana and Bella jumped up, each taking one of Maggie's hands. 'Mum, she squeezed my hand,' said Bella.

'Mine too,' said Diana.

'No fuss,' said Maggie, rousing on them in the way she sometimes did. 'Time?'

'Nearly five, Mum. You have been here since yesterday.'

'You both too. Go. Sleep.'

'No,' they chorused, 'we can stay.'

Gingerly, Maggie raised her good arm—her right arm—and pointed towards the door, her eyes closing again.

'Should we, Mum?' asked Bella.

'You wait here; I will check with the nurse,' responded Diana.

***

Having been given a commitment to be phoned if they were needed, Diana and Bella walked to the car park, talking about hot showers and something more solid to eat than sandwiches. They were parked on separate floors so went their separate ways, Bella accepting an invitation to stay at her mother's.

Diana thought she was okay. Until she closed the door of her car and in the pocket of solitude and safety it offered, was hit by a hammer of built-up stress and relief that her mother might be alright. She thumped her hands down hard on the steering wheel, tossed her head back and howled, her face crumpling and wet from the emotion pouring from her eyes.

She had come back to this same car park when James had died, stunned beyond belief, desperately trying to keep it together to be able to drive herself and Bella home. But this time she could let it out—not that she had a choice as it had turned up of its own accord. And she let it take its course.

She heard the double beep of someone unlocking the car next to her, and clapped a hand over her mouth, turning her head away so whoever it was would not see her distress. She heard the car start and back out, removed her hand and pulled down the vizor to see the puffy red eyes of pain looking back at her.

She wiped her eyes, took several deep breaths, and started the car to head home.

***

By the time she arrived home, she had it reasonably together again. Bella had kept her key and Diana could hear the shower running, which gave her more time to gather herself. She threw her bag on to the dining table, not noticing the page upon which she had written the relevant dates for her research this morning, slide out.

Bella appeared, one towel wrapped around her head, another around her body. 'That was *so* good. Your turn. Will I order the pizza while you shower?'

The normality of the scene was good but a weird-good when this two-year distance between them had not been dealt with. 'Yes, whatever you would like. Some garlic bread too, please? There is money in my wallet in my bag.'

Diana moved to the bathroom, peeled off her long-worn clothes and turned the taps on in the shower. The hot water was instantly soothing and calming and she stayed under it for a lot longer than she normally would.

She dressed in loose tracksuit pants and a sweater, putting on a pair of her favourite *Bamboozled* socks with bees on them, which made her smile. When she came back to the lounge room, Bella had turned the heater on, and more consoling warmth greeted her.

Bella was standing at the table with the page of dates in her hand. 'What's this, Mum?'

'They are dates I am using to find evidence of when Carrie, your great-great-great grandmother, sailed to New York. When you called yesterday, I was at the library trying to find a record of her travelling on a ship. Her family too, perhaps. Aunty Sophie suggested I look in these books that list ship voyages and logs, but I didn't find anything.'

'The ships log would tell you what happened on the voyage, right?'

'That's the idea. But I have to find what ship she sailed on first. No luck so far,' she said, tossing her hands in the air.

There was a knock on the door and Bella bounced up, returning with the pizza and garlic bread. It's smell and taste was tomato-cheese-herb goodness in a box, and they got stuck in. As they ate, Diana explained what each of the dates she had listed meant.

'Can I see the children's birth certificates and the letter to Carrie from Louisa?'

'Sure,' Diana said, moving to the drawer in the sideboard where she kept her research papers. As she opened the drawer, she saw the coin that had been in the trunk along with the letter and possum cloak. 'You might like to look at this too. The coin was wrapped in a lace hanky, but the hanky fell apart when I tried to untie the knot in it. It was in the trunk with the letter and cloak,' she said, handing them to Bella.

Diana watched her daughter pour over the birth certificates and the letter, then turn the coin in her hand. *Could their estrangement be over?*

It felt like the last two years had suddenly evaporated in terms of the distance between them. She just wanted to sit here and soak up being together, forever.

'Um, the coin could be valuable, do you think?'

'I doubt it, but who knows, I was going to take it to an antique dealer to find out how to clean it.'

'Okay, that's good,' said Bella. 'I think I am going to fall asleep now, whether I want to or not. I need to go to bed.'

'Me too. Everything is the same in your room,' Diana called, when Bella was at the door to her bedroom. She had left it that way in case her daughter returned. And now she had.

# Chapter Thirty-Eight

*Jenny Brother, 25 November 1866*

The child within her was restless. Carrie placed her hand upon her swollen stomach and made slow, circular movements, hoping to bring comfort to her child. She was six months pregnant with her fifth child, and this pregnancy was proving more difficult than the others. The nausea had persisted for far longer and the tiredness was at times close to being her undoing. She had calmed herself on occasion by reasoning that with caring for her four children and the long list of chores she faced each day, her tiredness was surely to be expected. But reasoning did not make it any easier.

Nor did what seemed an eternal struggle to procure enough coins and supplies to sustain their family.

She had done her best to comfort George when his efforts to breed cattle of his own had come to nothing. They had needed him to sell the small number of cattle he had, while surrounded by properties owned by other men who had accrued large numbers of both cattle and sheep. He had been disheartened for weeks and spoken little to either her or his children, in order, she knew, to keep his disappointment and, she suspected, anger, to himself.

She was grateful that at least they had not had to move for several years now, and for this hut being bigger than the others, several rooms accommodating their family more easily.

Carrie reached to wipe drops of perspiration from her brow, the day being warmer than usual for this time of year. While the children were outside playing, she would take the opportunity to make more damper.

As she stepped towards the flour sack, a cry rang from outside. 'Marmie, Marmie, Marmie,' eight-year-old Edward yelled.

She moved clumsily, but quickly, to the verandah in time to see Edward running along the dirt track leading to the hut, his six-year-old sister, Sarah, running behind him. Her two youngest children, William and Charles, rushed onto the verandah to hide behind her skirt.

Edward reached Carrie, breathless. He pointed behind him.

'Constables,' he gasped, sucking in air.

'Do not be concerned, Edward,' she said, with a calmness that threatened to leave her quickly.

Carrie could see the dust rising from the dirt track now. They rode at speed. Her heart skipped a beat. Edward's breathing slowed. 'Edward, ask your father to come,' she said, pointing to behind the hut. Edward nodded and ran off with the liveliness that only a child could muster.

'Sarah, take Charles and William inside. Give them milk and stay there, please, until I come to you.' Sarah—like her brother, Edward—nodded and did as she was bid, without protest.

As the police approached, Carrie stood alone upon the verandah. But it was only a moment before George appeared, Edward trailing behind him, to stand nearby. The sleeves of George's shirt were rolled up above his elbows, his arms slippery with perspiration produced by hard work. Carrie noticed the bulge of his biceps, the defiant look upon his unsmiling face and the rifle clasped in one hand. His other hand was clenched in a fist.

'Inside, Edward,' said Carrie, her son hesitating momentarily then following his mother's order.

Three men on horseback pulled up before the hut, the bodies of their horses glistening with sweat after being ridden hard. Dust swirled then settled around them. The men dismounted, tying their horses to the rail George had built for that purpose. They were of varying ages, from young to middle age, their mouths held in straight lines.

George laid his rifle upon the ground to signal his wish for no trouble. He took two steps forward. 'Inspector Battye, what brings you from Cooma to my door?' he asked, casting his eye in the direction of the constables. 'And with your man, Constable Ford, and Senior Constable McKee from Nimmitabel, no less.'

The weight of George's remarks hit Carrie as though one of her children had jumped into her arms. She felt her knees may give way but refused to sit upon the nearby chair. Instead, she stood still and straight. She would not show any weakness in front of these men whose intent was clearly unfriendly.

'George Henry Hedger, or should I say Perkins,' said the Inspector, his voice dripping with distain. 'You are charged with cattle stealing. You are to be taken into custody.'

The scene before Carrie blurred. She swayed. She had no choice this time but to steady herself by taking hold of the verandah post. George noticed and came to her. He put his arm around her and half-carried her to the chair. He bent to her ear, 'Say nothing, Carrie,' then stood and stepped back down to stand before the men, their uniforms crumpled and dusty from their journey.

*'I want the hide of the beast you killed last Saturday,'* said Senior Constable McKee.

*'You can't have it as it is made into ropes,'* said George.

*George knows of this. But I do not,* thought Carrie, a flash of anger rising then falling away as fast as a falling star disappears from the night sky. She stood to challenge all the men before her but got no further than the steps of the verandah before George said, 'Carrie, go inside. See to the children.' She wanted to protest but the stern look upon her husband's face and a piercing cry from her youngest son, Charles, from within the hut, stopped her from doing so. She looked at the inspector and the constables in turn, none of whom looked at her in return.

As she turned to leave, she saw the inspector had raised one arm and was pointing to the side of the hut. She entered her home and scooped up her crying two-year-old child, his cheeks flushed and wet with tears. She kissed Charles' cheek and held him close, soothing him with softly spoken words. When he had settled, she walked to the window, where the horses stood quietly, but there were no men in sight.

***

Carrie could hear nothing from inside the hut. No raised voices, no scuffle between men. While a need to go outside to see what was going on gripped her like an irritating itch; her need to see to and reassure her children proved greater. When Charles had stopped crying, William had started, needing his turn for her attention. Carrie had then turned her attention to Sarah, who quietly waited her turn for her mother's attention, while Edward kneeled on a chair by the window, keeping watch for the men to return.

As the wait continued, Carrie got on with making a damper that she would drizzle with golden syrup. It was a simple but tasty treat, that always comforted and quietened her children.

As the damper cooked in the ashes of the fireplace, Edward called out, 'They are back.'

Carrie fought her compulsion to run out the door, instead placing a hand on Edward's shoulder and saying to all her children, 'Stay here, please. Sarah, keep an eye on the damper; it will soon be ready.'

Any calmness she feigned left her when she stepped outside to see her husband's hands being bound behind his back with rope. She rushed down the steps to him.

'Stand back, Missus,' said a constable. She did not know which constable went by which name, as she had not been introduced. Those three words were the first acknowledgement of her presence.

'George, where are they taking you?' George opened his mouth but was pulled away before he could speak, Carrie having time only to see a mix of dejection and fury in his eyes.

'Where …' she pleaded to the inspector, '… are you taking my husband?'

A one-word reply was all she received. 'Cooma,' he said, before nodding at the constable to have George climb aboard the dray—George and Carrie's dray that one of the constables had strapped his horse to.

Carrie stood on the dirt track, watching as the men mounted and rode away, leaving her bewildered and alone to care for her four children.

The child within her was restless again. Once more, she placed her hand upon her swollen stomach and made slow, circular movements, hoping to comfort her unborn child.

***

Carrie could hear Charles crying again. As she reached for the handle of the door to the hut, she heard William begin to cry again as well. Her fingers slipped from the handle. She brought her hand to her mouth to still her trembling lips. She took a few moments to gather herself, then entered the hut, her movements purposefully unrushed to hide her alarm at her husband being arrested, from the children.

The sight of a single tear as it coursed down Sarah's face, almost undid Carrie's efforts. She pulled her daughter to her chest. She would not lie to her children. At less than two and four years old, Charles and William would not understand, but Sarah and Edward knew who the constables were and she would explain that their Pa had gone with them and would be away, but perhaps not for long.

When she pulled back from Sarah, she caught Edward's eye, and knew he already understood. 'Edward, please break the damper into pieces and help Sarah put syrup on a piece for each of us. We have missed our midday meal, and the damper will help settle the boys.'

Edward nodded and stepped forward to do as she asked. As she watched him and Sarah prepare the food, she rocked Charles and William in turn and offered each of her children what solace she could through a mother's gentle smiles.

***

The sugary sweetness of the syrup and the warmth of the freshly baked damper soothed them all and Carrie was able to lull Charles, William and Sarah to sleep in her and George's bed. Carrie decided to prepare the evening meal so that when the children awoke they would do so to the familiar sight and smell of their mother cooking for them.

She stepped from the hut and made her way around the back, to the lean-to beside the stables, where George kept the meat he provided for his family in a barrel-shaped harness cask. Edward followed her, as she suspected he would. She knew he would want to know what was to be done about his Pa being taken away by the constables. Lulling the children to sleep had provided Carrie with time to contemplate their quandry. There was only one option that she could see.

She turned to her son. 'Edward, would you ride to *Jimenbuen*? She paused. 'On your own?'

Edward looked directly into her eyes. 'Yes,' he said, his legs spread wide, his back straight, telling her of his conviction to do so.

Her heart went out to him. Her boy who continued to behave far older than his age. Whose father was instilling in him the resilience and skills required to be a stockman. Who had ridden his pony to *Jimenbuen* beside his father upon his own mount, and who was now to do the journey alone, for the first time.

With their dray gone, her only means of taking all her children with her to *Jimenbuen* had been taken from her. She could not do nothing, and she knew Edward would not want that either. Sending him was the only choice left to her.

Carrie nodded. 'Not today. It is late,' she said, reaching to stroke his cheek. 'Tomorrow, when the sun rises. I will write a letter for you to deliver to Mr Crisp. If you do not see him, then deliver it to Mrs Crisp. Do not come straight back; you are to rest at *Jimenbuen* first.'

Edward nodded. 'Yes, I will. He then moved to the harness cask, and removed its lid. He peered inside then turned to his mother with a perplexed look upon his face. 'The meat is mostly gone. There is only a small piece.'

'How can that be?' she said, stepping forward. But her son was right. She pulled the meat that remained from the cask. She would have to plump the stew she had planned to make with vegetables from her garden to feed them for as long as she was able.

# Chapter Thirty-Nine

As the second night passed since Edward had ridden from her—a water bag and a saddle bag containing nourishment and the letter Carrie had written, tied to his pony—Carrie's resolve to stay strong was all but worn away. She fretted for what may have befallen her son. A number of scenarios played over and over in her mind like a fiddle tune that stayed with you long after the fiddler had stopped playing. She fretted for the fate of her husband. Was he still being held in Cooma, or had he been taken further afield, perhaps to Goulburn? She questioned what would come next following his arrest? The image of him with his hands bound behind his back and being thrust into the dray, had haunted what little sleep she'd had.

Carrie searched for hope and calm in prayer and found enough to rise and prepare herself and her three youngest children for the day ahead. Like the last two days, she would fill this day with the reassurance found in undertaking their usual practices. She took up the kindling that lay beside the fireplace and lit a fire to prepare the children's porridge. There was no flour left in the sack to make damper today. George's plan to ride to Cooma to purchase more, had been thwarted by his arrest. There was still golden syrup she could add to their porridge though, which would help make their start to the day a pleasant one.

Sarah loved the vegetable garden so Carrie would ask her to help pick more vegetables that she could add to what remained of the stew, which was mostly gravy now. She would then walk to the creek—another tributary of the *Snowy River*—with the children, the journey slow because of Charles and William's ages, and return with a pail of water for drinking and cooking. Their supply of milk had run out the day before.

The washing would have to wait until she had help to retrieve enough water to fill a barrel, but she had been relieved to see that the trough for George's horse and Edward's pony was half full. Her own, beloved horse, Pony, had now passed from this earth, her memories of their many rides sustaining Carrie through the grief she felt over her loss.

By mid-morning, Carrie was brushing down George's horse in the stables, which had been restless in his absence. The children played nearby, when sounds came to her of someone arriving. She gathered the children and walked to the front of the hut in time to see a canopied buggy with Elizabeth Crisp driving, her son perched on the seat beside her, and Edward's pony tied to the back of the buggy.

Tears tumbled shamelessly down Carrie's face. Her Edward was safe, and her beloved friend was here and would offer help!

Edward jumped from the buggy and ran to her, wrapping his arms around her. She bent to kiss the top of his head, to smell his familiar earthy smell. The relief of having him safely back with her was overwhelming, as was her pride in what he had managed to do.

'Mr Crisp has gone to Cooma to help Pa, Marmie,' he said. 'And we have brought supplies,' he said, distracted then by his two brothers who wrapped themselves around his legs.

'That is right,' said Elizabeth, now standing before Carrie. 'Amos was away when Edward arrived, but Amos has ridden today to Cooma to help George.'

'Dearest Elizabeth. I am grateful for such true friends. And how very good it is to see you,' she said, stepping forward to give Elizabeth a hug that was warmly received.

'Now,' said Elizabeth, 'I will ask Edward to help me unload the supplies and see to the horses, then you and I can share tea and eat cake Mary has made for us. I will stay the night and ride back to my children at *Jimenbuen* tomorrow morning. But we have tonight to share and perhaps there will be news from Amos tomorrow.

***

Carrie and her four children waved heartily as Elizabeth drove away early the next morning. They had all shared a pleasant evening together, laughter coming to them all at times, and they had all slept well. Carrie felt renewed and hopeful that all would be well.

Elizabeth had brought mutton, potatoes, a sack of flour, milk, butter, cheese, sugar, jars of preserved fruit, jam, and in addition to the cake, biscuits that Mary had also made for them. Again, her gratefulness mingled with the relief that she was now assured of being able to feed her children.

Elizabeth's last gift had been a basket of fresh eggs, a true luxury for Carrie and her family. 'Perhaps,' Elizabeth said, 'you could proceed with your idea of keeping chickens yourself. George and Edward could build a coop for you.' Carrie warmed to that suggestion, 'Why, yes, I could,' she said, remembering her former hope to do so.

Edward busied himself gathering kindling and walking to and from the creek, each time returning with a pail of water. Carrie could not have been prouder of him. With his father away, Edward was helping wherever he could.

As the day wore on though, there was no sign of Amos arriving with news of George and when the last of her children to fall asleep had done so that night, her mind began the tumble into turmoil about what was to come.

***

Carrie's troubles were lightened the next day when Edward came running to her again, pointing to a swirl of dust that grew in size as the rider below it travelled along the dirt track to their hut. Carrie held her breath, her children clustered around her, her hope that it would be Amos uppermost in her mind.

It was not one rider though; it was two. It was Amos and George! Both sitting high in their saddles, George upon a borrowed horse, their hats pulled low over their foreheads. 'Pa, Pa,' yelled the children in unison, all of them jumping up and down on the spot, then quietening as the men pulled on reins to halt the horses.

'George,' called Carrie. 'Amos,' she said.

The men dismounted. A smile lit up Amos' face as he walked towards Carrie. The children ran to George, who bent down to greet them in return, Carrie unable to see the expression upon his face.

Carrie reached for Amos's hands. She gripped them tightly. There was a smudge of dust under each of his eyes, telling of the miles he had travelled to and from Cooma to help them. 'Carrie, you are a welcome sight,' Amos said. 'And I cannot describe how welcome a sight you are to me and the children,' she replied. You have brought George home to us. How can I thank you?'

A less joyous expression crossed Amos' face. 'Carrie, the charge of cattle stealing still stands. George is out of gaol on bail. He has been committed for trial at the next Quarter Session. In Cooma.'

For a moment, her breath was taken away from her. She was still holding on to Amos' hands when George came to her and kissed her softly upon the cheek. She let go of Amos' hands and turned to her husband. She could not read his face. There was no sign of anger or relief. She knew she would have to wait until he was ready before she would know more.

Carrie turned back to Amos. 'Will you stay the night?'

'Thank you, Carrie, but I must forge on to *Jimenbuen*. Elizabeth and the children await my return. Though a cup of coffee would be welcome beforehand, if I may.' The warm smile Carrie had received from him many times since the first day she had met him on the wharf at Port Melbourne, more than ten years ago, returned to his face and spread to her own.

'Yes, Amos,' she said. I have coffee, and also cake brought by Elizabeth. We are so grateful for the supplies gifted to us.'

'And you are all most welcome,' he replied.

Edward had stepped forward to hold the reins of the horses for the men and now he led them to the railing and tied the reins around it. Carrie slipped her arm through George's as she, Amos and the children walked towards the hut.

***

Carrie chose not to broach the subject of George's cattle-stealing charge and arrest with him over the following days. She knew her husband well and knew that his own choice not to talk to her about it meant he would not do so until he was ready. It was his way to remain silent until he had dealt with a matter within himself.

George was at home for ten days before he left to drive stock up into the high country to graze. As she had known it would, word of his arrest had spread but Amos continued to offer him work. His close association with Amos the younger, had not dimmed over the years regardless of the work George did for other men.

Before he rode from them, George had brought home a kangaroo for the harness cask and other supplies, ensuring his family would be well fed. Although George's impending trial was never far from Carrie's mind, the children's return to their playful ways was enough for her to carry on as she normally did.

Christmas was approaching and when the children were asleep, Carrie would sit quietly by the glow of the paraffin lamp, sewing a dress for Sarah, using pieces of material and lace she had purchased over time from her friend, Ann's store in Cooma. George had said he would return with gifts for their sons—toy horses he would carve from wood while he was away, for their younger boys, and a pair of boots, second hand, but better fitting for rapidly growing Edward. But when Christmas Eve dawned and her husband had not returned, her thoughts turned to what she would gift her sons. And how disappointed she and the older children would be if he was not with them for Christmas.

Carrie walked over to the pudding she had made weeks ago. It was hanging from a hook on the wall. She put her nose to it and inhaled its fruity and spice-filled aroma. She loved the tradition of a special Christmas pudding, and each year Ann always made sure her shop was stocked with dried fruit for the puddings her customers would make. The pudding would be too rich for William and Charles though, so their bowls would contain the custard she would make tomorrow, and for William, some pieces of dried fruit she had set aside.

The pudding would accompany a meal of roast mutton, recently delivered from *Jimenbuen*, and roast potatoes, turnips and carrots, gravy accompanying it all. And George had promised to hang a swing for the children to bring them more joy on the day.

The afternoon wore on. Carrie was sitting on the verandah, Charles upon her lap, when she looked up to hear before she saw, George thundering along the track on his horse. He was riding as though his eagerness to return to them dictated he do so, but Carrie knew this was how her husband rode—hard and with haste.

Edward, Sarah and William ran towards him, stepping to the side of the track, well aware of the caution needed around a powerful horse. Sarah and William jumped up and down. They called out in delight.

Carrie joined them, Charles upon her hip. When George reached them, he dismounted and handed the reins to Edward, her son's pride in being given the responsibility of taking his father's horse, displayed in his expression and stance.

It was not his children George first gave his attention to though. It was Carrie. He leaned to kiss her gently upon the lips, the children laughing as he took her in his arms.

***

*Cooma, 12 April 1867*

Carrie sat quietly in her friend, Ann's kitchen, her fifth child at her breast, sucking contentedly. Her second daughter, Alice, had been born around the time she had been expected—on 13 February 1867. Following her difficult pregnancy, Carrie had expected a difficult birth, but Alice arrived quickly and safely, soon nestled against her mother's breasts. With Alice's birth had come a wellness Carrie had not felt in months, and she had found herself re-invigorated.

Her renewal had continued, and she felt as prepared as she could be for George's trial for cattle stealing, which was to take place today. He had gone before the court in March, but he had not agreed to her attendance, sighting the recent birth of Alice as his reasoning. And his case had been deferred until the June court sessions, unless another time was decided upon. Which it had been, the date being today.

George had again not agreed to her being in attendance but this time she had stood her ground with him and declared that she would be doing so! As she sat feeding her baby, a memory of the timid sixteen-year-old girl who had stepped onboard the *B. R. Milam* at the Port of New York to voyage to Australia, came to her. She thought about how she had changed. How she had to change, not just in maturity but in the strength and determination needed to survive in a remote and isolated area of this country she loved, despite all the challenges it presented her with.

Little Alice pulled away from her, her feeding done. Carrie changed her napkin, wrapped her in cloth and walked through to the shop where Ann was, the back of a customer she had just served, retreating from her. Carrie handed her baby to Ann, who swayed gently as Alice fell into slumber.

'Thank you,' Carrie said. 'I hope I will return soon, that all will be well.'

Ann smiled at her friend, their voices mere whispers so as not to wake Alice. She bent to place the baby in a crate they had cushioned with a blanket that lay behind the counter and stood up again. 'Carrie, I am concerned that Amos Crisp cannot be there today to speak up for George.'

'Yes. If only he did not have need to be away. The unexpected timing of George's call to trial was unfortunate but at least the waiting is over,' Carrie said. 'And Amos has provided a letter which, it is hoped, will carry some weight.'

Ann reached to wrap her arms around Carrie and held her. 'Yes, Mr Crisp is held in high regard. We must hope that is the case,' she said, grateful that Carrie could not see the concern upon her face.

***

The heavy wooden door of the courthouse groaned as Carrie pushed it to enter the courtroom. This was a domain of men, a number of whom swung in their bench seats to look upon her. Their stares made her feel ill at ease, but she would not be forced away.

The only man who did not turn to look at her was her husband. *Perhaps he wished my attendance to the needs of our baby would not permit me to be here after all,* she thought. Although he had said nothing, she knew this trial must be humiliating for George. But in addition to his fate, it was the fate of her and their children that was at stake here. And she needed to see what happened for herself to gain an understanding of where they all stood. She moved to sit, alone, upon a bench at the back of the courtroom.

The trial began. The charge of George Hedger having, on 18 November 1866, stolen a heifer, the property of Mr Bodley, was read out. George—who it was stated was being defended by a Mr Dalley—pleaded 'not guilty'.

The Inspector of Police, Edward Montague Battye, who Carrie had last seen at their home when George had been arrested, commenced his testimony:

> *I went to the prisoner's residence accompanied by two constables. A short distance from the house I saw a dray turned in the direction of the prisoner's house. No one was with it. I ordered Constable Ford to go to the dray.*

Carrie remembered then, how the men had begun to disappear from where she could see them from the window in the hut.

Inspector Battye continued:

> *I saw on the dray some fresh hide ropes and some blood. Senior Constable McKee said to him, 'I want the hide of the beast you killed last Saturday.' The prisoner said, 'You can't have it as it is made into ropes.' The prisoner said the rest of the hide was at the stockyard and the meat is in the harness cask. I saw the meat; McKee took a piece of it.*

The meat Carrie had gone to fetch with her son, to feed her children, and found most of it gone. The constable had taken it.

> *I asked the prisoner what was the brand of the beast he killed. He said his own, GH. Afterwards, I said I hoped the beast had his brand on it and he said if it had not, it ought to have it. I went to the stockyard with Constable Ford and the prisoner, who pointed out the rest of the hide—also the head.*

Carrie twitched. She moved restlessly where she sat. No one noticed. She had realised—with alarm—that the cow in question was the one, already butchered, that George had brought home, to feed them. Although her heart beat rapidly, she would not believe herself foolish for trusting what her husband provided had been rightfully gained.

She leaned forward to be certain she heard each detail of what followed, clearly. She listened to Inspector Battye testify as to how the white mark upon the cow's face and pieces of the hide and ropes had been brought away. And how the brand of Mr Bodley had become apparent when the ropes were soaked in water and stretched upon a board.

As Constables McKee and Ford testified the same as Captain Battye, and three men employed by Mr Bodley testified to knowing his brand and knowing the cow in question, Carrie went to rise. Her fear that George would be condemned got the better of her for a moment, and a need to leave and not hear any more, assaulted her. She controlled herself and sat fully back on her seat. She would not cower!

As Mr Dalley's cross-examinations took a different turn, her heart began to beat more slowly, and her hopes began to rise. Mr Dalley cast doubt upon the brand being able to be identified as Mr Bodley's. He cast doubt upon Mr Bodley's men being able to recognise this cow among the many they cared for. 'A white star upon the head of a cow is surely not remarkable,' he said.

And then he put before Inspector Battye a letter and asked, 'Do you recognise the signature of Mr Amos Crisp upon this letter?' to which the Inspector replied, 'I do.'

Mr Dalley then turned to face the jury and read the letter—in which Amos attested to having always *known the prisoner as a hardworking, honest man*—out. 'This letter,' said Mr Dalley, 'from a man we all know to be of high character, attests to the high character of George Hedger. I remind you that there is one cow only in question here, and although he will not say from whom, Mr Hedger has told me he purchased it in good faith. I ask that you find him not guilty.'

The jury retired. The men in the room remained seated but murmured among themselves. Carrie was uncertain whether she should leave or stay. She decided upon staying, which proved worthwhile as the jury soon returned and a finding of 'not guilty' was declared.

When George came to her and they began walking back to Ann's shop, Carrie's arm in his, she asked him why he would not say who he had purchased the heifer from. 'A man who was in charge of cattle. He has children but his wife died.' That was all he said, and Carrie would ask for no more. She would not imagine how that had come to pass. It was enough to know that her husband had paid for the cow to provide for his family.

# Chapter Forty

Diana was getting ready to go to the hospital when Bella came out, tousled hair, still in her pyjamas. 'I'll be along in a couple of hours to see Nana,' she said.

'That's fine. We will see you then,' Diana replied, moving forward to kiss Bella, who took a step back from her. Diana sighed inwardly. *We're not there yet. I should have known.*

At the hospital, it was a relief to see her mother able to give a close-to-normal smile when Diana walked in; and while talking was still a great effort, they exchanged a few words as the morning went by.

It was close to lunchtime when Bella arrived. If Diana was still able to read her daughter correctly, the expression on Bella's face indicated that she was pleased about something. She said nothing though, moving to kiss her nana gently on the forehead and ask how she was feeling today, before taking a seat beside the bed and saying nothing more.

Maggie must have read Bella's expression similarly, as she turned her head towards Diana on the opposite side of the bed, raising her eyebrows. 'Cheese sandwich please,' she said, looking towards the door. It was a clear message to Diana that Maggie wanted a few minutes alone with Bella, to presumably quiz her granddaughter if she could manage to get the right words out.

*And what was that about?* Diana wondered, as she went off on her instructed errand to the café.

***

Thankfully, when Diana returned, the mood in the room was light. Although pale, Maggie was managing to smile, if somewhat crookedly, in Bella's direction as her granddaughter chatted away to her.

'Bella has news,' said Maggie.

Relief flooded Diana that the words had come out clearly. 'What's that?' she asked, as she passed around cheese sandwiches for all.

Bella put her sandwich down and dove into her backpack. She pulled out a small, flat, square box, opened the lid and held a shiny coin up between thumb and forefinger.

'I had Carrie's gold coin—you're coin now Mum—cleaned this morning.'

Diana reached over the bed for the coin, holding it up to the light coming through the window. The gold of the coin was like no other gold she had seen. It was rich, it was breathtaking; the coin was a work of art. 'It's beyond beautiful,' she said, passing it to Maggie.

'And not just that. The guy at the antique shop who cleaned it said not to let it out of our sight; that if he is right, it is valuable. Like, *very* valuable.'

Diana plonked down heavily in the chair. 'As in hundreds?'

'As in thousands,' said Bella. 'If he's right. He gave me the name of an expert in Melbourne that could value it. I could take it with me when I go back to Melbourne to collect my things. Even if I don't get the job at the university, I am moving back to Canberra,' she said.

'Coming home to us,' declared Maggie.

For Diana, the room swam, as though she had just stepped off from a fast-moving ride at the Canberra Show. It was not what the coin might be worth, it was the overwhelmingness of her daughter coming home and the relief that was surging through her that there was truly hope that whatever it was that had caused their separation, was to end.

She felt her eyes become watery and saw it was the same for Maggie and Bella. A single tear fell from Bella's eye and trailed down her cheek as she looked at her mother. 'Mum?'

Diana gathered herself. 'That is wonderful news that you are coming home … and yes, please take the coin with you to Melbourne.' Diana hoped her slight hesitation about the coin had not been noticed.

She recognised that she did feel an element of possessiveness in relation to the coin that was a tangible link to Carrie, but Bella had been a trustworthy child and teenager, and Diana knew that regaining her daughter's trust was what was most important.

***

Maggie had faded not long after her cheese sandwich had been slowly chewed and she'd had a stab at some of the lunch provided by the hospital. Diana and Bella sat quietly on either side of the bed as Maggie slept for several hours, then upon waking, waved a hand towards the door, signalling them to go home.

When Diana came out from her shower that night, Bella was making a vegetarian stir fry and had her head in the pantry searching for noodles and sauces. 'Any sweet soy sauce—*Kecap Manis*—Mum?' Still managing to keep her surprise at her daughter's what-must-be-fairly-new interest in cooking, Diana retrieved the sauce and the noodles for her. 'Smells good, that's for sure.'

'I don't think I cooked when I was at home, did I?'

'Not that I remember,' said Diana, 'good to see you doing so now though.'

Bella turned to face her Mum. 'I dated this guy—and before you ask, we are not dating now—but he liked to cook at home rather than go to restaurants. He was a good cook. I learned some things, found I liked cooking, etc.'

'Well, this smells divine. And I have a hunger fit to burst.'

As they ate, an awkward silence hung in the air between them—a stark reminder that there was still the matter of their not talking for two years to be dealt with. Diana broke the moment by saying, 'I don't think I will know what to do if the gold coin is as valuable as the antique dealer who cleaned it, thinks.'

'Well, let's see what the expert in Melbourne thinks first,' replied Bella, abruptly standing, picking up her empty plate and walking to the kitchen to deposit it among the pile of plates, pots and utensils she had used to cook dinner. 'Good night,' she said, retreating to her room and leaving Diana suddenly alone.

She shrugged, considered stacking the dishwasher, but was saved by the thought that she should check the Monaro Pioneers Facebook page in case there was any message in response to her request for information about Carrie and George. She wasn't expecting any replies to her message so was excited when she saw several. She read each of them, the last one causing her to lean forward and re-read it. A man—Ian—was offering a copy of several pages of a diary of Carrie's. Carrie was his great-great-grandmother too, he said. He could email it to her if she liked.

Her heart flip-flopped. *I certainly would like!* She replied straight away with a thank you and her email address.

*Ian must be a second cousin, maybe. How exciting*, she thought as she moved to the kitchen, trying not to let her anticipation at what she might be about to receive get out of control. She took the clean dishes out of the dishwasher, replaced them with the dinner ones, and pushed the button to start the cycle again. *What would the pages of the diary say? You just have to wait for a reply*, she told herself. She would check her email tomorrow morning. Perhaps he would have replied by then.

Two hours later, having reread the same pages of the novel she was currently reading a number of times because it didn't seem to want to stick in her mind, Diana, surprisingly, felt hungry again. She tip-toed to the kitchen trying to make as little noise as possible so as not to wake Bella, where she decided a cheese toastie was what she felt like. As she gathered the bread, butter, cheese, and a jar of her mum's homemade tomato relish, she put the toastie together and put it in the electric sandwich maker. Her mind wandered all over the place about what might be in the pages of the diary Ian was to email her.

The smell of the toastie roused her from her thoughts. As she slipped it onto a plate, took it to the table and blew on it to cool it, she reminded herself she would just have to wait to see. She took a small bite of the toastie. The vinegary sweetness of the relish was *so* good. Another bite and the melted cheddar cheese had cooled enough to enable her to take a bigger bite that filled her mouth with its gooeyness.

But even the luscious taste of the toastie was not enough to keep the pages of the diary from invading her mind. *Damn it,* she said, pulling her laptop towards her. She brought up her email, with one eye closed, which of course would make no difference. And there it was—an email from Ian with an attachment. She opened it and printed it off.

She read it more quickly than she had read anything else in her life. She was blindsided. Before her, on time-darkened, lined paper, was an entry about a voyage. She quickly scanned the three small pages, then looked up, not believing what she had in her hands. It was about the voyage she had searched in the National Library for evidence of. She could not believe it! How could she have been so lucky that the only three pages of a diary of Carrie's that she had learned about, were about this voyage!

Her eye went back to the date at the top of the first page. *2 August 1874.*

Now she had a rudder to steer her search for details of the voyage.

# Chapter Forty-One

*Rosebrook Station, 27 July 1874*

Carrie had not met Annie Clarke again in the eight years that had passed since the Clarke Brothers and their gang had robbed *Rosebrook Station*. Yet, each time Carrie visited her friend, Mary Anne, at the station, she found herself standing on the spot in the bedroom where she had stood face to face with Annie, exchanging intense words. And each time, a picture of Annie's face as clear in her mind as if she were there in the room with Carrie, came to her.

Carrie stood on that spot now, a different child, her sixth, on her hip—a daughter George had wished be named after his mother, Francis. The nearly four year old squirmed. Carrie bent to place her daughter's legs upon the floor, her own eyes, when she straightened, immediately drawn back to where Annie had stood when she had entered the room.

She had kept Annie's secret, telling no one of her presence that night when the robbery occurred. At odd times of a day or night, in a rare moment of quiet, Carrie had often pondered why she had told no one. She owed Annie no loyalty. Annie had been there to thieve what others had worked hard for and Carrie disapproved strongly of her seemingly cavalier approach to robbery.

But it was the images of Annie as a child with no shoes, rags dressing her little body, no food in her belly, and a mother struggling to care for her children, that Annie's words had lodged in Carrie's mind, and which refused to depart regardless of the time that passed, that Carrie had come to understand had led to her silence. A silence that she would continue to keep.

Carrie had followed The Clarke Brother's ongoing story through newspaper articles and word-of-mouth tales. Little came to her of Annie, one passing comment only of her continued extravagant dressing, that told Carrie nothing that would quench her intrigue. Had Annie played the same role in other crimes? Or had that night of confession and confusion affected her too? Or had it affected her at all? Carrie accepted she would never know.

A high-pitched, demanding cry came from the child at her feet, who tugged at her skirt for her mother to pick her up again. Carrie's attention returned to the present, to this last night before they were to leave for Sydney—for the journey she had doubted would happen—over the ocean to her home country, to New York and the family she had not seen in eighteen years.

***

Carrie clung to Mary Anne as though her shawl was not providing her enough warmth and she needed the closeness of another body. A subtle scent of the rose water her friend always wore brought the comfort of familiarity, as did the feel of her friend's hands gently patting her back. Mary Anne moved to pull away, but Carrie hung on, her friend stepping back into their embrace, sensing the fear that had overcome Carrie once the rush of preparing to leave this station this morning and journey into Cooma by buggy was over.

Fear of the journey ahead. Of whether she had made the right decision that all six of their children would accompany her and George. Fear of what would greet her in New York—family she still knew or people who had changed and who did not still feel for her as she still felt for them.

Carrie became aware of snuffling horses behind her, of a hoof stamped upon the dry ground signalling eagerness to begin the task of pulling the buggy away from the life she knew, back to the life she had known. 'Carrie,' insisted George's voice, not loud but firm in its demand. 'We must get to Cooma. The coach must leave on time.'

She acknowledged him with a nod, and pulled away from her embrace with Mary Anne, a knowing glance of a woman and mother's fear passing briefly between them. Carrie turned to see her husband and eldest son mounted on the horses they would ride beside the coach, on the first part of their journey from Cooma to Queanbeyan. She saw the rifle in her husband's hands and shivered. Guns may be a given in their lives, but her fear of their power would never cease.

She climbed into the buggy, pulling Francis onto her lap, leaning to wave to Mary Anne as the buggy jerked forward while the horses found their stride. She watched Mary Anne raise her arm higher so Carrie might see her wave for longer as the distance between them lengthened, until they could no longer see each other.

Carrie would miss her friends dearly, but they were women whose husbands' frequent absence, and their children's need for them, had taught them to be independent and strong. And Carrie reminded herself of this as the excitement of her children buoyed her mood. Francis squirmed upon her lap while seven-year-old Alice, nine-year-old Charles, eleven-year-old William, and fourteen-year-old Sarah, chatted and clambered to look around them. A calmness began to settle upon Carrie; an acceptance that they were on their way, that an adventure to be shared had begun.

***

They had arrived in Cooma in time for the coach. Now dust swirled around them as the horses picked up speed. Carrie gave herself and the children time to watch the rolling plains of the Monaro sweep by before she shifted her position to lower the blinds over the open windows of the coach. The children called to each other over the sounds of pounding hooves, creaking wood and a cracking whip until they had said all they wanted to say, and quietened.

As the day wore on, Carrie reassured them with the smiles of a loving mother and stirred their excitement again when she raised the blind beside her to encourage them to do the same, so they could see the thickly forested hills as they rose from the plains.

A stop along the way to hitch fresh horses to the coach, slowed their progress but gave them a chance to stretch their legs, take a little to eat from the wicker basket Carrie had prepared, and drink from the water bags her husband and eldest son had tied to their saddles.

As the sun began its downwards journey, Carrie's arms ached from holding Francis, who had long ago slumped against her in weariness. When, at last, the coach pulled up before the Inn at Bredbo, Carrie thought she might drop her daughter if she tried to move, and was grateful when Edward opened the door and lifted his sister from her arms. Not for the first time did the thought cross her mind that it would be easy to mistake his gentle nature for weakness but as his mother she well knew the quiet strength that was his foundation.

A meal of roast meat and potatoes restored their strength. Carrie readied her children for rest in the room they would all share, by reading passages from her treasured Bible that had travelled with her from New York when she was sixteen, and was now going on the return journey with her.

***

The arrival of a larger coach the next morning renewed the children's excitement. Carrie listened as they recited tales of wild rides upon Cobb & Co coaches through the bush to escape bushrangers and deliver passengers and mail on time—tales that had reached the ears of those who live beside and beyond the *Snowy River*. They climbed onboard as eager to begin the day's journey as the fresh horses were to pull them along.

Their heightened mood remained for most of the day, broken occasionally by the nodding heads and drooping eyelids of travellers becoming weary. When the children quietened, Carrie allowed herself to bask in the sunlight flickering through the leaves of trees, like the flame of a candle stirred by the movement of air.

Carrie's back ached, a deep throb began to gnaw at her awareness of what was passing by. George rode up to her window, the mouth of his mount frothy from the ride, to declare 'Queanbeyan is ahead' in a loud enough voice to capture all their attention. Gladness lifted her spirits—a chance to rest was close.

Rest was clearly not on her children's minds though as they scrambled to see what was ahead, heads soon poking from each window. Their joy fuelled her own. It caused her to forget her aching back, to lean forward in anticipation of her first glimpse of the town. She was not disappointed when she saw Queanbeyan, nor when the coach rolled along a wide street, the earth beneath them packed hard, both sides lined with shops and hotels. What she saw was like a mixture of Cooma on a larger scale, and again, smaller versions of the solid brick buildings of Melbourne she had glimpsed on her brief stay there when she had arrived in Australia from New York at just sixteen years of age. The same age her son Edward was now.

Her tiredness dissipated as the horses were pulled to a halt at the front of a hotel. Once again, Edward, who had quickly dismounted and tied his horse to a rail, came to help her with his youngest sibling. Carrie was grateful to feel solid ground beneath her feet, for the swaying of the coach to have stopped, although it took a moment for the swaying feeling to leave her body.

She stood back to see the sign announcing the name of the hotel. The *Royal Hotel.* She felt a giggle escape at the grandness of its name. The sound saw the children turn to her. 'What a fine home for us for the night,' she said, covering her mirth.

'Yes, Marmie, but can we explore before we have our supper and rest?' asked her second eldest son, William. 'We can indeed,' she replied. 'We will see our trunks delivered to our rooms, then take a walk together.'

***

The walk had eased the pain in her back, and the meal of roast mutton, turnips and potatoes was welcome, but the family had again crowded into one room, the children restless throughout the night. So, when the light of a new day dawned, Carrie did not feel at all rested and the children were subdued. Breakfast and climbing into the coach were a solemn affair, and the children's eyes were soon closed.

As the coach weaved its way around Lake George, Sarah stirred and raised the blind at her side. When she saw the lake brimming with water, she gently shook her brother, William, who in turn shook his brother, Charles, and so it went on until all the children were awake and bursting with excitement to see the lake which seemed to go on and on for miles.

The extra rest and the vista of the lake buoyed the children and Carrie as well, as they journeyed on to the city of Goulburn where they were to spend the night.

When the coach pulled up at Clifford's Hotel, Carrie sighed with relief for the comfort this hotel would provide them with, even if only for the night. It was a grand looking hotel of two storeys, with a verandah dressed in wrought-iron lace that ran the length of the second. She imagined guests walking from their rooms to view the goings-on below on Sloane Street.

A sturdy cedar staircase greeted them upon entry and her pleasure grew when she found that George had secured two rooms for them. This was then doubled when her eyes fell upon the sight of a large bed, its crisp white sheets, cotton bedspread and plump pillows calling her to it. She sunk into its softness, running her fingers over the raised design of the bedspread. It nearly undid her. It nearly caused her to curl up and welcome sleep into her world now. But she had children to care for, so she rose, her aching body trying to lure her back down again onto the bed. Having borne six children and done hard physical work since she had married at seventeen, she sometimes felt older than her thirty-five years. And this was one of those times.

Still, she kept going, scooping up Francis to perch upon her hip as she called her other children to her for another promised walk before mealtime. All except Edward, who had gone with his father to deliver their horses to the stables where they would be cared for while they travelled on.

She missed Edward on the occasions he was away with his father. She had come to rely on her very reliable son, and she often fought off the knowledge that he was growing up and may leave them to venture off on his own.

She fought off that notion again as her troop wound down the broad staircase of the hotel and stepped out onto the sidewalk to set off, in the direction of the church spire they could see.

The church was impressive, so much larger than the small church she had been married in and that her children and she had been baptised in. The church doors were open, and Carrie could not resist the invitation that offered, to enter. The children lowered their voices as they stepped inside, and Carrie basked in the sense of peace that washed over her in the cool quietness of the empty church. As the children found their way around the polished wooden benches, she took a moment to look upwards at the colour-filled led-light image of Christ on a cross and say a silent prayer of thanks for their safe arrival in Goulburn and a plea for their safety to continue.

***

Carrie woke during the night to the creak of floorboards outside the door of the room she was sharing with her husband and two youngest children. She had felt worn through by retiring time, and quickly fell asleep, Francis in her arms, Alice nestled beside them. Despite her tiredness, she was accustomed to having to be alert to the needs of her children through the night, so when she heard a sound, she slipped from the bed expecting to tend to a need of a child in the room next door.

She opened the door as quietly as she had removed herself from the bed, and saw the retreating back of her son Edward in the hall, a weave evident in his walk. 'Edward,' she whispered, the sound carrying easily in the absence of other noise, which told her it was late at night. Her eldest son stopped in his tracks but did not turn around. She could smell the alcohol as she approached him, and it shocked her. She stood in front of him, her face close to his, ignoring the urge to step away from the smell.

'You have been drinking,' she said.

His eyes were downcast. She felt his shame, and felt pity for him.

'Pa …' he said but didn't continue.

'Where is he?'

'Asleep in the lounge,' Edward said, his head hanging heavy, leaving Carrie to look at his forehead.

Her heart went out to him. She knew him well; knew he was embarrassed by his drunkenness. 'Go to bed, Edward. We have an early start; you will need your strength for the day ahead.' He nodded and stepped away upon the creaking floor. She followed him to the second room they had booked, checking on the other children who were fast asleep. She helped Edward off with his clothes and covered his prone form with a blanket. She tip-toed back to her own room, anger rising in her chest at her husband's obvious encouragement of their son's drinking.

***

When Carrie woke, Francis and Alice were breathing softly in their sleep beside her. Her husband had not returned to their room, and she had not expected him to. She knew the stockmen drank when they were droving. She had many times imagined them sitting around the campfire after a long, tiring day of pushing cattle along and retrieving strays, sharing company and rum. She did not understand the desire to drink alcohol. With the exception of the port on the eve of her wedding, she had never partaken of it, but when George was away, it brought her comfort to know he was enjoying the company of others.

A quiet tap on the door was enough to rouse Francis and Alice, who beamed happiness at her through sleep-leaden eyes, their cheeks touched by the colour of pink roses. Her eldest daughter, Sarah, entered quietly, as was her way, hugging her mother and sisters. An affectionate, intelligent girl, Carrie had begun to see glimpses of the woman her fourteen-year-old daughter would soon be.

'Marmie, Edward is not well. He is moaning and he smells odd.'

'We must be patient with him today. He will recover; believe me, Sarah.'

Sarah accepted her mother's advice, nodding, then stepping into her role of helping ready her sisters for breakfast, and the walk to the nearby train station. When they arrived at the station, Carrie found that her expectation of excited children had to be replaced by the perplexing view of children riveted to the spot as the mass of black metal, steam spilling from its sides, black smoke pouring into the sky from its funnel, pulled up in front of them. Carrie waved her arms around in a vein effort to dispel the steam and smoke, her children following her example.

She understood her eldest son's quietness, his paleness revealing the ill health he felt after his introduction to alcohol, but the younger ones' behaviour surprised her. Perhaps it was their first sight of a train that frightened them. If so, she hoped it would not last, that they could enjoy this part of their journey the way they had enjoyed the coach rides.

Carrie felt—and smelt—the presence of her husband, still reeking of alcohol beside her. She did not turn to look at him as she would not be able to hide her disappointment at his own behaviour and his leading their son to drink. She needed more time to decide if she was being reasonable or not. George did not address her. He knew her well. He had no intention of inviting an exchange of unsavoury words at this time. And especially not in front of their children.

Carrie stood quietly, children fanned out around her, as George moved to ensure their trunks were loaded onto the train. She was grateful when the awkwardness of this time was broken by the sound of a whistle to board and the distraction of shepherding and settling the children into their seats. Her husband and eldest son were the last to board, settling their unwell bodies at one end of the two bench seats, subdued miscreants, she decided, their eyes averted to looking out the window to avoid her gaze. Sympathy for their predicament rose within her, despite her need to remain upset with them for longer.

As the train departed, excitement finally bubbled within her younger children. Francis squirmed in Carrie's arms, leaning towards the window not far away. Each child scrambled to have a look as the final whistle blew and the train chugged out of the station. The windows were closed, but with a whoosh, nine-year-old Charles pushed one upwards, thrusting his head outside to get a better view, just as black smoke from the funnel rolled by. He yanked his head back inside the carriage, his face covered in soot. Mirth broke out among the family at the very sight of him. Charles took it on the chin. He was not one to complain, and Sarah took it upon herself to wipe his face with her handkerchief.

As they enjoyed the light-hearted moment, George caught Carrie's eye. She had never been able to resist those eyes. They had drawn her to him like a magnet all those years ago when, standing upon the front verandah of *Jimenbuen,* she had first come face to face with him. Their striking darkness had made her body quiver then, as it still did now. To her, they were like an invitation to a deep soul that lay behind them. She felt the corners of her mouth turn upwards into a slight smile, the tension between them beginning to thaw. Whatever it was that bound her to this stockman, would never break. She knew that in her heart. What lay between them was like the thickest, twisted, hessian rope that resisted being cut.

The children sensed the release of tension and chatted freely. They made *choo-choo* noises and hissed like the steam as the train gently rocked back and forth along the track.

The children's joy and the comforting movement of the train, created a sense of serenity within Carrie that she basked in, like when she stood taking in the sun's rays on the first days of spring as the snow began to melt in the *Snowy Mountains.* So far, her children were tolerating the movement of the train, as they had the coach, and she hoped it would remain so on this and the ocean part of their journey. A memory of how ill her mother had been on the voyage from New York entered her mind. She quickly pushed it aside. She must remain hopeful that all would be well.

***

Their train journey was long but uneventful, broken by a feast Carrie had asked the cook at the inn to prepare. When she opened the laden picnic basket, the peering eyes of her children widened at the sight of thickly sliced bread sandwiched with cheese and pickles and a large bottle of preserved peaches—all enthusiastically eaten as their journey continued.

It was nearing nightfall when the train pulled into Redfern Station. They had timed their coach and train travel to allow them a one-night stay in Sydney only in order to leave coin in their purses, after paying for the coach, train and ship voyage to come.

That her dream of returning to New York to see family was coming true, was still hard for Carrie to grasp. That dream had been her encouragement as she cared for the flock of chickens she had gathered over time, selling their eggs to whomever she could. She had kept her egg money in a tin, and over the years, the number of tins kept under the bed slowly increased. But her dream would not be coming true if her mother had not sent a generous contribution—most of what they required—her need to see her daughter embedded in the words of each letter she wrote. They were words that tugged at Carrie's soul, drawing memories of their once closeness, before she had denied her mother and chosen to marry the man she had fallen in love with and isolate herself on the other side of the world. Through the letters her mother had written to her after years had passed since Louisa had sailed back to New York; Carrie had come to understand that her own need to bridge the gap between them was as great as her mother's apparent need.

While George and Edward collected the trunks, Carrie and Sarah waited quietly nearby, each holding the hand of the youngest children in theirs. Francis twitched restlessly as tiredness set in. Only one buggy for the trunks could be found so the family walked the short distance to the hotel, this time aptly named *The Family Hotel.*

# Chapter Forty-Two

*Sydney, 1 August 1874*

Silhouettes, a shade lighter than the starless night above, lined their path as the cart they sat in travelled towards the harbour. Carrie peered to see the buildings on her right and left. This was her first journey to Sydney, and she wished to see more than shadows in the night.

Their time at the hotel had been uneventful. They had slumbered peacefully until George roused them to gather themselves and their belongings, for they were to board their ship—the clipper the *Windsor Castle*—at dawn.

Francis and Alice were slumped against Carrie, their eyes closed, their need for sleep a greater demand than seeing what surrounded them. There was a bite in the air and Carrie held the girls tightly to her body, beneath the blanket George had wrapped around them. She had learned to read the weather during her years on the Monaro, and she sensed a strong wind on its way. Perhaps it would follow behind them for part of the way, seeing their arrival in London earlier than the many weeks anticipated.

It would be a challenge to keep the children occupied during that time, but as was her want, she had prepared as best she could. One trunk brimmed with the books she had collected over the years, some of which she had used to teach all but four-year-old Francis to read and write. She hoped the ocean and creatures within it would capture her children's hearts the way hers had been captured on the voyage from New York all those years ago. Carrie hoped too that the ship itself would hold interest for them and that there would be other children for them to befriend. So many hopes. How precious hope had always been to her, having made a conscious decision years ago to hang on to it.

Charles was quick to jump out when the cart pulled up at the wharf. He stumbled, landing heavily on his knees. A rush of concern charged through Carrie like a runaway bull, but she knew better than to hurry to her son's side. George was soon there standing over his son but not offering a hand. 'On your feet lad,' he said, his voice laden with authority. While he took a softer tone with each of his daughters, Carrie had witnessed her husband being firm with each of his sons. After the birth of their third son, she raised this with him and had been rebuked. George had told her firmly not to mollycoddle them and reminded her that they must grow to be tough men who could care for themselves and their own wives and children. Once again, Carrie reminded herself of her husband's difficult childhood—the son of a convict, his father dying a tragic death, and George being separated from his mother at an early age. And once again she controlled her urge to argue with him. Instead, she would give Charles a mother's reassuring gentle touch when she could.

She watched Charles now, pull himself up to his full height, his fists clenched by his side, to meet his father's gaze. And in the growing light of dawn she witnessed, for the first time, the rebellion in her son's eyes. George would get his wish—his son would not grow to be at the mercy of other men.

The scene around them unfolded like the pages of a newspaper as the rising sun revealed details of sandstone buildings, gently lapping water, and their ship, its sails still furled, sailors scurrying about its decks. The familiar sounds of horses and people talking grew around them as more people gathered upon the wharf, and the offloading of trunks and passengers continued.

The *Windsor Castle* was larger in size than the packet ship she had voyaged on from New York, and Carrie took comfort in this as the concerns she battled to keep at bay fought their way into her head again. Was it madness to take six children, her youngest only four years of age, on such a journey? *The decision has been made. You are on your way; get on with it,* she told herself.

'How magnificent is the harbour, children?' she said, portraying a brightness she struggled to feel. 'Let us find a place to view it, while Pa and Edward see the trunks are loaded.'

Her children had not seen the ocean before, and Carrie was grateful they were easily distracted as she gathered her wits in preparation for boarding. When she received a signal from George that the time had come, she led the children to the gangway, scooping up Francis who hung on tightly, aware that a handful of her skirt was gripped in Alice's hand.

The ship felt sturdy under Carrie's boots—stable in the calm waters. A sailor led them to their cabins—two small rooms, with two bunk beds in each, the space in-between the beds sparse. But it was what they could afford, and they would make do. George, Edward, William, and Charles took one cabin, and she, Sarah, Alice, and Francis, the other. Their trunks were stored on a lower deck, where they would be allowed access to them from time to time.

The voices of William and Charles bickering over the same bunk came through the wall, followed by a short reprimand from their father, and then silence. It appeased Carrie to be reminded of how near they were. She was glad they had not been separated by other cabins.

As the day progressed and nightfall arrived, Carrie found herself questioning why they had been told to board so early in the day when there had been no expectation of sailing until the following day. Still, the time had given them an opportunity to settle in, to retrieve clothes and books from their trunks, and to be on deck viewing the sturdy, solid buildings aplenty, and the not-so-sturdy timber buildings dotted around the waterfront.

The next morning, Carrie woke to the sounds of orders called out to sailors, their feet pounding on the deck above. A knock came upon her door. She opened it to the sight of her husband and their sons standing around him in order of age and height, like different sized fence posts.

'Come above,' George said, 'we are to leave; the tug is beginning its work.'

'Is it safe for the children, George? Will we not be in the way?' Carrie asked, her words regretted as soon as they slipped from her mouth for she saw the eagerness for adventure on her sons' faces, and Sarah's too, who had come to her mother's side. Carrie had no doubt it existed within her husband as well, who had not at any point objected to this long voyage. She suspected part of his motivation was to see the man whose connection with his father had seen George brought from Van Diemens Land to the Monaro where he had learned his trade of stockman. That man, Amos Crisp the senior, had gone with his wife, Louisa—Carrie's mother—back to New York when she had chosen not to remain in Australia.

In that moment, seven pairs of eyes were upon her. 'Yes! Children let us see more of this glorious harbour as we sail away,' she said. George gave her another of his joyous smiles that she saw as hers alone, that always lifted her spirits and reminded her of their love for each other. He lifted Francis up in his arms and led the way up the stairs towards the bow of the ship, gathering them all close to avoid the rush of sailors at their work.

The grandness of the harbour, its waters deep, dark and mesmerising, left them speechless as they swung their heads in all directions, marvelling at its width and how far it seemed to stretch inland. Euphoria overcame Carrie as the ship moved, making its way towards the headlands of tall cliffs that towered above the unfurled sails of the ship. People on another ship waved to them and they all waved back.

As they neared the headlands though, a chill ran up Carrie's spine. It matched the chill that swept towards them on a wind that had sprung and whipped the tops of the waves to foam. Carrie pulled her shawl tighter around her body. The ship passed through the heads, and all she could see was nothing but open ocean and the reality of the long voyage ahead. 'Below decks it is for us, children,' she said, not looking at her husband in case he objected to her decision.

As they walked away, her decision was proven right as the ship negotiated a wave large enough for a spray of salty water to arc and land where they had been standing a moment before. As the up-and-down and side-to-side movements of the ship commenced in earnest, they weaved their way to their rooms to rest after the coach and train travel of the last days.

***

But no such rest was to be afforded them, as the ship encountered a squall, wind whistling around, and within the ship, rain falling upon its decks. Carrie prayed her children would inherit her tolerance for ocean voyage, but her prayer did not come to pass. Francis was the first to lose the contents of her stomach, followed by each of the other children—except Edward.

With only one wooden pail per cabin, George and Edward grappled with the tilting floors to battle the wind sweeping over the deck so they could empty the pails over the sides. But they had to choose their time to throw carefully. Carrie wiped her children's faces with cool water and changed their clothes, placating them with hugs and words of reassurance, lulling them to sleep to bring them relief in between the retching.

She didn't need to see the dishevelled looks of George and Edward to know the wind and waves were getting worse. She could feel the churning as the ship carved its way through both. On the fourth day, both George and Edward became ill too and the job of caring for all her family fell to Carrie alone.

She heard the sounds of others in nearby cabins who were as wretched as her own family, and met men and women on the stairs who, like her, were making valiant efforts to empty full pails. They looked as pale and exhausted as she felt. One day, when she stepped onto the deck, she lost her footing and began to slide towards the rail, her progress halted by two women who had dropped their pails to help her to her feet. The noise of the wind and the rattle of the sails was too great for them to speak and be heard, so a brief look of gratefulness was all she could reward them with.

She battled to drip drops of water into Francis' mouth, her jaws firmly clamped, belying the listlessness that portrayed her daughter's weakness. Sailors brought food and water to the cabins, with Carrie being the only one who could make herself eat. She must keep up her strength to care for her family.

She thanked God when George and Edward rallied after several days. She believed her prayers that they would find their sea legs had been answered. 'Carrie, Lass. You are a strong woman,' George said, as he spread his legs wide to find purchase on the rocking floor before putting his arms around her for the few moments they could find their balance. Their unwashed bodies grasped each other in a desperate need to tap into each other's determination to protect their children and survive what nature was throwing at them.

***

Carrie woke the next morning, Francis soundly asleep in her arms. As Carrie moved her aching limbs slowly, she became aware of a change. The sea was calmer, the ship's sway no longer savage, and the screaming wind and voices of men were reduced. Her body let go of a tension that had her as taut as a strung rope. A single tear of relief fell from her eye onto Francis' forehead, which she quickly wiped away with her finger. *Perhaps the sea has finished its rage against us, and the children can enjoy its beauty rather than come to fear its danger.*

'Marmie,' she heard Alice say from beside her, 'I am hungry.'

'Me too,' chorused Sarah from the opposite bunk.

They were words that buoyed Carrie's spirit. Perhaps all her family were feeling improved. 'Well then,' she said, 'shall we see what we can find?' But when she opened the door to do so, George greeted her with a tray of bread, cheese, a beaker of fresh water, and a treasured mug of coffee for her.

The bread was stale, but she and the girls did not care. They chewed happily, saying little in their eagerness. By the time Carrie had finished her hot, strong, sweet, coffee, she felt renewed as though what they had gone through was a bad dream she could now push from her mind.

***

But they had been tricked—their day of going on deck, conversing with other equally pale families, and reading from their books, was not followed by a like day. During their slumber that night, Carrie woke to the sounds of a squall whisking the sea into a frenzy again, further sleep evading her as the hours passed and her fear of what was to come did not.

As insipid light marked the beginning of a new day, Carrie saw restlessness stir in Alice. Carrie just managed to extract herself from her bunk, grab the pail and hold it before her daughter as her eyes sprung open and her stomach emptied. *We are not to be spared the might of nature. I must prepare my mind for what lies ahead.*

Francis became ill as well and within a short while the need to empty the pail often again, grew. 'Sarah, are you well? Can you care for them while I go on deck?' she asked. 'Yes Marmie,' was the reply, Carrie's gratefulness going out to her brave daughter, Sarah's own resolution to be strong and helpful visible in her eyes.

Carrie made her way from the cabin, falling to her knees as the rocking action of the ship became more violent. She struggled to keep the pail upright, pulled herself to standing, and took small steps, her legs astride, one arm flung out to the side to help her balance.

As she stepped gingerly onto the deck, she heard shouts from the captain who stood further along the deck, legs astride, face turned upwards. She followed his gaze to see sailors atop the masts, rolling the topsails in, reducing their resistance to the now heavy squalls.

A tremendous crash and crack marked the breaking of a great wave upon the deck and the breaking of rigging extending from the side of the boat. The ship tilted violently, and Carrie's legs were whipped from beneath her, the breath torn from her lungs as she was thrown on her side. Her hand released the pail which rolled towards and over the side, into the wild waves not far below. Carrie began to slide in that direction herself, feeling two hands madly grasping at her ankle. They were not the wide, thick hands of a man, but the narrower ones of a woman—ones that raised a memory of being saved from the flooded creek near *Jimenbuen*, by native women. She felt an arm that she knew belonged to her husband grasp her waist and the hands around her ankle let go.

She saw, rather than heard, George mouth the words, 'On your knees' as he pulled her up and they crawled the few steps back to the stairs where he swung her around to lower herself. At the base of the stairs was Edward, doing his best to keep another woman upright—the woman whose hands, Carrie had no doubt, had been around her ankle. Carrie reached out her hand to this woman she did not know, and for a fleeting moment, nature allowed them to clasp each other, before Edward led the woman, inch-by-inch towards her own cabin.

'Dry clothes, Carrie,' yelled George. 'The children,' she yelled back.

'I to the boys, you the girls,' he said, as his arm gripped her to him, and they battered their way along the corridor. 'The pail,' she cried. 'I will find another. Go,' he said as he flung open the cabin door to usher her in.

# Chapter Forty-Three

Diana didn't give her cousin, Sophie, time to offer a greeting when she picked up her ringing phone. Instead, Diana burst forth with the words 'I have it' and the croaky voice of her cousin replied, 'What exactly do you have, may I ask?'

'Evidence of the voyage back to New York! I am emailing it to you now.'

'Okay. Tell me more,' said Sophie, clearing her throat. 'Even though it is 2.00 am over here in London.'

'Oh, I'm so sorry. Why didn't I think of that?'

'I don't know, but I'm guessing excitement about what you have found is the likely cause. So go ahead.'

'Thanks Sophie. I found an article in the *Sydney Morning Herald*, dated 1 August 1874. It shows projected ship departures and clearances to depart. It lists a ship named the *Windsor Castle* as being cleared for departure to London. But it also lists "Mr and Mrs G. Hedger, Masters Hedger (3), Misses Hedger (3)" as passengers.'

Sophie had shrugged off sleep and her voice was now crystal clear in her response. 'So, if I remember right, that means they embarked on a journey to the other side of the world, with six children ranging from about four to sixteen years of age.'

'Yes, you have that right. And it turned out to be a dangerous voyage.'

'How do you know that?' asked Sophie.

'Because a second cousin I didn't know we had until the other day, has kindly given me three pages of a diary of Carrie's that just happens to relate to *this* voyage and it says they were *shipwrecked* on 17 September, after sailing from Sydney on 2 August 1874.'

'So, the passed-down story of Carrie being shipwrecked is true!' said Sophie. 'But that story didn't say George and *all* the children went too, did it?'

'No. All I heard was Carrie returned to New York. This is the first actual evidence we have that George and the children went too.'

'Gosh! Can you email me the diary too, please?'

'I can. It's a small number of brief entries; doesn't say anything about what they experienced on the voyage.'

'You said it was a dangerous voyage, so perhaps it was too rough to write much. I know how you can find out more though,' said Sophie. 'The ship's log. That's the captain's record of the voyage.'

'Yes but how do I find that?' asked Diana.

'I'm afraid it's back to those books on ship voyages at the National Library. Start there.'

Diana groaned. 'Well, it has to be easier, surely, now that I have the name of the ship. The *Windsor Castle*.'

'Only one way to find out,' said Sophie. 'Anything else in your bag of discoveries before I fall back into slumber?'

Diana laughed, feeling guilty now for phoning Sophie at such a ridiculous hour. 'Yes, I almost forgot. I will email you an article I found through TROVE. From the *Goulburn Herald and Chronicle*, dated 1867. It's about how George was charged with cattle stealing. Turns out it was *one* cow, and he was found not guilty. It comes across as though it became a bit of a big thing though. There was even a jury.'

'Especially for Carrie, no doubt. Maybe his convict heritage didn't help him.'

'What, you think he could have been targeted because of that?'

'Well, one cow makes me wonder if that could have been the case. From what I've read, there were thousands of cattle and sheep on the Monaro by then. And he was only charged with stealing *one*.'

'Umm, interesting. Okay, I am going to let you go now. Sleep tight,' said Diana.

'You too, let me know how you go with the Captain's Log.'

***

Not very well, as it turned out.

Diana and Bella were now taking it in turns to be with Maggie at the hospital, and today Diana was to be with her mum in the afternoon, so she had taken the opportunity to go to the National Library that morning. The desk in front of her was laden with all the books on ship voyages she could find but there was no reference to the voyage she was after.

She sat back in the chair and sighed, blowing out air through her mouth in frustration. She pulled two printouts towards her—two copies of what she had been able to find—a photograph of the *Windsor Castle*. To her it was a beautiful-looking boat. It was long and sleek, quite low to the water, multiple masts rising from its deck. Clearly a clipper ship, powered by sails. Not a steamer that Carrie's mother Louisa had hoped her daughter might sail back to New York on. *Perhaps clipper fares were cheaper than steamer fares, which, with eight of them travelling, you would think had to be a significant consideration,* Diana concluded.

Reluctantly, Diana returned the books, gathered up the printouts of the ship and made her way to her car and then the hospital for the afternoon. As she drove along, she contemplated where else she might be able to find the Captain's Log, if it was available, and she arrived at the possibility of museums.

Bella was still with Maggie when Diana walked into her mother's hospital room. Diana had filled both of them in, on the evidence she now had about the 1874 voyage and how she would go to the library today in search of the Captain's Log. 'Did you find it?' asked Maggie.

'No luck,' said Diana. 'Trawled my way through the books, but nothing, no reference to follow up even.' She took out one of the printouts of the photo of the *Windsor Castle* from her handbag. 'I did find a photo of the ship though.' She held it up then handed it to Maggie.

'Lovely looking clipper,' said her mother. It must have been a sight when all the sails were unfurled, churning through the waves.'

'Indeed,' Diana agreed, her mother's longest, well-pronounced sentence since her stroke, providing the release from any frustration she had been feeling about not finding the Captain's Log.

Maggie passed the photo to Bella, who held it up and examined it closely. 'Could I keep this one?'

'Sure. I made two copies,' said Diana.

***

The afternoon with Maggie passed peacefully, Diana finding herself dozing when her mother did the same. They were both surprised when, as Diana was preparing to leave for the night, Bella turned up again.

Bella handed Diana a large brown envelope with something thick inside. A wad of paper. 'What's this?' Diana asked.

'It's the ship's log for the *Windsor Castle*. I found it at the National Library, that's where I've been.'

'How? How did you find it? Did I miss something in all those books on shipping?'

'No. I didn't use those books,' Bella said matter-of-factly. I searched for more information on the *Windsor Castle* and I found out it was built by a company called Blackwall. I then punched that name into the search engine and found a book called *The Blackwall Frigates*, which the librarian had brought up to the Main Reading Room for me. And in the book was the log for our rellies' voyage.'

Bella's affectionate use of the term 'rellies' lifted Diana's spirits even more. 'Thank you. Have you read it?'

'No. It took all this time just to find it.'

'Read it now,' said Maggie from her bed. 'I want to hear too.'

Diana flipped through it. 'It's long, Mum. Is that okay?'

'Yes. I want to know it all too,' Maggie said.

The poignancy of the moment struck Diana. Three generations of women in a room, about to learn about a voyage, people they were descended from, took over one hundred and forty four years ago.

'Okay, here we go then,' she said settling back in the chair. 'It starts on Page 204 with an introductory opening paragraph:

*Dismasting of the Windsor Castle*

*In 1874, the Windsor Castle had a most disastrous voyage. On the passage out to Melbourne, she lost her mizen topmast and main topgallant yard, again she had trouble with her men, whilst the chief officer went mad and on arrival in Australia had to be taken to an asylum; whilst on the homeward passage she was not only dismasted, but could with difficulty be kept afloat until she was got into a Brazilian port. Her log records as follows:*

'Poor man,' said Maggie, 'the one who went mad I mean.'

'Indeed,' said Diana, turning her eyes to look at her always-thoughtful and caring mother, then back to the log. 'There are some brief entries for London to Melbourne, and Melbourne to Sydney, but here's Sydney to London—the one we want—so let's skip to there. And I might skip the more technical stuff, stick to what happened.'

'Wait, Mum,' said Bella, 'the ship got to a Brazilian port?'

'Yes.'

'Does that match with what Carrie said in the few pages of her diary that you have?'

'It does. Didn't I tell you that?' Bella and Maggie shook their heads. 'I guess my focus has been on finding the log. Sorry about that.'

Diana continued. 'The date the Sydney to London log starts matches the diary too. It reads:'

*2nd August.- 10 a.m., tug Mystery came alongside: proceeded in tow… Moderate gale and heavy sea. Ship labouring and straining heavily.*

'So not a pleasant start then,' said Maggie.

'Next entry is:'

*10th August…Wind E.S.E.(East South East) increasing with heavy squalls. P.M., fresh gale with hard squalls; reefed topsails, a tremendous sea broke aboard between starboard fore and main rigging, breaking in a great part of the bulwarks…*

As Diana read on, Bella used her mobile phone to look up terms they didn't know the meaning of. It seemed reefed means a sail had been rolled or folded and bulwarks were bits of rigging that stuck out from the sides of the front of the ship.

The three of them looked up when the door opened and a nurse, Susan, strode in, to check on Maggie and take her blood pressure. Susan picked up on the mood in the room straight away. 'All okay in here? You all look *occupied*, for want of a better word, by something.'

'Mum has begun reading the log of a truly wild ship voyage our family went on in 1874,' said Bella. 'The log is already showing how dramatic it was.'

'Goodness me. From where to where did they sail?' asked Susan, moving to the bedside to wrap the blood pressure cuff around Maggie's arm.

'From Sydney to London, on their way to New York,' said Diana. 'With six children, the youngest only four.'

Susan stopped what she was doing and turned to each of them, 'Six children! Did they all survive?'

Diana, Maggie and Bella looked at each other. 'Well, we think so,' said Diana. 'I guess we have assumed so.'

Susan nodded, turning back to Maggie, 'And how are you this afternoon? You do look a little tired.'

'I do feel a little tired now,' confessed Maggie.

Diana immediately felt guilty. They had all been eager to read about the voyage and missed that this was the time for Maggie to be on her own for the night. 'I'm sorry, Mum. We might leave now and let you rest,' she said.

'Well, it all sounds fascinating,' said Susan, 'when you know more Maggie, you can tell me all about it,' she said, leaving the room with a wave to the others.

Diana stood. She moved to kiss her mum softly on the forehead. 'See you tomorrow, Mum.'

'More of the log tomorrow?'

'Definitely, Mum. After your physiotherapy in the morning.'

# Chapter Forty-Four

*15 August 1874*

Only thirteen days at sea. Yet, if asked, Carrie would exclaim that surely it had been longer. She remembered the chill that had accompanied the thrill of sailing through the heads of Sydney Harbour. She had pushed aside that warning of what lay ahead but now she was under no illusions.

A leak six feet below deck had been discovered the day before yesterday, when cargo was being moved about. As she tended to her children, George had come to report that a carpenter had been lowered over the side in an attempt to repair the leak. Carrie brought her hands together to point to the heavens, saying a prayer to God for the carpenter's safe return on deck.

Prayer helped her to stay strong, and she followed the first with a second, asking for the carpenter's work to succeed. The winds and waves were less today, but still strong. *Would it take more than one attempt to fix the leak? Would nature gift them a chance to stop the water seeping onboard?* She looked down upon Francis, her face so pale, like all her children. *What will happen to us if not?* She must not allow her mind to journey there. She must stay strong for her family and pray for divine intervention.

***

*23 August 1874*

If only she could put pen to paper, for she knew the very act of doing so would provide solace, but the everlasting tossing of the ship and the needs of her children made all but a few hastily written words a dream only. All she could manage was a line or two here and there.

Carrie had finished the morning challenge of encouraging her younger children to eat, and acknowledging the achievement of her older children to do so when, not complaining, they forced down the porridge, which quickly congealed in the cold weather. She too found the effort to partake nourishment exhausting, beginning with swallowing small mouthfuls. Carrie wanted to eat as little as they did. But she must set an example.

Each day she was relieved when any meal time had passed. How she longed to be in her home again—the peaks of the *Snowy Mountains* in the distance, their beloved *Snowy River* a ride away—cooking a meal of meat and vegetables, watching her family gather and take delight in its flavour and sustenance.

She must push that thought from her mind. She must get on with the day, such as it was. While her eldest daughter, Sarah, wiped her younger sisters' faces, she must go to the next cabin along and check on her boys. She was concerned about the cough that had come to William. It was not the first time in his short life his chest had proved to be weaker than the others.

While the wind and seas were less rugged some days, today was not one of them, and her exit from the cabin became a challenging stagger like that of a drunken man. Carrie closed the door behind her, leaning against it. She took a rare moment for herself to let any semblance of a smile she donned for her children drop, as she took great gulps of air to steady herself. She refused to let any tears come to her. *There are weeks to go of this voyage; how will we manage? No! I must keep going!* She pulled away from the door and staggered the few steps to her sons.

William's cough was no worse, which gave her hope. She ruffled his hair and helped him change into fresh clothes. Washing and drying clothes was a struggle, but she had managed one set for each child. George had strung up a rope in each cabin and helped her take them on deck to flap in the wind when the rain retreated. Since her fall, he had banned her from going up on deck alone, insisting she be accompanied by either himself or Edward.

She lay beside William on the bunk. His younger brother, Charles, climbed up to be held by his mother too. It felt good to be able to give the boys this attention. The needs of their younger sisters, Alice and Francis, meant the boys sometimes had to wait for their turn.

Muffled shouts came to them from above as the wind whistled and the waves rolled the ship from side to side. Carrie opened her mouth to whisper words of reassurance to her sons, when a loud thud shook the deck above. Instinctively, she knew what it may well be, but she closed her eyes to pray that it was not. Her prayer was short, interrupted by an unfamiliar dizziness and Edward, who burst through the cabin door.

He looked straight into his mother's eyes, opened his mouth to speak then closed it again as his eyes turned to his younger brothers. Carrie extracted herself from the bunk and once again, staggered into the hall. Edward followed her.

'Did you hear?' he asked. She nodded. 'A sailor fell from the topsail,' he said. Carrie reached out to touch her son's arm. 'But with a hand, he got up!' The amazement in Edward's voice matched the expression upon his face. 'The captain said it was the layers of the sailor's clothing, to guard against the cold, that shielded him.' A smile came to her son's handsome face as Carrie returned his smile. 'Perhaps a miracle can happen anywhere,' she told him. 'Then perhaps we will survive this voyage, Marmie,' he said, turning from her to return to his brothers, leaving Carrie with a warmth in her soul that defied the coldness of the air around her.

***

*4 September 1874*

The cold had worsened as strong gusts of wind carried snow within them. Each time George and Edward returned below decks, their hair was adhered to their heads from both ocean spray and ice crystals, and they would peel off a layer of clothes in the hope of finding dry ones beneath.

They did so today, George signalling to Carrie afterwards to leave the cabin, no doubt to keep her informed but out of earshot of the younger children. Again, it was a battle to leave the cabin as the ship was 'knocking about', as Carrie had heard the captain say, in the whipped-up wind and waves.

George took her in his arms, and for the moments they could manage it, before the risk of tumbling became too great, Carrie took comfort in the sheer physical strength of his body. She longed to nuzzle her face into his neck and soak up the familiar smell of him, masked partly by wetness and saltiness. But he pulled back.

'The ship is taking much water,' he said. 'More of the starboard rigging has washed away.'

Carrie swallowed hard, forcing the little food she had in her stomach from rising to her mouth. She slumped as weakness threatened to take her legs out from under her. George leaned into her, managing to support her with one arm.

She needed to look into his eyes, to see something that would tell her not to be fearful, but what she saw was his own fear, and she knew she had frightened him. *Was he thinking that his wife, whom he had praised for her strength, was crumbling before him?*

He gave her what he could. 'The captain has ordered male passengers to assist with manning the pumps. Not Edward. I will not allow it. He will watch over you all. He is not to man the pumps, Carrie. Do you hear me?'

'I do,' she replied, knowing that Edward would object to his father's instruction.

But there was hope to be found in her husband's words that action was being taken, although his last words told her it was dangerous work. George was protecting his eldest son, who he would expect to be the man of the family if a fate were to befall himself.

Again, Carrie chose to hang on to hope. Her strength grew. She nodded and reached to kiss him, the ship's movement allowing their lips to touch only briefly before they slipped away. She turned and went back to her children, now clustered together in the one cabin.

# Chapter Forty-Five

The late autumn days of Canberra were often sunny days, the skies bright blue and cloudless. But the nights foreshadowed the winter, that lay just around the corner, with their crispy coolness. By the time Diana and Bella arrived home from the hospital, Bella felt the need to rush to turn the wall heater on and Diana was keen to jump into a warm shower.

As the water whisked away any hint of the colder weather to come, thoughts swirled in Diana's mind about what it would have been like for Carrie on that voyage. There was more to learn from the log but already it was portraying a rough journey. Diana was more than tempted to read the rest of the log tonight, but she would use restraint so it continued to be a shared experience with her mother and daughter.

*How did Carrie and her family stay warm or cool?* she pondered. Putting on more clothes or taking them off would have been one of the few ways they had. *When the seas were rough, could they have even made a hot drink for which they would have had to light a small fire somewhere on board?* Diana imagined they would have had to wear the same clothes for days at a time as washing and drying could only have been extremely difficult during such weather. How Carrie must have longed for a bath and to bathe her children. It must have been a nightmare for Carrie to try to keep her children clean, fed, and to say nothing of calm! How would Carrie have handled it if the four younger children all needed her to comfort and care for them at the same time?

*And did arguments among passengers, among sailors, between them both, break out?* Everyone must have been so tense; you would think there would have been some battling as to who knew best between them all. The captain would have won though, she presumed.

When Diana had dried herself and dressed in track pants and matching sweater, she made her way to the kitchen where Bella was cooking dinner again. A rich tomato aroma greeted her. 'Simple pasta tonight. But I make the passata myself,' said Bella, as she closed the fridge door, a bunch of fresh basil in her hand.

Diana loved the smell and taste of basil, and reached to break off a leaf. She held it up to her nose and inhaled. 'With garlic too?' she asked.

'Yes, and I add a tablespoon of Italian herbs, my not-so-secret ingredient.'

'Smells fabulous, Bella. I was going to be slack and suggest a pizza again, but your pasta will be way better.'

Bella began tearing the basil leaves and dropping them into the pot of passata. 'I read you tear the leaves—don't cut them—for more flavour. So the theory goes. Umm, different topic, don't suppose we can read the rest of the log tonight?'

Diana laughed. Bella was clearly as keen as she was to know what else they could find out. 'Sure would like to, but I'm thinking we should wait to share that with Nana.'

'Okay,' said Bella. 'That's what I thought you would say, and I think that's best too. Change of topic again—could I have your password for the ancestry website?'

'Of course. It's in that notebook on the table where I write down my passwords.'

'Mum, I don't think you're supposed to keep your passwords in a notebook, especially where people can find them.'

Diana shrugged. 'I know, I know. But so many passwords are needed nowadays, with upper, lowercase letters, numbers, symbols. How are we supposed to remember them all?'

***

When Diana came out into the kitchen the next morning, desperate for a coffee, Bella had left a note on the bench. 'Off to breakfast with a friend, then the library. Please wait until I get to the hospital to read the rest of the log.' The note wasn't signed with love, or kisses or hug symbols, but Bella had drawn a smiley face, which pleased Diana. She would take what she could get. And she was also pleased Bella was catching up with someone—maybe from her university days? *But why was Bella going to the library again?*

# Chapter Forty-Six

*16-17 September 1874*

George winced when Carrie touched him. She knew his muscles must ache from taking his lengthy turns on the pump. This last week had been better, the gales moderate, and the ice crystals they carried, less. The men were better able to stay on their feet while seeing to the pumps.

This day—a rare, calmer day—the sailors had been able to catch albatross. They offered around the cooked meet which at first the children were reluctant to try, but its juicy tenderness drew them in, offering them something to be happy about. Carrie was grateful for any food she could get into her children; such was the battle to do so since they had left Sydney over six weeks ago.

She consoled herself knowing they were heading towards the equator where warmer weather would come and perhaps the vicious wind and rain would cease. She was settling the children for sleep when her senses discerned the wind picking up again, warning her she must not let her guard down and that she must be prepared for what may be ahead. She busied herself checking if the pails needed emptying, seeing what clean clothes they had, and sending Edward in search of water and bread, before her concern that moving around the ship would become treacherous again, occurred.

***

At midnight, she was proven right. She woke in the pitch black, a shivering, squirming daughter pressed into each of her sides. She pulled them closer, blinking rapidly in an attempt to make out shapes in the cabin, but she could not. The blindness frightened her, almost as much as the rolling and pitching of the ship. Nausea that she could not allow surged. She swallowed, again refusing the little she had eaten to rise.

She could not see, but she knew that Sarah and Charles must be awake too. They would be huddled together on the opposite bunk. This journey was quickening her eldest daughter's journey towards womanhood. Carrie was grateful for the mothering of the younger children she now shared with Sarah.

Carrie prayed that with the light would come hope that the ocean and wind would decide to treat them kindly.

But the ocean and wind had other ideas, for with the dull light of dawn came squalls and rain that belied her muddled head's description.

She strained to hear the sound of even one man's voice from above, but could not. She turned her head to peer towards the opposite bunk, her children's faces coming slowly into focus. As no sound she made would be heard, she tried with her eyes to reassure them, but saw the fear they were unable to hide in their own.

Carrie ached for her children. George had instructed Edward to stay in the cabin next door with his brother, William. She did not know if her husband was there too at this time, and she could not stand not knowing. She could not! She must go to them and drag Edward and William back here if she had to, so at least all her children were together with her.

Leaden light penetrated the cabin, enough for Carrie to draw Sarah's eyes to her own, then down to the daughters in her arms. She screamed William's name, seeing comprehension dawn in Sarah's expression.

With great effort, Carrie pulled herself up, bringing her youngest children with her, one in each arm. She ignored the pain in her back caused by their weight and swung to place her bare feet to the floor. Numbing pain shot through her legs as bitterly cold sea water swirled around her ankles. She was horrified that water was seeping under the cabin door.

She was tossed forward as the ship leaned precariously to one side. She lurched across the narrow space between the bunks, pushing the children in her arms forward so they landed upon their older sister and brother. The effort drained her energy, and she sank to the floor, the numbing pain caused by the freezing water, rising to her thighs.

She crawled to the door and hauled herself up, her hands clawing at the wood. She winced as a splinter pierced her skin, but it was nothing when compared to the shivering that consumed her. She felt her sodden clothes pulling her downwards before she yanked on the rope handle of the door to swing it open and fall face first into the corridor. A moment's relief that the water was no deeper here, came to her. She righted herself and staggered the few steps towards the other cabin.

She flung open the door, a wave of dizziness from her exhaustion overcoming her as she realised the cabin was empty. Her heart may well sink within her before the ship did, she believed.

*On deck?* She turned back and inched her way to the stairs leading upwards. The ship dropped into a trough, flinging her from the steps. She landed on her side, winded. She rolled around in the water. She was so cold now, that more made no difference. The ship rolled to its other side, and she grabbed hold of a stair as she swept by, heaving herself up onto her knees and meeting the challenge each stair presented the only way she could—at a snail's pace.

A slush of water poured onto her head as she poked it above the manhole. Only her cast iron grip on the stair prevented her from tumbling backwards. She shook her head and slithered face down onto the deck. It took several attempts to raise her head and squirm to the side of a rope box, bracing her back against it, hanging on to a rope handle with one hand.

Carrie opened her eyes, rain stabbing at them like sewing pins. She closed them, and opened them, but she could only do so for a second at a time. A terrifying picture emerged—sailors struggling to haul a sail down from high above, their bodies lashed by wind and rain. They fought to hang onto the ropes tearing at their hands.

Another glimpse to see a sailor sliding towards her, his footing lost. Carrie closed her eyes, bracing for the impact of his body colliding with hers, but it did not come, and when she opened her eyes, he had disappeared. To where, she knew not, a wave bridging the deck, taking any thought from her. Spray filled her mouth with water so salty she choked and coughed, almost losing her grip; the pain of hanging on was wretched.

A crack not even the next vicious squall could mask, signalled the fall of the mainmast, which was carried off into the ocean without meeting with the deck. Carrie's breath refused to leave her, staying trapped within her chest. She was frozen in movement like the icicles she had seen dripping from stout snow gums in the *Snowy Mountains.*

She forced her eyes open to peer further away, to see an axe in the hands of a sailor come down upon a rope, splitting it in two, releasing the crate it held to disappear into the ocean, like the mast that had gone before.

In a brief lull, the fall of other axes came to her; the ships load was being lightened. Then, on all fours, she saw her eldest son, his young brother, William, clinging to his back, and in her haste to be with them, she stood and fell, her ankle twisting beneath her.

Later she would not be able to recall how, but all three of them made it to the below-deck entrance and scrambled down the stairs, where the pain from her injury took awareness from her.

***

Carrie came to, Edward's face above her. Her sodden outer garments had been removed, a blanket had been wrapped around her, and her two little girls were huddled against her side once more. She went to raise herself and felt the pull of rope tighten around her waist. She understood what that meant, they were tied to the bunk for their own safety, the danger posed by the storm unrelenting.

She moved her hands downwards and felt the rope that coiled around her daughters' waists. They were safe. She would not resist. Her children were together again. They would ride this out together, her husband would return to them, and they would be safe. She had to believe that!

Dizziness overcame her again, as the ship tilted violently. In a blur, she saw Edward fall to his knees in the ocean water swirling around the floor of the cabin. She struggled to focus, watching him drag himself over to the other bunk. His hands moved around his older sister and younger brothers. Carrie wanted to cry out when it struck her that he was tying them, but not himself, to the bunk.

She knew what that meant. Her son would not remain; he would go to be with the men on the pumps.

***

The days and nights passed in confusion born of fever. Carrie shivered with cold, but she burned as though her face were being held over a camp fire. Her ankle had been wrapped but throbbed with pain. Sometimes, there were children beside her, and sometimes there were not. She tasted broth or water fed to her by Sarah or her husband whose concerned expressions would pitch sideways with the movement of the ship, then come back into view. She heard mumbled voices. She struggled to rise on her own but could not, falling back into what she feared would be an eternal sleep.

She felt the ship still then the wind, rain and tilting begin again. Over and over. Until one day, she woke, the air humid, her fever absent. The faces of each of her children gathered around her. Behind them, stood her bedraggled husband, weariness presenting itself in crescents of puffy darkness below his drooping eyes.

'Carrie. You have come back to us,' George said, relief dripping from his words. He leaned closer. 'Listen, Carrie. Can you understand me?' Carrie nodded. We are in the Port of Bahia, in Brazil. We are to leave the *Windsor Castle*—to board a steamer that will take us to Liverpool.'

Carrie did not have the strength yet to speak, but within her mind, as the tears streamed down her face, she said, *Thank you, thank you* over and over again.

# Chapter Forty-Seven

There were seven more pages—crammed with often brief entries—of the Captain's Log that related to the time Carrie, George and their children had been on the *Windsor Castle* after it sailed from Sydney. Diana began to read each entry out and as they went along, Bella again used her mobile phone to look up any sailing terms they did not understand.

When Diana came to the entry for 17 September 1874, she stopped. 'This one is long. Let me read this to myself quickly first,' she said.

Bella took the opportunity to stretch her legs and ask her grandmother if she needed anything. 'A drink of water please,' said Maggie, which Bella poured from a jug sitting on the drawers beside the hospital bed, and handed to her grandmother.

'It looks like this entry is about when the shipwreck occurred,' Diana said. 'Although reading ahead, I think they are using the term *shipwreck* differently to how I have been thinking.'

'Have you been thinking ship-sinking-and-disappearing kind of shipwreck?' asked Bella.

'Yes,' said Diana. 'Me too,' said Maggie.

'Well, skipping ahead another few pages, it says, "*The Windsor Castle … did not reach Gravesend until 28th April … 269 days from Sydney.*" So that's well over nine months,' exclaimed Diana.

'Must have needed a bucket of repairs then,' said Maggie, 'before it could go the rest of the voyage to England after the shipwreck.'

'Indeed!' said Diana. 'Let's read on.'

The entry for 17 September 1874 began at midnight, with the captain describing the sailors' extreme efforts to *reef* or take the sails down, which Bella read from her phone, was to preserve the stability of the ship in strong winds. The log continued with:

> *The squalls were now coming down with violence beyond description. During a lull the reefed main topmast staysail was hauled down and immediately after the wind came with such awful force that the main-mast was carried away, close off to the deck, bringing with it the mizen topmast. The ship was for some little time with her lee rail under water, but as the squall passed over she righted.*

'Phew,' said Maggie. 'And remember, *reefed* means folded or rolled,' said Bella.

The tension in the room was palpable when Diana paused for a few seconds then read on:

> *8 am … the passengers were immediately set to work the pumps, not knowing what damage might have been done to the hull, when the mainmast was carried away.*

'There's a paragraph here with a lot of terms that you could look up for us, Bella …' said Diana, '… that appear to be about all the things that had been broken, different masts, etc. But I think we need the photo of the ship to mark all the broken bits on, to make sense of that paragraph.'

Bella nodded. 'I can do that later. Read on, Mum.'

'"*The ship was now in a sad plight …*" I'm not sure if that's the captain's words or a commentary from the author of the book that includes the Captain's Log,' said Diana. 'Anyway, it continues …' "*The foreyard and topsail yards were flying about without braces, as the ship rolled (and as the sea was now getting up, this she did heavily), causing her to strain very much. As many axes as could be found were brought into use at once; the ship fortunately was soon disentangled from the wreck …*"'

'That's interesting,' said Bella. 'By "the wreck", they must have meant all the things that had been broken.'

> *A royal was cut up to nail over the partners of the mainmast to prevent the water from getting on the lower deck, but before this could be done a great lot of water got below from the heavy seas which constantly broke aboard.*

'A royal is a small sail,' said Bella, looking up from her phone. 'Maybe there were holes left in the deck when the mainmast went that they were trying to cover?'

'Sounds like it,' said Diana.

'The wild weather continued as the ship limped on through the rest of the day and into the next,' Diana said, 'The Captain's Log reported that the *"ship (was) rolling to such an extent that at times it was impossible to get along the decks."* And the book also comments that *"... the ship (was) labouring and straining most violently; gear, etc was flying about the decks; also, hencoops, skylights and other fixings – all being broken to pieces, notwithstanding everything being lashed as well as possible under the circumstances."'*

'Only one fine day was reported in the weeks that followed,' said Diana, skimming ahead. 'And even on that day, it is reported that *'It was impossible to rig up a jury mainmast on account of the severe rolling of the ship.'*

As Diana read on, her mind was flooded with images of a weathered, wrinkle-skinned captain yelling orders that were swept away on the wind; of exhausted sailors grappling with what sails remained; of broken bits of wood flying about; of men fiercely pumping water while battling to stay upright. And of the women below deck, equally fiercely trying to protect their children—one of whom was her great-great-grandmother, Carrie.

And one of Carrie's children was Diana's great-grandfather, George Edward, always known as Edward. She wondered what role he had played when he had been sixteen at the time, close to adulthood in those days. Was he expected to behave as a man and help, or was that something he expected of himself at that age?

'On 3 October, it says the ship "... *was making upwards of 1 foot of water per hour—evidently from some fresh place having broken out in consequence of the heavy strain at the time the ship was dismasted.*" And the captain reported: *"Got water kegs filled and saw everything ready with boats, etc for an emergency; passengers and crew working at the pumps throughout the night. Ship's course set for Bahia.*"'

'Golly,' said Maggie, 'the captain thought they might have to put people over the side in a boat. Abandon ship, so to speak.'

'Indeed, said Diana. 'It goes on to say the next day an additional long boat was acquired from a passing ship—the *Eastern Star*—which kept the *Windsor Castle* company overnight, before sailing off. Then it says crew and passengers kept pumping and more cargo was thrown overboard. The *Windsor Castle* limped on, finally arriving in Bahia on 13 October.'

'And the last entry that is relevant for us,' said Diana, looking in turn to Maggie and Bella, says *"20th October – Passengers left in steamship Galileo." After that there are entries up until the Windsor Castle eventually arrived in Gravesend.'*

She put the copy of the log back in its envelope and placed it on the floor beside her handbag. Her mind was still swimming with images. Emotions were whirling.

'How long ...' said Maggie, '... from when they left Sydney?'

'Six and a half weeks from Sydney to the shipwreck, Nana ...' said Bella softly, '... then nearly five more weeks until they went off on the steamship.'

Maggie shook her head. 'What's the right word—mind-blowing, astounding, breathtaking? I don't know. And did they get to New York in the end, or did they come back to Australia?'

'We don't know that bit yet, Mum,' said Diana.

Bella stood, put her hands on her hips and took a big breath in. 'Actually,' she said, 'we do.'

'We do? How?' asked Diana.

'I used a computer at the National Library this morning and found the name of the ship they travelled from London to New York on and the date they arrived in New York—30 November 1874.'

Diana placed a hand on her chest and heaved a sigh of relief. 'They got there! Carrie got to see her American family. Thank goodness.'

But neither Maggie nor Bella responded likewise, with relief.

'What is it, Bella?' asked Maggie. 'Something's wrong, isn't it? Your face says so.'

Bella dropped her hands to her side and paced around the room nervously. When she turned to look Maggie, then Diana, in the eyes, her own eyes were watery.

'I went on to the ancestry website last night and looked at the family trees of several other people and started copying information into our … sorry … *your* tree, Mum. Information about Carrie and George's children,' she said, stopping to blow air through her lips, which were trembling a little. 'I saw that two of the children died young. William and Alice. I compared their dates of death with when the family arrived and left New York,' she said, pausing. 'William and Alice died when they were still in New York. Only weeks after they arrived.'

A cloak of silence descended upon the room, and for a few seconds there was no sound, not even in the corridor outside.

Maggie broke the silence. 'All that way. They survived that shocking voyage, got to New York, and two little ones died.'

'I don't know what of, but I have ordered their death certificates from New York,' said Bella. 'To come by email. So, we will know soon.'

'Thank you, Bella,' said Maggie. 'One child—that could be an accident—but two? That sounds like childhood disease, which was rampant in the 1800s.'

Diana could not have stopped the tears from tumbling and the whimper from escaping her, even if she had been given warning of their coming. She saw Maggie hold both her arms out, one to her and one to Bella, and they both rushed into them. Three generations of women cried together, shamelessly. They cried for the lost children, for their brothers and sisters, for George. And most of all, for Carrie, the mother who would have protected all her children with everything she had on the voyage, only to lose two of them when, they could imagine, she thought her whole family was safe.

# Chapter Forty-Eight

*Cooma, Winter 2018*

When Diana pulled her car up at the quaint church known as Christ Church, her imagination ran away with itself again. She pictured Carrie and George arriving with their presumed friends—listed on their marriage certificate as Edmund and Ann—on horses or in a buggy, or a mixture of both.

*Perhaps the tall, arch-shaped wooden doors were not such a vibrant red then,* she chuckled to herself, *but they certainly add to its character and announce how well cared for the church is.*

The caretaker of the church, Charles, met Diana and Bella at the wooden doors, and they shared a pleasant chat about Carrie and George's marriage here, before he pushed the doors open and stepped aside for them to enter. Three steps and they were standing in a small entrance upon roughly cut pieces of slate. 'They look original,' said Bella, looking down at the slate. 'They do,' said Diana, moving forward into the body of the church she thought was called a *nave.* 'But this wooden floor looks newer and so do the benches—see the modern bolts and nuts they have been put together with.' She pointed.

'Oh yeah,' said Bella, leaning down to look, then standing up again. 'Even so, the church has a definite *heritage* feel to it.'

'Cared for lovingly inside as well as out,' said Diana.

From behind them came Charles' voice. 'The church was first restored in 1936 and has been maintained since then. We open it occasionally for services.'

The *brriiing* of a mobile phone saw Charles raise his hand to them and leave the church to answer his call.

Diana took the opportunity to sit on the front-most wooden bench, and Bella sat beside her.

'What is it about churches, Mum? They always give me a certain feeling, like I should bow or something.'

Diana laughed. 'Sorry, I know what you mean. There's an atmosphere inside them that generates respectfulness—a feeling of peace for me too.'

'Guess sceptics might say they are designed to do that.'

'I suspect so,' said Diana. She turned her face to the wooden beams that stretched above. 'Regardless, they can be comforting places to be.'

Bella got up and moved towards the altar. 'Perhaps this is where Carrie stood when she married George. Or here,' she said, taking a couple of steps to the left.

'Most likely,' said Diana, her daughter's cheery disposition affecting her own. It had taken two days for the sadness that had come to her, Maggie and Bella, to begin to fade, after they had learned of the loss of two of Carrie and George's children in New York. During that time, Bella had her interview for the tutoring job at the university, which she reported went well, and Maggie, having been told she needed to stay in the hospital a while longer, had asked that Diana and Bella go to her home in Jindabyne to pick up some more of her things. A request Diana had no doubt was designed to have she and Bella spend more time together in the hope they might address the elephant in the room, as the saying goes—the reason why they had been estranged for two years.

In her own hope that visiting Christ Church on the edge of Cooma, where Carrie and George had married, might continue to reduce the gap between them, Diana had contacted the Cooma Visitors Centre, who had put them in touch with Charles.

'Carrie must have been very much in love with George to elope with him,' said Bella.

'Yes, it must have been an all-encompassing love for her to experience, knowing she was inserting a wedge between herself and her mother. That's my hypothesis anyway.'

'I wonder what she wore; how they got here from *Jimenbuen.*'

'Something simple probably—a dress she already had perhaps; and by horse or cart, or both. Whatever George had been able to organise, I guess.'

Bella sat back down and for a few minutes they sat quietly together, giving each of their minds time to generate imaginings of that time.

'Mum, complete change of topic—the doctor mentioned after Nana was admitted to hospital that her accommodation should be considered now that she has had a stroke. Have you thought about that?'

Diana rose and walked a few steps. 'I have managed to avoid facing it so far, because I don't know what to do,' she said.

'Okay. I have been thinking. How about this? You could stay with her to start with, and take it from there? I could help out on the weekends.'

Bella was right—there was nothing stopping Diana from doing that. And it might do her good to have a change of scenery—help both she and Maggie work out where to from here with their lives. Diana reached out and squeezed her daughter's hand, and Bella offered no objection. 'Yes. Yes, I could do that. And, you know what? I think I will talk to Nana about that.'

***

The visit to the church had been a special time—another link to Carrie, and another connection shared with Bella. Diana had left the church feeling touched by both Carrie in her absence, and Bella in her presence. And she was mightily relieved that, if Maggie agreed, they had the next step in helping her, worked out.

Maggie not being in her home when they entered was an odd feeling, but all the love her mother had given them from here, was still there, and so was the warmth and peace Diana felt when visiting. *Staying here with Mum will be good,* she thought, smiling inwardly.

The fridge door squeaked as Bella opened it. 'Nothing viable. I will head off to the supermarket. *So* hungry.'

'I'll come with you,' said Diana, grabbing her bag. 'How about we get a few things for tea as well as our very late lunch, stay here tonight and leave early in the morning. It will be too late for a hospital visit tonight if we go back today anyway.'

'I agree,' said Bella, not sounding particularly enthusiastic, but again, Diana would take what she could get.

As Diana drove the short distance to the shopping centre, a light sleet swished across the windscreen, announcing the arrival of winter in the *Snowy Mountains*. Soon, Jindabyne and the resorts would be throbbing with skiers, snowboarders and tourists. 'Remember those times we went on the ski lift at Thredbo, Mum, with Nana? To the café at the top, sipping hot chocolates with melty marshmallows?'

'And Nana scaring us that time when, halfway up on the ski lift, she threw her arms in the air and yelled, "Woo Hoo!"'

'Scaring *you*, you mean. I thought it was great.'

Diana laughed. 'Well, there *were* quite a few metres below us. But the view from the café, over the range of mountains, was spectacular.'

'And the time you and I, and James, went down the rapids on air mattress thingies?'

James's face, grinning at her as he zoomed past her that day, flashed into Diana's mind.

'I would have liked to do the horse ride too—the one up to one of the old huts.'

'Fun for sure,' said Diana. *And maybe we still could.*

It was midweek and mid-afternoon, and there weren't a lot of cars in the parking lot, or people around. The larger section of the shopping centre was long and rectangular in shape, it's middle occupied by an almost-as-long, brick-paved courtyard. Polished timber picnic-style tables with bench seats and several small gardens added a welcoming feel to the courtyard. 'How about we walk around, see what's here?' said Bella, setting off. Diana followed, noting the ski shops that would soon be opened for the season, a nice dress shop, and a café. She stopped at a 'To Lease' sign on a small, empty shop next to the café. She and Bella put their faces up against the glass, cupping their hands to get a better view.

'Looks like it opens up, narrow at the front, wide at the back,' said Bella.

'Wedge-shaped,' replied Diana.

'I wonder what shop or office was in there. Handy, right next to the café. The coffee smells delicious.'

'Very handy,' said Diana, wondering, fleetingly, what business would end up in there now.

***

They each woke early the next morning and, after making a coffee to drink along the way, were soon headed back to Canberra. Bella offered to drive, which gave Diana time to soak up the view of the Monaro and imagine the time of the pioneers. Bella dropped her off at the hospital and Maggie was delighted to see her. She was also delighted to see her favourite dressing gown, which she wrapped herself in immediately, and her woolly Ugg boots, which she slipped her feet into.

'I have had enough of hospital beds,' Maggie said, 'I would like to sit in the chair today.' She didn't wait for Diana to help her, rising from the bed and making her way to the chair alone, which both scared Diana a little in case she fell, but pleased her too, that her mother was able to do this on her own. It might take a while yet but Maggie was definitely on the mend.

'I have been thinking,' said Diana, sitting down in the chair on the opposite side of the bed, in the hope her mother wouldn't see her shaking hands. Although, as the words came out, she realised her voice was shaking too.

'Me too,' said her mother cheerily, apparently not noticing her daughter's nervousness.

*A minute of reprieve,* thought Diana. 'Okay Mum, you go first.'

'Remember I told you how my mum and dad would take us to the property named *Middleview* in the *Snowies* and I would watch Mum and Grandfather ride out across the plains?'

'I do.'

'Well, for the life of me, I don't remember that property being sold. Maybe it's still owned by a descendant, and you could see if they have anything of Carrie's there too. Like at *Snowy Vale*, which is a hop, skip and a jump away. Grandfather would have passed the property on. Worth a go, I was thinking. My Aunty Hilda lived there for some years after her marriage ended. She lived with her son, Noel. Lovely boy. But Grandfather Edward and Grandmother Bride had four boys, as well as Aunty Hilda, Aunty Clara and my mother, Caroline, so the property could have been handed down through one of them.'

Another lead! 'That's an excellent idea, Mum. We might find the property in the White Pages.'

Maggie smiled. 'I'm glad you like the idea. It's all rather addictive, fascinating and very moving to find out about the past. Now, what was it you wanted to say?'

Diana got up and moved her chair to be beside her mother's. She dived straight into the possibility of she and her mother living together, knowing she was talking too fast and saying too much because of her nervousness. But she need not have worried because when she finished, Maggie simply looked at her and said, 'Okay. I know I need some help. But what about you? You must not give up your life for me. I would not be happy about that.'

It was so like her mum to think of others, even when it was her who needed a hand. Diana stood to place a kiss upon her mother's forehead, then sat down again. 'A change—this change—will be good for me, Mum. I need a change. We will be helping each other.'

'Then let's do it,' said Maggie firmly, reaching for Diana's hand. 'But promise me one thing. One day I may need to go into care, and if that happens, there is to be no fuss. Promise?'

Making that promise right now was a tough call when Diana didn't even want to contemplate Maggie needing that level of care, but she was committed to respecting her mother's wishes. 'That's a promise, Mum.'

# Chapter Forty-Nine

Diana held the photo of her great-great-grandfather, George, at arm's length. *You did have a beard—a bushy one. And how handsome you were, with your voluminous dark hair and piercing eyes, oozing confidence as you looked away from the camera in a typical sculpture-like pose.*

She placed the photo back on her dining table, beside the one of her great-great-grandmother, Carrie, that had come with it, the second photo she now had of her. The black-and-white head and shoulder photos, tinted in a sepia colour, were copies of the originals, clearly taken at the same time—the background the same, both photos trimmed to an oval shape. Carrie looked younger in this photo than the first. Diana remembered how, in the letter found in the trunk, Louisa had asked her daughter for a 'likeness'. Perhaps these photos were taken before they sailed to New York on the *Windsor Castle* in 1874, or perhaps they were taken in New York. George and Carrie certainly appeared dressed and groomed very dapperly, more so than she imagined their usual attire in Australia. And Carrie's face was thinner, her hair shorter. Perhaps a haircut had been needed after the voyage?

Diana sat for a moment in the quiet—Bella had left for Melbourne several days ago—soaking up her amazement that she had these photos, given to her so generously by another second cousin, Ross, with some other photos that were not labelled. He had also given her some research his mother, Judith, had done that matched her own.

Judith owned the property *Middleview*. And the White Pages had indeed led Diana to talking to Ross. And Maggie had been right—

Judith was a descendant of Edward—his granddaughter through his son, John—and he had inherited *Middleview.*

As coincidences go, when Diana had contacted Ross, he was about to come through Canberra, and he had offered to drop off what he could find of his mother's paperwork on the family that she was happy to share. When he arrived and Diana saw what he had to give her, she had not found it easy to convey how grateful she was. She hoped she hadn't overdone it with her enthusiasm.

The family history research bug had captured her again, whisked hours away from her that day, and she now had a lead on her great Aunt Hilda's grandson, Chris. She had found a woman on the ancestry website who knew of him and suggested she try to get hold of him through his golf club. *Could she be that bold?* 'Yes, I can,' she declared out loud. 'Why not is the question.'

She picked up the photos of George and Carrie again, holding one in each hand, side by side. Carrie looked brimming with confidence too. *Would they have looked like that after the voyage on the Windsor Castle? Perhaps these photos were indeed taken before the disastrous voyage. Or after the voyage but before the loss of the two children.*

Either way, the photos would bring a little cheer to her mother and daughter following the arrival of the death certificates for the two children who had died in New York after the voyage. Alice had fallen prey to diphtheria and measles on 26 December 1874 at just seven years and ten months old. Only a month after the family had finally made it to New York. And William had died from measles and bronchitis on 13 March 1875 at twelve years of age. Both children were attended by a doctor, the certificates said, from 23 December, which meant Carrie had two sick children on her hands at the same time. *Or more? Perhaps the others were sick too—with measles being so contagious—but survived. What a frightful time it would have been for all of them. How Carrie must have hung on to hope and prayer.*

Diana's mobile phone was on silent so she could concentrate on her research and thoughts, but she couldn't ignore it when it began to vibrate. It was Bella. And Diana took it as a good sign that she was ringing, so snapped up the phone.

'Hi.'

'Are you sitting down? If not, I suggest you do,' Bella said.

Bile rose in Diana's throat. Had Bella had an accident? She tried not to panic, although that process had already begun. 'Yes,' she said, 'what has happened?'

What came across as a long pause on the other end of the phone, almost had Diana throw up. 'Bella. Please. Tell me.'

'It's the coin. I am at the valuer. He says it is an 1855 Sydney Mint sovereign, Australia's first sovereign. And it could go at auction for ninety or more thousand dollars. And he is offering to sell it for you.'

# Chapter Fifty

Diana had not been able to make a decision about what to do about the coin when Bella had phoned and told her its value. She had managed to get out, 'Please thank him. Could we let him know?' before politely ending the call. She had sat in stunned silence for five minutes then bounced unashamedly around the lounge room, whooping out loudly.

That didn't help at all with the decision she had to make, but it did help make the most of the joy that came with a possible solution to her financial worries. On top of how much she was looking forward to spending time with her mother, who was being released from hospital tomorrow, Diana felt better than she had in two years—since the loss of her beloved James.

Her acute hearing caught the key turning in the front door lock and Bella walked in. Or more to the point, *slumped* in. She looked tired and pale and a tad grumpy. 'Coffee?' Diana asked. 'Desperate for it,' replied her daughter.

Diana took a risk, 'New job not going well?'

'No, it's great. Students are great. Work is great.'

Away from her daughter's gaze, Diana raised her eyebrows. *Certainly doesn't feel like everything is going great.*

Their coffee was consumed in silence, prompting Diana to say, 'Would you rather not help with the packing this afternoon? I can do this myself if you need to have some time for yourself.'

'No, Mum. It's fine. I am fine.'

*Oh, oh, the "fine" word, which means everything is not fine.* But Diana decided not to say anything else. She had been touched when

Bella had offered to help her pack up the things she would be taking to Jindabyne. Bella had joked, saying, 'More room for my stuff, which I can bring from the storage unit, so this is not an altruistic move, Mum.' Then added, 'Thanks for letting me stay here while you are in Jindabyne. And I *do* know you refusing to let me pay rent is about helping me to save.'

In truth, that was part of it, but Diana didn't want to leave her home unoccupied for whatever time she would be away, so it was a two-way thing.

An hour after their coffee and non-chat, she was beginning to wonder if Bella was actually happy with the living-here arrangement, the stomping around and rough handling of boxes finally getting to Diana.

'Look, Bella. What's going on? You are clearly out of sorts.'

Bella turned, her face flushed red. 'He's not here,' she blurted out, angrily—so loud, Diana jumped.

'Who is not here?' she asked her daughter, in as calm a voice as she could muster.

'James. James is not here. I thought I would feel him here. I don't know, his presence, or something. I have been waiting for that to hit, but it hasn't. I needed to feel something of him here. But I don't and I *really* needed that!'

Diana watched the anger evaporate from her daughter's face, watched it crumple, watched tears turn up as though a dam of them had been sitting there for years, waiting for this moment to burst through. She opened her arms and Bella rushed into them.

Bella cried and cried, and Diana cried and cried too.

Finally, Bella pulled away. Her anger had returned. 'I loved him too. He was my father.'

'He …' Diana faltered, '… he was your stepfather. I didn't realise …'

'What? That I loved him. He was the father I knew. From three years of age. The other one left you to it, remember? James shared everything with you—the looking after me stuff, remember?'

Bella paced backwards and forwards, turning swiftly on her heels at each end of the lounge room. 'Making school lunches, dropping me off, picking me up. He always came to anything I did. Cared for me too when I was sick. Holidays. Walking the dog. The three of us together.'

'Oh Bella, I know …'

'Don't say that! When he died, you spent all that time arranging things, talking to other people, writing "thank you" cards. But *I* needed you! *I* needed you then. But it was like you were somewhere else,' she said, twisting the seed pearl and opal ring James had given her.

A collage of images, of special moments James and Bella had shared, flickered through Diana's mind. The laughter, the smiles, the way he made even the most boring of homework fun for her. It all came flooding back.

How could she have been so blind? She had kissed Bella, hugged her, fed her, wiped away tears. But Bella was right, she had not been 'there' for her when James had died. She had been in a different world—the world of grief so bad a natural disaster could have occurred and she would have barely noticed.

'You are right. I *was* somewhere else. I failed you. I'm so sorry. We both loved him. He loved both of us.'

Bella said nothing. She did not move. She stood where she was, looking utterly miserable. She stared at Diana, her mouth turned down, her face swollen.

Diana did not reach out to her daughter again. She went to the dining table, whipped up her handbag and pulled out her car keys. 'Come with me,' she said. 'Please.'

***

Diana ignored the beeps as she drove slowly along, over cautious, aware intense emotion could see her make mistakes. When she looked in the rear-view mirror, she caught a glimpse of a drawn, older-than-she-was woman, as pale as her daughter, but she didn't care. She hoped that being where they were going would help Bella the way it helped her—that she could at least give her daughter this gift.

They pulled into the car park, neither of them speaking, neither of them bothering about getting a ticket from the pay parking machine.

Diana took Bella's hand, Bella letting her, and led the way. When they stood in front of James's favourite bonsai tree at the National Arboretum, she turned to her daughter and held both her hands tightly. 'This,' she said, 'is where I feel him. Our last outing was here, and he was so happy. I can still see his face that day, in my mind, when I come here. So, I come here a lot.'

She tossed her head back, let go of Bella's hands and reached to gently stroke her daughter's cheek. 'It could be your special place too. You could come here alone, or we could come together. To feel him. To talk about him, to remember him and our love for him and his love for us. What do you think?'

If anyone was near them, if anyone noticed the two women wrapped, crying but smiling, in each other's arms, Diana and Bella were not aware of it.

# Epilogue

*Jindabyne, late Spring 2018*

Diana closed her eyes, reached up and ran her fingers over the letters of the painted sign on the window. She felt the smoothness and miniscule bumps of the letters which spelled out *The Little Bookshop of Dreams* in emerald, white and blue colours.

Her bookshop. She could hardly believe it. She had leased the wedge-shaped shop in the Jindabyne complex that she and Bella had walked past several months ago, that had remained vacant during that time as though it were waiting for her to join the dots.

Carrie's gold coin had been sold at auction for a staggering ninety thousand dollars. Quite a bit of the money had been used to outfit the shop, and stock it with books Diana, Maggie and Bella loved, and books their research showed others loved too.

Selling the coin had been a difficult decision to make. Diana had needed the help of her mother and daughter to do so, in a weekend of chats that included how much it must have meant to Carrie who had held on to it for so long and how its value would allow them to move forward in this new life they were creating.

The sound of meaningful chatter greeted Diana as she walked into the bookshop. Maggie and several of her CWA friends were busy laying out the last of their delicious homemade treats on a long table that had been set up at the back of the shop, near the wide window that shed light upon the feast. Acting as a centrepiece was a light-as-air vanilla sponge, filled with strawberry jam and whipped cream, and dusted with icing sugar. Around it were plates of fluffy scones with more jam and cream in antique green glass bowls, slices of sultana cake, chocolate cupcakes with frosting twirled on their tops, and plates of finger sandwiches with a variety of fillings.

Diana's heart sang with gratefulness for all they had done for this special day—the grand opening of *The Little Bookshop of Dreams.*

She savoured these final minutes before those invited, and those walking by that she hoped would pop in, began arriving. She cast her eyes over the white bookshelves and all they held. The bush-green painted walls with the framed photos of the old hut surrounded by forest that Bella had taken on their recent horse ride together up into the *Snowy Mountains.* The counter was fashioned from recycled timber. There was re-upholstered antique chairs occupying one corner—that she envisioned people sitting in reading—and the wall was covered by a curtain hung from a rod that would be swept aside to reveal a surprise during the opening.

'Is it time to throw in the aromatherapy,' Maggie said as she walked towards Diana, perfectly comfortable nowadays with using a flower-decorated cane Bella had bought for her.

'Definitely. The lemon myrtle scented candles should do the trick,' Diana said, automatically opening her arms for a hug. Since Maggie's stroke, there were a lot more hugs happening between mother, daughter and granddaughter. A lot more *I love yous* too. None of them were under any illusions—Maggie was elderly and they had to make the most of their remaining time together. Diana and Maggie were still happily living together—still 'going with the flow' on that score. Maggie had insisted on hiring a local lady to take the housework away from Diana and had asked Diana if she could do readings to children in the bookshop.

The warmth of a furry body leaned against Diana's legs, and they both reached down to pat Maeve. Diana, Maggie and Bella had gone together to the RSPCA in Canberra to adopt a rescue dog and there before them, in the first kennel, had been Maeve, a senior dog, a Staffy crossed with another breed they hadn't been able to determine yet. Her age had been a bonus. She was quiet and content to go wherever they did, including snoozing in her bed in the bookshop. It was the appeal and love in Maeve's eyes that had captured their hearts and they all agreed it was a fabulous decision to adopt her.

A sudden movement caught Diana's eye, and in through the door, like a burst of light and energy, came her cousin, Sophie, who had declared she simply *must* be there for the opening and that was *all* there was to it. And with her came Bella, who had volunteered to pick Sophie up from Canberra Airport after her flights from London.

Squeals of delight, hugs and kisses were exchanged, with Maeve weaving her way between legs and looking up lovingly for pats, her tail wagging madly. 'So here we all are,' said Sophie, 'I am desperate to have a look around before others arrive. 'Well, come with me,' said Bella. Sophie leaned in to give Diana and Maggie another kiss and as she and Bella bounced away, Diana thought, *No sign of jet lag there. Not yet anyway.*

*And how happy Bella looks.* Her beautiful daughter, their relationship steadily healing, her life in Canberra taking shape. Bella was still working as a tutor at the university and loving it but would soon be adding to that by starting on her path to achieve her own dream of a PhD that she had won a scholarship for. Bella had moved into a one-bedroom apartment close to the university that Diana had been able to help her with a good-sized deposit for. Diana's own home had been rented out until she conjured up enough courage to put it up for sale.

Diana could not stop another squeal of delight escaping as Chris, Ross and Ian arrived. Like herself, each was a great-great-grandchild of Carrie and George. She had only met Ross before—a strapping, friendly, down-to-earth farmer who had given her the precious studio photos of Carrie and George. It had been a joy to know all three of them would be coming today.

Chris lifted his arm to show the folio in his hand. 'I've got them,' he said.

'The letters!'

'If only we had the originals,' he said.

Both he and Diana had put a lot of effort into tracking down the originals but with no luck. Chris's father, Noel, had been given a copy of transcripts of the dozen letters many years before but the now-unknown person who'd had the originals in their possession, had not been willing to part with them. Whether the original letters still existed or had been lost—their importance not recognised by someone who came after the owner—may never be known, but they would keep trying to find them.

If only,' she said, 'but how good is it that your dad took and kept the transcripts of the letters sent to Carrie and passed them on to you, before he passed away himself? Did you see the chairs set up in a circle outside ready for your reading of the letters?'

'I did. And I am looking forward to it,' Chris said.

'Me too,' she said. 'Would you each like to help yourself to some CWA fare as we get underway? Molly, from the café next door, will be in soon to take orders for coffee and tea too.'

The discovery that Chris had transcripts of the original letters in his possession was like a dream come true for Diana. He had been happy to share them and had emailed copies to Diana. Together with his knowledge, she, Maggie and Bella had been taken on another journey of discovery and research. One letter had been from George to Carrie—a plea to his wife to return home from New York as soon as possible. It turned out that when Carrie's mother, Louisa, had passed away in 1878, she had left her apartment in Brooklyn to Carrie, who had to sail back to New York to claim and sell it. From a variety of resources, they had then learned that Carrie had taken two of her children with her—her seventh child, a babe in arms, Caroline Eliza, born since their return to Australia from their voyage in 1874; and her eight-year-old daughter, Francis—and she had given birth to her eighth child, a son, Henry Frederick, while in New York. Diana, Maggie and Bella had cried and held each other again, when a death certificate Bella obtained revealed that little Caroline Eliza had died of scarlet fever in New York, at just two years and seven months of age.

That meant, that by the time Carrie sailed back to Australia to spend her remaining years, until her death, aged sixty-five, in the *Snowy* region, she had left three children behind her, all buried in New York. And in total she had had eight children. Diana, Maggie and Bella had asked themselves how could she have borne the pain of losing three children. They had stood together at Carrie's graveside near Berridale, and lain flowers to pay tribute to her, her strength and all she had gone through.

*The Little Bookshop of Dreams* began to fill with people. Sophie passed around a visitor's book for all to sign. Maggie handed out more-than-what-was-asked-for plates of treats, and Bella guided people around the shop.

Her friend, Ruby, from *Snowy Vale* came to stand beside Diana as the deep, spiritual sound of a didgeridoo heralded the arrival of a local elder wearing the possum cloak that had been found in Carrie's trunk. The sound and sight moved Diana more than any words she could find to express what she was feeling. Diana had made the decision to return the cloak to Indigenous owners, and elders in the region were helping identify where it should be kept. They may never know how Carrie came to have the cloak in her possession, but it was Diana's hope, that occasionally, like today, an elder would bring it to the bookshop to show and talk to people about the significance of possum cloaks to Indigenous people.

As the elder moved further into the bookshop, three *National Parks and Wildlife Service* rangers quietly entered. Diana was glad to see they wore name badges so she could whisper a welcome by name and introduce herself as Diana Walker. The two younger rangers, both women, nodded and moved towards the gathered crowd. The third ranger, a man about her own age, reached out to shake her hand. 'Thank you for coming, Peter,' she said, having looked at the badge on his chest. His good looks were impossible to miss—he was tall, slim, broad-shouldered, and his greying hair had a dressing of cute curls on top. But it was when she looked up into his dark blue eyes that she felt a flutter, and any words that should have been forming, slipped from her mind. He was still holding her hand when Diana heard Bella call, 'Mum, Mum,' trying not to sound too loud, while waving Diana over.

'Excuse me, Peter,' she said, nodding in the direction of Bella and the crowd.

She moved to the wall covered by the curtain and waited for everyone to gather around when they were ready. Bella joined her. 'As some of you know,' Diana began, 'this bookshop—my dream—would not have been possible without the sale of a coin that belonged to my great-great-grandmother, Carrie. But there is much more to the story, both her story and our story,' she said, looking at Bella and Maggie. 'Learning as much as we have been able to about Carrie's life—and our imaginings about her life too—has been a very moving experience for us. And, without further ado, we would like to unveil our tribute to Carrie, George and their family, who some of us here today, are descended from.

Bella, as practised, swept the curtain to the side, revealing a wall of various-sized and shaped frames. In prime position were the photos of Carrie and George. There was a family tree, showing Carrie and George's children, grandchildren and great-grandchildren. Side-by-side photos of the back and front of the polished gold sovereign were accompanied by a potted history of its manufacture. A rectangular frame held a copy of the three surviving pages of Carrie's diary about the disastrous 1874 voyage, with another showing a photo of the *Windsor Castle* they had sailed on. There was a photo of the little church Carrie and George had been married in, and another of the possum cloak. And in a large frame to the side was an overview of Carrie's life, titled, 'The remarkable life of an every day woman.'

It was the words— 'every day woman'—that brought back to Diana the pull she felt towards putting everything they had found out about the lives of her great-great-grandparents into a family history book that would be available for all to see, should they choose. For it had been quite a shock to find that there were few writings remaining of every day people from the time of Carrie and George.

Diana and Bella moved to the side to enable their now-happily-chatting and peering guests to step up to the wall.

'Mum,' said Bella cheekily, placing an arm around Diana's shoulders. 'It's fantastic, but we missed a spot,' she said, pointing to a large square of space, close to the window.

'Umm,' said Diana, 'Did I ever tell you about my great-grandmother on my father's side? Christina was her name. She sailed to Australia from Scotland in 1856 when she was only seven years of age.'

Bella threw back her head and laughed, and Diana thought it was the most beautiful sight and sound she had ever witnessed.

# Author's Note

This story is inspired by Caroline (Carrie) Amelia Hedger (née Marston) and George Henry Hedger Perkins, who were my great-great-grandparents on my mother's side. Louisa Marston was Carrie's mother, and Nathaniel Marston was her father. Louisa did marry Amos Crisp, who was a convict, and Amos did use his mother's maiden name of Vince to escape and return to Australia years later, after he had met and married widowed Louisa in New York. Carrie, Louisa and Amos did arrive from New York in 1856 onboard the *B.R. Milam.*

It is believed they did travel by ship from Melbourne up the coast of Victoria and New South Wales, but it is possible they travelled overland by dray to *Jimenbuen* on the Monaro (known as *Maneroo* at the time) from Tathra, rather than Two Fold Bay, as described in this story.

Carrie and George's story is based on as many facts as possible, with my imaginings building upon them to create a fictional story. The disastrous 1874 voyage upon the *Windsor Castle* did occur and a Captain's Log of the voyage does exist. Some paragraphs of the log included under Diana's story have been taken from the log (they are in italics), and I have used the log in some descriptions of what happened to Carrie and her family on the voyage. I found the log in *The Blackwall Frigates* by Basil Lubbock (1922 edition).

I have used Carrie and George's eight children's real names, with the exception of their first son, George William, who I have named George Edward and chosen to call him 'Edward' so as not to have two prominent characters with the name of George. I did not use the name William, as Carrie and George also had a son named William.

Carrie did voyage back to New York in 1878 to claim and sell the apartment her mother bequeathed to her. And three of the children did pass away in New York, as described in this story. And her son, Henry, was born in New York, as also described in this story.

There is a considerable amount of information in the public domain about the convict Amos Crisp and his extended family. Included in what I have read are the in-depth family histories of *Defend the fold : Cartwright family history : Richard Cornelius Cartwright, Thomas Cartwright, John Cartwright and their descendants / researched and compiled by Edward W. Northwood*; and *Brecon to the Monaro and Beyond. A history of the John and Sarah Williams Family 1807-2007 Volume 2.*

My naming of Carrie's friend, Maria, is a tribute to Maria Crawford, who was indeed a midwife who rode far and wide to tend to women during birth. Although I do not have evidence that it is so, I like to think that perhaps Carrie and Maria did not know each other in real life. Thanks go to Denise Dovey, who provided information on Maria, who she is descended from.

The *Snowy Vale* homestead does not exist. It is modelled on the heritage homestead *Numbla Vale*, which a heritage report says was built for George Hedger by Amos Crisp. However, other sources indicate Hugh Mugridge had the homestead built and his family lived there for many years. As is so often the case with research—we learn more as time passes.

A number of sources indicate that after their return from New York following the disastrous ship voyage, George and Carrie continued to move around. Locations where they lived are given as Bushy's Park Buckley's Crossing (Dalgety), Delegate, Bombala, and Matong. *Matong Station* and homestead are in the region of *Numbla Vale* but to date I have not been able to find evidence that George and Carrie lived at *Matong Station*. He did have a lease in the area, which was cancelled in 1896 due to failure to pay.

Annie Clarke was a sister of the bushrangers known as the Clarke Brothers and their gang, and it is thought she may have sometimes 'cased' potential robberies for her brothers. But, while the robbery at the *Rosebrook Station* by the gang *did* occur on the date stated, I have no knowledge that George, Carrie or Annie were present at the time. I have added that scene both to build upon the impression of the time I was portraying, when bushrangers were a real presence and threat, and to add to my portrayal of what women's lives were like at the time, particularly by bringing out Annie's difficult childhood, which I understand to be true.

In this story, I have Carrie, George and their children travelling from Goulburn on the train to Sydney to board the *Windsor Castle*. It is likely they went to Sydney from Queanbeyan on a coach. The railway did not reach Queanbeyan until 1887, so in order to include train travel, which was an important addition to life in Australia at that time, I have the family catching the train from Goulburn. I also, to aid the flow of the story, have the family spending one night in Sydney before they sailed when, from the three pages of Carrie's diary that exist, we know the family spent several weeks in Sydney before they sailed and left home earlier than what I have indicated.

Diana's story is not mine, with several exceptions—the opening scene where Maggie gifted Diana the very old book is similar to what I experienced with my mum. I am lucky to have that same book in my possession today. And I have used my family history research experiences in portraying how Diana and Bella discover information.

There are elements of my mum in Maggie. That was not intentional, as I was writing, that came into play by itself.

My three second cousins—Chris, Ian and Ross—are real and did indeed provide the materials mentioned in the book—and more—for which I am incredibly grateful. Chris's father, Noel Gray, was given a transcript of the letters mentioned in this story by his cousin, and the letters in Chapter Thirty (to Carrie from her sister, Anna) and Chapter 33 (to Carrie from her mother, Louisa) are two of those letters with minor grammatical changes. The current whereabouts of the original letters is not known.

A trunk of Carrie's belongings did exist, but it is believed it perished when the shed it was in on the property *Middleview*, was burnt down.

Chats with my mum and an article written on my great-great-grandmother by Ian Burke, published in *The Snowy Echo* in 2012, started me on this journey to write Carrie's story. As did the encouragement of author Fiona McIntosh.

*The Snowy Echo* article contained a lot of information which, after my own research to confirm facts, I revealed gradually in this story, in order to create a novel.

Was George Henry Hedger really *The Man from Snowy River*? Some think so. Others do not. There are at least eleven other contenders. Perhaps only Banjo Patterson knew the answer to that one? Or perhaps it truly was the many stockmen he met and their stories that inspired his model of *The Man* and the famous ride?

The story of the Perkins brothers, as portrayed here, is real. I wish to acknowledge that there is a belief in my family that George Perkins' medical condition may have been due to him being beaten by soldiers when he was a prisoner in Port Arthur.

It is also true that his son, George Henry, was given the surname Hedger when his mother, Francis (Fanny) became the partner, then wife, of John Hedger. And that Amos Crisp senior had a hand in George Henry being brought from Tasmania to the property *Jimenbuen*, where he became a stockman at a young age.

George Henry Hedger Perkins was accused of stealing a heifer and was found not guilty, though he did have the remains of said cow in his possession. I have used that occurrence to highlight what it must have been like for his wife, Carrie, to have her husband taken into custody when they lived a remote existence with young children. While I have used the real names of the inspector and constables involved in his arrest, I have not used the real name of the landholder who is listed as accusing George of theft. My understanding is that he was a usually-absent owner of land on the Monaro. I have changed the dates George was charged and found not guilty, to one year later than actually occurred, in order to place some time between the *Rosebrook Station* robbery and the cattle stealing events, to aid the flow of the story. And I have used details, including actual words from *The Goulburn Herald and Chronicle* (14 April 1866) article on George's trial—to write the chapters relating to the cattle charge incident.

While George Henry Hedger Perkins has a significant part in this story, I didn't want the focus to be on him, but to be on the women of two different time periods, and to encourage readers to think about how remarkable every day women and their lives are.

There must be so many every day women's stories from the past and present still to be told.

# Acknowledgements

My heartfelt thank you to author Fiona McIntosh for her amazing Masterclass, Inaugural Masterclass Conference, encouragement and support.

I also completed online courses run by the Australian Writers' Centre, which I learned a great deal from. And I tapped into services offered by the Australian Society of Authors.

To the three second cousins I didn't know I had before beginning my research—Chris Gray, Ian Weston and Ross Walters—thank you! I am very grateful not only for the insightful information you provided but your willingness to do so. I have benefited greatly from the conversations Chris and I shared, and also the incredible legacy of family history research his dad, Noel Gray, achieved at a time when the resources available today were not.

It was an absolute pleasure to be able to talk to Mrs Lois Crisp, who is married to a descendant of the Amos Crisps included in this story. I am so grateful for the valuable information she provided too.

Thank you too, to Linda Warren, who kindly gave me entries from the diary of her great-great-grandmother, Catherine Blyton (née Wright) about daily life on the Monaro. Also, to Jane Glasson, a more recent owner of *Jimenbuen,* who talked to me about the property.

And to the Pioneers of Christ Church Maneroo who organised my access to the church where my great-great-grandparents married.

I am very grateful too, to members of the Monaro Pioneers for their extensive local history knowledge, which they willingly shared.

During the extensive research I have done for this story, I have tapped into many resources. I have also sidled up to librarians and archivists either in person or online. I am sure some of the people realised I only half knew what I was doing but were very polite and helpful.

Resources I am grateful to have been able to tap into include the National Library of Australia, including TROVE; NSW State Archives; NSW Registry of Births, Deaths & Marriages; Museums of History NSW; Public Record Office of Victoria; NSW Government Gazettes; Mariners & Ships in Australian Waters; City of New York Department of Records & Information Services; Monaro Pioneers website, Snowy Monaro Regional Library; Cooma Monaro Historical Society, Goulburn Mulwaree Library; Goulburn District Historical & Genealogical Society; ancestry.com.au; newspapers.com; and Find My Past.

To Andy McDermott, founder of the publishing provider company, Publicious, and his team, thank you for your professional and friendly assistance, which has made making my dream to publish this story come true.

To Julie Guthrie of Say It Write, who did the manuscript assessments, copy editing and proofreading of my story, your excellent work is greatly appreciated.

To my family and friends thank you for your interest and support and for not saying, 'Just how long is it going to take you to write this story?'

To my husband, Christopher, thank you for your belief in me and for sitting quietly and not allowing your eyes to glaze over when at times you asked me a question about my story, and half an hour later, I was still talking.

It seems a fitting tribute to my great-great-grandmother, Caroline Amelia Hedger, to give her the final words through the following poem she wrote and left behind for us:

*"My Wish."*
*"Wherever you dwell may content be your lot,*
*And friendship like ivy encircle your cot,*
*May each rosie morn dressed in a mantle of peace,*
*Shed health o'er your dwelling. Your blessings increased,*
*May gay smiling plenty adorn the fair spot,*
*May sorrow ne'er enter the door of your cot,*
*May your honest endeavour be crowned with success,*
*May you ever live happy, ne'er witness distress,*
*On your neat humble roof may these blessings descend,*
*Tis a wish free from guile, Tis the wish of a friend."*

# About the Author

Ann Connolly lives on a rural block in Murrumbateman, New South Wales, with her husband and animals. She had a career in natural resource management following studies at the Australian National University where her degrees majored in wildlife ecology and biological anthropology. Other strong interests include animal welfare, being in nature, family history research and the untold stories of every day women.

www.ingramcontent.com/pod-product-compliance
Lightning Source LLC
Chambersburg PA
CBHW020538020726
47494CB00006B/1809

*9781764298902*